FURY

HEATHER ATKINSON

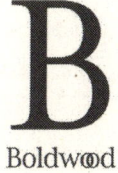

Boldwood

First published in Great Britain in 2025 by Boldwood Books Ltd.

Copyright © Heather Atkinson, 2025

Cover Design by JD Smith Design Ltd.

Cover Images: Shutterstock

A CIP catalogue record for this book is available from the British Library.

Paperback ISBN 978-1-83703-563-2

Large Print ISBN 978-1-83703-562-5

Hardback ISBN 978-1-83703-561-8

Trade Paperback ISBN 978-1-80656-082-0

Ebook ISBN 978-1-83703-564-9

Kindle ISBN 978-1-83703-565-6

Audio CD ISBN 978-1-83703-556-4

MP3 CD ISBN 978-1-83703-557-1

Digital audio download ISBN 978-1-83703-559-5

This book is printed on certified sustainable paper. Boldwood Books is dedicated to putting sustainability at the heart of our business. For more information please visit https://www.boldwoodbooks.com/about-us/sustainability/

Boldwood Books Ltd, 23 Bowerdean Street, London, SW6 3TN

www.boldwoodbooks.com

1

Virgil sat with his eyes closed and legs crossed, enjoying the warmth of the grass under him, the gentle sigh of the wind and the scent of wildflowers in the air. Peace reigned in his heart and all was right with the world. He smiled as blissful thoughts filled his mind.

The image of his bloodied fists pounding the face of his opponent smashed his sense of peace, the memory of the coppery stench of blood and the feel of the man's bones disintegrating beneath the blows eradicating his calm. Virgil's large, scarred hands formed into fists, the veins popping out in his arms as the excitement of the violence rose to claim him once again.

'Breathe,' he murmured to himself. 'Just breathe.'

After a few slow, deep inhalations, the violent images vanished and his body relaxed. The serene smile returned to his lips.

'Hey, Virg,' called a voice.

Virgil sighed as the sense of serenity vanished entirely. Turning, he saw his next-door neighbour, Cecil, approaching. The man was tall, thin and slightly stooped. The white vest he wore was a little too large for him and hung low, revealing his pale, scrawny chest covered in thick grey hair. He also wore cargo shorts, his skinny legs sticking out the bottom. Cecil's face was long and sad-looking, like a basset hound, and his grey hair was shaggy and unkempt.

'How are you finding my breathing technique?' Cecil asked him in his slow, languid way.

'Aye, great,' replied Virgil. 'It helps me get back on track when the violent thoughts start intruding.'

'Glad to hear it,' he said, unlocking the door of his caravan. 'Want to join me for a wee smoke?' he added, referring to the marijuana he consumed on a daily basis.

'Maybe later. I need a shower.'

'Aye, it's bloody hot today,' said Cecil, squinting up at the sun before vanishing inside his caravan, letting the door bang shut noisily behind him.

Virgil huffed with annoyance. Cecil was a good man, but he could be incredibly thoughtless. Fancy interrupting someone mid-meditation. Not so long ago, he would have knocked Cecil out for that, but he was a new man now, living the quiet, violence-free life in the countryside.

He rose and turned to face his own caravan, smiling fondly. It was only small but pretty, the top half neatly painted white, the lower half yellow. It even had its own garden with a small patch of lawn, colourful flowers and a vegetable patch. His washing on the line to the right of the van waved in the warm, gentle breeze. The caravan might be small but it was his haven, his retreat from the world, the place where he'd been reborn. No longer was Virgil MacGregor a bare-knuckle boxer and bodyguard for hire who revelled in carnage and violence. Now he was all about calm and peace and doing harm to no one.

His happiness only increased as he stepped inside the caravan. The interior was as neat as the outside, everything freshly painted and clean, the kitchen tiny but spotless. Best of all, it was all his. Virgil's privacy was very important to him after growing up with seven siblings.

After enjoying a cool shower, he slipped on a pair of shorts and a black vest. He stared down at his stomach, his little paunch visible through the material. Once his stomach had been rock hard and muscular, but that had meant an enormous amount of time spent at the gym. He'd rejected that way of life and now he had much more free time to do the things he actually loved. He hadn't let his boxing skills rust thanks to the punching bag around the back of the caravan; it kept his arms and shoulders in shape and he did a lot of walking, but his stomach was a bit neglected. He had intended to start doing sit-ups again but had been unable to find the enthusiasm. At first, his paunch had filled him with shame but now it made him feel liberated. He'd broken free of the shallow expectations of society and he liked it; it made him feel rebellious. Gone were his smart trousers and shirts too. Now he perpetually lived in T-shirts, shorts and jeans.

Virgil stared at his reflection in the mirror hanging on the wall of his compact bedroom. The face that stared back at him had been called handsome many times, although he couldn't see it himself. His Italian heritage through his mother was strong – his hair was black, eyes dark and skin olive. His height and strength had been inherited from his Glaswegian father, who'd had a fixation with the Wild West, particularly the Earp family. He'd been so obsessed with the history he'd named his children after all the Earp siblings, hence his own name, which had been the bane of his life at school where he'd been constantly taunted by the nickname *Virgil the Virgin*. The taunts had stopped when he'd turned fifteen, shot up in height and breadth and unleashed his frenzied temper, which had built up after years of bullying. He'd put his primary tormentor in hospital and no one had messed with him ever again. It was hard to believe that had only been eleven years ago. He felt to have lived a lifetime since.

This hotchpotch heritage of Italian and Scottish with a dash of the American West had made Virgil feel like a bit of an odd mix, neither one thing nor the other. The Earp names had been hard on most of his brothers. Their one sister, Adelia, had never gone through what he and his brothers Newton, Morgan and Wyatt had at school. How they'd envied their younger brothers and sister their normal names. There were two years between each sibling with Newton being the oldest. His parents had always been sticklers for punctuality.

He wandered into the kitchen and made himself a cup of chamomile tea because it helped keep him relaxed. Just as he'd sat down at the small table to read his latest self-help book, his eyes settled on the photograph on the wall. It was of himself and his wife, Ember, whose fiery temper certainly lived up to her name. In the photo they were on a beach in Cyprus, arms wrapped around each other. That had been in the days when they'd been happy. He loved that woman with all his heart, but two people with such volatile tempers should not be together. He'd learnt that the hard way.

Virgil sighed heavily at the sight of her brilliant green eyes and fiery red hair. Ember approached everything in life with great energy and determination, which was why it had hurt when she hadn't bothered to fight for him when he'd told her of his intention to leave the suburb of Garthamlock north-east of Glasgow city where they'd both been born and raised. She'd just coldly told him it was a good idea, that they both needed some space, before getting into her bright red sports car and driving off, leaving him standing alone and despairing on the pavement.

That had been six months ago and he hadn't heard from her since. Every day he expected divorce papers to land on his doormat but so far it hadn't happened, so he'd been living as a married man without a wife. He wished he could move on and find someone else, but the irony was he couldn't bring himself to do it even though their relationship had broken down. He'd always hoped she'd follow him and that they'd be able to work out their relationship away from the pressures of home and their families, but she hadn't bothered, which told him it really was over.

Just as Virgil returned his attention to his book, he heard a car door slam. He'd only had a total of four visits in the six months he'd been here, the majority of his family and friends deciding to give him the cold shoulder, considering him to be a traitor for putting his mental health first and leaving Garthamlock, so he didn't think the visitors would be for him. But to his astonishment, he saw his mother, grandmother and Ember getting out of the latter's bright red car.

Virgil tossed the book onto the table and leapt to his feet, frantically looking around to ensure the place was straight, which it always was. He took great pride in his little home. Should he wait until they'd knocked or open the door anyway? Had they seen him peering out at them? God, he wasn't used to feeling so uncertain, but he hadn't seen them in months and he knew all three would give him some pain for his so-called betrayal.

Deciding it would be better to wait for them to knock, he was kept waiting when it didn't happen. Curious, he peeked out to see the three women he loved most in the world standing in a line, studying his caravan and garden. He pushed open the door and two pairs of dark eyes and one pair of bright green eyes snapped onto him.

'Hello,' he said.

The three women frowned back at him.

'So this is your new home,' said his grandmother, resting her large bulk on the walking stick she held in her big, wrinkled hands. Even though she'd moved to Glasgow over fifty years ago, she had never lost her thick Italian accent. Despite his mother's inner strength and Ember's phenomenal temper, Ludovica was the scariest of the three.

'It is,' he replied. 'What do you think?'

Ludovica nudged a pot plant with the toe of her thick, sensible shoe. 'It has a little charm, although it looks very small.'

'It suits me well enough.'

Virgil was unable to keep his eyes off Ember. She wore one of her usual 1950s-style rockabilly dresses. This one was an off-the-shoulder number, black with red cherries. It should have clashed with her jaw-length red hair but somehow it didn't. She wore one of her chunky beaded necklaces, this one green, and a matching bangle on her wrist. Those fascinating eyes of hers regarded him curiously.

Maria, his mother, strode up to him and rested her hands on his shoulders. 'I have missed you, son,' she said.

'Then why didn't you come out here before?' he replied. 'I invited you often enough.'

His mother was a beautiful, regal woman who always held herself tall and proud. Her dark brown hair was streaked with grey and held back in a long plait. Her large, dark eyes could be warm and full of love, or cold and hard, depending on her mood. In contrast to her mother's accent, Maria's was pure Glaswegian.

'Let's talk inside,' she said, glancing sideways at Cecil, who was watching them curiously through the window of the caravan next door while smoking a joint.

Virgil nodded and led the three women inside. He refused to lose pride in his home when they regarded it with disdain.

His grandmother banged her walking stick on the floor. The woman didn't need a stick to get around – she was sturdy and as strong as an ox – but she liked it, mainly because she could thump it off the ground when she wanted everyone's attention, or she could hit people with it.

'You're needed back in Garthamlock,' announced Ludovica. 'Your brothers are running riot.'

'That's hardly news, Nonna,' he replied. 'Our family isn't known as The Bloody MacGregors for nothing.'

'This is worse than usual. You'd think Nick being sent to prison for assault would knock some sense into their heads, but it hasn't. They're wilder than ever. You have to return and put them into order again.'

'If you can't control them then what chance do I have?'

'They listen to you, Virgil; they always have.'

'Can't you just put one of your curses on them? A couple of weeks with boils and sores will keep them too busy to cause trouble.'

'I never curse my own family, as you well know,' she spat. 'And where are your manners? You were raised to be a good host, or is there no room for politeness in this new life of yours?'

'I take it that means you want a cup of tea, Nonna?'

Ludovica nodded and thumped her stick on the floor once more before taking a seat.

'Maw?' he asked Maria.

'Yes, please.'

'Ember?' he said, addressing her directly for the first time.

His estranged wife just nodded while continuing to regard him curiously. Virgil knew she was trying to work out whether he was a changed man or still the husband she had once known.

Virgil switched on the kettle and began preparing the mugs. 'So, what have my brothers been up to now?'

'Morgan took on a bodyguarding job for Liam McNeil and he half killed one of Liam's own men,' replied Maria.

'Good. Liam's a walloper and why does he need a bodyguard when he has his own crew?'

'Because there's a certain amount of kudos in having a MacGregor as a bodyguard,' she replied with a proud tilt of the chin. 'Unfortunately, Liam's man was stupid enough to make fun of Morgan; apparently he was jealous of his presence.'

'So he got the hiding he deserved? I don't see what the problem is. It's only what I would have done.'

'Aye but you wouldnae have put him in intensive care. The polis got involved. It was only thanks to the man refusing to talk that nothing happened. Then Wyatt and James got into a fight in a nightclub and practically smashed the place up, which cost our family more money and Warren beat up three men in the barber's.'

'The barber's?' He frowned.

'Aye. One of them was Adelia's ex and they made sexual comments about her in front of him. Even Newton, the most sensible one out of the lot of you, headbutted someone on the local bus for nicking his seat. They're out of control and if you don't come back and sort them out then they'll all end up in prison. So far it's only the threat our name carries that's meant that hasnae happened, but one day it will; I can feel it.'

Virgil sighed. 'You have to understand that I'm no' the man I was. I took an oath of non-violence.'

His mother arched a thin, perfectly plucked eyebrow while his grandmother raised both of her thick bushy brows. Ember continued to regard him with that detached curiosity.

'Non-violence?' repeated Maria.

'Aye. I've done a lot of deep inner work these past few months to control my temper. It doesnae overwhelm me any more and it's brought an amazing sense of peace into my life that I don't want to lose, which I will if I go back to Garthamlock. I'll be sucked back into my old ways and I don't know if I'll ever find my way back to peace again.'

'Your brothers need you and you're refusing to help?' demanded Maria, anger glittering in her eyes.

'I want to help them, of course, but I don't think I'm the right person to do it.'

Maria opened her mouth to yell back at him, but Ember got there first.

'So how do you spend your days here?' she said.

Virgil smiled, glad she was taking an interest in his new life, which was more than his mother and grandmother had done.

'I like going for hikes,' he said. 'There are some beautiful woodland walks around here. I meditate, read and I've got a job as a guide at the whisky distillery down the road. It's really interesting; I meet people from all over the world.'

'I bet you enjoy the free whisky too?' Maria frowned.

'No. I don't drink any more and I quit smoking too. Neither do I eat meat.'

Ludovica slammed her stick on the floor so hard Virgil winced, afraid she would put a hole right through it. The woman might be in her mid-seventies but she was freakishly strong.

'What is this nonsense I hear?' she barked. 'This family was raised on meat. What about my tagliata di manzo? Or my porchetta? My beef braciole used to be your favourite meal.'

'I'm no' denying they're delicious, Nonna,' he replied as he poured out the tea. 'But I don't want to consume the bodies of slaughtered innocents any more.'

'Slaughtered innocents? Oh, I see. You're on drugs, aren't

you? I saw that scarecrow of a man in the caravan next door. Don't you think I know a joint when I see one? He's addled your brain with his dirty drugs.'

Virgil sighed inwardly but he wasn't surprised. He'd always known they wouldn't understand. 'I don't take drugs. I don't take anything that doesnae enhance my body.'

'Oh, aye?' said Maria as he carried the mugs over to the table and placed them before the women. 'Then how come you're carrying this tyre if you're so health-conscious?' she added, prodding him in the belly with her finger.

'Because I'm no' slaving away in the gym six times a week and I'm much happier for it,' he replied, placing a protective hand over his stomach. 'I'm still fit and healthy.'

'A vegetarian in our family.' Ludovica sighed and shook her big bull head. 'The shame.'

Virgil rolled his eyes and leant back against the kitchen counter, out of reach of her walking stick. He glanced at Ember, whose opinion he was most anxious about, but she continued to regard him with those curious green eyes.

'I have to admit that you do look healthy,' said Maria.

'How can he be healthy without any meat inside him?' said Ludovica. 'He will soon start to fall apart. Meat is vital to our health.'

'No, it's not,' said Virgil.

'Nonsense,' she snapped, banging her stick on the floor again.

'We're no' here to discuss his diet,' said Maria. 'Virgil, your family needs you to come home.'

'So you ignore me for six months, practically disown me all because I wanted to better myself and suddenly I've got to drop my new life at your command. I'm sorry, Maw, I love you, but don't you see how unfair that is? Where were you when I needed you?' he yelled, dark eyes blazing.

The three women smiled as the old rage consumed Virgil. He took several deep breaths, concentrating on the breathing techniques he'd learnt, consigning that rage back to the shadows that lurked inside him.

'So the old Virgil still lives?' said Maria.

He'd noted that their smiles were dark. They didn't want this new, kinder, peaceful Virgil because he was no use to them. They wanted the hard, violent one who would crush anyone who got in his way. He'd always known the three women in his life were wicked.

'That man's gone,' he replied. 'My brothers are all adults. If they get themselves into trouble that's their problem.'

The women's smiles dropped.

'We are MacGregors,' hissed Maria. 'And MacGregors support each other.'

'If that's true then why did none of you support me in my new life?'

His mother just stared back at him coldly.

'Your brothers have got back into the underground fighting scene,' Ember told him. 'For Toni McVay.'

'You're fucking kidding.' He sighed, dragging his hands down his face. 'How the hell did that happen?'

'I thought getting back into the fights would allow them to channel their aggression,' said Maria. 'I negotiated with Toni in exchange for helping out some of her people.'

'Why would you do that when those fights were the reason that I came out here in the first place? I nearly killed someone, for Christ's sake.'

'You weren't there, so I did what I had to do. Their first fight is in two days' time and I hope you'll be there to support them.'

'Who's fighting?'

'Morgan and Warren.'

'I cannae believe you've done this. You've made our family beholden to that psychotic bitch again. Why would she even let our family back in? She said we were ruining the odds because we always won our fights.'

'Toni realised she had no choice if she wanted her people saving.'

'What people?' he exclaimed.

'It doesnae matter; it was just her latest gang war. She's always going through them. Anyway, she owes us and letting your brothers back in the fights was the payment we demanded.'

'No, something's no' right. Toni was delighted when she managed to push us out of the underground fights. If she's let our family back in then it's only because she's found a way to turn the situation to her advantage, which will hurt us.'

'She knows better than to mess with us,' hissed Maria.

'Toni McVay is scared of no one. She's the most powerful and dangerous woman in the whole of Scotland. Something bad is going to happen to Morgan and Warren. You have to pull them out of that fight.'

'Impossible. It would hurt our reputation too much.'

Virgil groaned and screwed his right hand up into a fist, about to slam it down on the counter. It was only the gleam in the women's eyes that stopped him from doing it.

'Don't you see that this fight is the real danger to our family?' he said, voice low and controlled.

'It will let them get the violence out of their systems,' said Ludovica. 'And that can only be to everyone's benefit.'

'Are you going to come back to Garthamlock then?' said Ember with her same casual curiosity.

'I can't,' he said through gritted teeth.

'So be it,' replied Maria. She got to her feet. 'We'll let you know how the boys get on.'

Virgil turned his back on them and placed his hands on the counter while he wrestled with himself. It would be easy for him to keep out of it and stay here, but he knew his brothers were walking into some sort of trap. Toni had lost a lot of money betting against his family and she would want revenge, even if his brothers had helped out her people. Toni McVay was a very clever tactician and she would have found some way to turn the situation in her favour. His mother was just as clever as Toni, though, and had decided to use this to lure him back home.

Virgil turned back to face them, looking longingly around his little van before speaking.

'Fine, I'll come back.' He sighed.

'Wonderful.' Maria smiled. 'I knew you wouldn't let us down.'

'But I want to make it clear that it's only temporary. This is my home now.'

'Aye, of course,' she replied dismissively.

'I mean it, Maw. I don't even know how much help I'll be. As I said, I've changed.'

'No one ever really changes,' said Ludovica. 'Deep down, they're always the same.'

'No' me. I really am different.'

'That remains to be seen.'

'When will you return?' Maria asked him.

'Tomorrow. I need to pack and let my job know.'

'Very well. Your old room will be waiting for you.'

'If you don't mind,' Ember told the older women, 'I'd like a word with Virgil in private.'

'Of course,' said Maria. 'We'll wait for you in the car.'

Ember nodded and handed her the key. She didn't speak until Maria and Ludovica had left.

'Why don't you sit down, Virg?' Ember told him.

He nodded and took the chair opposite her at the table.

'We haven't talked and we should have,' she began. 'I considered driving out here to see you many times, but I thought I had no place in your new life.'

His expression softened. 'There will always be a place for you in my life, no matter what.'

'I understood you came out here to fight your anger issues and I didn't want to get in the way of that. My temper's just as bad as yours and I thought I wouldn't help.' Her green eyes narrowed suspiciously. 'Have you really got a handle on your temper?'

'Aye. It's so much better; it doesnae rule me any more.'

'All because of meditation and chamomile tea?' she said, gesturing to her mug.

'It helps keep me calm,' he replied.

'You really don't want to come back to Garthamlock, do you?'

'No. I've made progress these last few months. I'm really no' the man to put my brothers in line. Why can't Newton do it? He's the oldest, for God's sake.'

'Because he's weird and introverted and he doesnae have your air of authority. The boys listen to you.'

'They listen to Maw and Nonna.'

'Maria's grip on them has been slipping lately. She knows she won't be able to control them for much longer and Ludovica's getting on. She doesn't need this shite in her life.'

'Come on, Ember, you know Nonna thrives on trouble. Besides, I've lost my air of authority. My brothers will see me as weak.'

'Oh, I see,' she said with an amused smile.

'See what?'

'You're not afraid of being unable to control your brothers any more. You're afraid of them taking the piss out of you.'

'I am not.'

'You can't fool me, Virg; I understand you far too well. You don't want to lose face in their eyes. It's nothing to be ashamed of. They've looked up to you your entire life. It's only natural that you don't want to lose that.'

'All right, I admit it's true, but that's no' my biggest worry.'

'Then what is? Please, talk to me. After all, I'm still your wife.'

'You know what almost killing Mark Stewart did to me.'

'I do. It nearly destroyed you.'

'I'm terrified that if I come back, I'll lose control and do the same thing to someone else, or maybe next time I'll go the whole way and take someone's life. That's my worst fear.'

She placed her hand over his. 'As you said, you're different now. You've got coping mechanisms you didn't have back then. Maybe you'll return to Garthamlock and be stronger than ever?'

'Maybe,' he said, knowing it wasn't true.

'Your return means we need to discuss us. Do you still love me, Virg?'

'Of course I do,' he said, giving her hand a gentle squeeze. 'I'll always love you.'

'I love you too. The question is – do we try again or get a divorce?'

The thought of divorce sent pain lancing through his entire body. 'I don't want a divorce.'

'So you want to try and make it work?'

'Aye but we both know the old problems will still be there.'

'I've had an idea. We could try couples counselling.'

'You'd really do that?'

'I think it's worth a shot.'

'But you were always against therapy before.'

'I've had time to think since you've been away. I've missed you and if therapy could help us then we should try it. That's if you agree?'

'Absolutely I do. I've become a big believer in therapy lately.'

'Great. I've found a good counsellor who comes highly recommended. I do think we should still live apart and not do anything physical. Let's just see how we get on first.'

'Okay,' he said, although he was disappointed. He hadn't had sex in six months and he found Ember as desirable as ever, but it was worth it if it saved his marriage.

'I'd better go. Maria and Ludovica will be getting impatient and it's not wise to keep women like them waiting.' Ember got to her feet and rested her hand on his shoulder. 'I want things to work out for us, Virg.' She bent over to kiss his neck. 'I still want you,' she breathed in his ear. 'I've dated other men but none of them can measure up to you.'

He was so enjoying her touch that it took him a moment to process what she'd said. 'What other men?' he demanded.

Ember just gave him an enigmatic smile before leaving.

'Wait,' he called, leaping up. 'What other men?'

He rushed to the door but she was already getting into the driver's seat of her car. As he ran outside, she started the engine and sped off, the wheels kicking up gravel, spraying his plants and vegetable garden like shrapnel.

The thought of his wife with another man disturbed the calm balance of Virgil's mind. He picked up a plant pot containing a geranium he'd been nurturing and hurled it at the window of his caravan, smashing it.

The sound of breaking glass brought him back to his senses and he rushed inside to find the tender plant sprawled across the floor, soil and glass everywhere, the pot broken. He wasn't even back in Garthamlock yet and already the old shite was turning him back into the man he didn't want to be any more. Now Ember had left, the spell she usually cast over him had gone and he started to wonder why a woman like her would even suggest therapy in the first place. Was Ember really that willing to do anything to get their marriage back on track, or did she have an ulterior motive?

Virgil knelt beside the geranium, being careful to avoid the shards of glass and broken pot and tenderly picked up the injured plant.

'I'm sorry,' he breathed, shoulders sagging, not sure whether he was apologising to the geranium or himself.

2

Virgil rose early the next morning and drove to the distillery where he worked. They'd been so good to him that he felt they deserved nothing less than an explanation in person as to why he wouldn't be in work for a while. They accepted his story of a sick family member without question, even sympathised with him and told him his job would be kept open for him until his return and that he wasn't to come back until he was ready. He felt horrible lying to these good people, but he could hardly tell them he was going to save his brothers from an underground boxing match run by the biggest gangster in the country. He then drove back to the caravan park and went to visit Cecil, who promised to look after his van for him, as well as his plants and vegetable garden and to let in the glazier who was coming that afternoon to replace the broken window. It was only a thirty-minute drive from Garthamlock, but events back home had the habit of tangling him up in their web. Although technically it wasn't far, it felt like a world away.

After packing his bags, Virgil took one last, lingering look around the caravan that had been his home for six months. He'd been so happy here and had intended to make this place his permanent home. It had made him realise that he didn't need the big house, the designer clothes or all the other crap he'd thought was important for so many years. This little nook was his haven and his instinct was screaming at him not to leave it.

With a regretful sigh, Virgil picked up his bags and carried them outside, pausing to check on the geranium he'd lovingly repotted. Thankfully, it didn't seem to be suffering from the violence inflicted on it and stood tall and proud in the sun.

He dumped the bags in the boot of his black twelve-year-old Peugeot 208. His nearest neighbours had come out to wave him off, people he'd become close with in this small, peaceful community they'd created together. He felt choked up as he got in the driver's seat and started the engine.

As Virgil drove away, he continually glanced in the rear-view mirror, watching his little yellow and white van getting smaller, along with all those kind, happy faces until the scene vanished entirely, causing a pang in his chest.

Swallowing down his emotion, he concentrated on what he was about to face. Already he knew it wasn't going to be pleasant.

* * *

The first sign that Virgil was nearly home were the Garthamlock and Craigend Water Towers that looked like a couple of enormous grey UFOs with legs. The three terraced houses his family owned were just down the street from these towers, which dominated everything around them and gave the area a slightly claustrophobic atmosphere.

His family's three houses sat together in a row. Initially, they'd only owned the house in the middle, but when the neighbours either side of them had got sick of their antics and put their homes up for sale, the MacGregors had purchased them, not wanting to leave the area where they'd lived for nearly thirty years. The fences and hedges dividing the front gardens of the three houses had been taken away, creating one long garden.

The houses didn't have driveways, so he had to park at the kerb at the end of a long line of cars. The majority of these motors belonged to his brothers, and were pretty high-end cars too – a BMW, two Audis, a Tesla M3 and a Lexus. His own little car looked completely out of place.

Virgil parked behind a white Audi A1 that he recognised as belonging to his younger brother, Warren, and climbed out of the car. The front door of the middle house in which his mother and grandmother lived was opened and out poured his brothers, loping towards him with big grins on their faces, looking like eager Labradors.

Warren was the first to reach Virgil and threw his arms around him.

'Maw said you were coming home today but I didnae believe it until now,' he said, slapping Virgil on the back before releasing him. 'It's fucking great to see you again.'

'You too,' replied Virgil, hoping he looked more enthusiastic than he felt.

Morgan was the next to hug him, followed by twitchy, edgy Wyatt and then James. Only Newton remained in the garden, arms folded across his chest, looking his usual grim self. All the brothers closely resembled each other, their Italian heritage obvious. Their father had also been tall and strong, something all his boys had inherited.

'So you're back?' Newton casually asked him.

'Seems so,' he replied.

Virgil was close to all his brothers, except this one. Newton had always resented the influence he had over their siblings, especially as Virgil wasn't the eldest. In fact, James was older than Virgil too, but he'd never held any animosity against him as Newton had, accepting the fact that Virgil was a natural leader. James didn't want the hassle of trying to keep them all in line; Newton, however, was a different kettle of fish. There was something of the snob about him and he'd always been cold and a little creepy. He was handsome and strong just like his brothers, but Newton's dark eyes were haughty and indifferent, lacking the fire his siblings possessed.

'Maw said you were coming home but I had my doubts,' said Newton.

'As you can see, she wasnae wrong,' replied Virgil.

'Is this a permanent return or just a temporary one?'

'It's temporary. I intend to go back to Milngavie as soon as all this shite is sorted out.'

'What shite?'

'The bare-knuckle boxing.'

'Don't tell me you're against it?' said Morgan.

'Let's discuss it inside,' he replied when he noticed one of the neighbours staring at him from their window. That particular neighbour wasn't at all afraid of any of the brothers, having got into scuffles with them several times, but he was terrified of Ludovica and her Italian folk magic and her curses.

The men all piled into their mother's house where a feast awaited them in the kitchen, which was the heart of the house. Ludovica loved to cook; it was how she showed her love and spent the majority of her days. There was always something simmering on the stove or warming in the oven and the house was perpetually filled with delicious aromas.

The dining table groaned with a variety of dishes, all home-made and Italian. As with all the walls in the house, the ones in this room were covered in pictures and old photographs of the

Wild West. Thanks to their father's fascination with the Earp family, the majority of them were various scenes from Tombstone in Arizona. Pride of place at the head of the room was an enlarged photograph of their father, Jimmy MacGregor, in his usual uniform of ten-gallon hat, blue jeans, cowboy boots and blue denim jacket. He was standing outside the OK Corral, scene of the infamous shootout between Wyatt, Virgil and Morgan Earp along with their ally, Doc Holliday, against five members of a gang known as the Cowboys. Beside him in the picture was Maria, looking impossibly elegant and out of place. She looked radiantly happy wrapped in her husband's arms, pleased because he'd finally visited a place he'd wanted to see his entire life. Jimmy had died of a sudden heart attack two years after that photograph had been taken, which had been almost a year ago.

'I knew you wouldn't let us down,' Ludovica told Virgil with a rare smile, patting his cheek so hard it was almost a slap. She gestured to the table. 'Sit, eat. You must be hungry.'

'It seems he's liking the food a bit too much.' James grinned, prodding Virgil's stomach.

'Piss off, you cheeky bastard.' Virgil smiled back, smacking his hand away.

The men ranged around the table, Newton being quick to take the chair at the head of the table, the one their father had occupied until his death. Virgil had to hide a smile. Once such behaviour would have annoyed him but now he just saw it as petty.

'So what's this I hear about you getting back into the underground fights?' said Virgil, plucking a slice of focaccia from a plate and tearing off a piece before popping it into his mouth.

'It's great, isn't it?' Warren smiled. 'Me and Morgan are fighting tomorrow night.'

'Do you know who your opponents are yet?'

'Nope but there will be some big names there, men we've never fought before, so hopefully we'll get to beat the living shite out of them and take their titles from them.'

'Toni McVay's running them.'

'Aye, we know. We helped save some of her people from a battering, not that those people couldnae hold their own, but they were outnumbered at the time. The Savage Sisters from Haghill, you ever hear of them?'

'No.'

'They're sexy as hell and hard as nails. I've been dating Rose, the youngest sister. Christ, she's something else.'

Warren cringed when his grandmother smacked him hard around the back of his head and began swearing at him in Italian for taking the Saviour's name in vain. Warren apologised in Italian. All the siblings had been taught from a young age to speak the language and were fluent in it. This heartfelt apology caused Ludovica to simmer down and lower her raised fist.

'I cannae believe you want back into the fights after what happened to me,' said Virgil.

'We havenae forgotten,' replied James gently. 'How could we? We all saw how it affected you, but we don't lose it like you do in the ring.'

'It's no' just that,' said Virgil, forcing down the traumatic memory of watching his opponent lying on the canvas bleeding from his mouth and nose, eyes rolling about in his skull while his wife screamed in horror beside her fallen husband. 'Toni didnae like us taking part in the fights because we always won and no one would bet against us. It ruined the odds for her, so why would she let you back in?'

'Because we made a deal to protect her people.'

'That's shite and you know it. Toni never does anything that isnae to her benefit. She's setting you up somehow and I don't think you should go through with it.'

'We've no choice. If we back out, then not only will we piss off Toni, but we'll look like cowards as well. Everyone will think we've lost our bottle. You know we have to go through with it, Virg.'

He sighed, the terrible feeling that his brother was right sinking over him like a ten-ton weight. 'This is such a mess.'

'Perhaps if you'd been here then this wouldn't have happened,' Maria told him as she joined her sons at the table.

'I had to leave, Maw, for my own sanity. You know that.'

'You're a very strong man; you would have got through it with your family's support. Instead, you chose to run away.'

'It wasnae running away. I needed to get my head straight.'

'To be fair,' said James. 'We don't know what it's like to nearly kill someone.'

'I do,' said Ludovica, savagely tearing a piece of ciabatta in two.

The difference between his mother and grandmother had always been a startling contrast to Virgil. While Maria was tall, beautiful and elegant, Ludovica looked like she could strangle pigs with her bare hands. Her features were fierce and coarse, her face heavily lined. Ludovica's body was very stout, although she was quite tall like Maria, which made her seem even more imposing.

'I don't think Virg is talking about your curses, Nonna,' said James.

'Neither am I,' she replied. 'His name was Matteo Barbieri and he was my lover when I was a girl. He cheated on me with that slut Elena Amato, so I stabbed him in the belly with a pitchfork.'

Morgan spluttered into his glass of orange juice. 'A pitch-fork?' he gasped, wiping the spilt liquid from his chin.

'Yes,' she said casually. 'He lived, by some miracle. Believe me, that is not what I intended. Whenever he saw me coming after that, he would run away.'

'I'm no' surprised.'

'Didn't you stab Elena too, Nonna?' said Warren.

'No, because she didn't promise to love me until the stars fell from the sky.'

'Hey, that's a good line. I'll use that on Rose.'

'You're in love?' said Virgil with surprise.

'Aye, I think so. You'll understand when you meet her; there's no one else like her.'

Virgil glanced across the table at Wyatt, who was quiet and sullen, as always. He'd struggled from a young age with the pressure of being named after a legend. 'Are you involved in these fights too, Wyatt?'

'I'm waiting to see how Morgan and Warren get on first,' he muttered, which was his usual way of speaking.

'At least someone's being sensible about all this,' Virgil told the table.

Morgan rolled his eyes. 'Will you relax? Everything's fine. Your problem is you've been living the quiet life too long. You've lost your bottle.'

The other brothers all regarded Virgil with wide, worried eyes. Just a few months ago, anyone accusing Virgil of losing his bottle would have been pulled to pieces but now he just sat there, seemingly unaffected by the accusation. Their jaws all dropped open in astonishment, even Newton's.

'As you can see, I really have changed,' said Virgil with a touch of smugness.

'Just wait until you've been back here a week,' replied

Newton with a knowing look. 'Then we'll see the old Virgil again.'

'I suppose you think getting back under Toni McVay's thumb is a good thing too?' retorted Virgil.

'Like Wyatt, I'm waiting to see how tomorrow night goes.'

'Everything will work out,' said Morgan with his usual optimism. 'It always does.'

'No' for me, thanks,' said Virgil when James picked up the bottle of red wine that sat in the centre of the table and attempted to fill his empty wine glass with it. 'I've given up the drink.'

They all gaped at him again.

'You don't drink?' spluttered Warren.

'Nope.'

'No' even pints?'

'No' even pints and I'm healthier than I've ever been.'

'If that's true then how come you've got a gut on you?' said Warren.

'You cheeky wee bastard, it's no' a gut. I just stopped going to the gym and it's a big relief.'

'Ember won't like that stomach. She's no' interested in any man who's no' ripped.'

'I like to think that our marriage is based on something deeper than what each other's bellies look like,' replied Virgil while trying not to think about the dates Ember had said she'd been on. His brother could smell weakness a mile off and if he found out, Newton would never let him live it down.

'You might be deeper but she's no'.'

'Don't worry about me and Ember; worry about yourself. You're about to walk into Toni McVay's trap.'

'Who cares?' said Warren. 'As long as I get to twat people, I'm happy.'

'She'll soon have you dancing to her tune just like all her other puppets.'

Morgan's expression darkened. 'I'm no one's fucking puppet.'

'You will be by the end of tomorrow night.'

'No' gonnae happen.'

Virgil sighed. It had been pointless coming back here. His brothers had decided they were taking part in the fights and nothing would change their minds. He recalled Ember's words and thought perhaps his return hadn't been a complete waste of time. It would be worth it if it got his marriage back on track, but that would mean giving up his new life in Milngavie. He still wasn't sure how he felt about that.

'I hear you've been up to other stuff too,' said Virgil, deciding it was time to move the conversation on from the underground fights. 'Why did you beat up Adelia's ex?' he asked Warren. Their sister had moved away from Garthamlock after their father had died and now shared a flat with a friend in Edinburgh, wanting to escape her overprotective brothers.

'Because the wanker started mouthing off about all the stuff they'd got up to in bed right in front of me. He thought it was funny because he had his pals with him. They got a good fucking twatting too.'

'Do you want to end up in prison like Nick? Because that's where you're going if you carry on down this path.' There had never been an Earp brother named Nick. As there had only been six Earp brothers, Maria and Jimmy had named their seventh son after the Earp brothers' father, Nicholas.

'I bet Rose wouldnae hang around waiting for you to be released,' Newton told Warren. 'She'd soon be after a new man.'

'What the fuck did you say?' he barked, shooting to his feet while Newton smirked back at him.

'Sit down,' Virgil told Warren. 'He's only trying to wind you up.'

Warren glared at Newton before retaking his seat and stabbing angrily at his food with his fork.

'You've all got to learn some self-control,' Virgil told the table.

'Coming from you?' replied Morgan. 'Seriously?'

'As I said, I've changed.'

'We'll see,' said Newton. He leant back in his chair and clasped his hands behind his head. 'We'll fucking see.'

* * *

After dinner, Virgil wanted to take a walk to exercise off the enormous amount of food he'd consumed. He'd missed his grandmother's amazing cooking. He also wanted to familiarise himself with the place again as it felt like he'd been away a lot longer than six months. Virgil had intended to take the walk alone, but James and Wyatt insisted on accompanying him. Morgan and Warren were heading to the gym to get some practice in before their big fight and Newton was working as a bodyguard to a local drug dealer on a neighbouring scheme.

'Are you glad to be back?' James asked Virgil.

Out of all his brothers, James was his favourite. He was the most sensible and down-to-earth of them all. Virgil had always thought he would be much better at keeping their brothers in line than himself, as James tackled situations with logic and reason whereas Virgil went at them with anger and violence, but it did mean he was much more feared than his laid-back older brother. James had always refused to take on the responsibility, saying he was in charge of himself and no one else, which only went to prove how sensible he was.

'It's great seeing you all again,' replied Virgil. 'But I miss my wee caravan and the peace and quiet of the countryside.'

'Have you really given up the drink?'

'Aye.'

'Even though you were working at a distillery?'

'Yep.'

'So what do you do for fun?'

'I read, meditate, go hiking.'

'I said fun, no' punishment.' James grinned wryly. 'You do realise that you will turn back into the man you used to be if you hang around here for too long? Our younger brothers alone are enough to drive a saint to drink. Then there's Nonna cursing everyone left, right and centre, and Maw determined to do whatever it takes to earn some cash.'

'Aye, I know but I've nae choice.'

'You could go back to your caravan.'

Virgil stopped and turned to face James. 'You really mean that?'

'Aye. Don't get me wrong, I love having you back, but I think for the first time in your life you're truly happy and coming back here to all the shite will only ruin that.'

'Thanks, pal, I appreciate that and I've got the horrible feeling you're right.' Virgil glanced at Wyatt, wondering what he thought about it all, but he just walked alongside them in silence. That was just Wyatt's way. He wasn't as vocal as his brothers.

'Maw said Ember went to see you too,' said James.

'She did and she wants to try couples counselling,' replied Virgil.

'Seriously, Ember wants to do that?'

'Why do you look suspicious?'

'Because it doesnae sound like her at all.'

'Maybe she's changed too? Aye, all right,' added Virgil at James's sceptical look. 'You think she could have an ulterior motive?' he said, curious to get a second opinion. He wasn't sure if he was being paranoid or not.

'Maybe. This is Ember we're talking about after all, but you never know.'

Unconsciously, Virgil had been wending his way towards the three-bedroomed house he and Ember had lived in together for the last six years, two of which they'd spent married. Most of the houses in Garthamlock were pretty recent. The majority of the old, dilapidated tenements in the area had been demolished in the 1980s and replaced with new builds. His and Ember's home was a rather elegant-looking three-bed semi of red-brick and white stone complete with a two-car drive and a decent-sized back garden. It was also on the opposite side of Garthamlock to the rest of his family, something Ember had insisted on. Although she got on well with the MacGregors, she didn't want Maria and Ludovica coming round every five minutes to criticise her housekeeping skills or Virgil's brothers turning up whenever they felt like it. Virgil had been in agreement with this as he'd thought a little privacy from his overbearing family would help calm his and Ember's volatile relationship, but strangely it had the opposite effect and he'd never been able to work out why.

He stared up at the house as he recalled the happy times he'd shared there with Ember.

'Are you gonnae see her?' Wyatt asked Virgil.

'No' yet. Besides, I don't think she's in. Her car's no' on the drive.'

Virgil's gaze turned wistful. Despite their unstable relationship, he and Ember had shared a lot of good times, many of them in that very house that he now felt cast out of. He got the feeling it would never be his home again.

3

The underground fights changed venue each time so the authorities couldn't catch up with them. The fight Morgan and Warren were participating in was being held at a fire station that had shut down a few years ago. Toni McVay had bought it intending to turn it into a pub but instead she'd decided to use it for more nefarious purposes.

A large boxing ring had been set up where the fire engines used to be housed and already quite the crowd had assembled, word having got around that two members of the MacGregor family would be fighting that night. No one liked to bet against them, but they loved watching the sheer speed and savagery with which the brothers fought.

Virgil arrived with James, Newton and Wyatt. Morgan and Warren were already present. Maria and Ludovica never came to these fights, so they'd remained at home. Everyone greeted the brothers cheerfully, shaking their hands and patting their shoulders. Such were their reputations for violence that no one would risk offending the brothers and becoming a victim of their retribution. Wyatt, however, hated being touched; it made him twitchier than usual. One man who dared put his hand on his arm recoiled when Wyatt whipped round to face him, left eye frantically twitching, outrage written across his face. The man stammered an apology before melding into the crowd.

They found their younger brothers loitering at the side of the ring. Warren had his arm slung around a very attractive woman in her late teens with long dark hair and large hazel eyes. Even though she looked completely out of place, she appeared to be relaxed and confident, not at all intimidated by some of the large, violent individuals in the room.

'I didn't think you were coming,' Morgan told Virgil. 'Seeing how you were so worried.'

'I'm here because I am worried,' he replied.

'Virg, this is Rose,' said Warren, regarding his girlfriend with adoring eyes. 'The youngest of the Savage Sisters.'

'Nice to meet you,' Virgil told her with a nod of the head.

'You too.' She smiled back.

'Isn't she gorgeous?' Warren grinned, before kissing her cheek.

'Are your sisters here?' Wyatt asked her with a leery smile.

'Naw,' replied Rose. 'They're both working.'

'Rose's family work for Toni,' Warren told Virgil in a low voice.

Virgil sighed inwardly. Great, another connection to the psychotic Queen of Glasgow.

'I don't though,' said Rose. 'When I leave college, I'm setting up my own business as an events planner. No one's gonnae dictate to me.' She looked to Warren and winked. 'And that includes you.'

'I wouldnae dream of trying.' He grinned, sliding his arms around her waist and kissing her.

'Do you know who you're fighting yet?' said Virgil, interrupting the passionate moment.

'Nope, it's no' been announced,' replied Morgan. 'There are another six fighters, all fucking awesome ones too, so it could be interesting.' He nodded at a beefy man whose chest and back were covered in thick black hair. 'I hope I get Harvey the Hammer. That twat called me a wee dick once, so it would be nice to get some payback.'

'Do you know when your fight is?'

'No' yet. We're waiting for Terry.'

Terry Donovan was the man who ran the underground fights on Toni's behalf. She'd employed a few different people over the years for this purpose, but most had fallen by the wayside, usually because they'd ended up stealing from her. Toni had tortured them all before removing their eyes – her trademark – and then killing them. Terry was the only one who'd gone the distance, mainly because he wasn't stupid. He was an ex-boxer and it showed with his cauliflower ears and bent nose. Although he was now in his late fifties and had retired from the game years ago, he was still more than capable of laying out any fighter who tried to go too far. It was thanks to his intervention that many fighters had left the ring alive. Before he took over, there were too many deaths and life-changing injuries, something Toni McVay didn't want as it made her life more difficult.

As Terry jumped into the ring, the entire room went silent without him having to utter a word. He spotted Virgil and frowned. Virgil was the only man who'd knocked Terry out while trying to break up a fight. It was the day he'd almost killed his opponent, and the shame and horror of it washed over Virgil once more. Never again would he step inside a boxing ring.

'Thanks for coming out tonight in this shitey weather,' Terry told the crowd. His voice naturally boomed, meaning even those stuck right at the back of the room could hear him. 'You'll see two fighters here tonight who've been absent for a while,' he began. 'Two members of the infamous Bloody MacGregor clan – Morgan and Warren.'

In response, the crowd erupted into applause.

'Now I know what you're all thinking,' continued Terry. Even though his face looked like a map that had been folded too many times, he possessed plenty of charisma and a charming smile. 'What's the point in even having a wee flutter if those two maddies are fighting because, let's face it, they flatten anyone in their paths.'

The other six fighters all grumbled at this compliment to their opponents.

'But here you're gonnae see the fight to end all fights because tonight it's MacGregor versus MacGregor. Morgan and Warren will fight each other,' announced Terry, raising his arms in the air for dramatic impact.

While the two men in question stared at each other in astonishment, the room erupted into wild applause, everyone loving the idea.

'And there it is,' said Virgil, feeling the anger start to rise inside him. 'I knew something like this would happen.'

'What the fuck do we do?' said Warren.

'We can't back down,' replied Morgan. 'We'll look like fucking cowards.'

'I don't want to fight you.'

'I don't want to fight you either but what choice do we have?'

'What did I tell you both?' spat Virgil, hands curling into fists as his rage rose. He took a deep breath and uncurled his fists. 'Now you've put our family in an impossible position. You're damned if you do and damned if you don't.'

'What would you do, Virg?' said Morgan.

'I wouldnae have been here in the first place, you fucking idiots.'

'You have to fight,' Newton told them.

The room began to grow restless, everyone wondering why the brothers weren't in the ring yet.

Terry's expression turned positively hostile when Virgil waved him over.

'What the fuck do you want?' Terry snarled at him. 'Because you're never getting back in here, I'm telling you that.'

'I know and I don't want to,' replied Virgil. 'But you cannae force them to fight each other.'

'This isnae my idea. If you want to tell Toni McVay that they don't want to do it then be my guest, but keep me out of it. And if they don't fight each other then your family's never getting in this ring again and your wee brothers will probably lose their eyes too.' Terry grinned with malicious pleasure. 'Toni doesnae like being told no.'

With that, he jumped out of the ring and told his people to begin taking bets.

'Newton's right,' Virgil told Morgan and Warren. 'You have to do it because it's either fight each other or have your eyes gouged out by Toni McVay.'

'And you have to make it realistic,' said Newton. 'You cannae get away with dancing around each other.'

'We can do this,' Morgan told Warren.

'Aye, all right but don't hit the nose. Rose won't want me any more if it ends up splattered across my face.'

The two brothers grinned at each other and fist-bumped.

'I knew you wouldnae let me down, boys.' Terry smiled as they stepped into the ring. 'Hurry up and finish placing your bets,' he told the room. 'The fight starts in two minutes.'

'I'm no' sure I can watch,' said Virgil.

'What are you talking about?' said Wyatt eagerly. 'This is gonnae be epic. Don't fucking touch me,' he barked in the face of one man who had accidentally nudged him in the shoulder. Such was the ferocity with which he spoke and the frenzy in his eyes that not only did that man leap backwards but the two men beside him did too.

'Take it easy, Wyatt,' said Virgil. 'Starting a rammy won't help our brothers.'

Morgan and Warren pulled off their tops and tossed them aside before their hands were wrapped with tape, ending one inch below the knuckles, to cushion the bones and tendons against the impact of the blows, allowing the fight to last longer. In official bare-knuckle matches, punches with a closed fist were the only types of blows allowed, but in Toni's underground matches other moves were permitted such as kicks and strikes with elbows and knees. However, the more dangerous techniques were strictly banned. Groin protectors were the only other protection Toni permitted her fighters to use.

As the bell rang, Virgil set the timer on his watch for two minutes, which was the length of each round, of which there was a maximum of five. Part of him hoped one of his brothers would do the decent thing and go down quickly, but he knew them too well and neither would want to lose face, especially Warren with Rose watching. They both loved to win and he worried that need might make them go too far.

They danced around each other for a bit first, each brother unwilling to land the first punch. It was only when the crowd started booing and demanding that someone do something that Morgan lashed out, catching Warren on the jaw, snapping back his head. The blow was delivered with such speed that murmurs of appreciation ran through the crowd. The main reason the MacGregor brothers were so unbeatable was their speed. Even the most experienced fighters had enormous trouble defending themselves against them.

Warren didn't appear to be in the slightest bit injured by the blow but he did seem surprised that his brother had hit him. Determination filled his eyes and he swung back at Morgan, who dodged the first punch, but the second immediately following it caught him on the left cheek.

Virgil glanced at his watch. Forty-five seconds already gone. Perhaps his brothers would get through this relatively unscathed?

His hopes were soon dashed. As more blows were exchanged, the brothers' blood got up, filling them with the fighting frenzy the MacGregors were famous for and they were soon trading furious punches. When the bell rang, Morgan's left eye was swollen and blood trickled from a cut to Warren's lower lip. Both men were coated in sweat, their dark eyes alight with the intoxication of violence. To show that battle lines had been drawn, both men went to the opposite side of the ring to take a break, glaring at each other across the canvas.

'For Christ's sake, Morgan, don't go too far,' Virgil told him. 'Remember he's your brother.'

He just gave him a hard nod in response.

Virgil then rushed over to the other side of the ring to talk to Warren, who was being tended to by Rose. She handed him a bottle of water and when he'd drunk his fill, she gently dabbed at his cut lip with a cloth. Virgil had to admit that she did seem to genuinely care about him. He repeated the same message to Warren that he'd given Morgan.

'Aye,' he replied dismissively, more concerned with Rose.

'I mean it, Warren. I don't want you two causing each other any permanent injury.'

'Yeah, yeah, yeah,' he muttered, waving a taped hand dismissively.

The bell rang for the second round and Virgil restarted the timer on his watch. To his dismay, Morgan and Warren went at each other even harder. It was clear they were both enjoying themselves, even though they were fighting a beloved sibling. Their love of battle had overcome them and their brotherly bond meant nothing.

'Fucking kill him, Warren,' yelled Rose when a punch from her beau sent Morgan staggering back against the ropes. She saw Virgil frowning at her. 'Sorry,' she told him. 'I got carried away.'

He shook his head and returned his attention to the fight. The bare chests and backs of both men were now smeared with blood from their various cuts, each determined to prove they were the better fighter. Virgil and James glanced at each other, both equally worried, while Newton, Wyatt and Rose cheered along with the crowd, who were going out of their minds with glee at seeing MacGregor fight MacGregor.

Morgan managed to get Warren against the ropes and began pummelling him in the face and stomach. Virgil glanced at his watch. Ten seconds. 'Hurry up,' he breathed as Warren's head was snapped from side to side by the blows.

With just four seconds to go, Warren managed to kick Morgan away and launched himself at his brother with a roar, swinging his fist into his face. The bell rang and they broke apart.

'I don't know how much more of this I can take,' breathed Virgil as both fighters retreated to their corners, dripping blood.

'I know what you mean,' replied James. 'And we're no' even halfway through yet. I'm hoping one of them will see sense and back down before it goes too far, but I doubt it.'

'Me too. Look at them – they've fucking lost it.'

Virgil recognised the bloodlust in his brothers' eyes only too well. It was the same feeling that had possessed him so many times and that had driven him to nearly kill someone. It had also made Morgan and Warren forget that they were brothers. What fresh damage could it do to his family?

The bell rang for the third time and the two fighters practically sprang at each other. Despite the two rounds they'd already endured and the injuries they'd sustained, they were more determined than ever to win and their fists started flying.

'Jesus, we have to do something before they kill each other,' said Virgil.

'I agree, but what?' replied James. 'Any tampering will incur the wrath of Toni McVay.'

Warren punched Morgan hard in the face, the blood that burst from his mouth spraying a spectator standing at the ropes. The man barely seemed to notice, too caught up in the excitement of it all. Bloodlust had gripped the crowd too, their eyes bright with the fever of it.

'Warren!' yelled Virgil. 'He's your brother. Don't forget that.'

Warren ignored him and punched Morgan again and again. To Virgil's relief, Morgan managed to block his next punch and kicked him in the side of the face, sending him stumbling backwards. Morgan gasped with relief that the onslaught was over and staggered forward a few paces, raising his bloodied fists again.

The brothers tore into each other once more, but their movements were more lethargic as tiredness began to set in. However, both were still on their feet and ready for more by the time the bell rang at the end of the third round.

Virgil rushed up to Morgan, who was leaning against the ropes for support and attempted to jump over the ropes, but Terry jabbed a digit in his direction. 'Don't you fucking dare.'

Virgil sighed and remained on the outer edge of the ring. 'Morgan,' he called. 'What are you playing at?'

'Winning,' he mumbled before taking a drink of water. 'He's going at me just as hard.'

'If you back down then so will he.'

'I cannae back down.'

'Morgan...'

'No,' he snapped. 'We're going on to the end.'

Virgil rushed over to Warren, who was once again being tended to by Rose, but his pleas continued to fall on deaf ears. Both men were determined to see the fight through to the end.

'Have you thought about what happens when you leave this building?' Virgil hissed at Warren. 'That's if you're both lucky enough to get out of here without severe brain damage. It will hurt your relationship.'

'We'll be fine,' he replied. 'The only difference is we'll know who's the better fighter.'

'That's no' worth killing each other over,' he exclaimed.

'Relax, Virgil. The same thing won't happen to us as it did to you.'

'You don't know that; you're both getting carried away. Tell him, Rose.'

Before she could reply, the bell rang again and the brothers rushed back into the fight.

'God, two more rounds to go,' groaned Virgil, resetting the timer on his watch.

'I'm sure they'll be fine,' said Rose. 'They know what they're doing.'

'You're optimistic,' he sighed.

The brief rest had given Warren and Morgan their energy back, but their handsome faces were both distorted with bruising, swelling and blood. It was Morgan's fist in Warren's ribs that put an end to the proceedings. Virgil saw his brother's face pale as the bones cracked.

'Don't be a fucking idiot,' Virgil yelled at Warren when he drew back his fist to strike his brother while grimacing in pain. 'What if you get a punctured lung?'

Thankfully, he finally saw sense and nodded. Terry grabbed Morgan's arm and raised it aloft, proclaiming him the winner. Between them, Virgil and James helped an injured Warren out of the ring.

'Sorry, babe,' he told Rose with his swollen, split lips. 'I lost.'

'No, you didn't; you were amazing,' she said. 'Any other man would have been wiped out in the first round.'

He smiled and wrapped an arm around her, grimacing at the pain in his ribs. 'Sorry, babe,' he said. 'I've got blood on your top.'

'I don't care,' she said, kissing his bruised cheek.

Morgan eventually climbed out of the ring once he'd finished basking in the glory. Everyone watched as he approached Warren, eager to see if the fight had caused a rift between them.

'Sorry, pal,' he told Warren. 'I think you would have had me if I hadnae got in that lucky hit to your ribs.'

'Aye, I would,' he retorted.

They stared at each other before grinning and hugging.

'Ow, mind my ribs,' grimaced Warren.

'Sorry,' said Morgan, releasing him. He turned to the rest of his brothers. 'You've got to admit, that was an epic fight.'

'I think I aged ten years watching it,' sighed Virgil.

'I thought it was fucking awesome,' exclaimed Wyatt.

'Me too,' said Newton. 'Nice punch, by the way,' he told Morgan. 'I heard the crack when you hit him in the side.'

'Aye, thanks,' scowled Warren, who was leaning a little on Rose for support.

'You need to sit down,' Virgil told him.

Warren nodded and sank into a fold-out chair Terry's assistant provided for him, while Rose started to wipe away the sweat and blood with a towel.

Terry leapt down out of the ring, a big grin on his face. 'Fucking nice one, boys. People will be talking about that fight for years to come. It's the first time they've seen anyone last longer than two rounds against a MacGregor. If it hadnae been for that rib shot, I'm sure we'd have made the full five rounds. Cheer up,' he told a frowning Warren. 'We've all made a fortune tonight, including you and Morgan. Hang about and I'll get your share for you.'

'Who was the money on?' Morgan asked him curiously.

'It was split fifty-fifty. No one could decide who to back. I saw a few punters tossing a coin just to pick a name.'

Even people who'd betted on Warren and had consequently lost approached to congratulate him on a great fight, which buoyed his spirits, as did Rose's tender care.

* * *

The MacGregors left the old fire station and drove back to their mother's house, accompanied by Rose. Virgil watched her interactions with his mother and grandmother very carefully. Between them, the two women had driven away most of the brothers' partners over the years because they could be so domineering and, in Ludovica's case, scary. Ember was the only one to have gone the distance, mainly because she could be scary too. Rose, however, was relaxed and happy in the older women's company and not at all intimidated; indeed, they looked to be very fond of her. It seemed the Savage Sisters deserved their reputations.

'Maybe you should get checked out at hospital,' Virgil told

Warren. 'Cracked ribs can damage the lungs.'

'Nonsense,' said Ludovica. 'I can care for him better than any hospital. All they will do is give him an X-ray, tell him what he already knows and send him on his way. My remedies will heal him much faster. Anyway, it won't be the first time I have nursed one of you boys through cracked ribs with all the fights you've had over the years.'

Virgil didn't want an argument about it, so he took a seat in the scrupulously neat lounge, which was usually reserved for visitors, but Ludovica had decreed that Warren and Morgan would be much more comfortable in there with its soft couches.

As Ludovica set to work tending to her grandsons' injuries, Virgil once again studied Rose, wanting to see how she reacted to his grandmother's remedies as Ludovica constantly muttered charms under her breath while she worked. Her ways were the old ways, passed down through generations of her family from Naples, and they were very effective too, but a lot of outsiders found them strange and unnerving. Rose, however, was enthralled, watching with wide, eager eyes. His mother was also watching Rose and she was smiling. It seemed Rose had gained her good opinion too. Ember likewise had taken an interest in Ludovica's ways, but she'd only wanted to use them for her own nefarious purposes, so Ludovica had refused to teach her, despite her repeated requests. What were Rose's intentions?

'I cannae believe you fought each other,' said Maria once Newton had explained the evening's events. 'That is not something MacGregors do.'

'We had no choice, Maw,' said Morgan. 'It was either that or have our eyeballs scooped out by Toni McVay.'

'She wouldn't dare.'

'Course she would because she's a psycho,' said Newton. 'And she's afraid of no one, no' even us. Anyway, Morgan and Warren both made a ton of cash tonight.'

'Aye, we did,' said Warren, managing to muster a smile, despite how tired and sore he was. 'And we need the money.'

Virgil sighed. His family was perpetually short of cash and it didn't seem that situation had changed in the time he'd been away. It wasn't that they didn't earn much because they did, they raked it in through their bodyguarding sideline as well as the underground fights, but they had expensive tastes – nice cars, designer clothes and watches, top-of-the-range phones. He'd been the same once, but since he'd left Garthamlock he'd realised how useless all that crap was, enabling him to get some savings behind him.

'At least something good came out of this mess,' said Maria. 'I cannae believe Toni would do this to our family.'

'I can,' said James. 'You've got to admit it was clever though and it made her a fortune too.'

'This is just the beginning,' said Virgil. 'She'll try to rope the rest of you into fighting each other now.'

'No' you?' said Morgan.

'No. You heard Terry say he won't allow me back in the ring.'

'He'll have to if Toni orders it.'

'Perhaps not – she respects him too much. Anyway, even if she does get him on board, I'll just refuse.'

'You know you cannae refuse her.'

'Yes I can and I don't care what she threatens me with. I won't do it,' he said while trying not to think of all the ways Toni McVay could force him into obeying her formidable will.

'The woman's smart. She'll find another way to force you.'

'I hope you realise what a mess our family's in. We're now beholden to a psychopath.'

'Oh, stop worrying, for God's sake.' Newton sighed. 'Rose's family work for Toni and they're doing really well.'

'Really?' Virgil asked her.

'Aye,' she replied. 'My sisters, cousin and uncle all debt-collect on her behalf. They even have their own crews now.'

'Maybe we should get involved in that?' said Morgan.

'No,' replied Virgil firmly.

'It's no' just your decision,' retorted Newton. 'We all have the right to a say and we need to start earning some serious money.'

'Correction, we already earn good money. It's our spending we need to get under control.'

'Why, what's wrong with our spending?' Morgan frowned.

'You're saying that when you have a sixty-five-thousand-pound BMW sitting outside?'

'Better that than the portable toilet you drive.'

'It does what I need it to do, which is what's important. Car finance is such a massive financial trap.'

'What the hell happened to you in the countryside?' Wyatt demanded of him. 'You've come back all boring and pompous.'

'Amen to that,' said Newton. 'And all this coming from a man who used to own a seventy-grand Audi.'

'Aye and I couldnae wait to get rid of it,' said Virgil. 'I'm just saying that if you all cut back on the luxuries a bit then you'll have a hell of a lot more money.'

'I'm no' giving up anything,' said Warren. 'I like all that stuff. I'd rather earn more money to afford it.'

'You won't be earning anything until you've got over those cracked ribs. Does anyone have any more bodyguarding jobs?'

'Me and James are working tomorrow night,' said Newton. 'For Adam Parker.'

'The dealer?' replied Virgil.

'Aye.'

'Why do we always end up looking after scumbags?'

'Because only the scumbags will hire someone unlicenced. Anyone legit wants someone with all the paperwork behind them.'

'Maybe you should get that paperwork? I was thinking about it while I was away. What's to stop you from getting properly licenced and opening a real business instead of doing ad hoc work for wallopers?'

'I don't want to go legit,' said Newton. 'Having to obey the rules and pay taxes. Fuck that.'

'Why, what's wrong with it?'

Newton rolled his eyes. 'You're no' the man you were, are you?'

'That's what I keep telling everyone. You could make decent, regular money and you wouldnae be guarding drug dealers and gangsters any more.'

'No, we'd be guarding lawyers and politicians who are even worse.'

'That's a good point,' said Morgan. 'I don't want to work for pricks like that.'

'What do you think, James?' said Virgil, turning to the most reasonable of the brothers.

'I can see both sides,' he replied. 'Aye, it would be good to have a steady, reliable income but I don't want to be tied down to something, restricted by rules and regulations.'

Virgil looked to Warren for his opinion but he was starting to doze off in the armchair, resting his head on Rose's shoulder.

'I noticed you didn't include yourself in this grand vision for our family's future,' Maria told Virgil.

'Because I intend to go back to my caravan when everything around here's calmed down,' he replied.

'Then you'll never go back, because things will never calm down in Garthamlock.'

Virgil went to his bed that night feeling troubled. The Queen of Glasgow was involved in their lives and they would have to fight each other again at her command. There was no avoiding that. Hopefully Terry's objections would be enough to keep him out of it, but he knew nothing would stop Toni if she wanted something enough. He had to face the fact that one day soon he might have to get into that ring again and be pulverised by one of his own brothers because he would never raise a fist against any of them.

The memory of that terrible fight returned – the cheers and yells of the crowd fading into shocked silence, the coppery stench of blood, the screams of Mark Stewart's wife...

Virgil shook the memory away and turned over onto his side, seeking sleep, but it eluded him.

If refusing to fight meant having his eyeballs scooped out, then so be it. Someone had to make a stand against Toni McVay.

4

Virgil managed to drop off around two o'clock in the morning, his fragmented dreams torturing him with images of Ember. She kept appearing before him, beckoning to him enticingly, but every time he was about to reach her, she would disappear. He was rudely woken at the crack of dawn by the sound of raised voices. For a moment, he thought he was back in his cosy little caravan, so he turned over and attempted to block out the sounds, until he realised it was his brother Morgan who was shouting.

He flung aside the duvet and rushed to the window. Looking down at the front of the house below, he saw Morgan and Wyatt squaring up to a group of four men. James was between them all, attempting to calm the situation, but his efforts seemed to be in vain. Virgil knew that James would soon give up all thoughts of diplomacy and resort to violence.

After pulling on a jumper and jeans, Virgil hurried down-stairs. As he exited the house, he saw the rest of the family emerging from the other two houses, all in pyjamas or wrapped in dressing gowns. Even Warren was there, left arm wrapped around his injured ribs, Rose by his side.

'What is this nonsense at this time of the morning?' demanded Ludovica. She wore her thick grey towelling dressing gown and furry bootie slippers. 'Go home and stop waking decent people at this ungodly hour.'

'Decent people?' spluttered one of the men, all of whom were around the same age as the brothers. 'Decent people don't go around shagging other people's wives,' he added, pointing at Morgan.

'You might want to round it down a bit,' replied Morgan. 'Who are we talking about?'

'Isla Carter,' exclaimed the man.

'Oh, aye, her.' He grinned. 'She's a right wee raver.'

'And she's married to me,' screeched the man.

'Hey, she didnae tell me, so it's no' my fault. As far as I was aware, she was single. And I don't know why you're having a go at me. I'm no' married to you.'

'Stay out of it, the rest of you,' the man told the other MacGregors. 'This is between me and him.'

'Then why did you bring that lot?' replied James, nodding at the man's friends.

'Because I know what your family's like.' The man's eyes settled on Virgil and widened. 'Virg,' he said, nerves creeping into his voice for the first time. 'I didnae know you were back.'

'Obviously,' he replied, moving to stand beside Morgan. 'And Nonna's right. You shouldnae be here at this time of the morning, shouting the odds.'

'I've only just found out. Don't tell me you wouldnae have done the same if Ember had been cheating on you.' The man took a step backwards when Virgil's eyes suddenly blazed, which everyone knew was a warning sign. 'No' that she has, I'm sure. Everyone knows she loves you to bits.'

The man's wheedling, conciliatory tone annoyed Virgil. 'Why don't you fuck off before you and your pals end up as red stains on my maw's nice grass?'

'Aye, all right,' he replied, holding up his hands. 'I'm no' really bothered anyway, she's a daft tart. I mean Isla, no' your maw,' he cried when he realised what he'd said. 'We'll go now.'

'Good and don't come back.'

They all watched the four men turn and run down the street.

'How come everyone's shit-scared of you when I was the one who won a bare-knuckle boxing match last night?' demanded Morgan.

'Because Virgil almost killed someone,' said Maria casually. 'Now, who wants breakfast?'

'What's all this rammy about now?' demanded a voice.

They all turned to see the neighbour who lived to the right of the three houses they owned. He stood there in just a T-shirt and boxer shorts.

'It's just endless trouble living next door to you noisy bastards,' the man added.

'How dare you stand around in your underwear in front of my maw and nonna?' snarled Wyatt.

The neighbour squeaked with fear when he saw Ludovica and slammed the door shut. He was quite happy to stand up to the brothers despite their reputations, but Ludovica and her curses terrified him. Her dark cackle filled the early morning air. How she enjoyed people's fear.

Newton appeared in the doorway of the house to the left of Maria's home, yawning and running a hand through his hair.

'Oh, finally,' said Morgan sarcastically.

'What's going on?' said Newton. 'Why are you all standing outside at this time of the morning?'

'There was a little trouble, but you missed it,' replied James.

'What trouble?'

'It was to do with a woman Morgan's been pumping.'

'Oh,' he replied, this being nothing out of the ordinary. 'I'm starving. Any chance of some breakfast?' he added, looking to his mother and grandmother.

'You're a grown man; you can feed yourself,' retorted Ludovica.

'Aye but it never tastes as good as your cooking.'

'No one's cooking is as good as mine,' she replied proudly.

'Let's go inside,' said Maria. 'We're making a spectacle of ourselves out here.'

'Our neighbours got used to that years ago,' muttered Morgan.

Virgil was relieved about going back inside. After living quietly in the countryside among sweet, gentle people, it was a little jarring to be amid all his family's noise and chaos again. However, part of him had missed it. His family might continually squabble and bicker, but at the end of the day, they were a tight unit who had each other's backs, although Newton still remained to him an unknown quantity.

They all piled into the house and headed straight into the kitchen. The men ranged around the table while the two women began cooking.

'You stay with Warren, sweetheart,' Maria told Rose when she moved to help. 'He needs you.'

Rose nodded and sat beside her boyfriend, who was slumped at the table, looking tired and pale. He was, however, consoled by the fact that Morgan had more bruises to his face than he did.

'Since you two are gonnae be out of commission for a while,' said Newton, looking from Warren to Morgan. 'We need to rearrange our work schedule.'

'That's shite,' said Morgan. 'I can still work.'

'You're walking like an auld biddy,' he replied. 'Our clients don't want to be guarded by someone who looks like a strong breeze could knock him over.'

'You cheeky bastard.'

'No arguing,' spat Maria, pointing at them with a wooden spoon. 'We've had enough for one morning.'

'Sorry, Maw,' said Morgan.

'Newton's right,' said James. 'You two need to take it easy and recover.'

'The problem is,' said Newton. 'It leaves us a bit short-handed.'

They all turned to look at Virgil.

'No way,' he told them.

'It would just be the once,' replied Newton.

'We both know that's no' true.'

'So you won't do it?'

'Naw. I'm just here because Maw and Nonna asked me to come, but I am not getting back into the bodyguarding business.'

'There's nothing wrong with it; it's honest work.'

'You call protecting criminals and drug dealers honest work?'

'It's better than being the criminals and drug dealers.'

'You cannae argue with that, Virg,' said Wyatt.

'I suppose not but I don't want to get involved again.'

'Fine,' replied Newton. 'I get it, but I don't know what Tam Kiernan will say when no one turns up tonight to act as his bodyguard.'

'You mean Tam Kiernan who burns people's houses down if they piss him off?'

'Aye. I'll just have to tell him that Warren cannae dae it

because he got his ribs smashed in and there's no one else to cover. Me, Wyatt and James are all booked out on other jobs.' He sighed regretfully. 'It's a shame because we do love our houses.'

'Fine, I'll do it,' muttered Virgil, his eyes flashing.

'Great.' Newton smiled.

Virgil sighed and slumped back in his seat. He'd had the feeling this would happen.

'Cheer up,' Morgan told him. 'It'll be more exciting than working in a distillery.'

Virgil caught his mother's eye and saw the gleam there. This was what she wanted, him back in the saddle keeping his brothers in line. Between his mother, his grandmother, Ember and Toni McVay, he wondered what would become of him. These women were going to kill him.

The MacGregors received a visitor just as they'd finished eating breakfast. James led Ember into the kitchen. She wore one of her usual rockabilly dresses with a cropped leather jacket and black high heels.

Virgil shot to his feet and ran a hand through his uncombed hair.

'Sorry to interrupt your breakfast,' she said sweetly.

'You're family,' replied Ludovica. 'You don't need to apologise. Sit, eat.'

'You can have my chair,' Warren told Ember while slowly getting to his feet. 'I need a hot bath.'

'What happened to you?' She frowned back at him.

'Bare-knuckle fight last night.'

'Your opponent must have been fierce to do that to you.'

'I was,' said Morgan.

Her eyes flicked between the two. 'You fought each other?'

'Aye.'

'Wow, brutal. I bet you made a lot of money on the bets though.'

'Just a bit. It makes all the pain and bruises worth it.'

'I'll come with you,' Rose told Warren as he ambled to the door. 'Give you a hand.'

'Give you a hand doing what?' called Morgan with a cheeky grin as they left the room.

'Can I have a word in private?' Ember asked Virgil.

'Aye, course,' he replied before leading her into the lounge.

He stood while she took a seat on the couch.

'Why don't you sit next to me?' she said.

'Okay.'

She smiled as he sat down. 'Why do you look so nervous?'

'Because I don't want to push you away from me even more than I already have,' he said softly.

Ember pressed a hand to his face. 'You won't.'

Virgil turned his head to kiss her palm. He was disappointed when she lowered her hand.

'I've booked an appointment with the couples counsellor tomorrow afternoon at two o'clock,' she said.

'Oh.'

'You don't seem keen?'

'No, I am. Everything just seems to be happening so quickly. I've already been roped into a bodyguarding job tonight because Warren's too injured.'

'But you're so good at bodyguarding.'

'I'm no' that man any more. I don't want to inflict violence on anyone again.'

'You're good at that too. There's no harm in using your talents to earn some money.'

'It's no' what I want.'

'And what do you want, Virg?' she said, a touch of impatience in her voice. 'To lead tourists around a distillery for the rest of your life?'

'What's wrong with that?' he exclaimed, frustrated that no one seemed to listen to what he wanted any more. It hurt even more that even his own wife was ignoring his thoughts and feelings. 'It's a great place to work with nice people and the pay's no' bad. Whisky's big business. Who knows what it could lead to?'

'If you and your brothers had any organisational skills or ambition you could have your own crew by now. Look at Rose's family – they're raking it in.'

'All the while beholden to Toni McVay. At least our way, we're free.'

'Your brothers just fought in a match arranged by Toni and it made her a lot of money. Your family's already lost its freedom and you know it.' Ember leant into him. 'You're not returning to your little caravan or your distillery. You're staying right here because you have no choice. Don't look so down,' she added when his eyes flashed. 'You belong with your family not hiding out in the sticks.' Virgil gasped with desire when she straddled his lap and took his face in her hands. 'Once you wanted so much more and I know that man still lives inside you. If he was dead, he wouldn't have been persuaded to come back here.'

'I like who I am now. Maybe I don't want to go back to being the old Virgil?' he countered.

'The old Virgil was the man I married.'

'And we couldnae live together because we kept clashing. Maybe now, we'd stand a better chance?'

He tried to kiss her, but she sighed and climbed off him. 'I want my fierce husband back, not this weak pacifist.' Ember smiled when his eyes flashed.

'I am no' weak,' he retorted. 'Sometimes it takes a lot more strength to back down from a fight.'

'We can go through all this with the therapist,' she said, turning to the mirror on the wall and running a hand through her hair.

Virgil came up behind her and wrapped his arms around her waist. 'Was there anyone else while I was gone?' he said, kissing the curve of her neck.

'Just one man,' she replied.

His turbulent eyes met hers in the reflection of the mirror. 'Who?'

'It doesn't matter. You weren't here,' she said with a casual shrug. 'And I do have needs.'

Virgil released her. 'Who the fuck is he?' he snarled. 'I'll rip his fucking head off.'

'Stevie Moorburn.'

'You slept with that pathetic, scrawny dick?'

'As I said, I have needs and I find him very attractive.'

'Right,' he barked before storming to the door.

'Where are you going?' she called after him.

'To rip Stevie's heid off his fucking shoulders,' he bellowed.

As he stormed to the front door, all his brothers except Warren dashed into the hallway as he pulled on his jacket and stuffed his feet into his trainers.

Ember appeared in the hallway with a smile. 'He's going to kill Stevie Moorburn because I slept with him.'

'What did you do that for?' Morgan yelled at her.

'My husband ran off and left me. What was I supposed to do?'

'No' shag scummy little dealers.'

'It was only one dealer, singular.' Her lips curved into her trademark cruel smile. 'But he fucked me several times.'

'What is this filthy talk?' hissed Maria, emerging from the direction of the kitchen.

'Ember slept with Stevie Moorburn,' replied Wyatt.

'Have you forgotten the sacred vows you took?' Ludovica demanded of her.

'Maybe you should ask your grandson that?' she replied. 'He was the one who deserted me.'

'Don't get involved,' Ludovica told Maria. 'It is between her and Virgil.'

'Don't get involved?' she replied. 'She cheated on my son.'

'It is between a husband and wife. No good will come of interfering.'

'She's a MacGregor and MacGregors do not betray each other.'

'Virgil betrayed me first by abandoning me,' said Ember.

'I didn't abandon you,' he countered. 'You knew where I was and now I'm gonnae go and kill Stevie,' he spat before storming outside.

'Why are you smiling?' James asked Ember.

'I didn't really sleep with Stevie.'

'Then why did you say you did?'

'Because Stevie's a nasty wee worm who I'd like to see take a beating. And I want my husband back.'

'For God's sake,' he exclaimed before rushing outside after Virgil.

'You're got a vicious streak,' Morgan told her before hurrying after his brothers along with Wyatt.

'Aren't you going to run after him too?' Ember asked Newton.

'Why bother? I'd like to see Stevie get a battering too. He cheated at a card game I had with him once.'

'Virg, wait,' called James. 'Virg,' he yelled again as he caught up with his brother.

'You're better staying out of this,' replied Virgil. 'Because I'm gonnae kill the bastard.'

'Ember told us she lied. She didnae sleep with Stevie.'

This caused Virgil to stop and whip round on his heel. 'You fucking what?'

'She only said she did because she hates Stevie and because she wants you back the way you used to be.'

Virgil sighed and planted his hands on his hips as the anger drained away, leaving him feeling foolish. Ember had always been manipulative and it was important he remembered that. 'Thank Christ she didnae sleep with him, but I cannae be the man she wants.'

'You really were gonnae kick the shite out of Stevie, weren't you?'

'Aye, because I thought he'd slept with my wife,' he said as though James was stupid.

'You've no' changed,' Wyatt told him. 'You're just the same Virgil, and I'm fucking glad about it because we need him.'

'Piss off, Wyatt,' he said before striding away, making his brother grin.

'Where are you going?' James called after him.

'For a walk,' he called back over his shoulder. 'I need to think.'

'Is he all right?' Morgan asked James as they watched Virgil go.

'He's far from all right,' he replied. 'The poor sod should have stayed in his caravan.'

* * *

Virgil found himself wending his way towards the pub. Before, it had always been his haven in times of trouble. When he realised what he was doing, he veered off in another direction, tramping the streets, thoughts whirling furiously through his mind. How he wished he was back in his little white and yellow caravan. He could have gone for a hike through the countryside but then again, if he'd been back there, he would have had nothing to worry about. Ember didn't want the man he'd become. It didn't matter how much couples counselling they had, he was no longer good enough for her, which made him wonder why she'd even booked the counselling in the first place.

It was tempting to jump back in his car and return to Milngavie. His brothers were all adults and could sort out their own lives. He could also finally divorce Ember and move on. The thought of an entirely fresh start was an exciting one. Yes, he loved Ember – he always would – but their relationship was a burden. It would also mean he had one less link with Garthamlock, one less thing to bring him back here. Her cruel tricks made him want to escape her, but he was also continually drawn back to her, his ever-present torment.

'Virgil,' called a voice.

He turned and sighed when he saw four men approaching him. They belonged to the Carter family. Two were brothers to Isla, who Morgan had been sleeping with. The third man was a cousin and the fourth one of their friends.

'What do you want, Jordan?' said Virgil.

'I want to know what the fuck you think you're doing back in Garthamlock?'

'Visiting my family.'

'If you were smart you would have stayed away.'

'Aye, well, my family need me. And why are you so angry with me? It's no' my fault my brother's been shagging your sister.'

'This is nothing to do with that. I...' Jordan's flabby, jowly face twisted with confusion. 'Wait – Isla or Isobel?'

'Isla.'

'And who's been shagging her?'

'Morgan.'

'Oh, I didnae know. Anyway, that's no' what this is about. Before you left, you battered my pal, Ian. He spent four weeks in the hospital.'

'Aye, sorry about that. I was in a bad place.'

The four men all looked at each other in confusion. The last thing any of them had expected was an apology from Virgil MacGregor.

'That's no' good enough,' continued Jordan. 'You broke his knee and his wrist. It took him ages to get over it and he's still having physiotherapy.'

'Ian's only himself to blame. I was minding my own business, just taking a wee walk, when he attacked me because he wanted to be known as a hard man and he thought taking me on would be the right way to do it.'

'Aye but you didnae need to go so far. You could have easily knocked him out with a single punch.'

'That would have been too easy. He needed to be taught a lesson and he's fucking lucky he got off so lightly. The old me could have done a hell of a lot worse to him.'

Jordan frowned. 'What do you mean, the old you?'

'I'm a changed man. I've renounced my life of violence.'

The four men looked at each other, not sure whether he was taking the piss or not.

'You found religion or something?' said Jordan.

'No but I have found peace.'

'My God, it's actually true. You've lost your bottle. Everyone was saying it after you nearly killed Mark Stewart, but I didnae believe it.'

'Aye, it's true, so if you've come here looking for trouble, you're gonnae be disappointed.'

With that, Virgil turned and continued on his way.

'Hey,' called Jordan. 'I'm no' finished.'

'Well, I am.' Virgil found he no longer had the stamina or patience for people like Jordan. Just a few months ago he would have rejoiced at this situation because it would have been another excuse for a fight, but now it just bored him.

Virgil felt his shoulder grabbed and he was whipped round.

'You've got to pay for what you did to Ian,' said Jordan.

'Why?'

'What do you mean why? Because...'

Virgil regarded the man with a raised eyebrow as he frantically tried to come up with a reason.

'Because Ian's my pal,' Jordan eventually said.

'Your so-called pal shagged your girlfriend while you were serving five months inside for attempted burglary.'

'Aye but...'

'But what?' pressed Virgil. 'It sounds to me like he's using you to do his dirty work but you don't owe him anything.'

'He's the one I should be kicking the shite out of. I'm gonnae hit him right in his gammy knee.'

'Good for you. That reminds me, how's your da doing? The last I heard he was in hospital with chest problems.' Virgil knew how much Jordan loved his dad, so he thought this topic would be a good diversion.

'He's been diagnosed with emphysema,' said Jordan, hanging his head.

'I'm so sorry to hear that. Gavin's one of the best.'

'Aye, he is and he doesnae deserve this,' he said passionately.

'I understand,' said Virgil, placing a sympathetic hand on

Jordan's shoulder. 'I watched my grandda' fight cancer. It was so hard.'

Jordan nodded, swallowing down the lump in his throat. 'I want to help him, but I don't know how.'

'Just be there for him. There's nothing else you can do.'

* * *

Ember watched from up the street, furious that her plan had obviously failed. She'd got Virgil riled up by telling him she'd cheated on him then added to that turmoil by letting him know that she'd lied. She'd wound him up and sent him out to inflict bloody violence on someone and when Jordan and his friends had come along – who she'd tipped off about Virgil's return because she'd known they wanted revenge for Ian – he'd somehow managed to talk them down. She was too far away to overhear what was being said but it looked like Jordan was actually crying, wiping a tear from the corner of his eye.

'Where have all the men gone?' she huffed with disgust before turning and stomping away.

* * *

Virgil donned his black trousers and a stab vest, which he had to adjust to accommodate his paunch, but at least it held his gut in a bit. Over this he wore a smart black shirt, ready for his body-guarding job that evening. It was the same outfit all his brothers wore for this sort of work. He studied his appearance in the mirror and sighed. He had not intended to get dragged back into all this. He'd envisioned himself standing firm and saying no but he couldn't negatively impact on his family's business. Just because he didn't want to be a part of it any more didn't mean he should ruin it for them too.

After strapping on his watch and sliding his mobile phone and wallet into his trouser pockets, he jogged downstairs.

'You remember what to do, don't you?' Newton smirked at him as he headed to the front door.

'Aye,' replied Virgil as he slipped on his shoes. 'It's no' exactly rocket science, is it?' he added, satisfied when Newton's smirk fell.

He'd never understood what his older brother's problem was. For as long as he could remember, Newton had been hostile to him. Newton loved his mother very much but sometimes he could be scathing even to her. The only person he was very careful to be polite to was his grandmother, but only because she'd once threatened to curse his manhood if he ever backchatted her again and, as everyone in their family knew, Ludovica's threats were far from idle. Newton only had a couple of friends. He didn't seem to like people very much and he rarely sought out their company. He'd had a few girlfriends, but each one had soon fallen by the wayside when they'd realised he was cold and uncaring.

Virgil drove to Tam Kiernan's house on the other side of Garthamlock. Tam's garden was the only one that wasn't neat and well tended like everyone else's, with its overgrown lawn, broken trampoline and the old, stained mattress lying beside it. In sharp contrast, the cars sitting on the driveway were pristine and expensive – a gleaming black Range Rover and a Porsche SUV. It seemed Tam had risen in the world.

Virgil parked at the kerb, got out and knocked on the front door. It was opened by a man in his late thirties with black hair and a black beard. Tam's neck was covered in large spots, as was his forehead and what could be seen of his cheeks. His face was a little flabby and greasy, and he was spreading around the waist. Tam was on the phone when he answered the door and he bid Virgil enter with a twitch of the fingers of his free hand.

Virgil nodded and stepped inside, closing the door behind him. Thankfully the interior of the house was much nicer than the front garden. It was messy, children's toys littering the living room, but it was clean. The sound of kids charging about upstairs was audible. They were so rambunctious the light in the centre of the ceiling swayed. Virgil knew Tam had four children and they were just the ones who lived here. The rest were strewn all around Glasgow living with their various mothers. He noted Tam had swapped his usual tracksuit and trainers for smart grey trousers and a white shirt. There was an expensive Tag Heuer watch on his wrist. He, however, still sported the tacky gold chain around his neck that had become his trademark.

'Sorry about that, Virgil,' said Tam pleasantly after he'd hung up. 'A bit of unexpected business cropped up.'

'No problem,' he replied, shaking his extended hand. 'And business is looking prosperous.'

'I cannae complain,' smiled Tam, pleased that he'd noticed. 'I heard you were back. What happened to the new life in the countryside?'

'My brothers happened.'

'Aye, I heard about Morgan and Warren's fight. It's a shame I missed it. I bet it was epic.'

'That's certainly one word for it, which is why you've got me tonight. Warren's in no fit state to work and the others are all booked out.'

'I'm no' complaining; I've got the fiercest of the lot of you.' He smiled, clapping Virgil on the shoulder.

Virgil wondered what Tam would say if he knew his bodyguard was a vegetarian pacifist who meditated. 'So where are we headed tonight?' he said instead.

'We're going to the Leopard Club. I have a wee bit of business there.'

Virgil knew that meant he would be dealing drugs. 'Aye, I know it. Nice place.'

'It used to be until it was taken over a few months ago. Now it's a bear pit, which is good for me because I wouldnae have got through the door before.'

'Are you expecting any trouble?'

'Possibly. I've got a rival called Kenny Brown. He's fucking mental. Likes stabbing people in the kidneys. We've butted heads recently, so it's only a matter of time before something kicks off between us.'

This was not what Virgil wanted to hear. 'Aye, I've heard of Kenny.'

'He's a wee mad rocket, so watch my back, literally.'

'Understood. Are you wearing a vest?'

'How do you mean? Like a string one? Who am I, fucking Rab C Nesbitt?'

'I mean a stab vest.'

'Oh,' said Tam, spotty cheeks colouring. 'Naw. Actually, that would be a good idea. Are you wearing one?'

Virgil nodded.

'Can you get me one?'

'I can see if you can borrow Warren's since he won't be needing his for a while.'

'But we're different sizes. A racing snake I am not.'

'It's adjustable. We can pick it up on our way to the club.'

After collecting Warren's stab vest for Tam, which he pulled on under his shirt in the car, they headed to the Leopard Club.

'There, I feel much safer,' said Tam, fastening his shirt back up. 'I need to buy myself one of these.'

'It would be a good idea,' said Virgil. 'Especially if you're regularly going into bear pits.'

'Maybe you should get a suit of armour,' joked Eric; Tam's friend and driver was a cadaverous individual who looked like all the fluids had been sucked out of him. It made him appear a lot older than his forty years.

The Leopard Club had been a favourite of Virgil's and Ember's when they were dating and it had always been a nice place. Now its signage was fading and the 'p' in Leopard had dropped off and lay propped up against the wall. The doormen had always been professional and had looked very smart in their suits and long black coats. Now the door was being worked by two ageing thugs in tracksuits who were roughing up a couple of neds.

'Come on, boys, move out of the way,' said Tam as the three of them approached.

'Aye, sorry, Tam,' said one of the thugs as he stepped aside, dragging one of the neds along with him by the collar. When he saw Virgil was following, he blocked his path. 'Where do you think you're going, big man?'

'It's all right, Davey, he's with me,' said Tam. 'This is Virgil MacGregor.'

Davey's dull, stupid eyes widened. 'Oh aye, I've heard of you. You nearly killed someone at that illegal fight, didn't you?'

'Aye, that's right, shout it down the street, why don't you?' said Tam, rolling his eyes.

'Oh, sorry,' said Davey. 'Good to meet you,' he added, extending his hand to Virgil.

'Yeah, you too,' he replied, shaking his hand while attempting to hide his disdain for the man.

'In you go and have a good night.'

Virgil entered the club with Tam and Eric and was shocked by how quickly the place had deteriorated. The club had got its name from the interior decor, which naturally was all leopard print. Before it had been classy, subtle and understated rather than in your face, but whoever had taken it over had decided to go all out and now it resembled Del Boy's bedroom, the leopard print accompanied by garish pinks and limes. It wasn't just the bad taste, but the general lack of care. The place didn't look very clean, the tables were damaged and stained, and the staff clearly didn't care about providing customer satisfaction. On top of that, there was an air of sleaziness overlaying everything. It was such a shame because this used to be one of the best clubs in the city.

'This place has changed a lot,' commented Virgil after Tam had placed their order at the bar, the barman clearly in no rush to provide them with their drinks.

Virgil found it rather sad. This club held a lot of warm memories for him of his time with Ember but the fact that it had changed so much made it hard to relive them.

'Aye, the owner lives in Spain,' replied Tam. 'He made his brother-in-law manager but he couldnae gi'e a shite. He's hardly ever here, so the staff don't put in any effort. On the bright side, it's made it easier for people like me to ply my trade. Are you sure you won't have anything stronger than an orange juice?'

'No' while I'm working. The last thing you want is a pished bodyguard.'

'Aye, good point.'

Virgil decided not to tell Tam that he was teetotal. He didn't think it would go in his favour.

Finally, they were served their drinks and Tam and Eric moved about the room together, chatting with people and shaking hands, which was when the exchange of drugs for money was slyly made. Virgil felt dirty as he followed them about. Not that he was whiter than white when it came to drugs. He'd experimented as had all his brothers, mainly with marijuana and cocaine, but they'd all got into fitness and decided to reject drugs, apart from a bit of weed now and then. The whole thing was seedy and sordid and made him long for his little caravan even more.

'Any sign of Kenny?' Tam asked Virgil after concluding his fifth transaction of the evening.

'Nope,' he replied, eyes constantly scanning the room, remaining vigilant. He may hate this job, but he was determined to do it well for his brothers' sakes.

'The night's still young and I've got the feeling the wee ferret will soon make an appearance, so stay sharp.'

Tam's prophecy was proved correct an hour later when a short, skinny man with a shaved head, an extremely pointed nose and sharp cheekbones strutted in with two friends. The eyes of all three men homed in on them immediately and they stormed over to their group. Kenny's friends were short and thin too and they were all bristling with aggression.

'You cannae go any further,' said Virgil, putting his hand against Kenny's chest when he tried to storm up to Tam.

'If you don't stop touching me, big man,' growled Kenny, 'I'll chop your fucking hand off.'

'There's no need for violence.'

'No need?' he barked. 'Who the fuck are you, Ghandi?'

'I'm Mr Kiernan's bodyguard.'

'Mr Kiernan?' he spluttered. 'That rancid thing's no' a mister.'

'Who the fuck are you calling rancid, ya wee prick?' retorted Tam.

When the two drug dealers attempted to rush at each other, Virgil placed himself between them and pushed them apart.

'Don't fucking touch me,' snarled Kenny, drawing a knife from the back of his jeans and pointing it at him.

'Go on then,' said Virgil.

'Go on then what?'

'Stab me.'

'I will, I mean it,' he spat, eyes wild.

'I know you do, so get on with it.'

'Right, you asked for it.'

Kenny jabbed the knife into Virgil's chest, where the blade was deflected by the stab vest. All Kenny could do was stare back at him stupidly.

'You put a hole in my nice shirt,' said Virgil flatly.

'You told me to, ya dick.'

When Kenny made another lunge at him, Virgil grabbed his wrist, twisted and tore the weapon from his hand, pocketing the knife.

Kenny rounded on Tam when he laughed. 'It's no' fucking funny.'

'Aye it is, fanny baws.'

'I seriously suggest you both calm down right now,' said Virgil. 'Because two undercover polis have just walked in.'

They all whipped round to see two tall, rather hard-looking individuals heading to the bar.

'How do you know they're polis?' said Kenny.

'I saw them lift someone for dealing on a bodyguarding job I was on a few months ago.'

'Well, that's reassuring,' commented Tam.

'The person they arrested wasnae my client, but I do suggest you both sit down and have a chat, see if you can agree to no' stab each other. Or you can go back to waving knives around and we can all get lifted.'

'I only got out of prison a year ago,' said one of Kenny's friends. 'And I'd rather kill myself than go back.'

A surprising amount of sympathy filled Kenny's eyes and he patted the man's shoulder. 'Aye, I get it, Dermot.' He looked to Tam. 'Maybe he's right? Tearing lumps out of each other is affecting business and there's a newcomer encroaching on both our patches. Perhaps we should team up to take them down?'

'Like it.' Tam smiled.

The men bought a fresh round of drinks and sat down at a table together. As they talked, Virgil remained vigilant in case this was a ploy on Kenny's behalf to sink a blade into Tam, but as the drinks flowed the tension between them eased and soon it was as though they'd been best friends all their lives. Eric also got on very well with Kenny's two friends. Virgil smiled inwardly; once again, his peaceful approach had produced results.

* * *

Ember watched her husband from across the room. Maria had given her the details of where he would be and when, along with who he was working for, and Ember had passed a message on to Kenny through a mutual friend letting him know that Tam Kiernan would be dealing in a club on his turf. Certain violence would ensue, she'd been astonished and infuriated when Virgil had not only talked Kenny down but negotiated a truce between him and Tam.

She narrowed her eyes at her husband's turned back. 'You should work for the UN Peacekeeping Force,' she muttered.

Ember hitched her handbag up her shoulder. It was time to

go back to the drawing board and figure out another way to breathe fresh life into Virgil's darker side.

'Where are you going, sweetheart?' said an ugly, drunken creep when she tried to leave, exhaling beer fumes in her face.

'Get out of my way,' she retorted, eyes flashing.

'Stay and I'll buy you a drink,' he said, reaching out to touch her. 'We can have some fun together...'

Ember produced the small blade she kept secreted in her stocking top and expertly slashed the top of his hand, causing him to hastily retract it. She then pressed the tip of the blade to his crotch.

'If you touch me again,' she said, 'I will drive this deep into your tiny, pathetic balls. Is that what you want?'

'N... no,' he rasped.

She tilted back her head. 'Then get out of my fucking way.'

He stood aside and she strode past him towards the door, stuffing the knife into the pocket of her jacket. The man looked down and whimpered when he saw the small bloodstain on his jeans.

5

'How did it go last night with Tam?' Warren asked Virgil the next morning at breakfast.

'Good,' he replied. 'He managed to negotiate a truce with Kenny Brown.'

Warren's eyes widened and he looked to his brothers, all of whom were also ranged around the kitchen table. 'Kenny Brown?'

'Aye.'

'But they've been tearing lumps out of each other for ages.'

'So I believe but no' any more. They've got a mutual enemy, so they agreed to work together to take them down.'

'How did you even get them talking in the first place?'

'When it looked like they were gonnae start fighting, I told them a couple of undercover polis had just come into the club.'

'Had they?'

'No, they were just two random customers, but it did the trick and got them talking to each other. Turns out they get on pretty well. Tam was so pleased he paid me double.'

'I bet it's only a matter of time before they're back to trying to stab each other in the eyes,' said Newton.

'I don't care if they do; it's no' my problem. The job's done. Here,' added Virgil, tossing some money across the table to Warren. 'There's half of what Tam paid me. You'll need it while you get better.'

'Cheers, pal,' replied Warren, tossing it back to him. 'But you can keep it. I got a ton of cash from the bare-knuckle fight, so I'm all good.'

Virgil shrugged, picked up the wad of notes and placed it in his pocket.

'Me and Newton have been asked to fight each other,' said Wyatt.

Virgil nearly choked on his coffee. 'What?' he croaked.

'Toni was so pleased with how the fight between Morgan and Warren went that she wants to arrange another asap.'

'I thought she didnae hold the matches any more than once a month so the polis won't clock on.'

'Aye but everyone's still talking about the last fight, so she thought it good to use that publicity for this one. The betting will be even bigger.'

'That doesnae sound like Toni; she's usually so cautious.'

'She's seen the potential for our family and she wants to make the most of it. Besides, this fight won't be at the fire station. She's got another venue for us to use.'

'I think this is a very bad idea.'

'How no'? It's no' hurt Morgan's and Warren's relationship.'

Virgil didn't like to say that Newton was a very different kettle of fish to their more laid-back younger brothers. He'd never forgive Wyatt if he lost to him.

'It doesnae matter what you think,' Newton told Virgil. 'We're grown men and in charge of our own lives. Why don't you run away back to your shitey caravan if you don't like it?'

'No,' said Maria firmly. 'This is Virgil's home; it's where he belongs.'

'Actually, Maw,' said Virgil, getting to his feet. 'Newton's right. I should go back to my caravan because me being here is pointless. You want me to put them all in line and stop the violence before they end up like Nick, but they don't want to listen to reason.' He turned back to Newton. 'Fine, take part in the fight, beat the living shite out of each other and then get arrested and flung into prison for years. At least my life might be a bit more peaceful,' he yelled before storming out.

Maria scowled at Newton. 'I hope you're happy.'

'Actually, I am. Things would be a lot easier without the family conscience constantly having a pop at us. I mean, where does he get off? He was the most violent out of the lot of us.'

'Your brother's going through a lot. You should be more sympathetic.'

'He's lost his bottle, Maw, which means he's dead weight.'

Maria snatched up the rolling pin on the counter and slammed it down on the table. 'Don't you talk about your brother like that,' she yelled. 'Blood is more important than anything, including money. Do you understand?'

Although his lips twitched, Newton nodded graciously. 'Anything you say, Maw.'

'Good. Now finish your breakfast. You need your strength for the fight.'

'Aye,' Wyatt eagerly told Newton. 'Especially because I'm gonnae win.'

* * *

Virgil stormed outside, deciding to once again walk off his anger. If he stayed in Garthamlock for much longer all his old demons would rise to claim him and he'd be right back where he started but, despite what he'd said, he didn't want to abandon his brothers. He had to stay and figure out a way to get his family out from under Toni McVay's thumb. He couldn't believe his mother had voluntarily thrust them back into this situation and he wondered if she had an ulterior motive, one more than simply wanting to give her sons an outlet for their considerable aggression. She was a clever woman, so he was certain there was more to her actions than she'd so far let on. His instinct was telling him that it was probably a lure to get him back here, but he didn't want to believe that of his own mother, especially as he'd told her repeatedly of his mental health struggles after almost killing a man.

Virgil stayed away from home until it was time for his appointment at the couples counsellor at two o'clock with Ember. He found himself sitting in a beige room in front of a woman dressed entirely in beige with all the personality of a soggy chip. Ember was already waiting and she regarded him with one of her mischievous little smiles, which made him worry about what she had in store for him.

'Thank you for coming, Virgil,' said the beige woman, who was called Sandra. 'Please take a seat beside your wife.'

Virgil placed himself in the chair beside Ember's and regarded the counsellor expectantly.

'I think what we need to do first is decide what you want to get from counselling,' continued Sandra. 'Ember informs me you've been estranged for a few months now, mainly due to your volatile temper, Virgil?'

'*My* volatile temper?' he exclaimed. 'She's the one who threw a knife at my head when I said I didn't want to go to her friend's birthday party because her pal's a massive arsehole.' When he saw his wife smiling at him, her green eyes twinkling, he realised he'd let his temper get the better of him and he took a deep breath to calm down.

'If you would please let me finish,' replied Sandra with a condescending smile. 'I'm only repeating what Ember told me. I'm making no accusations. That's not what this space is about. I just want to get to the bottom of the issues that have been dividing you. It's quite clear there's been volatility on both sides.'

'You make it sound like we're at war.'

'Is that how you feel?' said Sandra, tilting her head to one side.

'Sometimes.'

'Do you feel the same way, Ember?'

'Yes, I do,' she said. 'Especially when he gets angry, which is all the time.'

Virgil frowned. His wife sounded meek and timid, not at all like the firecracker he knew her to be. 'It's no' all the time,' he said.

'It feels like it's all the time,' replied Ember, eyes wide and sad. 'And I never know what's going to set him off,' she told Sandra. 'I'm constantly walking on eggshells.'

'You what?' he said, half laughing, the idea that Ember would ever walk on eggshells highly entertaining to him.

'Please don't laugh when your wife is sharing, Virgil,' said Sandra.

'You don't understand,' he replied. 'She's even more angry than me; she's constantly shouting and yelling. I've got a scar on my arm from where she stabbed me with a potato peeler.'

'That was in self-defence,' retorted Ember. 'I was scared for my life.'

Once again, Virgil was so astonished he laughed. 'Come on,

Ember, you've never been scared in your entire life. It's one of the things I love about you.'

For the briefest moment, her green eyes softened before the sad, frightened look filled them again. 'He's got terrible anger issues, and I'd hoped we could come here and work through things together. I do love him and I want to get our marriage back on track.'

'Even though you're frightened of him?' said Sandra.

'She is not frightened of me,' insisted Virgil. 'The Devil himself wouldnae scare her.'

'I love him,' said Ember, a tear slipping down her cheek. 'What more can I say?'

Virgil rolled his eyes at the sight of that tear. 'For Christ's sake.'

'You don't like it when your wife expresses emotion, do you?' Sandra asked him in rather a hard, clipped tone.

'She's no' expressing emotion; she's putting it on. Why can't you see that it's all an act?'

'He's always like this when I get upset,' rasped Ember. 'He prefers to pretend that I'm faking it, so he won't have to deal with the fact that he's upset me.'

'I see,' said Sandra sympathetically.

'This is ridiculous,' said Virgil, shaking his head. Ember did love to play the victim when usually she was the perpetrator.

'You must allow Ember to express herself,' said Sandra. 'Repressing emotion is so damaging. It's important you allow an open and free exchange of opinions and feelings, otherwise your relationship will fail. Do you want your marriage to work, Virgil?'

'Aye, course I do, but we've both got really bad tempers, despite what you seem to think,' he added with a touch of bitterness. 'We constantly argue and believe you me she's no' shy about letting me know how she feels. I'm the one who's taken steps to work on my temper. I went to live in the countryside where I cut out drinking and I started meditating. My temper's under control for the first time in my life.'

'That's very good to hear, Virgil. Well done.'

'Ember's the one who refuses to work on herself.'

'You don't think the fact that she's booked this appointment indicates she's willing to do her own self-work?'

'I've no' seen any evidence of that so far. She's just used it to make me look like a total shite.'

'That's no' true, Virg,' said Ember softly, placing her hand over his. 'I just want us to reconcile and finally get along without all the shouting and fighting.'

He arched an eyebrow when her lower lip wobbled and her eyes filled with fresh tears in an Oscar-winning performance.

'Here you go,' said Sandra gently, handing her a tissue.

'Thank you,' replied Ember in a trembling voice, accepting the tissue from her and dabbing at her eyes with it.

'Can't you see when you're being played?' Virgil demanded of Sandra. 'You're supposed to be a trained professional, for God's sake.'

'I see what Ember means about you deflecting whenever she gets upset. Now you're choosing to blame me for her pain.'

'I'm no' blaming you,' he exclaimed, his temper rising in his exasperation. 'It's just that she's putting on a performance and you're too stupid to see it.'

Sandra's lips pursed. 'Please don't call me names, Virgil. I'm only trying to help.'

'If you want to help then you have to listen to me as well. So far all you've done is take Ember's word for everything. What do you know about this anyway? I see you don't wear a wedding ring. Are you even married?'

'No, but I...'

'Have you ever been married?'

'No, but that doesn't affect my ability to do the job.'

'Of course it does. How can you counsel people on marriage when you've no idea what being married is like?' He turned to Ember. 'Find a counsellor who knows what they're talking about and I'll meet you at their office. This woman's an idiot.'

With that he left, Ember watching him go with narrowed eyes. She'd known Sandra would get on his tits, but she hadn't worked him up into one of his furies as she'd hoped. Once again, one of her plans had failed. Ember lowered her head as her hands curled into fists, nails digging into her palms and she bit her lower lip so hard she tasted blood. She was not used to failure and the fact that it was becoming a constant in her life was intolerable to her.

'Are you okay, Ember?' said Sandra, reaching out to pat her hand.

The counsellor hastily retracted her hand when Ember's head snapped up, green eyes brilliant and fierce, blood on her lips.

'Virg is right,' yelled Ember, shooting to her feet while hitching her handbag up her shoulder. 'You are an idiot.'

With that, she stormed out, leaving behind a bemused Sandra. So intimidated was the counsellor that she didn't dare ask Ember to pay her fee.

* * *

'Where are you going?' a voice asked Ember as she stomped outside.

She stopped and turned to see her husband lounging against the exterior wall of Sandra's office, hands in his jeans pockets. At the sight of him, some of her rage eased; he looked so handsome and strong. If it hadn't been for that flabby stomach he could have been the man she fell in love with.

Ember didn't reply; she just watched as he straightened up and approached her.

'I'm beginning to wonder if you booked that counsellor on purpose just to rile me up,' he added, towering over her.

'I didn't. I really thought she could help us.'

'Don't give me that innocent look; it doesn't suit you. Are you purposefully trying to make me angry?'

'Of course not, Virg. I'm just trying to find a way for us to reconcile so we can finally be a proper married couple and no' have to live apart any more.'

'I really want to believe that, but I don't.'

'You don't believe that I want to be with you?' She frowned.

'It's the bit about no' provoking my temper that I'm finding hard to swallow.'

'Why are you always so suspicious of me?'

'Because I know you.'

'You haven't seen me in six months. I might have changed.'

'You havenae changed. The blood on your lower lip makes that clear. What brought that on? Was it me walking out or Sandra's stupidity?' He smiled when her eyes flashed. 'Probably both. The strange thing is, I don't want you to change. The irony of that statement means we still won't be able to be together.'

Ember sighed and glanced up and down the street before turning back to him. 'Do you want to go to bed?'

'I'm no' sure that's a good idea.'

Her eyes flashed fire. 'Don't you fancy me any more?'

'Course I do, more than ever. I've always thought you're the most beautiful woman I've ever seen and that's no' changed, but our relationship is so...'

'For Christ's sake, Virg, I just want sex. It's been six months for us both. At least,' she added, anger filling her eyes, 'It had better be six months for you too.'

'It is. I've no' played away. I couldnae do that to you.'

The fire that constantly raged inside Ember simmered down a little. 'Good. Then come back to our home and have sex with your wife.'

Virgil shrugged. 'Aye, all right.'

* * *

Virgil grunted when Ember raked her sharp nails down his bare back. Even though he knew she'd drawn blood he didn't cease his caresses. He'd got used to her scratches and bites years ago.

He kissed her and she bit hard on his lower lip, both of them tasting blood.

'Why don't you just get your knife out and have done with it?' he breathed as he moved on top of her.

'Don't put ideas in my head,' she moaned, wrapping her thighs even tighter around his waist. 'Faster,' she cried as he kissed her neck.

He obeyed and soon they came together, the room filled with their cries, as well as the scent of hot, sweaty sex tinged with the coppery smell of blood from the wounds to Virgil's back.

'Mmm, that's better,' breathed Ember, sinking back into the pillows. 'You've neglected your marital duties for far too long.'

Virgil rolled onto his side, pulled her to him and kissed her. 'It's been torture. I've been thinking about being here in our bed with you constantly.'

'Have you been dreaming about me?' she purred, brushing his lips with her own.

'Night and day.'

'And there's really been no one else?'

He heard the danger in her voice and smiled. 'Really. Who could compare to you?' Virgil took her right hand in his own, stroking the palm where her nails had cut into the pale skin. 'I love you, Ember, and I want our marriage to work.'

'Then come home,' she replied, sliding her hand down his chest. 'Things will be different, I promise.'

He cradled her face in one hand. 'You've no idea how much I'd love to believe that, but we both know it's no' true. Have you tried meditation?'

'What?' She frowned.

'It really helps me. So does mindfulness. We could practise them together and we can get out into the countryside more too. Being away from all the people and noise makes a huge difference. It's so calming lying in bed at night listening to nothing but the hoot of an owl or the screech of a fox. We can start right now, actually,' he said, sitting up. 'Shall I show you some meditation techniques? What's wrong?' he added when she stared at him coldly.

Ember sat up too. 'I don't know who you are any more. Meditation, mindfulness? Have you heard yourself, Virg? You sound ridiculous.'

'Ridiculous?' he repeated, coldness filling his eyes.

'Where's my fierce man, the one everyone in Garthamlock was terrified of? Now you're just a joke. I've heard them talking about you behind your back. You're a laughing stock.'

'I don't get what everyone's problem is. What's wrong with me trying to improve myself?'

'You were the top man around here, even more so than Newton who thinks it should be him just because he's the oldest. You were in charge around here, but you've thrown it all away to become a veggie-munching tree hugger. It's pathetic.'

Virgil shot to his feet and began pulling on his clothes, looking away so she wouldn't see the hurt in his eyes. Why couldn't his wife just support him? 'Then you might as well just divorce me, Ember, because this pathetic man is here to stay.'

'Fine, I will then,' she retorted. 'I'll call my solicitor first thing in the morning.'

'Why wait? Do it right now. I'd hate to continue being an embarrassment to you.'

'Good because I'm sick of taking pelters about you. I want a real man, one who's no' afraid of sticking up for himself or fighting when he has to. Newton's always fancied me. Maybe I'll finally give him a chance.' The corner of Ember's mouth lifted when Virgil's eyes blazed with that sudden, violent rage that had possessed him so often in the past. In that moment she knew she was in no danger. He never had and never would lay a finger on her, but she suspected that if Newton had been here, he would be in some danger.

Virgil raised his fist to punch the wall. It was only the zeal in Ember's eyes that snapped him out of his anger. He screwed his eyes shut and took in a few slow, deep breaths. Finally, he released one long breath and lowered his arm while slowly opening his eyes.

'Go for it with my blessing,' said Virgil as he pulled on his shoes. 'See how long it is before Newton's smugness drives you up the wall and you smash his face in with an iron, something you threatened to do to me often enough.' Virgil's eyes twinkled when he saw how furious she looked. He'd called her bluff. 'I wish you both all the best,' he said before leaving.

As Virgil jogged downstairs, he heard her scream the word *bastard*, the sound accompanied by something breaking. While Ember began systematically smashing up their bedroom, Virgil was smiling to himself as he left the house.

* * *

Virgil returned home to find his brothers rushing out of their mother's house.

'What's going on?' he asked them.

'We've had word the fucking Wilsons are back in Garthamlock, so we're gonnae sort them out,' Wyatt told him before hurrying after his brothers towards their cars.

'Wait,' called Virgil, running after them.

'You coming too?' Morgan grinned. 'Nice one. We're a body down because Warren's still no' ready for a fight.'

'No, I'm not coming. I want you all to stop and think.'

'Oh, God,' groaned Newton. 'He's gonnae gi'e us another of us his pacifist speeches about how we should love the Wilsons and all live in peace and harmony together.'

'No, I'm not actually,' he retorted. 'But I am asking you all no' to charge in like you usually do. It is possible to reason with people, you know.'

Newton shook his head. 'You might have lost your baws but we havenae. Stay here with Maw and Nonna. You can help them with their baking.'

With that, Newton hopped into the front passenger seat of Morgan's car while James and Wyatt got into the back.

Virgil watched the car set off down the street and growled with frustration. 'For fuck's sake,' he exclaimed before jumping in his own car and following them.

The two cars drove to the north end of Garthamlock where a collection of red-brick semis were ranged around an expanse of grass. Virgil's heart sank when he saw it was indeed the Wilsons, a family from Easterhouse who kept coming onto their patch to cause trouble. They'd stayed away for the last year ever since Virgil had hammered the oldest brother, Gary. Now the five of them were back with reinforcements, their numbers bolstered to ten by their friends. When he saw his brothers leap out of Morgan's car and storm up to the group, Virgil was left with no choice but to follow.

Gary Wilson stood before them holding a baseball bat. The Wilson brothers were one extreme or the other – either very tall and skinny or short and tubby. Gary fell into the latter category, belly protruding from under his T-shirt. The Wilsons always wore black clothes because they thought it was intimidating. Those black clothes were usually jogging bottoms and T-shirts with zip-up hoodies. The Wilsons' friends in contrast wore brightly coloured tracksuits and sported baseball caps. Gary wasn't the only one with a weapon. The Wilsons and their allies wielded crowbars, tyre irons and wrenches.

'Well, look who it is.' Gary smiled when Virgil joined his brothers. 'I did think for a moment you were gonnae hide away in your car. I got word you were back and that you've gone fucking soft.'

'Virgil will never be soft, you prick,' retorted James.

'That's no' what we heard. He managed to broker peace between Kenny Brown and Tam Kiernan. I'll give you your due, Virg, that took some good negotiation skills and you managed to talk down Jordan Carter too. The old Virgil would have put them in intensive care.'

'I'm no' the old Virgil any more,' he replied.

'Aye, so it seems and now it's time for you to pay for what you did to me.'

'Are you talking about the time he beat the shite out of you and made you cry?' growled Wyatt.

'I didnae fucking cry,' Gary snarled back.

'Aye ya did, like a wee lassie.'

'Shut your hole before I shove this down your throat,' yelled Gary, pointing at him with the bat.

'You're only acting big and hard now because you think Virgil's gone soft and that you might actually have a chance at beating him,' said James. 'But you're wrong and you'll only end up back in hospital. Leave while you can still walk.'

'Oh no. We're gonnae have this out right here, right now. No one gets away with humiliating me.' He looked back at Virgil. 'Let's go, Virg. We'll see who's really the better man.'

'And you think that's you, you silly, fat bastard?' sneered Newton.

'Who are you calling fat, you fucking fanny? Get the mouthy shite, boys,' he told his men. 'But leave Virgil. He's mine.'

While his brothers ran to meet Gary's friends, Virgil remained where he was, looking pissed off.

'Come on then,' Gary yelled at him, waving the bat around.

'No,' he replied while chaos erupted around them.

'I'll come to you then. I fucking mean it.'

'I know.'

'Right, well, here I come,' said Gary, drawing back the bat before charging at him. He stopped several feet away from Virgil, looking confused. 'Aren't you gonnae fight?'

'No. I'm done with all that. It doesnae help anyone.'

'Aye, but aren't you gonnae at least defend yourself?'

Virgil shrugged. 'I don't know. Why don't you try hitting me and we'll see?'

Gary hesitated, unsure whether this was a trap or not. Virgil looked calm and relaxed, like he wasn't on the verge of one of his violent frenzies, but he feared it was a trick to make him get closer.

Virgil noted his brothers were already getting the upper hand. The Wilsons and their friends simply couldn't compete with their speed and strength, the brothers throwing the men around like they weighed nothing. Morgan had taken a crowbar from one of Gary's brothers and was swinging it around his head. James and Newton fought coolly and methodically, while Wyatt revelled in the violence, unwittingly paying great homage to the namesake he constantly felt inferior to. The only ones not partaking in the violence were himself and Gary.

'You're trying to trick me, aren't you?' said Gary.

'Get closer and find out,' replied Virgil.

There was a darkness in Virgil's tone that Gary didn't like and he began to regret his rash decision to come here. He'd already noticed that his backup was losing the battle. When he looked back at Virgil and saw those hard eyes were fixed on him, he had to fight the urge to run.

'Well,' said Virgil. 'Are you gonnae dae something, or are you intending to stand there all day?' He shook his head when Gary didn't move. 'I thought so.'

Virgil turned and headed back to his car. His brothers didn't need any help; they'd already won the battle. When he heard footsteps rushing up behind him, Virgil whipped round and snatched the bat from Gary's hands.

'Now take it easy, Virg,' he said, holding up his hands and backing away.

'You're a stupid fucking bastard,' he roared, eyes blazing.

Virgil sounded so much like his old self that all his brothers turned to look. Virgil had also caught the sound and he began taking in long, deep breaths. The anger retreated, the red mist leaving him, and calm settled over him once more. Seeing this, Gary sighed with relief.

'Get the fuck out of here,' Virgil told him. 'And don't come back.'

'Aye, all right. Cheers,' he said before turning and running away.

Virgil began making his way back to the car, turning when he heard a loud crack behind him. Gary was splayed on his front and Newton stood behind him holding a wrench.

'What the fuck did you do?' Virgil demanded of his brother.

'Covering your back,' he retorted. 'He was sneaking up on you from behind.'

'That's shite. He was done.'

'He was far from done. He had this,' said Newton, picking up a piece of lead pipe.

'Did any of you see this?' Virgil asked his brothers.

They all shook their heads.

'We were too busy mopping up the rest,' replied James.

'So only you saw Gary produce that pipe?' he asked Newton.

'Are you accusing me of lying?' he retorted.

'No, course not,' Virgil said, cynicism in his voice.

The two brothers stared at each other, ignoring the bleeding and injured men lying on the ground around them.

With one last hard look at his brother, Virgil strode back to his car and drove off, Newton glaring at him as he went.

* * *

'The plan's not working,' said Ember. 'Virgil's determined to stick to his new, peaceful ways.'

Knowing the brothers were all out, she was in conference with Maria and Ludovica at their home.

'I didn't think he'd stick to his new principles so much,' said Maria. 'I'd assumed just being back at an underground fight among the violence and the smell of blood would reignite it all inside him again.'

'Well, it didn't and he's going around Glasgow spreading peace.'

'Virgil's gone out with his brothers to see off the Wilsons. That should be enough to bring back his old self. He hates that family.'

'I wouldn't bet on it. He's probably got them all sat in a circle singing "Kumbaya". Everything I've tried has failed, even the annoying therapist.'

'Then we must think of something else. If only we could get him back in the ring at the underground fights, then I'm certain it would all come back.'

'You need to raise his hot blood out of the ring,' said Ludovica. 'Feed it and nourish it. We know messing about with his old enemies doesn't work. To really get his blood up, someone he loves and cares for needs to be in real peril. Instead of playing on his hate, play on his love.'

Maria smiled. 'You're so wise, Maw.'

'I'm very well aware of that fact,' she replied.

The two older women watched Ember as she lapsed into thought. They were content to let her come up with a plan to finally bring Virgil back to himself, knowing she was more than capable. They also realised that she was the best bait for Ludovica's idea.

'There's only one option,' said Ember. 'Virgil has to come to my rescue.' The corner of her mouth lifted. 'But you already knew that, didn't you?'

'One thing I've always liked about you, Ember, is your intelligence,' said Maria. 'There are far too many stupid people in this world.'

'I know just how to do it too.'

'Then don't waste time here with us. Go and carry out your plan and finally bring Virgil home. Permanently.'

Ember shot to her feet. 'I'll let you know when it's done,' she said before rushing out.

'I'm surprised you havenae told us to leave Virgil be and let him follow his own path,' Maria said to her mother when Ember had gone.

'I'm curious to see whether he can resist your attempts,' replied Ludovica. 'If not, then he hasn't really changed but if he does, then you and Ember will have to accept that he is indeed a new man.'

'I don't suppose you could...'

'No,' she said firmly, wrinkled brow creasing. 'I will not use my skills on a family member; you know that.'

'You made Da's hair fall out.'

'No, I didn't. That was natural. He just thought I made it happen when he slept with the viper on the next street. You just have to tell someone you have cursed them so they think anything bad that happens to them is down to you. I have told you this before.'

'I know but in Da's case I really thought you had. You never pass up an opportunity for revenge.'

'And his own mind did it all for me.'

'I remember walking in on him in the bathroom. He was crying on the floor with clumps of his own hair in his hands.'

Ludovica's lips curled with pleasure. 'Stress did that to him. How I enjoyed his torment. It was nothing less than he deserved.'

'I agree,' said Maria, patting her hand. She'd never liked her father very much. She'd been a mother's girl from the day she was born.

* * *

It was with a huge sense of relief that Virgil drove up to his little yellow and white caravan. He got out of the car and took a moment to breathe in the fresh air and drink in the peace and quiet. All the worry and stress his return to Garthamlock had caused him dissipated. Even his torturous thoughts of Ember felt to ease. He was pleased to see that his little repotted geranium appeared to be thriving and the broken window had been replaced.

Unlocking the door with the spare key, he stepped inside to see everything was in order. In fact, it looked like Cecil had gone over the place with a vacuum and duster. He must remember to thank him.

Virgil took a seat on the couch and gazed out of the window at the woodland. This was where he belonged; this was the place where his soul sang. Perhaps he should go back to Garthamlock, pack his bags, tell his mother he was sorry; he'd tried but there was nothing he could do to control his brothers. They were adults after all. They were entitled to follow whatever path they wanted and if they ended up in prison then they had no one to blame but themselves.

Virgil's shoulders slumped as he recalled the time Nick had been sent to prison for assault, the fear in his eyes despite his bravado, the pain etched on their mother's face. Did he really want to see any of his other brothers go through that? No, but if he stayed in Garthamlock, there was a strong possibility he would go through it himself.

He sighed, wondering what his father would have said about all this if he'd been here. Then again, if his father was still alive his brothers wouldn't be running riot. Jimmy MacGregor had been the hardest bastard of them all, perfectly capable of controlling seven wild sons. For some reason, that duty had now been placed on his own shoulders when he wasn't even the oldest son. Why couldn't Newton and James bear the burden? He already knew why – because they joined in the mayhem with just as much glee as their younger brothers. If Virgil decided to return to his caravan permanently, then his brothers would all get back into the underground fights, beholden to Toni McVay until they stopped being useful to her, a situation which was dangerous in itself.

No, he knew he couldn't return here in good conscience until he'd done something to set his brothers on the right path or at least get them out from under the stiletto heel of the Queen of Glasgow, a task that seemed impossible.

Virgil pulled on his hiking boots and waterproof coat and delved into the woods behind the caravan park. There was nothing but the rustle of leaves underfoot and the caw of the birds around him. The raucous call from a large rookery made him smile. He looked up and saw the big black birds flitting from nest to nest and envied them their freedom. He wished he could soar into the sky and escape all the crap that happened on the earth below. He loved his family but sometimes they felt such a burden to him. The only one who'd ever supported his new life was James. The others seemed to think he was a coward, that he'd been running away, failing to realise that he'd been trying to protect his mental health. None of his brothers knew what it was like to think you'd killed someone. None of them understood that awful, cold feeling when your stomach plummeted into your feet and your blood froze in your veins. The entire world seemed to stop, the only sound the scream of a woman who thought she'd lost her husband forever.

The memory made him walk faster, as though he could escape it, but he knew he never would. He would have to live with it for the rest of his life, which was only right and fair. It was his punishment, his daily penance. If his brothers knew this feeling then they would change their ways, just as he had. All except for Newton – he'd always been cold and strange – and perhaps Wyatt too simply because he was so unpredictable.

Virgil delved into the darker part of the woods, the place where the shadows crept and strange scurrying sounds echoed through the undergrowth, made by creatures he could never see. He always came here when he was locked in a battle with his darker self. His thoughts turned to Ember, the woman he loved but who he couldn't be with. What had happened earlier had proved that. The stinging in his back reminded him of her sharp nails, the predatory look in her green eyes, the sly curve of her lips. The woman was dark and aggressive, yet he still longed for her. His wife's darkness spoke to his shadow self; it was that part of him that craved her. He would never be a new man while he was married to her, even if they were estranged. She would always have a hold over him.

Suddenly his path was clear and it was time to take the first step on it.

Virgil turned and headed back the way he'd come, the shadows giving way to the light. He hiked through the woods and returned to his caravan. The moment he was back inside, he took out his phone and called his solicitor.

'Hi, Raymond,' he said. 'I want to divorce Ember. Can you draw up the papers for me?'

6

Ember went to visit Lucas Blair, her husband's long-time rival. He owned three nightclubs in the city. His flagship was a rather seedy club that played eighties and nineties music. The decor was in keeping with the period but it was done in a cheap, tacky way. She was confident she could parley with him as they'd known each other since childhood and had gone to the same schools.

Lucas and Virgil had butted heads ever since they were teenagers. Lucas had been the one responsible for coming up with the nickname *Virgil the Virgin* and the two had got into many fights all through school. Their rivalry had never ended and their most recent encounter had been eight months ago, not long before Virgil's infamous underground fight. The two had both been rather drunk in the local pub and had come to blows. Lucas's resentment had only increased when Virgil had humiliated him by overpowering him and forcing him to drink the contents of the drip trays all mixed together in a pint glass. Ember was banking on this to encourage Lucas to agree to her plan.

She found him sitting at a table in his nightclub, which wasn't yet open. He was flanked by a couple of members of his crew and they appeared to be going through some paperwork together. The sound of her high heels clicking across the dance floor caused them all to look up.

'Hello, Lucas,' said Ember.

'What the fuck are you doing here?' he demanded.

'I need to talk to you.' She looked pointedly at the two men. 'Alone.'

'Leave us, boys,' Lucas told his friends.

'You sure, boss?' said one of them. 'She carries a knife.'

Lucas's face creased with anger. 'Of course I'm fucking sure. Do you think I cannae handle a wee woman?'

'Aye, but that wee woman is a psycho,' he replied.

'Get tae fuck, ya walloper,' he roared, smacking the man across the back of the head.

The man rose and left with a scowl, rubbing his head, his friend following.

'Take a seat, doll,' said Lucas magnanimously, gesturing to the chair opposite him.

Ember nodded and took the proffered seat. She studied him carefully, gauging his mood. Lucas was quite a good-looking man. He wasn't in the same league as Virgil and his brothers, but he was still attractive and he was never short of female attention. In looks, he was the opposite to Virgil with his fair hair and blue eyes that contained a charming twinkle. He also had a very winning smile. However, there was no sign of that smile or twinkle as he stared back at her. In fact, his demeanour was rather icy.

'What ya wantin'?' he said.

'It's about Virgil.'

Lucas's face immediately twisted with anger. 'You can tell

that prick that if he tries to humiliate me again then I'll cut off his...'

'Hear me out before you start throwing threats about.'

'What's wrong, doll? Does he no' do it for you any more? Are you looking for a real man?'

Ember scowled when she felt his hand on her knee under the table. 'If you don't get off me, I'll stab you.'

He felt the small knife she was known for carrying pressing against the top of his hand, so he carefully retracted it.

'That's better,' she said, retaining hold of the weapon under the table. 'Now, can we talk sensibly?'

'I never could say no to a lady,' he replied, leaning back in his seat, attempting to look casual while being eaten alive with curiosity.

'Naturally Virg doesn't know I'm here,' she said. 'None of his family do. I need your help.'

'I swore to never help anyone with the surname MacGregor.'

'I think you'll change your mind when you realise that what I propose will be to your benefit.'

'Oh aye?' he said as though he was bored, when in fact he couldn't wait to hear what she had to say.

'You and my husband have been rivals for a long time.'

'Aye, years. I hate him and he hates me.'

'How would you like an opportunity to get your own back on him?'

'Now why would you offer me a chance like that?'

'You must have heard by now that Virgil's changed. He's no longer the man I married.'

Lucas chuckled. 'I did hear he's been going around making peace like he's the fucking Dalai Lama. Tam Kiernan and Kenny Brown are best pals now.'

'So I believe,' she said disdainfully. 'I want my husband back but it's plain to me now that he's never coming back.' Her eyes glittered. 'I want revenge instead and I thought you'd want in on that.'

'You're right, I would, only there's one problem, sweetheart – I don't trust you. I think you're here at Virgil's behest. I don't believe this act he's putting on, swanning about the place like a saint, spreading peace. I think it's all part of a ploy.'

'To what purpose?' She frowned.

'Me and my crew have been stopping your family from taking over Garthamlock entirely. With me gone, there would be nothing standing in your way. Years ago, Virgil promised he'd bring me down and finally he's making his move. What's his plan, Ember? Send you in as a distraction so he and his brothers can target my men? Or are you a honeytrap? Get close to me, put me off my guard, seduce me, make me think you want to leave Virgil for me and when I eventually do let my guard down, he charges in and gets me out of the way once and for all?'

'You seem to be labouring under the delusion that Virgil constantly thinks about you when he doesn't. In fact, I can't recall the last time he even mentioned you. Besides, if he met you, he'd only try and make friends with you.' Her eyes glittered with anger. 'He's so pathetic.'

'So it really is true?' he said, noting her anger was genuine and not at all an act.

'Unfortunately, yes.'

'Now that is interesting,' he said before lapsing into thoughtful silence. 'Right, you're gonnae be my guest here.'

'Why?'

'To lure your husband into a trap.'

Lucas smiled when Ember glared at him, the green in her eyes turning bright, which everyone knew meant her temper was close to the surface.

Ember shot to her feet and raced towards the door.

'Stop her, boys,' called Lucas.

The two men who'd left the table earlier rose from their bar stools and blocked her path. She scowled at them, gripping the knife tightly.

'You could have a go, sweetheart,' said one of the men. 'But by the end of it, I promise you'll have lost most of your teeth and that pretty face will never be the same again.'

When he held his hand out for the weapon, she threw it across the room, making him sigh in irritation.

'No,' said Lucas when the man drew back his fist to hit her, Ember glaring at him fearlessly. 'We don't treat our guests like that. And we're no' gonnae maim her either. We have to make the bait as tempting as possible. Come and sit back down, Ember. Have a drink or even a few on the house. Don't worry, you'll be treated nicely. It's your husband I hate, no' you.'

Ember tilted her nose in the air, stomped back over to his table and retook her seat, the essence of hauteur.

'I'll have a gin and tonic,' she sniffed. 'Large.'

'Brian, get the lady her drink,' he called.

'Want me to piss in it?' called back the man who'd threatened her.

'That won't be necessary. I'll have a whisky while you're at it and no, I don't want you to piss in that either.' He looked back at Ember and smiled. 'Relax, princess. It'll soon be over.'

'What have you got planned?' she replied.

'You already know. I'm gonnae lure your husband here. You're the maggot on the end of the hook.'

'I beg your pardon?' She frowned.

Lucas chuckled. 'This will be fun. I've always admired you, Ember. You take absolutely no shite from anyone, do you?'

'Not until this moment, no. Usually by now my knife would be buried in your crotch.'

'But you don't have your knife and there's no need for violence. I promise me and my men won't harm you, so don't be afraid.'

'I'm afraid of nothing.'

'I think you're afraid of one thing – losing Virgil. Christ knows why because he's an arsehole. You can do way better.' His eyes bored into her meaningfully. 'Such as a loaded nightclub owner.'

Ember's expression was scornful. 'You mean you?'

'Aye, how no? I'm pretty good-looking, I've got plenty of money, way more than Virgil's ever had, and I can be very witty. Things are only on the up for me. I've recently made a deal that will put me in the big league and I need a woman by my side, a smart woman who'll gi'e me a kick up the arse if I'm about to make a bad move. That woman is you, Ember. Virgil's nae idea what he's got in you. How could any man leave a cracker like you to live in a caravan in the sticks? He must be fucking mad. I promise I'd always appreciate you and I would never leave you and humiliate you like he has. I can see how deeply that hurt you,' he added when her eyes flashed with a fiery pain. 'I will treat you like a queen.'

Lucas went silent when Brian plonked their drinks down on the table before returning to his friend at the bar, in earshot in case their boss needed them. They all knew what Ember MacGregor was capable of.

Lucas picked up his whisky glass and took a sip. 'So, what do you say, doll?'

'I'm not sure,' she slowly replied. 'To be honest, I wasn't expecting this.'

'You don't have to answer now. Take some time, think it over. I understand it would be a big change for you.'

'And you would get double revenge on Virgil?'

'What's the point in denying it?' He smiled. 'That prick's been a pain in my arse for years.'

Ember picked up her drink and smiled. 'I won't deny that your offer's an intriguing one. I'm sick of struggling to pay the bills. Some stability would be nice.'

'You'll never have that being a MacGregor. That lot are always scrabbling about for whatever scraps of cash they can get from their fights and bodyguarding.'

'It makes me furious that they've never been able to organise themselves into something more. They could set up a really good business but they cannae be arsed. They're either too lazy or have never grown up, messing about like they're still wee boys. No wonder Adelia moved to Edinburgh; the rest of them were dragging her down.'

'And they're dragging you down too. It must be frustrating for a woman like you, doll. Old Jimmy MacGregor had more ambition than all his boys put together, but in the end his health let him down. I bet you thought you could encourage Virgil to make more of himself, but he always ignored your advice.' He smiled with satisfaction when her hands curled into fists and he knew her nails were digging into her palms with anger. He'd admired Ember ever since they'd been at high school together, so he'd observed her carefully over the years and he understood all her ways. He was willing to bet he knew her better than her loser of a husband did. Sure enough, when she opened her hands, he saw the blood there.

'Brian, a tissue,' he called.

'I don't have a tissue.' He frowned.

'Get some of that kitchen roll from behind the bar then.'

Brian obeyed and wandered over to the table with the full roll.

'No' me, ya tube,' snapped Lucas when he held it out to him. 'Give it to the lady.'

Brian held the roll out to her and she took it from him, tore off a piece and dabbed at her palms with it.

'You've always been fiery,' Lucas told Ember as Brian once again retreated to the bar. 'But you were never this angry when we were younger and I know a lot of that is driven by your relationship with Virgil. Imagine how much happier you'd be without that constant torment. Imagine how much freer you'd be.'

Her eyes swept up to meet his and Lucas smiled at what he saw there. It was hope. He raised his glass to her in a toast. 'To the future.'

Ember raised her glass in response. 'To the future, whatever it may be.'

These last four words contained so much promise that inwardly Lucas rejoiced. He couldn't imagine a better revenge on Virgil MacGregor than stealing his wife from him.

* * *

It was with some reluctance that Virgil returned to Garthamlock, heading straight to his mother's house. Warren was curled up on the couch in the lounge with Rose, the two of them watching a film together. His brother had a bit more colour in his cheeks and seemed more alert, although it was clear his cracked ribs were still causing him pain. Rose, however, was on hand to tend to his every desire.

'Don't let him take advantage of you, doll,' Virgil told her.

'I won't,' she replied with a sunny smile. 'He knows I'll twist his baws right off if he messes me about.'

'And she means it,' said Warren, smiling adoringly at his girlfriend. 'This beautiful goddess is a fierce warrior.'

When the two kissed, Virgil left them to it. He wandered into the kitchen where James and Morgan were sitting at the table. To his relief, Newton was absent. His grandmother was cooking at the stove.

'There you are, Virgil,' said Ludovica as he took a seat at the table. 'Just in time for my sfogliatelle,' she announced proudly.

'Riccia or frolla, Nonna?' replied Morgan eagerly.

'Riccia.'

'Great, my favourite.' He grinned.

'None for me, Nonna,' said Virgil. He patted his stomach. 'I need to lose a little weight.' He took in the furious scowl that made her small black eyes burn like coals. 'Or I could have one.'

He was treated to a hard pat on the cheek that was almost a slap. 'Good boy. They are nearly ready.'

'Where are Newton and Wyatt?' Virgil asked his brothers.

'On a bodyguarding job,' replied James. 'Gordon who owns the corner shop is taking a load of cash to the bank and he doesnae want to get mugged by a bunch of neds again. He's no' the first business owner around here to go through that. Pete the bookie's had some hassle too. It's getting so bad that Gordon's thinking of starting a card-only policy.'

'Gordon of the tall tales.' Morgan grinned. 'He'll be filling Wyatt and Newton's heids with all sorts of shite, making out he was a big-time gangster who served seven years in Barlinnie for GBH when everyone knows he only served three months for shoplifting.'

'I always found it ironic that a shopkeeper got done for shoplifting.'

'He was seeing a high-maintenance bird who wanted him to keep buying her luxury shite. When he ran out of money, he decided to start nicking instead.'

'What a prick,' said James.

'I'm no' arguing with you there. A tenner says Wyatt ends up punching him just to shut him up.'

'You're on.'

Virgil rolled his eyes. One reason his brothers were terminally short of cash was because they kept having stupid bets with each other. They were overly fond of the online casinos too. Virgil had been just as bad but he'd managed to wean himself off gambling during his time away, and it had saved him a fortune. It had been rather frightening to discover just how much of his money he'd thrown away on it.

'Here we go,' said Ludovica, placing a large plate piled high with shell-shaped pastries in the centre of the table. The perfect layers in the pastries resembled stacked leaves, which was where the name came from.

Ludovica watched with a proud smile as the three men eagerly tucked in.

'I forgot how good they were,' said Virgil after swallowing a bite, relishing the semolina, ricotta, cinnamon and candied peel filling. After finishing the first pastry, he tried to resist temptation, but he was soon reaching for a second, to his grandmother's satisfaction.

They all looked at each other when there was a loud bang at the front door.

'Sounds like trouble,' commented James.

'Let's check it out,' said Virgil.

Morgan regarded the pastry on his plate with a regretful sigh. 'Talk about shite timing.'

The brothers headed to the door, Virgil pulling it open to

reveal a middle-aged woman with thick black hair piled on top of her head. She wore black trousers and a black shirt with a gold heart pendant, gold hoops in her ears. Her make-up was smudged from crying.

'Is Ludovica here?' she demanded in Italian. 'I need Ludovica,' she added before wailing loudly.

'She's here, Lucia,' Virgil replied in the same language. 'Come in.'

He opened the door wider and Lucia, who had been a neighbour of theirs and a client of Ludovica's for years, rushed inside past them. Ludovica supplemented her meagre pension by performing tarot readings and spiritual cleansings for the local community. They also came to her for advice, treating her as the wise woman of Garthamlock.

'Ludovica, you must help me,' cried Lucia as she ran into the kitchen, the brothers strolling in after her. 'Martin is leaving me for my cousin, Bianca. She is a slut and a viper. She has cast a spell over him – I just know it. You have to reverse it.' Her eyes settled on the plate in the middle of the table and widened greedily. 'Sfogliatelle. Perfect.'

Lucia snatched up one of the pastries and tore into it savagely. It was gone in a few bites and she immediately picked up another and made that disappear in record time too before reaching for a third.

When Morgan opened his mouth to object about this assault on one of his favourite foods, Ludovica glared at him with such ferocity he decided not to comment.

'We'll get out of your way,' Virgil told his grandmother as she seated a wailing Lucia at the table and poured her a strong coffee.

Ludovica just nodded in response.

'Why did that daft cow have to come along just when the

pastries had been brought out?' grumbled Morgan as he wandered down the street with James and Virgil. 'I bet the greedy bitch could smell them.'

'It would serve her right if Martin really was leaving her,' said James. 'She's cheated on him enough times.'

'I've come to a decision,' announced Virgil.

'Oh, aye?' said Morgan, kicking a stone down the street, smiling when it hit one of the neighbour's cars.

'I'm divorcing Ember.'

His brothers stopped to regard him with shock.

'Seriously?' said James.

'Aye.'

'I never thought I'd see the day. You were mad about her once.'

'I still am but she doesnae want the man I've become. She wants the old violent Virgil and I am no' going back to being him again. I'll never be able to make her happy.'

'So you're saying you're doing it for her more than yourself?' James frowned.

'Aye and why are you looking at me like that?'

'Because we all know that's shite. You're doing it so there's one less link between you and this place. You've been desperate to escape back to Milngavie ever since you got here and no' being tied to a wife will make it easier for you to leave again.'

'You're right,' Morgan told him before regarding Virgil with cold eyes. 'We know you don't want to be here, with us.'

'It's nothing personal,' Virgil told them. 'But you know what I've been through and I refuse to go through it again. I'm only trying to protect myself.' He really did love his family and spending time with them, but they were all harbingers of chaos, even his nonna. Peace would never be his again if he stayed around them.

'That's shite. You're scared and you don't want to admit it.'

'I am not,' he retorted, the comment denting his pride.

'Aye, ya are. You loved it here before that fight with Mark Stewart. You never once mentioned leaving. You said Garthamlock would always be your home. Then all that happened and you've been running away ever since. I never had you down as a coward, Virg. Out of us all I always thought of you as the toughest and strongest, but now I see that you're actually the weakest. Well, go on then, divorce that absolute cracker of a woman and run away back to your shitey wee caravan, you coward. See what becomes of you then because you'll never find another like her.'

'I think that's the point,' James told Morgan drily. He looked back at Virgil. 'None of us are good enough for you any more, are we?'

'I didnae say that,' replied Virgil.

'You don't need to; we get it. You're only here because Maw forced you to come. Well, piss off back to your caravan because we don't want you either.'

'James,' began Virgil, shocked at this reaction. He'd thought James at least would understand.

'Come on, Morgan,' said James. 'Let's go for a pint.'

'Aye,' he replied, eyes flashing. 'Where the company will be better.'

Virgil watched his brothers walk away while throwing glares back at him over their shoulders. He considered going after them to explain, but what was the point? In a way, they were right: he did want to be free of this place and that was part of the reason why he was divorcing Ember. He thought his brothers' reactions a little unfair but if that was what they chose to believe then he couldn't force them to change their minds.

Instead, he headed back to his house. Lucia's wailing was

audible as he passed his gran's house, so clearly Ludovica was still struggling to calm her down. It was only a matter of time before Lucia got slapped hard across the face.

He returned to his bedroom and began packing his stuff. He could achieve nothing here. It was time to return to his real home.

When his phone rang and he saw it was Ember, he was almost tempted to ignore it but James's jibe about him being a coward had struck its mark. He should talk to her, let her know he'd started divorce proceedings. It was only fair.

'Hi, Ember,' he said when he answered. 'I'm glad you called because we need to talk... Lucas?' He frowned when he heard the voice on the other end. 'What are you doing with Ember's phone?' Virgil's eyes blazed, all the tendons popping out of his neck. 'What the fuck did you say?'

'I said I've got your very lovely wife here at my club,' he replied. 'And if you don't want her to get hurt then you'll come here alone and unarmed. If you break those rules, then I will start torturing her and you know how creative I can get when it comes to stuff like that.'

Virgil did indeed know. Lucas had had a sick fascination with torture ever since he was a teenager. He vividly recalled a presentation Lucas gave in the third year of high school on the Spanish Inquisition that was so disturbing it led to him being sent straight to the head teacher's office.

'On my way,' growled Virgil.

'Good. Don't take too long because that won't go well for poor Ember. And don't tell your family because she will suffer for that too. You've to come alone.'

With that, Lucas hung up.

Virgil unleashed a primal roar of rage as his temper exploded out of him, all his calm dissolving beneath the hot force of his anger, like a volcano that had been dormant for years before violently erupting.

He raced downstairs and outside, jumping in his car and starting the engine. He hit the accelerator so hard the wheels spun as he sped away. So furious was he that he failed to notice that he passed Morgan and James.

'There goes the coward,' said Morgan. 'He's probably already packed his stuff and is heading back to his crappy caravan.'

'I don't think so,' replied James as he watched Virgil's car screech around a corner and vanish from sight. 'Didn't you see his face? He looked really angry and I mean the old anger.'

Concern filled Morgan's eyes. 'Do you think we pissed him off that much?'

'No, I don't. If we'd got him into that state, we would have known immediately. Something must have happened.'

'In the ten minutes since we last saw him?'

'I reckon so. I'll try calling him.' James phoned Virgil, but to no avail. 'He's no' answering.'

'Because he's sulking.'

'Virgil's no' the sulking kind. He couldnae have seen anyone else in so short a time. No one's in at home apart from Nonna and she's sorting out Lucia. Someone must have phoned him.'

'Who, Ember?'

'Possibly. Let's head over to their house.'

'Why bother? They'll probably only argue and then have loud sex.'

'I want to make sure they're okay. We'll need your car,' added James before turning and rushing back the way they'd come.

'But I want to go for a pint,' groaned Morgan as he jogged after his brother.

'Later,' James snapped back at him.

7

Virgil slammed on the brakes outside the tackily named Old Skool, the club owned by Lucas Blair. He jumped out of the car, slammed the door shut and stormed inside the nightclub. He encountered a man at the door who was clearly waiting for him, but the man made no move to intercept him. Despite how furious he was, Virgil realised he was walking into a trap but he didn't care.

Virgil stalked through the reception area and into the night-club proper. His sharp, fury-filled eyes scanned the darkened room, which was even gloomier than usual. He saw Ember sitting at a table at the back, her red hair like a beacon. Sitting beside her was Lucas. The way Lucas slid his arm around Ember's shoulders, as though claiming possession, only infuriated Virgil even more.

'She's mine now, Virgil the Virgin,' Lucas called to him cheerfully. 'She wants a real man after being stuck with you for years.'

Lucas had expected Virgil to stop and parley, to try and broker peace with him as he had with Jordan, but instead he continued his relentless march across the dance floor towards him. Lucas's smile only dropped when he realised the rage he'd seen in Virgil's eyes so many times in the past was still very much present.

'I thought you said he was a changed man,' Lucas asked Ember.

She smiled at the worry in his eyes. 'He is. Virgil has renounced violence.'

'He doesnae look like he has. In fact, he looks like he wants to rip my heid off.'

Ember just shrugged, enjoying Lucas's discomposure, as well as the fact that Virgil once again resembled the man she'd married.

'Stop him, boys,' cried Lucas.

Brian and his friend were the first to charge at Virgil, who batted them away as though they were annoying flies. Brian was knocked against the bar and his friend was thrown into a table, which he upended, knocking him out. Brian, however, wasn't so easily overcome. He charged at Virgil again with a roar, his big, bulky body looking awkward and a little ridiculous. Virgil whipped round, fist raised, and hit him with so much speed Brian was unconscious before he'd even realised what had happened.

Lucas got to his feet, gaping at his fallen friends. 'He's no' changed, ya daft tart. He's exactly the same.'

'I knew it.' Ember smiled with satisfaction. Her eyes glittered as she turned to Lucas. 'And he's gonnae kill you.'

'Get him, ya fucking wallopers,' yelled Lucas, waving his hand at his men. 'Don't just stand there.'

More men emerged from the shadows holding pool cues and baseball bats. One man attempted to jab Virgil in the stomach with his cue. Virgil grabbed the end and yanked it out of his hands before flipping it around and smacking him across the face with it. He used the cue to block another man from hitting him with a baseball bat before he too received the full force of the weapon in his stomach. Virgil smacked one man across the back with it and the cue snapped in half. He retained hold of the broken end and slashed another man across the face, who screamed, shattered splinters sticking out of his face. The shock of seeing his friend that way caused the heavy standing beside him with a bat to hesitate and he was knocked off his feet by Virgil's fist in his face.

'Jeezo, look at him,' exclaimed Lucas. 'He's a fucking loon.' He rounded on Ember. 'You lied to me. You made out he was a peace-loving wuss.'

'Because I thought he was,' she replied, regarding her husband with unconcealed delight. 'But my Virgil is back.'

Her smile made Lucas's jaw clench. His last man was taken down with punches so fast he didn't even have time to defend himself.

Lucas pulled a knife and pressed it to Ember's neck when Virgil's blazing eyes settled on him.

'Stay back,' he told him. 'Or I'll cut her, I swear. I mean it, stay the fuck back,' he cried when Virgil continued to march towards him. He only stopped when Lucas nicked the pale skin of Ember's throat with the tip of the blade.

'Good,' said Lucas, sweat standing out on his forehead, breathing hard with fear. 'Now, me and Ember are leaving and you won't follow us.'

'You do know, that wherever you go, I will find you,' growled Virgil. 'You will never be free of me. I will keep coming after you. You know that I never, ever stop.'

The dark, disturbing desire for violence that shone out of Virgil's eyes had never failed to terrify Lucas, ever since he'd

seen it for the first time at high school and Virgil had beaten him
to a pulp for bullying him.

Virgil's chest heaved, his fists covered in blood. 'Let her go
and I might reconsider ripping your fucking head off.'

Ember was so delighted by this turn of events that her green
eyes were positively luminescent in the gloom.

'We're going now,' said Lucas. 'And I suggest you don't follow
us if you want to protect your wife.' He looked to Ember when
she didn't move. 'Get up,' he said.

'No,' she retorted.

'I will cut you, I swear.'

'Go on then. I'm not stopping you.' She smiled in Virgil's
direction. 'But he will.'

'He won't be able to reach me before I do it.'

'Maybe not but he will still tear you into tiny little pieces.'

Lucas looked back at Virgil, who appeared even more predatory. The only thing holding him back was fear of doing something that would hurt his wife. That was Lucas's only advantage
and he knew he had to use it.

He grabbed a handful of Ember's hair and yanked back her
head, putting the knife to her throat. Lucas screamed in pain
when a fire started up in his left thigh. Looking down, he saw
blood trickling down his leg and a flash of silver in Ember's
hand.

'You didn't even think that I might have a second knife, did
you?' she hissed before slashing at his hand holding her hair.

Lucas yelped and released her, and Ember threw herself
sideways as Virgil flew at her captor, leaping over the table to
reach him. Virgil used the broken pool cue to knock the knife
from Lucas's hand before landing on top of him and knocking
him to the floor. He began smashing Lucas repeatedly in the face
with his fists.

Ember looked on, practically purring with satisfaction. This was the Virgil she loved, the strong, powerful animal who no one could stand up to, not even his own brothers. She knew that he would triumph if he was ever put in the ring with any of them because none of them had this wild beast inside them, the beast he'd tried to leave behind.

Lucas had fallen unconscious during the beating, which was probably all the better for him. Ember had thought that Virgil would keep going until he was dead, but it was only when Lucas stopped moving and screeching that the red mist finally left him. Virgil stared down at Lucas's battered face in horror.

'Oh, Christ, what have I done?' he cried, leaping to his feet.

'You did what needed to be done,' replied Ember.

'I think I've killed him.'

The small, terrified way he spoke annoyed her. 'You've done nothing of the sort. I can see him breathing from here.'

At that moment, Lucas coughed and spluttered, his eyes rolling open and Virgil sighed with relief. 'I should call an ambulance.'

'Are you fucking insane? They'll arrest you for assault and how will you explain all this?' she added, gesturing to the injured men around them.

'I'll call the polis too and tell them the truth…'

'Wake up, Virgil,' she snapped. 'You'd be arrested and flung into prison. All the polis know of your reputation, so you wouldn't stand a chance. And fuck this lot anyway. Have you forgotten that they abducted me? Now, we need to leave before the staff start to arrive.'

'Aye, you're right,' he murmured, studying Lucas carefully, making sure he really was okay. He was reassured by the way Lucas was trying to sit up. He wasn't lying in that disturbingly still way Mark Stewart had.

Virgil was stunned by the carnage he'd caused, wounded men lying all around him. Thankfully all were conscious but the worst injury he'd inflicted was to the man with all the wooden splinters sticking out of his face. He was sat on the floor with his back against the bar, shaking and whimpering like a kicked dog.

'Jesus,' murmured Virgil.

'Let's move before they get back on their feet,' said Ember, taking his hand and pulling him towards the door.

Virgil allowed himself to be led. The man they'd encountered on the way in was still standing there, his jaw hanging open, having witnessed the entire thing. He hastily leapt out of their way, not wanting to share his friends' fates. Realising he was no threat, Virgil and Ember ran past him and outside. Virgil stopped, blinking against the sudden sunlight, still trying to process what he'd done.

'Where are your car keys?' Ember demanded of him.

He produced them from this jeans pocket and she snatched them from him.

'Get in,' she told him.

Virgil was happy to obey and to let her drive. He was still far too shocked to do it himself.

'Won't you say something?' demanded Ember when Virgil had been silent for a full five minutes.

'Sorry,' he said, dragging his attention from the window and onto her. 'I still cannae believe that just happened. How did I take down all those men on my own?'

'You were furious that they'd kidnapped your wife and held a knife to her throat. I'm fine by the way,' she added venomously.

'God, I'm sorry,' he said, noting the dried blood on her neck. 'I should have asked that sooner. Did they hurt you, apart from what Lucas did to your neck?'

'No. I was just the bait to lure you there.'

'For what purpose?'

'Lucas doesn't believe this new peaceful act of yours.'

'It's no' an act.'

'He thinks it is and you've just proved him right.'

'I never wanted to raise my hand to anyone again and then this happens.'

'The last time you went on a rampage like that you only took down five men on your own,' she added sardonically. 'It's because you're trying to suppress your natural urges. They all came spilling out at once. You can't hide who you really are, Virg. Bad things happen when you try.'

Ember parked outside his mother's house and the two of them climbed out of the car. Virgil still felt a little shaky and in shock, which he thought went to prove that he was a different man now. The old Virgil would have revelled in the violence he'd inflicted.

James and Morgan were just pulling up in the latter's car.

'Virg,' exclaimed James, leaping out of the car and dashing up to him.

'I'm no' in the mood for another row,' he retorted.

'Neither are we. We've been looking for you. We were worried.'

'Why?'

'Because we saw you speed away looking really pissed off about something. We've been all over Garthamlock trying to find you.'

'What happened to your neck?' Morgan asked Ember, noting the blood.

'Come inside,' replied Virgil in a weary voice. 'There's a lot to explain.'

They entered the house to find Ludovica in the kitchen with Maria. Lucia had gone.

Maria was also quick to spot the blood on Ember's neck, as well as how pale Virgil was and the cuts to his knuckles.

'What's happened?' she demanded, getting to her feet.

'Lucas Blair kidnapped me,' replied Ember.

'What?' exclaimed Morgan and James in unison.

'He'd heard Virgil was a changed man so he decided to take him down, thinking he wouldn't fight back. Virgil burst in to save me. He was magnificent; he took down eight of them all on his own.'

'Wow, Virg.' Morgan grinned. 'That is impressive.'

Warren and Rose, alerted by all the chatter, joined them in the kitchen and the story was relayed to them too.

'Eight?' said Warren. 'That's incredible, Virg.'

Virgil didn't reply. He just looked down his hands, which he'd only just noticed were cut, bruised and coated in dried blood. 'I need to wash my hands,' he muttered, heading to the sink.

'No, not in here,' Ludovica told him savagely. 'In the bathroom.'

He nodded, understanding that the kitchen was a sacred place to his nonna, so he rushed down the hall to the small toilet.

Virgil frantically scrubbed his hands under the water, watching it swirl away red. When he raised his head to look into the mirror, he saw the same pale, haunted face he'd seen the night he'd almost killed Mark Stewart. He'd never wanted to look at that face ever again.

Flashes of the fight came back to him – smashing one man in the face with the pool cue, kicking another, repeatedly slamming his fists into Lucas's face. A tiny bit of satisfaction rose inside him at that last image. Lucas had been his nemesis for years. He also recalled Lucas pressing a knife to Ember's throat and some of his guilt vanished. Lucas had kidnapped Ember and threatened her. A beating was the least he deserved. The fucking idiot should think himself lucky he was still alive.

Anger blazed in the eyes of his reflection. Virgil closed them and shook his head.

'Deep breaths,' he said, willing his thumping heart to slow.

When he opened his eyes again, he looked calmer. It was time to get out there and discuss the consequences of his actions with his family, because this would affect them all.

Newton and Wyatt had returned and were being brought up to speed. The former had an insufferable told-you-so look in his eyes.

'Well, he's back.' Wyatt smiled, patting Virgil on the shoulder. 'I knew he would be.'

'No, he's not,' retorted Virgil. 'That was just a one-off. The creep kidnapped Ember.'

'You did the right thing. You couldnae leave your wife to that dirty perv. If Lucas got the shite kicked out of him in the process, then it's his own fault.'

'There's just one problem,' said Newton. 'Lucas has started working for Toni McVay and we all know she gets pissed off when someone under her protection is attacked. It makes her look bad.'

'Toni McVay?' exclaimed Virgil.

Maria glanced sharply at Ember, wondering if she'd known Lucas had been working for Toni all along. Ember's answering look was impossible to read.

'Aye,' said Newton. 'He's dealing for her through his nightclubs. She's no' gonnae be very happy about this.'

'But he kidnapped Ember,' replied Virgil. 'Surely she'll understand?'

'You expect a woman who scoops people's eyeballs out of

their heids to be understanding? Toni's a psychopath. All she cares about is making money. I'm willing to bet you can expect a visit from her very soon.'

Virgil began wondering if it was too late to make a run for it to Outer Mongolia. 'This day just gets worse and worse.'

'Tell him about Toni, Rose,' said Newton.

'I'm no' so sure she won't understand,' replied Rose. 'Aye, she can be terrifying but she's shown my family compassion when she didnae have to. If she likes someone then she will try to help them or at least no' take the revenge you think she might.'

This coming from someone who actually knew and had interacted with Toni McVay made Virgil feel slightly better.

'Sit down, Ember,' said Ludovica. 'I will treat your neck. Then I will sort out your hands, Virgil.'

'Thanks, Nonna,' he replied, slumping into a chair at the kitchen table.

'Are there any sfogliatelle left?' said Morgan.

'Lucia finished them off,' replied Ludovica.

'Greedy cow,' he muttered. 'I hope you cursed her?'

'No, but she thinks I cursed her love rival. It made her feel much better.'

'Never mind all that,' said Maria. 'Everyone, sit. We need to talk.'

The rest of the siblings obeyed and they all gathered around the table.

'There is a possibility that Toni may no' come after Virgil for this,' continued Maria. 'It was personal between Virgil and Lucas and she is known for keeping out of personal disputes.'

'That's true,' said Rose. 'She's done the same for my family.'

'But if she does want revenge then you can guarantee it won't be in the usual way. She will get Virgil to do something that will be to her advantage. That is the way the woman's mind works.'

'Nae offence, Maw,' said Newton. 'But what do you know about the way Toni McVay's mind works?'

Maria glanced at Ludovica, who nodded. 'Very well, I shall tell you something that may come as a shock to you all. Perhaps I should have told you sooner, but it was something I preferred to keep to myself. Toni and I used to be friends.'

'Seriously?' said Morgan.

'Aye, seriously,' she snapped. 'Why would I lie?'

'I didnae say you lied. I'm just shocked. Go on.'

Maria scowled at him before continuing. 'We met through a mutual friend at a party and found we got on very well. We had similar dreams, similar ambitions,' she said wistfully. 'Toni found it very hard to get along with other women. Men were a different matter, she could weave her spell around any man she wanted but women resented her. No' me though. I met my Jimmy when I was seventeen and I knew he was the man for me, so I was never a threat to Toni for the attention of other men, which meant we were able to form a friendship. We even remained friends after her brother disappeared and she took over leading the family. Then she began to become greedier and in turn colder and more ruthless. I started to find she was bad company, so I saw her less until we stopped meeting up altogether.'

'So you never worked for her or anything?' James asked her.

'No.'

'Why did you never call her and ask her to let us back into the underground fights?'

'Because she would have said no. Toni lost money because of our family. She finds things like that hard to forgive, and don't expect her to do anything out of sentiment because she doesnae feel things like that.'

'We must prepare because darkness is coming,' said

Ludovica. 'I have seen it many times in my dreams lately, but I can't see the outcome. It comes to us on black beating wings. Many ill omens have I seen. Whether this darkness arrives in the form of Toni McVay or something else remains unclear, but today is the beginning. I have had dreams of blood and wood and splinters.'

Virgil and Ember glanced at each other.

'Why do you say splinters?' Virgil asked his grandmother.

'Because that is what I have seen in my dreams. Wood shattering, splinters flying through the air and then blood.' She frowned. 'You have seen the blood and splinters, haven't you?'

'Aye, today. I hit one of Lucas's men with a broken pool cue and left him with splinters sticking out of his face. And yes, there was blood.'

'Fucking awesome,' said Morgan.

'Then it has definitely begun,' said Ludovica. 'I was hoping it would not happen yet, but it has. We must be ready.'

'For what?' said James.

'For the darkness to arrive on black beating wings.'

James had very little time for his grandmother's mysticism and stifled an irritated sigh. 'Let's just focus on the danger we can see and that is possible retribution from no' just Toni but Lucas too.'

'No way will Lucas try and hit back at us,' said Morgan. 'He'd be mad to after his entire crew was taken down by just one of us.'

'He can be sneaky when he wants to be. We need to stay on our guard.'

'I hope you realise that you cannae return to your caravan, Virgil,' Maria told her son. 'No' yet at least. Isolating yourself from your family would be dangerous.'

'I know,' he said tightly, grinding his palms together. 'We

need to consider Nick too. He's vulnerable in prison. I've got a visit booked with him today.'

'Then you need to explain to him what has happened. In the meantime, I can get a message to him warning him to be on his guard.'

'What else can we do?' said Wyatt.

'Nothing except remain vigilant,' said Ludovica. 'For already I can hear the beating of wings.'

They all regarded each other in silence.

'Right,' said Ludovica, placing her palms flat on the table and pushing herself to her feet. 'I need to tend to Ember and Virgil. Everyone else leave.'

The others rose and left. No one ever questioned Ludovica. Their grandmother delved into a cupboard and produced a variety of herbs and oils, Ember and Virgil watching in silence as she ground them all up before mixing them into a thick paste, which she then smeared on the wounds to Ember's neck and Virgil's hands.

'There,' she said, nodding with satisfaction. 'They will soon heal.'

Ember tried to ignore the pungent smell, knowing Ludovica's remedies always worked and a lot faster than conventional medicines too.

'This Lucas has also placed the evil eye on you both,' said Ludovica. 'In your case, Virgil, it is full of hatred and jealousy. Ember, it is frustrated passion and possessiveness.' As she spoke, she filled a white porcelain bowl halfway with water and placed it on the table before Virgil. To the water she added five drops of olive oil, which immediately burst and covered the surface of the water. Ludovica muttered something under her breath before producing a second bowl, which she placed before Ember. The process was repeated and this time the drops clustered together in the centre of the bowl.

'There, malocchio in you both,' Ludovica announced, referring to a curse whether consciously or unconsciously transferred from one person to another by a look or a glare.

She then recited a charm in Italian over Virgil and Ember, invoking the protection of Archangel Michael. As she spoke, she made the sign of the cross in the oil then slashed the air over the bowl before Virgil with a pair of scissors before tossing some salt into the bowl. The process was repeated with Ember's bowl, then the contents of both were poured down the drain in the backyard.

By the time Ludovica had finished, Virgil didn't feel any different, but it seemed to satisfy his grandmother, who studied them both carefully.

'Yes, good,' she said. 'All gone.'

'Thanks, Nonna,' replied Virgil. He turned to his wife. 'Can I talk to you in private?'

Ember nodded and they exited the kitchen, leaving Ludovica to tidy up. They entered the lounge, which was empty, the rest of the family having gathered in the front garden to enjoy the sunshine and chat.

'I havenae thanked you properly yet for saving me.' Ember smiled.

Virgil took a step back when she tried to slide her arms around his neck.

'What's wrong?' She frowned.

'I'm glad you're safe but you should know that this morning I told my solicitor to start divorce proceedings.'

Ember blinked up at him in surprise before anger filled her eyes. 'What the actual fuck?'

'I cannae be the man you want me to be.'

'But you just were back at Lucas's club. You were everything I've ever wanted. Apart from that,' she added, prodding his belly.

'Only for those few brief moments. I don't intend to ever do it again.'

'You did though, Virg,' she said ardently, taking his hands. 'You did it for me because you love me and you were protecting me, which is what a husband should do for his wife.'

'You never did tell me how you ended up at that club in the first place.'

Although Ember forced a look of innocence, Virgil caught the mischief that briefly filled her eyes, which always became more luminous when she was up to something. He'd never informed her of this tell because it was the only advantage he had.

'I was walking home when Lucas's men pulled me into a van,' she said.

'Really?'

Ember managed to maintain the innocent look when his face hardened with suspicion.

'Yes,' she said. 'Why would I lie?'

'Because you know how much me and Lucas hate each other and you wanted to use that to bring back the old me.'

'Actually, Lucas had heard the rumours about you and decided now was a good time for some revenge. That makes much more sense than me willingly putting myself in a dangerous situation. I'm not stupid.'

'I'm well aware of that. I'm also aware of how manipulative you can be. Lucas has been in love with you for years; it's one reason why he hates me so much. You must have known he wouldnae hurt you.'

'I don't believe this. I was kidnapped and you're trying to blame me for it.'

'I'm just trying to figure out exactly what happened.'

'I've already told you, or are you calling me a liar?'

Ember revelled in the way his eyes ate her up, assessing the slightest expression and gesture, weighing up her words. Gently she cupped his face in her hands. 'I was so proud of you today. You dealt with Lucas and his men as though they were nothing. You have so much power, Virg, but you don't realise it. You could do anything with it and I can help you,' she breathed, brushing his lips with her own. 'Together, we'd crush pricks like Lucas Blair. Wouldn't you like that?' When something sparked in his eyes, she decided to press a little harder. 'You might have found a temporary peace in your wee caravan, but it wouldn't be long before you got bored and started wanting more. It was never going to make you permanently happy and you know it.'

'You're wrong. I'd be very happy to stay there for the rest of my life. It's what I want and I will go back there.' He gestured around him. 'This is what's temporary.'

Her gaze hardened. 'And that includes our marriage, doesn't it?'

'We both know it's no' been working. We're best cutting ties now so you can find someone who can give you the life you've always wanted – money, a mansion and a line of flash cars on the drive, because I don't care about all that and one day you will hate me for it. In fact, I know you already do. It's why our marriage became so unstable. I do love you, Ember, but I cannae be with you. Now go, and please, be happy.'

Ember was so surprised her plan had failed that for a moment all she could was stare at him in shock, her quick brain paralysed by surprise. She'd thought reawakening what he truly was would automatically throw him back into her arms, that he'd come home and everything would go back to how it had once been. 'You're serious, aren't you?'

'Yes. It's over.'

Overwhelming rage swept over Ember, crashing down on her like a tidal wave.

'So much for me always having a place in your life, you lying bastard,' she screamed before punching him repeatedly all over his body. Virgil didn't retaliate; he just raised his arms to fend off the worst of the blows.

'What's going on?' demanded James, bursting into the room along with his brothers.

'Ember's just getting something off her chest,' replied Virgil wryly.

'Don't you dare fucking smile,' she yelled. 'Or do you think divorce is something to laugh about?'

'Divorce?' Newton frowned.

'This shitebag's started divorce proceedings against me,' she cried, ceasing her assault on her husband to turn to them with a martyred look. 'He doesn't want me any more,' she added, face crumpling.

Newton rushed to wrap her in his arms. Ember buried her face in his chest and sobbed. Wyatt and Warren frowned at her like she'd run mad, while Morgan and James appeared sceptical. Rose's eyes, however, were filled with knowing. She understood exactly what trick Ember was pulling. Virgil thought she was very shrewd for someone who wasn't yet twenty years old.

'Why don't we all clear out and leave them to it?' suggested James.

Ember rounded on him. 'No. I want you all to bear witness to this. I want you to see how Virgil uses women and casts them aside.'

'Uses them? He just rescued you from Lucas Blair.'

'Why did you agree to the counselling if you'd no intention of repairing our marriage?' Ember demanded of Virgil.

'I wanted to give it a try,' he replied, icily cool. 'But that was until you set me up. Today you made me do something I'd sworn I would never do again.'

'I was kidnapped, for God's sake,' she cried.

'I don't believe you. I know what you're like, Ember. You knew that what I did to Mark Stewart almost killed me, but you didnae care. All you saw were your own selfish needs. Today made me realise that you don't care about me.'

'That's no' true, Virg. I love you.'

'I could have done to Lucas what I did to Mark and it would have completely destroyed me, but that didnae matter to you. That is no' love.'

'You should have killed him after he abducted me.'

'Have some dignity and stop lying. I know exactly what you did; I just wish I'd taken a minute to think it over after getting that call from Lucas.'

'Virgil,' began James. 'Are you sure?'

'Aye, I'm sure,' he snapped back, gaze fixed on Ember. 'I can see what she did in her eyes.'

'I'm no' sure that'll stand up in a divorce court,' said Newton.

'Stay out of it,' Virgil told him.

'You're gonnae regret doubting me, Virgil,' said Ember. 'I swear to the Almighty that I will get you back for this.'

'I look forward to seeing what other trick you can pull to make yourself look the victim, but I promise you this – if you somehow end up getting kidnapped again then I won't be coming to your rescue.'

'You smug prick,' she snarled, cheeks bright red with rage. 'I'm gonnae kill you,' she screeched before running at him.

James and Morgan grabbed her and held her fast. Ember fought and struggled to free herself while Virgil looked down at her coolly.

'We can sell the house and split the profits,' he told her. 'You're welcome to stay in it until it's sold. I'll collect the rest of my stuff tomorrow.'

'You do know that all your stuff will have been destroyed by the end of the day?' James asked him.

Virgil shrugged. 'So what if it is? I don't want it any more.'

'Aye because you've got everything you need, haven't you?' snapped Ember. 'Your stupid wee caravan. I hope the fucking thing burns down with you in it.'

'Hey.' Morgan frowned. 'I know you're upset, doll, but there's no need for that.'

'You'd better leave before you lose all your dignity,' Virgil told her. He looked to his brothers. 'Let her go.'

They released Ember although they remained close in case she tried to do anything stupid. They all knew she always carried at least one knife.

Ember glared at Virgil, as though contemplating bloody violence before turning on her heel and storming out, slamming the lounge door shut behind her. In the hallway she was confronted by Ludovica, who studied her closely with her coal-black eyes.

'You pushed him too far,' the older woman told her. 'I always knew you would one day. I'm surprised it took this long.'

'Your grandson wants to divorce me. Isn't that against your religion?' retorted Ember, spotting her chance to gain a powerful ally.

'I follow my own religion, not what others tell me I should believe. And don't try and use me as an instrument of your revenge. I'm far smarter than Lucas Blair.'

'I was only trying to bring him back to us,' she rasped, expression softening, tears spilling down her face.

'I know,' said Ludovica, patting her arm. 'But as usual, you lacked subtlety. That has always been your trouble.'

'I had to do something because you and Maria weren't bothering to try.'

'I wonder what you will do now? You are a child-woman, Ember, who has a tantrum when she doesn't get her own way.'

Ember stood her ground when Ludovica's eyes bored into her soul. It was unnerving sometimes looking into the old woman's eyes. You got the feeling there was far more beyond them, such as stars and galaxies and ancient things the human race had long forgotten.

'I like you,' Ludovica continued. 'And until your divorce you will still be one of the family, but I warn you – do not seek vengeance on my grandson. You know what I will send your way if you do.'

'One of your curses?' she replied with a mocking smile.

'No. I know you don't believe in them, which reduces their power. I will think of something far more insidious. Something...' Ludovica's lips twisted '...deforming.'

'What?' Ember frowned, appalled by this statement.

Ludovica patted her cheek, Ember grimacing at the touch of the old woman's cold, wrinkled hand. 'I know how you prize your looks, my pretty. I do hope nothing damages them.'

'You evil old crone.' She scowled.

'That is what you fear the most about me, isn't it, Ember? Not how wicked I can be but old age.' Ludovica held up her hand. 'Take a good look because this will be you one day, with the wrinkles and the liver spots. You can't avoid it, no matter what you do.' Ludovica dropped her voice to a whisper. 'And that terrifies you more than anything.'

Ember tilted her chin defiantly in an effort to hide the fact that Ludovica's arrow had struck its mark perfectly. 'I'm leaving now. I've been humiliated enough by this family for one day.'

Ludovica took a step back, giving her room to depart, a smile playing at the corners of her mouth. 'Go then.'

Ember, exhausted by the day's events, stomped towards the front door without another word.

'I mean what I say,' Ludovica called after her. 'Do not seek revenge against Virgil.'

Ember turned to look at her, the confidence back in her green eyes. 'I make no promises,' she said before flinging open the front door and stepping outside, slamming the door shut behind her.

Virgil stepped out of the lounge. 'Has she gone?'

'Yes,' replied Ludovica. 'I warned her not to seek revenge against you.'

'I appreciate that, Nonna, but I know that God himself won't be able to stop her.'

'You're no' wrong,' said James as he and his brothers also exited the lounge. 'You need to watch your back, Virg.'

'And you really think she set up that kidnapping?' an incredulous Newton asked Virgil.

'I do,' he replied. 'If I hadnae let my anger overwhelm me, I would have realised it sooner. All of you at one time or another have said it's the bloodlust and anger that makes me strong and has given me my reputation, but it takes me over so much I cannae even think. Now, thanks to that and Ember's scheming, I might have just opened Pandora's box and got our family into a whole heap of shite.'

'But what if you're wrong and Ember really was abducted?' pressed Newton.

'I didnae think you were gullible,' he retorted.

Newton's lips pinched. 'I'm no' gullible but there is a possibility that she was telling the truth.'

'She was lying; I could see it in her eyes. If you knew her as well as I do you'd have realised it too.'

'I just hope you havenae ruined your marriage for nothing.'

'I started divorce proceedings before that even happened. If Ember had known, she wouldn't have bothered going to Lucas. Anyway, it's done now and cannae be changed. We'll just have to deal with whatever happens next.'

'I don't envy you,' Wyatt told him. 'A scorned woman's a dangerous thing. She'll probably cut off your cock.'

'I wouldnae put it past her to try.' Virgil glanced at his watch. 'I have to go. I've got a visit booked with Nick in an hour.'

Virgil headed out to his car and sighed when he saw both tyres on the driver's side had been slashed, no doubt with one of the small knives Ember habitually carried. He went back inside and asked Morgan if he could borrow his motor.

'Don't you dare laugh,' Virgil told his grinning brother. 'I'll call my breakdown company to come and sort it out.'

'Leave me the key in case they turn up while you're out.'

'Cheers,' said Virgil as the brothers swapped car keys.

'You should think yourself lucky she didnae use her knife on you.'

'Believe me, that has crossed my mind.'

8

Virgil was shocked by Nick's appearance. The last time he'd visited his youngest brother he'd seemed rather happy-go-lucky, determined not to let his incarceration get him down, but now he looked sullen, pale and unwell, which was a shock as he was usually the picture of health.

'Are you okay?' Virgil asked Nick as he took a seat opposite him in the Visits Centre.

'Just feeling a bit under the weather,' he mumbled back.

Virgil studied him carefully. 'You're on drugs, aren't you?'

Nick immediately looked around to make sure no one had overheard. 'Keep your fucking voice down, will you?'

'So I'm right?'

Nick sighed. 'You don't know what it's like in here. I need it to get me through.'

Virgil's heart nearly broke for his little brother. 'You've only a few months left to go. If you get caught, you'll have time added onto your sentence.'

'I cannae get through those few months without it. This place is hell.'

'Is someone giving you a hard time? Because if they are I'll sort them out for you.'

'No, it's just this place in general – being locked in, the clang of the doors, the shouting and screaming of the other prisoners.' He ground his palms together furiously. 'I'm so sick of it. I just want to hear silence for one fucking second.'

'Look, I know it cannae be easy...'

'What the fuck do you know?' he spat back. 'You've never been inside and I havenae heard anything from Debbie in over a month,' Nick added, referring to his girlfriend. 'She promised she'd wait for me, but it seems she's forgotten all about me. Have you seen her?' he asked earnestly.

'No, sorry, but I havenae been back in Garthamlock long.'

'Have the others heard from her?'

'Nae idea.'

Nick sighed and slumped back in his chair miserably. 'I'd feel much better if she paid me a visit.'

'I'll have a word with her, get her to contact you.'

'Thanks,' he said, looking a little relieved. 'That would be great.'

'On one condition.'

'What?'

'That you gi'e up the drugs.'

'I can't,' he hissed. 'Without them, I wouldnae even be able to get out of my bed in the morning.'

Virgil leant forward in his seat, eyes hardening. 'Aye ya fucking will. All you've got to do is keep your heid down for another five months and you'll be back home.'

'Five months on the outside is five years in this shitehole.' He ran an anxious hand through his hair. 'I cannae go the distance.'

'Jesus, Nick, what's happened to you? You were so strong once, even stronger than the rest of us.'

'It turns out I'm no'.'

'Tell me what happened.'

'Nothing's happened.'

'Aye it has. Now spill.'

Nick dragged both hands down his face. 'Someone touched me.'

'Touched you?' He frowned.

'Aye.' Nick glanced around before leaning in closer, lowering his voice. 'Down there,' he added, nodding at his crotch.

'Did they...'

'Naw, I didnae let it go that far. I threw the prick across the room, but he's got a crew around him and they've been threatening me.'

'Threatening how?'

Nick sighed in agitation and shook his head.

'Tell me,' pressed Virgil.

'They're threatening to gang-rape me,' he whispered.

'Jesus,' said a shocked Virgil. 'I thought that sort of thing only happened in films.'

'Well, it turns out it happens in real life too.'

'Who are they?'

'The leader's called Henry Allan. He's one of the Allans from Garrowhill. Have you heard of them?'

'Aye, I know of them. Me and the boys will pay them a visit. Don't worry, Henry will soon be off your back. It'll all be sorted by tonight. Then will you be able to kick the drugs?'

'Well, it might help,' he said, looking doubtful.

'It better because if it doesnae, you'll be stuck in here a hell of a lot longer than five months. Do you hear me?'

Nick nodded seriously. 'Aye.'

'Good.'

Virgil then went on to relate to Nick everything that had

happened in Garthamlock. By the time he'd finished, visiting time was over.

'You really will sort things out for me?' Nick asked Virgil as he got to his feet.

'I promise. Just hang in there.'

Nick nodded but he didn't look as if his big brother's pep talk had fuelled him with any fire. He appeared limp and defeated already. Virgil left the prison feeling troubled. He'd never seen chirpy, happy Nick look like that before and he feared what would become of his brother if he couldn't kick the drugs. He was determined on one thing though – the Allan family would pay for what Henry had done.

* * *

Virgil drove back to Garthamlock to visit Debbie Mitchell, Nick's girlfriend. Before he could get out of the car, the front door of her home opened and Newton emerged. At first, Virgil wondered if Nick had also asked him to speak to Debbie on his behalf, until Newton turned to kiss the blonde woman standing behind him, which was Debbie herself.

Virgil leapt out of the car, slammed the door shut and stormed up the garden path. Neither of them had noticed him as they were still kissing.

'What the fuck is this?' he demanded.

They jumped apart, Debbie paling with horror.

'All right, Virg?' said Newton casually.

'What the hell do you think you're doing? She's your brother's girlfriend.'

'She was lonely. I was only giving her some company.'

'I know what you were giving her. Get inside both of you before someone sees us.'

'Fine,' said Newton, looking bored while Debbie's eyes were wide with panic.

The three of them stepped inside the house, Virgil slamming the door shut behind him. Debbie was very pretty with her thick blonde hair and blue eyes. She was wrapped in a pink dressing gown and her hair was mussed up from lovemaking.

'Listen, Virgil,' she began, hands held out before her in a placating manner. 'We didnae mean for this to happen. I was just so lonely after Nick got sent down. Me and Newton got talking and one thing led to another.'

'Did you ever think about Nick?'

'Of course I did. I love him.'

'You've got a funny way of showing it.'

'It's been so hard for me since he was sent down.'

'You promised to wait for him. Shagging his brother is no' waiting for him.' Virgil felt the rage shift inside him, seeking escape, but he was fighting hard to keep it contained. Newton's smirk, however, was not helping.

'And what about you?' he demanded, rounding on his brother. 'Did you ever think of Nick?'

'Like Debbie said, one thing led to another,' he coolly replied.

'How long has it been going on?'

'About a month.'

'Is that why you cut off all contact with Nick?' he asked Debbie.

'I couldnae face him,' she replied. 'I was too ashamed.'

'So you should be. Cheating on him was bad enough but with his own brother...' He shook his head. 'Disgusting.'

'Coming from the man who abandoned his own wife to live in a crappy caravan in the countryside,' said Newton. 'You're such a hypocrite.'

'I never cheated on Ember.' The thought that his brother could have slept with his wife while he was away suddenly occurred to Virgil.

Newton noted the way his hands formed into fists, divined what he was thinking and smiled. 'Men really shouldnae leave their women unattended.'

Virgil grabbed Newton by the front of his shirt and slammed him back against the wall. 'Have you shagged my wife?' he snarled.

'No, of course not,' he replied, maintaining his aloofness.

'I don't believe you,' growled Virgil, his grip tightening on his brother.

'I cannae help that.'

Virgil inhaled deeply before releasing him. 'Naw, Ember wouldnae touch you with a bargepole. She always said you were a pompous wanker.' Satisfaction rolled through Virgil when annoyance finally flickered in his older brother's eyes.

'Are you gonnae tell Nick?' Debbie asked Virgil in a timid voice.

'I should but it would destroy him. You've no' seen the state he's in. I'm afraid it will push him over the edge.'

'You mean he might hurt himself?'

'Aye.'

'But Nick's always seemed so strong.'

'Prison's close to breaking him. A visit from you would go a long way to helping him.'

'I'll book a visit with him as soon as I can. I promise.'

'Do you still want to be with him? Because if you don't then you're best waiting until he's been released to tell him.'

'Yes, I still want him. I love him,' she said ardently. 'I... I was lonely and I missed male company. I have needs too.'

'It would have been better if you'd discreetly shagged a stranger, but you had to choose his own brother. That's fucking twisted.'

'I don't see what business it is of yours,' said Newton. 'We're both consenting adults.'

Virgil rounded on him again. 'When was the last time you visited Nick?'

'Dunno, probably about three weeks ago.'

'You must have noticed he was deteriorating.'

'He seemed pale and quiet but he told me he'd been poorly.'

'Well, he's no' poorly, he's on drugs.'

'Drugs,' gasped Debbie.

'Aye. He said it's the only thing that gets him through each day. I told him to stop taking them, but I don't know if he will. He'll stop for you though.'

Debbie nodded, clearly shocked by this news. 'I'll contact him right now, ask him to book me a visit.'

'You'd better because you're the only one who can save him.'

She nodded before scurrying into the living room and closing the door. When she'd gone, the two brothers stared at each other in hostile silence.

'Right, you,' Virgil told him. 'We need to talk to the others. We've got to do a favour for Nick.'

'What favour?'

'He's getting hassled by a member of the Allan family. We need to force him to back off.' His brother's apathetic look irritated Virgil. 'After what you've done, you should be jumping at the chance to help Nick.'

'I'll help. Now get off my back.'

'Get off your back? You betrayed your own brother. How could you do that? You know what Debbie means to him.'

'You don't get to talk to me like that. I'm the oldest brother, no' you.'

'What's age got to do with it?'

'You're always taking over, bossing everyone about. You've no' been back five minutes and already you're telling everyone how to live their lives when you don't have a clue how to live your own. If you did, you wouldnae be divorcing your wife. I know far more about satisfying a woman than you do.'

Virgil's eyes burned and he drew back his fist.

'Go on, hit me,' goaded Newton. 'See where that fucking gets you. I'm no' some pussy like Lucas Blair.'

Only the thought of what his mother would say if she found out he'd punched his own brother forced Virgil to lower his fist.

The living room door opened and Debbie appeared.

'I've got a visit booked with Nick tomorrow afternoon,' she told Virgil, eager to please.

'Good and you'd better be there,' he retorted.

'I will be, I promise.' She looked past him to Newton. 'This between us has to stop. I want to concentrate on Nick.'

'Aye, whatever.' He shrugged.

The pain his words caused her showed in her eyes. 'Why did I ever cheat on Nick with you? I must have been mad.'

'I didnae hear you complaining all the times I made you come.'

'You disgusting pig,' she yelled.

'Get in the car,' Virgil told him.

'You don't get to tell me what to do,' retorted Newton. 'You're just my wee brother,' he added before striding out, not even deigning to look back at Debbie.

'I hope you've learnt your lesson?' Virgil asked her.

'Aye, I have,' she replied. 'He just used me, didn't he?'

He nodded.

Debbie grimaced and wrapped her arms around herself. 'I'm such a daft cow. I don't deserve Nick,' she said, the tears starting to fall.

'It's no' too late. If you convince him to get off the drugs, then your debt is paid.'

'I will, I swear. I'll be there for him every step of the way.'

'Good.'

The hard look he gave Debbie caused her to swallow nervously. Out of all the MacGregor brothers, Virgil was the one she found the most intimidating.

With that, he left and found Newton already sitting in Morgan's BMW as Virgil had failed to lock it in his haste to confront them both.

'So how are we gonnae tackle this Allan situation?' said Newton.

Virgil regarded him incredulously, wondering how his brother could sound like he hadn't just been caught shagging his brother's girlfriend. 'We need to discuss it with the others first,' he replied, starting the car.

Silence reigned as Virgil drove them back home. He could feel the hostility radiating off Newton, who was no doubt pissed off that he'd spoiled his fun. It wasn't his relationship with Debbie that he was upset about losing but the fact that he'd been getting one over his brother. He and Nick had been butting heads over the slightest thing before Nick had been sent down and sleeping with Debbie had been Newton's way of getting revenge.

'Are you gonnae tell the others about me and Debbie?' said Newton.

'No, but I'm no' keeping your dirty secret to protect you or her. I'm doing it to protect Nick. He's struggling enough as it is. I'm no' mentioning the fact that he's on drugs to anyone else either. It'll only break Maw's heart.'

Newton nodded, looking unconcerned, although Virgil sensed he was relieved about that. It wasn't their brother's or even their mother's reaction he was worried about, it was their nonna's, who hated disloyalty between family members. If she ever found out she would come up with a dark and unusual way to punish Newton for his misdeed.

They arrived home to find their brothers ranged throughout the three houses. Virgil and Newton told them all to gather in the kitchen of their mother's home. As usual, Ludovica fussed around them with food and coffee, having made a fresh batch of sfogliatelle.

'I don't care if the Pope comes to the door,' said Morgan, plucking one of the pastries from the plate. 'He's no' getting one of these bad boys.'

'Don't talk about the Holy Father like that,' said Ludovica, clipping him around the back of the head.

'Ow.' He frowned.

'So what's this meeting about?' said James before biting into one of the pastries.

'Nick,' replied Virgil. 'I've just been to see him in prison and he's in a bad way.'

'I saw him three days ago and he looked ill,' said Maria. 'I hoped he would have improved by now.'

'He's getting harassed by Henry Allan and his cronies. I said we'd sort them out for him.'

'How will you do that if they're in prison?'

'We're gonnae threaten Henry's family.'

'I hope you don't mean his wife and children?'

'He doesnae have a wife and weans, Maw. He's single. But he does have a younger brother and a da, and they live together.'

'Oh. That's all right then.'

'We'll all go,' he told the table. 'It's time we gave everyone a good reminder of just what our family can do.'

'We need the old Virg back,' said Morgan.

'Don't,' James told him.

'What? We all know it's true. It doesnae matter about the rest of us or what we can do. Our family's entire reputation is on your shoulders, Virg.'

'We're here to discuss the Allans, no' me,' he retorted.

'Do you know where they live?' said James.

'Aye.' He took out his phone and brought up the Allan home on the map. 'Here, in Garrowhill.'

He placed his phone in the middle of the table and they all leant in to peer at it. They found themselves looking at a white pebble-dashed semi.

'There's a lot of houses around it,' said Newton. 'Plenty of people to call the polis.'

Virgil just nodded, finding it hard to look at that particular brother.

'It doesnae seem a good spot to tackle them,' added Newton.

'What do you suggest?' said Virgil, forcing himself to look at him before someone noticed something odd. Fortunately, he and Newton had never got along very well, so no one would think it strange if they were a little cool with each other.

'We could follow them, learn their movements so we can tackle them somewhere quieter.'

'We don't have time for that. Nick needs us to do something now.'

'Why, what have they threatened him with?' said Warren.

'Are they gonnae batter him? Because I'm sure he can handle this Henry walloper and his pals.'

'There's too many of them even for Nick.' He was telling no one about the threatened gang rape.

'I blame Debbie,' said Maria, face hardening. 'She's practically abandoned him since he was sent down. She's made my poor boy miserable. I don't know what's got into the silly wee coo.'

Virgil glanced at Newton, who didn't react to this statement. He thought there must be something missing inside his brother that meant he couldn't feel guilt or shame.

'I bumped into Debbie earlier,' said Virgil. 'She's already got a visit booked with Nick tomorrow. She was just finding it difficult seeing him stuck in prison.'

'Then she should toughen up a bit,' said Maria. 'I always said she was too soft for one of my boys. Any woman coming into this family needs to be made of iron.'

'Like my Rose.' Warren smiled.

'Aye, like that lassie. The same goes for Ember. Debbie's too doughy, no backbone. I keep hoping Nick will see sense and dump her for someone more suitable.'

'Well, hopefully she can cheer him up a bit,' said Virgil, keen to move the topic of conversation off Debbie. 'We have to go to the Allans' house. There's nae choice but we can still be discreet about it. Me, Newton and James will go in. Morgan, Wyatt, you wait outside with the car, keep an eye out.'

'What about me?' said Warren.

'You're no' up to this.'

'I bloody well am. I'm feeling much better.'

'Aye but your ribs havenae healed properly yet. One knock to them and you'll be back at square one.'

'This is for Nick. I won't be left behind, Virg.'

'Let him come,' said Newton. 'He can wait in the car with Morgan and Wyatt. They'll keep an eye on him.'

'No, because it'll mean taking two cars and that will make us stand out more. Sorry, mate, but you're gonnae have to sit this one out.'

'Fine,' sighed Warren, folding his arms across his chest and wincing at the pain in his ribs.

'How do we approach the house?' said Wyatt. 'Wait till night?' he added with an eager smile, left eye twitching.

Virgil regarded him uncertainly. Wyatt had always had a disturbing obsession with the dark. When he was younger, he used to go around drawing all the curtains in the house during the day, saying he couldn't stand sunlight, no matter how weak. The house had a cellar and he would often go down there just to sit in the dark, and he loved to go out walking at night.

'Aye,' replied Virgil, broadening his grin. 'It's a Friday night; people like going out then. We burst in and play some loud music to drown out any sounds.'

'What if they won't open the door to us?' said James.

'Then we'll kick it down. Remember, we're doing this for Nick. We have to provide him with as much protection as we can while he's inside.'

They all nodded.

'What do you think?' Virgil asked his mother.

Their father had once been at the heart of every scheme their family had come up with. Jimmy MacGregor had been an excellent strategist and Virgil had learnt at his feet, eagerly absorbing his words of wisdom. Jimmy had always listened to Maria's counsel and Virgil had resolved to do the same. If it hadn't been for the fact that their family was terrible with money and let it flow through their fingers like water, they could have risen to great heights by now, but bad spending habits and debt kept them down.

'I don't think you have a choice,' replied Maria. 'We must do everything we can to protect Nick, but Newton does have a point. I don't want any more of my boys being sent to prison.'

'We can be caught just as easily following them somewhere,' said Virgil.

'Yes, I know. I just worry about you all. I also worry about you losing control like you did back at Lucas's nightclub.'

'I won't, Maw. That was sudden; it happened so fast. This will be properly planned out and I'll have my brothers with me.'

'Well, okay, but be careful. Do not lose control.'

'I won't, promise.' Once Virgil would have thought he could keep that promise, but now he wasn't so sure.

* * *

Morgan parked his car just down the street from the Allans' home on the opposite side of the road.

'Good,' said Virgil, studying the house. 'The lights are on but it doesnae sound like they're having a party. I was worried they'd have guests. Wyatt, Morgan, wait here while we go in. We'll let you know if we need any help and behave yourselves, okay?'

'We'll be as good as gold,' replied Morgan with a mischievous smile.

Virgil, Newton and James got out of the car.

'I hope they don't take matters into their own hands and cause their usual chaos,' said James as they walked across the road to the Allan home.

'Relax,' Newton told him. 'You're always bloody worrying.'

'Can you blame me? Morgan and Wyatt are the least stable of us all.'

'You wouldnae say that if you'd seen the state Nick was in,' said Virgil.

'That bad?' replied James.

'Aye, that bad.'

'Hopefully this will improve life in prison for him.'

Newton knocked on the Allans' front door, which was pulled open by a grossly obese middle-aged man wearing just a white vest and a pair of navy blue tracksuit bottoms, a can of lager in one hand. He opened his mouth to speak and instead a loud belch came out so potent it caused the three MacGregors to grimace and take a step back.

'What?' He frowned.

'Are you Stan, Henry Allan's da?' replied Virgil.

'Aye, what about it?'

'Can we have a word?'

'Why? Who are you?'

'We're Nick MacGregor's brothers.'

Stan's eyes widened. 'The MacGregors from Garthamlock?'

'Aye. Don't even try it,' he said, pushing the door open wider when Stan tried to close it on them.

The three brothers entered, Newton closing and locking the door behind them.

'Who else is here?' Virgil asked Stan.

'Just my younger son, Danny. You don't need to bother him; he's nothing to you.'

'We'll decide that. In there,' said Virgil, pointing to the door leading into the living room.

Stan sighed heavily and shambled into the small, stuffy room. It was relatively clean but the room hung heavy with smoke. There was a cigarette smouldering away in an ashtray. Virgil snatched the can of lager from Stan's big paw and poured the contents over it, extinguishing it.

'Where's Danny?' said Virgil, letting the can drop to the floor.

'Upstairs in his room,' replied Stan with forced cheer. 'He'll be playing on his games; he's addicted. There's no need to disturb the boy. We can talk in private.'

'Bring Danny down here,' Virgil told his brothers. 'And check the house for anyone else.'

They both nodded, although Newton did look put out about being given an order by his younger brother.

'Drink?' Stan asked Virgil. 'I've got a few cans in the fridge.'

Virgil shook his head.

'So, why are you boys here? Anything I can help with?'

'Why are you sweating, Stan?'

'I cannae help it. I'm always sweating. It's one of the reasons why my wife divorced me, the miserable old bitch.'

James and Newton returned downstairs, the latter leading a sheepish man in his early twenties by the arm.

'What's going on, Da?' said Danny.

'These boys want a word with us,' replied Stan, his smile becoming strained.

'Sit down and shut up,' Newton told Danny, shoving him into a chair.

'No one else is in the house,' said James.

'Good,' replied Virgil before turning to Stan. 'We want a word with you about Henry. He's been giving our brother Nick some hassle in Bar-L.'

'I'm no' surprised, the shite lives for causing other people hassle. I've had two heart attacks thanks to the prick. I had to have a bypass. Look at my scar,' he said, pulling down the vest to reveal pendulous man boobs coated in sweat.

Stan's look said he hoped the scar would provide him with some sympathy but the faces of the MacGregor brothers were like granite.

'We cannae get to Henry,' said Virgil. 'So we're gonnae get to you instead.'

'Now wait, please,' said Stan, holding up his hands. 'There's no need to get rough.'

'There's every need,' replied Virgil as the three of them advanced on him. 'Our family takes no shite off anyone.'

'Danny, run,' cried Stan. 'Get help.'

Danny shot to his feet and ran for the door but James was faster. He grabbed him by the back of the shirt and yanked him backwards so hard he fell to the floor.

'Don't hurt my boy, please,' cried Stan.

Virgil's eyes blazed. 'Your fucking son's been threatening to hurt our brother. What goes around comes around, ya prick.'

'I'll speak to Henry, get him to back off.'

'That's no' good enough. There's only one way to hammer the message home.' He drew back his fist. 'And that's by hammering you.'

'No, don't,' he wailed, holding up his hands. 'I'm no' a well man.'

A pang of compassion got Virgil right in the chest and he hesitated.

'What are you waiting for?' hissed Newton. 'Gi'e him a doing.'

Virgil clenched his fist with determination but he found he couldn't do it. The old Virgil would have already turned Stan into paste by now but what if he had a heart attack? The man was sweating even more and had turned a frightening shade of red.

Newton's fist met Stan's face, knocking him off his feet.

'What the fuck's wrong with you?' Newton barked at Virgil.

Virgil didn't answer. All he could do was stare down at Stan wheezing on the floor.

Newton didn't share his brother's pity. He kicked Stan twice in the ribs before straddling him and punching him repeatedly in the face.

'Da,' cried Danny helplessly.

James hastily hit the button on the stereo that sat on the sideboard and techno music burst into life, so loud it drowned out Stan's cries of pain and Danny's anguished howls.

'All right, he's had enough,' Virgil told Newton.

His brother ignored him and punched him again.

'I said stop,' exclaimed Virgil, grabbing his arm.

Newton glared at him over his shoulder before yanking his arm free and getting to his feet. Newton nodded at James. 'Gi'e him a battering too,' he said, nodding at Danny.

Before Virgil could object, James tore into Danny, a punch to his chin snapping back his head, blood spurting from his mouth. Danny's eyes rolled to the ceiling and he collapsed back onto the couch. James laid into him as mercilessly as Newton had attacked Stan.

'No, please,' said Stan weakly, reaching out a shaking hand to his son. 'Don't hurt him.'

'Shut it,' said Newton, kicking him in the stomach, silencing his protests.

'Stop,' yelled Virgil, grabbing James and pulling him off Danny, who was a crumpled heap on the couch. 'We've made our point.'

Unlike Newton, James took a deep breath and nodded.

Virgil knelt beside Stan, who flinched from him, expecting more violence. 'Tell Henry that if he doesnae leave Nick alone, then we'll come back here again and again and take it out on you and Danny. You'll be the ones to suffer for his sins and you'd better hope to God he cares about you and his wee brother because it will never end until he ends it.'

'I'll get him to back off,' he gasped. 'Just don't hurt Danny any more, please.'

'We'll uphold our end of the bargain if you uphold yours.'

'I will, I swear.'

'And if you ever forget the deal,' began Newton before snapping one of Danny's fingers, making him scream.

'No, Danny,' cried Stan.

'Calm yer jets,' said Newton. 'It was just his pinkie. He's lucky it's no' his kneecap or his fucking neck.'

Stan's face crumpled, as though he was about to cry. Virgil got to his feet, sickened by the entire situation. He looked to his brothers. 'Let's go.'

The three MacGregors left the house. No one spoke until they were back in the car where Morgan and Wyatt waited, anxious to get away before they were seen.

'What the fuck was that all about?' exploded Newton as Morgan drove them away from the scene.

'Jeezo, my ear,' grimaced James, who was sitting in the back between him and Virgil.

'Never mind your bloody ear. You froze, Virg.'

'I didnae freeze,' he retorted. 'I was being cautious after Stan told me he had heart problems.'

'Fuck his heart problems.'

'What would have happened if he'd died of a heart attack because of us? We'd have been banged up along with Nick.'

'That's an excuse because you've lost your bottle.'

Virgil's countenance darkened. 'I've no' lost my bottle.'

'Aye, ya have. Me and James had to do everything while you just stood there like a fucking dummy. You weren't even gonnae gi'e Danny a kicking. It's no' like he was a wean; he was a fully grown man.'

'I have not lost my bottle,' Virgil hissed through gritted teeth.

'That's shite and you know it. You're a fucking pussy.'

'Err, Newton,' said James, noting the gathering storm in Virgil's eyes. 'I think you should stop talking.'

'No,' he barked. 'Someone needs to tell him that he's a liability; useless, weak.'

'Seriously, Newton, stop it,' said James when Virgil's hands bunched into fists and his lips curled back over his teeth.

'You might be scared of him but I'm no',' continued Newton. 'He's dragging us down, damaging our reputations. He should sod off back to his wee caravan and grow flowers, the big jessie, because he's no' fucking use to us. I don't know what Ember ever saw in him.'

'Newton, shut your face,' yelled James.

'Why, what's he gonnae dae? Nothing. He's too weak. At least Ember's free now to find a real man.'

With a roar, Virgil lunged across James and grabbed a handful of Newton's hair. He yanked him downwards, so he was lying across James's lap and began slamming his fist into the side of his face.

'Jesus, what's going on?' cried Morgan when the car began to violently rock.

'Pull over, for fuck's sake,' exclaimed James as he attempted to defend Newton from the savage blows, Virgil roaring all the time with rage.

Newton managed to block one of Virgil's punches and hit him in the stomach. It didn't injure him but it did cause him to momentarily pause, enabling Newton to sit upright, but Virgil still fought relentlessly to get at him.

'Jesus, stop it, both of you,' cried James, trapped in the middle of the struggling men.

The car screeched to a halt at the kerb and Morgan and Wyatt leapt out, the former pulling open the rear door on

Newton's side while Wyatt opened the one on Virgil's side. The two brothers leant in, wrapped their arms around their older brothers and yanked them both out of the car, leaving James inside to breathe a sigh of relief.

'What the fuck are you doing, ya mad bastard?' yelled Morgan, desperately trying to keep hold of Newton when he fought to tear himself free. 'Look at him,' he added, nodding at Virgil, who managed to shove Wyatt away in his rage. 'He'll tear you apart.'

'I'm no' afraid of him like the rest of you are,' he retorted.

Morgan let Newton go and rushed to help Wyatt hold back Virgil. James also got out to assist. Virgil fought and snarled to get back at a bruised Newton, who stood there, goading him.

'Fucking calm down,' James yelled in Virgil's face.

Virgil took a deep breath and nodded. James was relieved when the sanity returned to his brother's eyes. Despite this, Wyatt and Morgan still kept a tight hold of him.

'You should know better than to wind me up like that,' Virgil told Newton.

'All I did was gi'e you a few home truths,' he retorted, wiping the blood from the corner of his mouth. 'It's no' my fault you cannae take it.'

'Let it go, both of you,' said James. 'Now let's go home. It's late and we're all tired.'

'I'm no' getting back in the car with that fucking loon,' said Newton, pointing at Virgil. 'I'll make my own way back.'

'But you're bleeding.'

'It's nothing.'

'No, you go in the car,' said Virgil. 'I'll call a taxi. I could use some space.'

'Fine by me,' snapped Newton before getting back in Morgan's car and slamming the door shut.

'I'll wait with you,' James told Virgil.

'Please, Jamie. I just want to be alone.'

James nodded and patted his shoulder before getting back in the car, as did Wyatt and Morgan.

Virgil watched his brothers drive off, Newton giving him the finger through the back window. The car turned a corner and vanished and he looked down at his hands, which were once again bruised but thankfully weren't stained with his brother's blood. So much for the new him, but Newton had been asking for it for a while. He couldn't deny that part of him was rather satisfied at the memory of punching in his smug face. Virgil was just ashamed that he'd lost control again and disgraced himself in front of his brothers.

Virgil shook himself out of his gloomy thoughts and studied his surroundings. He was still in Garrowhill on a strip of grass with trees opposite some houses. All was quiet and no one seemed to be about.

Taking out his phone, he called a taxi and sat on a bench to wait. Fortunately, it was a mild night, so he wasn't uncomfortable and the taxi didn't take long to arrive. He was tempted to ask the driver to take him to his caravan but he had to face up to the consequences of his actions. His mother and nonna were not going to be impressed about him attacking Newton, no matter the provocation. They'd drummed it into all the brothers' heads from a young age that MacGregors stick together, even though Newton himself had chosen to ignore that teaching. Virgil felt ridiculous worrying about his mother's and grandmother's opinion at his age but he couldn't help it. He supposed you were never too old to want the approval of your elders.

As the taxi pulled up outside the family's houses, he was dismayed to see all the lights were blazing inside. He had hoped everyone would be in bed as it was almost eleven o'clock, but he supposed that was a vain hope.

With a weary sense of resignation, he opened the door and stepped inside. He could hear murmurs from the kitchen that immediately stopped as he removed his jacket and shoes. Silence reigned as he padded into the kitchen where the family was gathered around the table. Newton was sitting in a chair, Ludovica applying her salve to his bruises. The smirk had once again returned to his older brother's face, which didn't help Virgil's mood.

Maria's look was cold while Ludovica's, although similarly cool, was not hostile.

'I hope you're ashamed of yourself?' Maria demanded of Virgil.

'Aye,' he sighed. 'I shouldnae have attacked Newton but he winds me up, Maw. He started talking about Ember.'

'I don't care. We do not attack each other, no matter the provocation. Yes, I know that Newton can sometimes be so smug it makes you want to smash his face in with a hammer...'

Newton's smirk dropped at this statement.

'But you still shouldn't have done it,' continued Maria. 'He's your brother.'

For a moment, Virgil was tempted to tell them that Newton had been sleeping with Debbie. Newton read this in his eyes and concern briefly filled his gaze, but Virgil held his tongue because he knew that revelation would not help Nick's situation.

'Newton also said you couldn't bring yourself to hit either Stan Allan or his son,' said Maria. She slammed both hands down on the table, eyes blazing in a way very reminiscent of Virgil's. 'What is happening to you, Virgil? We need you strong. After your father died, God rest his twisted soul, you kept everything together and now you are so weak you cannae even beat up two nobodies.'

'One of them had a heart bypass recently,' he retorted. 'What would have happened to us if he'd died of a heart attack? I was thinking over my next move to make sure we wouldnae all be done for murder, but Newton wired right into him.'

'I couldnae gi'e a shite about his stupid bypass. His son is threatening our Nick and MacGregors take that from no one.'

'You said you couldnae bear for any more of your sons to go to prison. I was trying to stop that from happening.'

'That's shite, Virgil, and you know it,' said Newton. 'Your bottle went. Me and James both saw it.'

'Don't drag me into it,' replied James.

'Tough because you're already in it,' Newton snapped back. 'Unfortunately, he wasnae lying when he said he's a changed man.' He looked back at Virgil. 'Piss off back to your caravan. You're no use to us.'

'Is it true, Virgil?' Maria demanded of him. 'Are you no longer able to lead this family like you used to?'

'We don't need him to lead us,' said Newton. 'We can lead ourselves.'

'Hush,' Maria told him without looking his way, her gaze locked on Virgil.

Newton scowled but remained silent.

'I've told you repeatedly that I'm a changed man,' said Virgil. 'But you wouldnae believe me.'

'Because you proved that wasn't true when you went after Lucas Blair and his men,' replied his mother. 'You took down eight of them alone. Why could you do that but you couldnae deal with a couple of useless pricks like the Allans?'

'I don't know,' he sighed.

'I do,' replied Newton. 'It's because Lucas kidnapped Ember. She means more to him than Nick does.'

'That isn't true,' barked Virgil. 'Don't start trying to turn everyone against me.'

'I'm not. I'm just telling it like it is. You've lost your edge, Virg. You should leave while you still can.'

'Is that a threat?'

'Naw, but you know that if any of the many people around here who hold grudges against us hear about what happened at the Allans' house, they'd see you as fair game. They'd all come for you.'

'Newton makes a good point,' said Maria. 'You're putting not just yourself at risk but all of us too. Losing your reputation damages us all.'

'Fine. I'll go back to my caravan,' said Virgil. 'I never wanted to leave it in the first place. You and Ember were the ones who convinced me to come back, but if you insist, I'll happily go and you lot can sort out all this shite.'

'Stay right there,' barked Maria when he turned to the door.

Virgil sighed but obeyed.

'Sit down,' she said, gesturing to one of the free chairs.

Virgil took the seat between James and Wyatt. Morgan, Warren and Wyatt seemed to find it hard meeting his eye and he knew they were ashamed and embarrassed by his actions. Only James seemed to still be warm towards him.

'There's another problem,' Maria told Virgil. 'Newton was supposed to be fighting in one of Toni's matches tomorrow night and now he cannae do it thanks to what you did to him.'

'I thought Newton and Wyatt were fighting each other?'

'The arrangements were changed yesterday. There's a well-known local boxer who's been after taking on a MacGregor for a while and his name pulls in the crowds. Toni had placed him to fight Newton but now he cannae do it thanks to you.'

'How no'? I didnae break a bone.'

'No but he looks battered and bruised and Toni likes all her fighters to be in peak condition. If someone steps into the ring looking like they've already taken a beating then it ruins the odds because no one will back that fighter. When I called to let her know that Newton cannae do it because of his injuries, she said she'd heard you were back in Garthamlock and that you've to take his place.'

'Oh no,' said Virgil. 'I am no' stepping in that ring again.'

'You have to.'

'Have you forgotten that Terry won't let me?'

'Aye, that's right.' Morgan grinned. 'He's still pissed off that you knocked him out.'

'This isn't funny,' Maria snarled at him. 'So wipe that stupid smile off your face.'

Morgan's grin dropped.

'Terry's been told it's happening, so he's accepted it just like you have to, Virgil,' continued Maria. 'If you don't do it then Toni McVay will not be very happy. You're fighting, so deal with it.'

Virgil's eyes turned into hard shards. 'No.'

'You would put this entire family in danger because of your selfishness?'

'This isnae my fault. I said it was madness getting back under Toni McVay's thumb. You set that up, so don't blame me for this mess.'

'I wouldn't if you hadn't beaten up Newton.'

'He didn't exactly beat me up,' frowned Newton. 'He'd be the one covered in bruises right now if he hadnae taken me by surprise.'

'Aye, course,' said Maria, patting his shoulder in a patronising way, making him frown again. She looked back at Virgil. 'The fact of the matter is that our family's involved in the underground matches again and thanks to you Newton cannae take part, so you're our only option. If you refuse, then we will all suffer the consequences.'

'I'm no' doing it.'

Maria's lovely face twisted with anger. 'You're as stubborn as your father,' she yelled.

'What if he freezes in the ring like he did at the Allans' house?' said Newton. 'It would humiliate our entire family.'

'That won't happen,' she replied, looking directly at Virgil. 'Because his opponent will attack and he'll be forced to defend himself. That will bring out the beast in him.'

'Who is this fighter?' said Wyatt.

'Callum Young.'

'Holy shit, he's awesome,' said Morgan. 'He'd stand a good chance of beating one of us. His speed matches our own. I'd like to fight him myself. He'd be a great challenge.'

Warren, who had remained silent throughout this exchange, narrowed his eyes at him.

'I won't do it,' said Virgil. 'I don't care who I have to fight.'

Maria sighed and looked to Ludovica. 'You're being very quiet, Madre. What do you think?'

Ludovica dropped the cloth she was using to dab the paste on Newton's face onto the table and wiped her hands on the apron tied around her waist. 'I want to talk to Virgil alone.'

The rest of the family immediately left the room.

'Do you want something to eat?' she asked Virgil when they'd gone.

'No, thanks, Nonna. I'm no' hungry.'

'You need something. It will warm you and make you feel

better. I have made some ciambotta, vegetable stew, just for you. No meat.'

'Really? I thought you were against me being vegetarian?'

'I am. That has not changed but you are a man entitled to make his own decisions, so I have decided to graciously accept it. Besides, arguing with you is a waste of the precious time I have left.'

Ludovica dished him up a bowl of stew and placed it before him, along with a couple of her home-baked crusty rolls. The delicious smell soon stirred Virgil's appetite and he tucked in. Ludovica took the chair beside him, enjoying watching him eat and the obvious pleasure it was giving him.

'There,' she said. 'You look better already.'

'Thanks, Nonna,' he replied. 'I didnae realise how cold I was.'

'You are in shock after attacking your brother. I could see it in your eyes. Now you look stronger, so we can talk properly.'

'You're gonnae try and convince me to do the underground fight, aren't you?'

'No. As I said, you are a man. I won't try to convince you to do anything. You need to follow your own path.'

'But if I don't fight, then our family will be in trouble.'

'Perhaps, perhaps not. I think Maria and the others overestimate how much we matter to Toni McVay. She has much bigger things on her mind than us. And what your mother is failing to consider is that it would be much worse for our family if you did get into the ring and what happened tonight at the Allans' house happened there. Toni McVay can be reasoned with but once you lose your reputation there's no getting it back.'

'So you're saying I shouldnae fight?'

'It doesn't matter what I think. All that matters is what you think.'

'They're all disappointed in me, even James. I could see it in their eyes. I'm losing all their respect. Have I lost yours too?'

'No, but I see things differently to everyone else.'

'How do you see me then?'

'Someone desperately fighting against the tide. If you keep struggling against it, you will drown.'

'Great,' he sighed. Virgil clenched his hands into fists before extending the fingers and clenching them again as he fought to deal with the encroaching sense of being trapped. 'So, what should I do: go back to the caravan or fight in the ring?'

'Only you can answer that. Stop trying to get the answers from others.'

'I want to go back to the caravan.'

'Then go back.'

'The rest of the family will hate me.'

'Yes, they will. If you can live with that then it is fine.'

'Would you hate me if I left?'

'No, but you will always be pulled back here. It is in your nature.'

'Perhaps. I thought you would be furious at me for attacking Newton.'

'I've no doubt he asked for it. Sometimes I have to fight not to hit him myself.'

'But you're always saying we shouldn't attack each other.'

'And I stand by that but sometimes things happen.' Ludovica shrugged her sturdy shoulders. 'You and Newton have never got along. I'm surprised it has never happened before. You were the one who kept us all going when Jimmy died. I never forget a debt, even if all the others have.' She pushed herself to her feet and picked up Virgil's empty bowl. 'Now, it is late and you need to rest. No important decision should ever be made late at night.

That is some of the wisest advice I was ever given and I pass it on to you.'

'Thanks, Nonna.' He smiled fondly. 'A lot of people find you scary, but you've always been good to me.'

She squeezed his cheek fondly. 'Because I love you, Virgil, and you are very special. For now, fear is getting the better of you, but one day soon you will break free of the prison it has placed you in and, when you do, no one will be able to stop you and you will never be afraid again.'

Virgil wasn't sure what to say to that, but it seemed a reply wasn't necessary because Ludovica turned her back on him. The sense of the otherworld that permanently hung around his grandmother and which frightened a lot of people seemed even stronger than usual.

Without another word, he quietly slipped out of the house, the rest of the family oblivious to his departure.

9

Ember leant over Lucas Blair, who was in his hospital bed in the private room he'd been given. The man's face was a mess, all swollen and puffy. His right hand and wrist were in a plaster cast.

'Lucas,' she said.

He didn't respond.

Sighing with annoyance, she prodded his injured arm.

Lucas gasped with pain and jumped awake. His eyes widened. 'Ember?'

'Aye, it's me.'

'Oh, God, go away.'

'I wanted to see how you were.'

'Are you for real? Your nutter of a husband beat me up. Why the hell would you think I want you anywhere near me?' His left eye widened. The right one couldn't as it was swollen shut. 'Is he here? He hasnae come back for more revenge, has he?'

'No, of course not,' she replied, taking the empty chair by his bed. 'I came alone. I brought you some grapes.'

'I hate grapes.'

'Fine. How about this though?' she said, producing a small bottle of vodka.

'That's more like it.'

Ember smiled and poured some of the alcohol into a beaker sitting on his bedside cabinet. He snatched it from her with his good hand and knocked it back in one go.

'That's better,' he said. 'I've been stuck on tea and orange juice in this place.'

'When are you being discharged?'

'Tomorrow. I'm still sore as fuck but I'll be fine.'

'What about your arm?'

'Fractured wrist but it'll heal. I cannae believe you've just swanned in here after what you did to me and my men.'

'I take it you haven't told the polis what really happened?'

'No, course not. We said we were attacked by a gang of sixteen masked men.'

'I suppose you couldn't stand the embarrassment of everyone knowing you all got taken down by a single man. It wouldn't go down very well with Toni McVay either. That is who your new deal's with, isn't it?'

'How the hell do you know about that?'

'You cannae keep anything a secret around here. What's her take on all this?'

'I told her it was personal, no' business, so she doesnae care. Don't worry, your precious Virgil won't have his eyeballs scooped out of his heid, more's the pity.'

'He's no' my Virgil any more.'

'Eh?'

'He doesn't believe you abducted me. He thinks I set it up, so he's divorcing me.'

'So he's no' as stupid as I thought.' Lucas chuckled humour-lessly. 'He's got your number, hasn't he, sweetheart? He's seen you for the poisonous, manipulative bitch you really are and now he's kicked you into touch. Your big plan backfired.'

Ember merely smiled. 'I never thought I'd hear the day you stuck up for him.'

'That's because I actually feel sorry for the bastard. No wonder he's so angry. I was with you for a few hours and look what happened to me. He was stuck with you for years.'

'I don't believe you mean that, Lucas,' she said, leaning forward, giving him a good view down the front of her dress. 'You've always wanted me.'

'That was before you used me. So jog on, bitch. I don't want anything to do with you.'

'I don't believe that. You always get what you want, don't you, Lucas? First there was your crew, then your nightclubs and now your deal with Toni McVay. What else is there for you to conquer except me?' she breathed, leaning in closer to him.

Despite how rotten he was feeling, lust overtook Lucas. He'd never been able to resist that beautiful red hair and those sharp green eyes. Those eyes had haunted his dreams for years.

'Get away from me, you witch,' he said.

'I'm no' a witch. That's Ludovica.'

'You're setting me up to get hurt again. What's the plan, Ember? Let Virgil catch us together so he can batter me once more?'

'I hate him, Lucas. I want revenge on him.'

'Revenge for what? Finally seeing sense and dumping you?'

'Yes,' she glowered.

'If he's divorcing you then it's your own fault and if you came here looking for sympathy then you'll get none from me. Now piss off. I need my rest.'

When Lucas closed his eyes, Ember glared down at him, green eyes almost luminescent with anger at being so easily dismissed by this man whom she considered to be her inferior, but she swallowed down that anger. Lucas was the weapon she was going to use against Virgil either to get him back or take him down. At that moment, she wasn't sure which she wanted more. All she knew was that she needed Lucas Blair to do it.

Lucas gasped when he felt something on his crotch. Opening his good eye, he saw Ember had her hand under his blanket and it was moving back and forth. Even though he was feeling sore and miserable, he reacted immediately.

'Impressive.' She smiled. 'I admit, I was expecting something considerably smaller, so this is a pleasant surprise.'

'You mean you thought I'd have a wee maggot in my pants,' he groaned, fighting the rising tide of pleasure.

'Perhaps. It turns out you have a king snake.' It wasn't a lie – the man was very well endowed – but she still got no pleasure from the act. It was merely a means to an end.

'Stop it,' he rasped. 'Get away from me. I was right, you are a witch and you're casting your spell over me.' Lucas moaned, head sinking back into the pillow as the pleasure overtook him and his resistance began to fail.

'Think of it as an apology for what I put you through,' she said, hand moving faster. 'I just want to make you feel better, Lucas.' Ember was relieved that it didn't take long. His body jumped, he groaned and that was it.

'There,' she said, hurrying to the sink to wash her hands. 'All better.'

'I wouldnae say that but you've brightened up my day,' he murmured.

'I'll be back to see you later,' she said, gathering up her handbag and jacket. 'Think about what I said,' she added before leaving.

Lucas stared up at the ceiling, smiling to himself. Ember

Douglas had just given him an orgasm. He always liked to think of her by her maiden name and not the name of the wanker she'd married. Unfortunately, he hadn't been able to reciprocate but he anticipated that wouldn't be far off in the future, probably when he'd recovered sufficiently from his injuries. He knew he was playing with fire with Ember, but he couldn't resist getting one over Virgil fucking MacGregor.

'Oh shit,' he said when it occurred to him that he would have to explain the explosion in his underpants to the male nurse who always helped him change because of his injured hand.

Lucas shrugged, enjoying the pleasant afterglow of the orgasm. Who cared? He was on top of the world once more.

* * *

Virgil walked into his mother's kitchen the next morning to a very sombre mood. Only Warren and James greeted him cheerfully. Newton was his usual smug, hostile self and Morgan seemed to have joined him in that, no doubt allowing himself to be influenced by his older brother. Wyatt just regarded everyone with confusion, unsure which side to take. Maria was also unfriendly, plonking Virgil's breakfast down before him unceremoniously. Ludovica continued to work at the stove, as though not wanting to influence what was going to happen.

'Have you packed your bags?' said Newton, the first one to address Virgil directly.

'No doubt you'd love me to say yes,' he replied. 'But I've decided to stay.'

'I knew you wouldnae let us down.' James smiled.

Virgil nodded at him before looking back at Newton. 'You look disappointed.'

'No' disappointed, just surprised. I thought you'd run away. Again.'

'I'm done running. It's time to stay and finally face everything.'

Ludovica placed a cup of strong coffee before him and patted his cheek. Clearly this was the conclusion she'd been hoping he'd reach.

'You're a brave man staying to face Ember,' said Morgan, who appeared friendly to him again.

'She will want to punish me for divorcing her, but I'll be ready for whatever she throws my way.' He hid the pain this statement caused him very well. It felt like he was going to war with the woman he loved and that was the last thing he wanted, but Ember had forced his hand.

'You have to fight Callum tonight,' Newton told him. 'And you cannae freeze.'

'I won't, don't worry,' he replied with more confidence than he felt.

'We'll see.'

Maria slapped Newton around the back of the head. 'Don't dent his confidence. This is wonderful news. I'm sure you'll do well in the ring tonight, Virgil. Now eat. You need to build up your strength.'

As Virgil tucked into his breakfast, he glanced at Newton, who clearly wasn't pleased with the news that Virgil had decided to stay. He'd probably hoped he'd leave so he wouldn't have to continually see the person who knew his dirty secret. It made Virgil wonder what else Newton was hiding.

* * *

Virgil constantly expected Ember to turn up at the house to either shout the odds, beg him to take her back or set fire to all three houses. The fact that she did none of those things made him nervous. He understood her well and knew she wouldn't be able to accept the situation gracefully. Many times he'd wondered why he'd married her. She'd always been unstable, right from being a teenager. She'd stabbed another girl with a compass in high school for daring to style her hair in the same way and she'd pushed another girl down the stairs because she'd also fancied Virgil. Ember had pulled some crazy and often violent stunts over the years, and it was amazing that she hadn't killed anyone yet. Virgil knew she was more than capable and now he would be her prime target.

However, as the day passed, his thoughts were drawn away from his estranged wife and onto the fight that night. Virgil stood before the mirror hanging from his bedroom wall, willing the dark thing that made him so violent to rise to the surface, but it refused. Instead, he felt flat and unenthusiastic.

'Great,' he muttered, dragging a hand down his face.

He didn't think his mother had been right when she'd said the smell of blood in the air would unleash his inner beast. It certainly hadn't at the Allans' house but then again, he'd been too worried about giving Stan a heart attack. There was only one thing for it.

Virgil left the house and headed to the one on the other side of his mother's. He entered and found Newton sitting on the couch in the lounge, alone.

'You've got to wind me up,' Virgil told him.

Newton looked up from the newspaper he was reading and frowned. 'You what?'

'At the fight tonight. You need to piss me off.'

'Oh aye, so you can go off on one and attack me again?'

'I won't attack you. I'll attack Callum.'

'How can I know that for sure? You don't think when you're in that state. You're just some wild monster.'

The term *monster* cut Virgil to the core but he didn't let Newton see that. 'Back at Old Skool I only went for Lucas and his men. I didnae lay a finger on Ember and she knew I wouldn't.'

'Aye, but I now know that you're no' afraid to lay a finger on me. Sorry, Virg, I won't risk strangers seeing us fighting. It would weaken our family's reputation.'

Virgil sighed. Newton was right, which was annoying. 'Aye, all right. I don't know what else I can do though.'

'Then you'll have to hope that Callum finishes you quickly,' he commented before returning to his newspaper.

'You're a big help, thanks,' said Virgil sarcastically before leaving the room, almost walking straight into James.

'Hi, Virg,' said his brother. His face creased with concern. 'You okay?'

'No,' he muttered, eyes flashing. 'I'm worried about no' being able to perform tonight.'

'I bet Ember thought the same thing often enough,' called Newton.

To Virgil's dismay, this comment did nothing to provoke his anger.

'Shut it, you,' James called back to him.

Newton responded with an amused chuckle.

'Let's get out of here,' James told Virgil. 'We can have a chat about it, work something out.'

'Okay.'

Virgil and James left together on foot and headed down the street.

'I thought Morgan had turned against me,' said Virgil. 'Until I said I was staying. I bet Newton was winding him right up.'

'You're right about Newton winding him up, but Morgan has never once been against you. He was confused. He's idolised you ever since he was a wean and now he's seen that you're no' invincible, that you're just as fallible as the rest of us and he's struggling with it. His faith in you was restored this morning when you said you'd stay and fight.'

'He'll lose all faith again if I don't win tonight.'

'Don't worry about what Morgan or the rest of us think.'

'That's easier said than done. You're my family.'

'You've got to get your mind off this for a while. The more you think about it the worse you'll feel. Let's go and blow off some steam.'

'I'm no' in the mood. I'm worried that if I fuck things up tonight then I'll put us all in danger...' He trailed off and stared down the street.

James followed his line of sight and saw Ember walking towards them. 'Oh, shite,' he said.

'She's smiling,' replied Virgil. 'I don't like it.'

'Me neither. I hope you're wearing a stab vest and a groin protector.'

'Morning, boys,' said Ember pleasantly. 'Lovely day, isn't it?'

'Aye,' replied Virgil uncertainly. 'Lovely.'

'Are you just going for a wee walk, doll?' James asked her.

'Yes. I want to enjoy this gorgeous sunshine. It makes me feel really positive and uplifted. Don't you agree?'

Virgil and James frowned at each other before looking back at her.

'Suppose,' said James mistrustfully, expecting her to pull a weapon and launch herself at them with a scream.

'Well, I'll be on my way. I've got to be at work soon.' She winked at them both. 'Bye, boys.'

'Bye,' said Virgil as he and his brother watched her walk off in the direction of the beauty salon where she worked.

'That was very weird,' said James.

'Aye, it was,' replied Virgil. 'I don't like it. Shouting, screaming, even hitting and kicking me like she did before would have been normal but that was just creepy.'

'You need to watch your back, pal,' said James, patting his shoulder. 'Because that woman is building up to something big.'

* * *

A different venue had been chosen for the underground fight that night. Anticipating an increased crowd, Toni McVay had decreed this match be held in a larger building and, as usual, she was right. The place was packed, everyone eagerly putting on their bets. They weren't just here for the MacGregors. Callum Young was a big name in the underground fight scene, having only lost once and that was just because he'd been told by Toni to take a dive. Callum was as hard as nails and the odds were split right down the middle between him and Virgil.

Terry was not at all happy about Virgil getting back into the ring and he glared at him, muscular arms folded across his thick barrel chest.

'I want you to know that I'm doing this under protest,' Terry told Virgil. 'If it was up to me, I'd throw you out of here heid first, but someone much more powerful than me says you're in, so I've nae choice. But just know that if you lose the plot like you did before then I will make it my personal mission to see you crippled for life. Do you fucking get it?'

Virgil nodded contritely. 'I do and I don't blame you, Terry.'

'Aye, well,' said Terry, a little disappointed that he hadn't got the argument he'd been hoping for. 'Just fucking watch it. Now get ready. The fight starts in five minutes,' he added before striding off to bark orders at his subordinates.

'You can do this,' James told him. 'You just need to tap into that rage.'

'What if I do and I nearly kill Callum like I did Mark?'

'Callum's a much better fighter,' Warren told him. 'You're a lot more evenly matched. That was the problem with that fight – Mark wasnae in your league. Terry was mad to put him in the ring with you.'

'That's true,' said Morgan. 'Callum's a real threat to you but you've got to win. If you don't, our family will look like losers.'

'So no pressure then,' muttered Virgil, pulling off his jacket and jumper and handing them to James.

Some of the crowd standing closest to Virgil noted the change in his physique and hastily switched their bets to Callum while those already betting on Callum smiled, pleased with their very wise decision. Others noticed the scratches down Virgil's back left by Ember's nails and grinned.

'For God's sake, make sure you take him down,' Newton told Virgil.

'Thanks for that,' he retorted. 'I hadnae thought of it myself,' he added before reluctantly climbing into the ring and holding his hands out to Terry's lackey to be bandaged.

'Please tell me you've got one of your sly tricks up your sleeve to piss him off?' James quietly asked Newton.

'Nope, nothing,' he replied.

'You've always been able to wind him up and the one time we really need you to do it you won't?' he said, arching an eyebrow.

'It's his own fault. If he hadnae lost the plot last night, I'd be the one in the ring and he'd be standing here, so sod him.'

James turned to his other brothers instead. 'We've got to do something to get Virgil angry,' he told them.

They all looked to Virgil, who stood limply in the ring. His expression said he was not happy about being there.

'Newton...' began Wyatt.

'He says he won't help. All we can do is hope the killer instinct kicks in when the fight starts,' said Morgan. 'I mean, he won't just stand there when Callum starts laying into him.' He frowned at the doubt in James's eyes. 'Will he?'

James shrugged.

'I've got an idea. Hey, Virg,' called Morgan, jumping up onto the edge of the ring. 'Did I ever tell you that two years ago I used your toothbrush to scrub the algae off the inside of my fishtank?'

'Aye, I know you did,' he casually replied. 'I saw you and swapped my toothbrush for yours.'

Morgan grimaced and climbed down off the ring. 'I feel sick.'

'That backfired on you.' Warren grinned.

The crowd began to cheer when Callum strutted towards the ring. He was the same age as Virgil and of the same height and build, although every muscle in his body stood out in high definition, a contrast to his opponent's body. He was square-jawed and his blue eyes were bright with the prospect of violence. He wore a pair of blue shorts and a purple boxing robe while most of the fighters in the underground matches usually just wore a pair of jeans or jogging bottoms.

'Is that boxing robe silk?' Wyatt frowned as they watched Callum parade through the room, basking in the adulation of the crowd.

'Aye,' replied Warren.

'What a fucking jessie.'

Callum gave the brothers a hard look as he approached the ring.

'What's his fucking problem?' demanded Wyatt, the tic in his eye starting up. 'I'll make him eat that poofy robe.'

'Take it easy,' said James as he and Warren grabbed his shoulders and pulled him back. 'This is Virgil's fight, no' yours.'

'Aye, all right,' he muttered, glaring at Callum.

Callum grinned, finding Wyatt's anger amusing, before lithely jumping into the ring.

'You ready to have the shite kicked out of you, Virgil?' said Callum.

'I am if you are,' he replied with more confidence than he felt. 'Unless you've changed your mind about this fight?' added Virgil, seeing a possible way out of the situation.

'Oh no you don't. I've wanted to take on a MacGregor for a while now, so stay right where you are.' Callum hastily appraised his opponent, noted he looked a little out of shape and decided that, despite Virgil's ferocious reputation, he had a good chance of winning.

Terry strode up to the brothers. 'Right, you lot – if he goes fucking mental again then you can break up the fight. That's the deal.'

'Don't worry, Terry,' said Morgan. 'You won't have to risk getting knocked out again.'

'The twat got lucky, that's all, you arrogant wee dick,' he spat before waving a hand at his lackey. 'Let's get this show on the road.'

The bell rang and the room went expectantly quiet as the two fighters began jogging around the canvas, sizing each other up.

'This is good,' said James, trying to convince himself more than anyone else. 'Virg looks strong and alert.'

'Aye he does,' replied Morgan. 'He's got this.'

Callum was the first to lash out with a punch that forced Virgil to jerk back his head to avoid being hit.

'Christ, you weren't joking when you said Callum hits as fast as we do,' said Warren.

James nodded, eyes glued to the fight.

Callum threw a few more punches to test his opponent but Virgil evaded them all.

'Virg has still got his speed,' said Warren.

'He hasnae tried to hit him yet though,' replied Morgan.

This thought had clearly occurred to the crowd too because they began to boo, demanding that blood be spilt.

Callum struck twice more. This time the second blow caught Virgil on his jaw. As he hadn't been hit in several months, he staggered back a couple of paces.

'Oh, hell,' breathed James.

Virgil recovered quickly enough to block Callum's uppercut but he got the full force of his fist in his gut. Virgil managed to move through the pain and struck back, catching Callum in the shoulder.

Newton chuckled. 'At least all that padding around his stomach came in useful.'

'That isn't helping,' James told him.

The determination to win overtook Callum. He'd already sensed Virgil's reluctance to fight. With a growl, Callum began throwing punches hard and fast and all Virgil could do was concentrate on blocking them.

'Callum left himself wide open there,' said Morgan. 'Virg could have got a hit in, but he chose not to.'

'Because he's gone soft,' said Newton, who was looking forward to watching Virgil take a beating. It would be payback for what he'd done to him. 'I keep saying it but no one wants to listen.'

James ignored him and continued yelling advice at his brother. He could see the reluctance in Virgil's eyes and it broke his heart. He didn't feel any anger that his brother was letting them all down; after all he'd warned them that this would happen. It was just sad seeing such a ferocious man reduced to this.

'Oh, Christ, he's gonnae lose, isn't he?' groaned Morgan.

'There's still time for the beast to be unleashed,' replied Warren. 'Just have some faith.'

'Are you serious? Look at him, he's getting battered,' he said when Virgil's head was snapped left and right by Callum's fists.

'Maybe Virg is luring him into a false sense of security?'

The bell rang, indicating the end of the first round.

'I think we're lucky he's still on his feet,' commented Newton.

'And I suppose you would have beaten Callum by now?' James snapped back at him.

'Course I would.'

'That's shite and you know it. He's a fucking awesome fighter.' James rushed over to talk to Virgil, who was drinking from a bottle of water. 'How are you holding up?' he asked him.

'I'm no' feeling any rage,' replied Virgil. 'In fact, I'm no' feeling much of anything except being pissed off that I'm here.'

'I'm sure it'll kick in at the right time,' he replied, hating the scepticism in his tone.

The bell rang again and the two fighters retook their positions. Callum laid into Virgil with renewed vigour, sensing an easy victory was close. The spectators were in uproar, Callum's supporters cheering him on while those who'd backed Virgil yelled at him to pull his finger out.

'It's a shame Ember isnae here,' said Warren. 'She'd have wound him right up.'

All the brothers could do was watch helplessly as Virgil

began to falter beneath the onslaught of Callum's fists. Blood trickled from his lower lip and a cut to his right eyebrow. It dripped into his eye and as he raised a hand to wipe it away, Callum was left with an opening that he took full advantage of, punching him again in the face.

'Shit, Virgil's gonnae go down any minute,' said Morgan. 'We have to think of something to make him angry.'

Newton chuckled. 'Who do you think he is, the fucking Hulk?'

'Oh, shut it, Newton, you're getting on my tits.'

Callum delivered a blow to Virgil's face that had such power behind it he was spun around one hundred and eighty degrees. A hush fell over the crowd, everyone wondering if Virgil was done and the fight was over.

Just as Terry was climbing over the ropes, preparing to declare Callum the winner, Virgil whipped back round to face his opponent. The smell of blood in the air was finally pumping lava through his veins and his love of the fight rushed to the surface.

Callum found himself confronted by a pair of blazing eyes. He'd fought some of the hardest bastards in Glasgow, but he found that look intensely intimidating. Recognising the look, Terry hastily retreated out of the ring.

Virgil's fist shot out, catching Callum in the side of the face, and he was almost knocked over by the force of it. Virgil lashed out again and again, each powerful blow knocking Callum back a step. Callum raised his arm to deflect a punch to the left side of his face and drove his fist into Virgil's stomach but his opponent didn't even seem to notice and continued the onslaught, the blows now coming at Callum so rapidly he had no chance of avoiding them, especially as there was enormous strength behind each punch. Soon Callum felt woozy, the room starting to blur.

One forceful uppercut put Callum on his back and Terry hastily climbed back into the ring to begin the count.

'Oh, shit, he's going at him again,' said James when Virgil lunged at the supine fighter. 'Come on.'

James, Wyatt and Morgan all leapt into the ring. Warren was unable to because of his healing ribs, while Newton didn't bother.

'Aren't you gonnae help them?' Warren asked him as they watched their three brothers grab Virgil and drag him backwards, keeping him off Callum so Terry could finish the count.

'Naw,' replied Newton. 'They've got it under control.'

Virgil fought so hard to get back at his opponent that his brothers lost their grip on him and he charged back at Callum, Terry yelling at them to get him under control. Fortunately, they managed to get a firmer hold on him.

The red mist left Virgil as quickly as it had come and he looked down at his opponent.

'Oh, Christ,' he gasped when he saw another man lying on the floor unconscious before him, covered in blood. He threw himself down by his side. 'Callum, are you okay? Callum,' he repeated louder when he didn't respond. He wanted the crowd to shut up; their stupid cheering was getting on his nerves.

Callum gasped and coughed before his eyes rolled open. 'You hit like a fucking train, Virgil. Do you know that?'

'Oh, thank God,' he breathed.

Callum held his fist out to him. 'Respect.'

Virgil smiled and bumped the proffered fist with his own. 'So do you. You've loosened a few teeth.'

'That's nothing,' he groaned before slowly sitting up and spitting out a couple of his own teeth onto the canvas.

'Come on, mate,' said Virgil, holding his hand out to him.

Callum nodded, grabbed his hand and Virgil helped haul him to his feet as Terry proclaimed Virgil the winner.

Virgil felt elated. He'd done it; he'd won and he hadn't killed or seriously injured anyone. His nonna had been right.

The fear had gone.

* * *

It was Virgil's turn to be smug as he basked in the praise of his family. Back at home, they enjoyed a few drinks, Maria and Ludovica celebrating along with them. Virgil, however, still refused to touch any alcohol. Newton sat quietly at the kitchen table, lacking the enthusiasm of the rest of his family.

'He was awesome, Maw,' said Warren. 'Callum stood nae chance.'

'Yes, it's wonderful.' She smiled, patting Virgil's cheek fondly. Other than the loose teeth, he had a few bruises and a cut to his forehead but that was it. He'd got off very lightly. Even though Callum had lost, his reputation was still intact because he'd shown such sportsmanship, congratulating Virgil and telling everyone who would listen what an amazing fighter he was.

'I thought you might have got rusty while living in your caravan,' Morgan told Virgil. 'But you're faster than ever. It must have been twatting Lucas and his men that did it. They got you back on form. You should thank Ember for setting that up.' His grin dropped. 'Oh, shite. Sorry, Virg, I didnae mean...'

'It's okay,' he replied. 'I know what you meant.'

'Thank God for that. You're top dog around here again, mate.'

Everyone cheered when Ludovica placed a series of her home-made treats on the table – panna cotta, tiramisu, semifreddo and a selection of cannolis.

'It's a wonder they're no' all obese, Maw,' said Maria.

'They're good boys and they deserve a treat,' replied Ludovica, smiling with satisfaction as the men eagerly tucked into the food.

They all looked at each other when there was a knock at the front door.

'Anyone expecting visitors?' said Virgil.

Everyone shook their heads.

'It's nearly ten o'clock,' said Maria, glancing at the clock on the wall. 'Who would be rude enough to call at this time of night?'

It occurred to Virgil that it could be Ember and her inevitable vengeance. 'I'll go,' he said when the knock sounded again.

'I'll come with you,' replied James, thinking the same thing.

Wyatt and Morgan also said they would accompany them to the door and the four brothers trudged down the hall en masse.

Virgil pulled the door open and the four big men all appeared uneasy when they saw Ember standing alone on the doorstep, a creepy smile on her face and a cardboard box in her hands.

'Hello, Virgil,' she said sweetly. 'I saw your fight and I wanted to congratulate you on winning.'

'Wait, you were there?' He frowned.

'Of course. Like I'd miss your big moment. I knew you could do it, especially after the way you tore through Lucas and his crew.' She held the box out to him. 'I got you a present. I thought this was a moment worth celebrating. Well, aren't you going to take it?' she added when he stared at it uncertainly.

'I suppose,' he replied, taking it from her and holding it away from his body. 'You couldnae have just bought this tonight because everywhere is shut.'

'Oh no, I ordered it online. I never had any doubt that you would win.'

'That's very kind. Thank you.'

'You're welcome. See you around,' she said cheerfully before walking away, humming to herself.

James hastily shut the door and the four men all stared down at the box Virgil held.

'You should get rid of it,' said Morgan.

'Don't be a walloper,' replied Wyatt. 'It could be something really awesome in there.'

'Or it could be something really deadly.'

'Ember was being nice,' said James. 'Did anyone else find that weird?'

They all nodded.

'What are you gonnae do?' Morgan asked Virgil.

'I suppose I'd better open it,' he replied. 'After all, she went to a lot of trouble to get it.'

'Get what, a bomb? A scorpion? A rabid honey badger?'

'Don't be a daftie,' said Wyatt. 'The box isnae moving and it's no' ticking.'

'Maybe a mallet shoots out and whacks whoever opens the box in the face?'

'You'll get my toe up your arse if you don't shut it,' James told Morgan.

Virgil ignored them all, continuing to stare down at the box.

'I'm gonnae open it,' he said.

Virgil placed the box on the floor. Morgan handed him a small penknife that he used to slit open the tape sealing it shut. Virgil handed the knife back to his brother and they all moved backwards as he slowly opened the box.

Virgil sighed with relief. 'It's just a bottle of whisky. A twenty-year-old single malt. Ember knows I don't drink any more. Is she trying to get me back on the booze?'

'Pour it down the sink,' said Morgan.

'Why?'

'It's probably poisoned.'

'Don't be ridiculous,' said James. 'No' even Ember's that crazy.' He frowned at the bottle. 'But it's better to no' take any chances.'

'You're right,' said Wyatt.

'Aye,' replied Virgil. 'Shame though, it's my favourite.'

They all returned to the kitchen and explained to the others about Ember and her gift.

'Give it to me,' said Ludovica, holding her hand out for the bottle. 'I will know if it has been tampered with.'

They all watched as she snatched the bottle from Virgil. She stared at it for a few seconds before unscrewing the cap and sniffing it. Ludovica scowled at the bottle again and then took a few deep gulps.

'Nonna, you shouldn't have done that,' said Morgan.

'Why not?' she replied, wiping her lips on the back of her hand. 'It is very good stuff.' She took another deep drink before handing it back to Virgil.

'You drank a quarter of the bottle in one go,' he exclaimed.

'Oh, Maw,' said Maria. 'Sit down before you fall down.'

Ludovica waved a dismissive hand. 'I will not fall down. I have always been able to drink any man under the table. Just because I am an old woman doesn't mean I still can't. Now, sit back down and eat,' she said gesturing to the table.

'Who wants some?' said Virgil, holding up the bottle.

'Aye, go on,' replied Wyatt. 'I'll risk it.'

'I still don't like it,' said Morgan.

'Ember is capable of doing something nice just for the sake of it,' said James.

'Aye, but to the man who's divorcing her? Does that sound like the Ember we all know and fear?'

Wyatt snorted. 'You're scared of her.'

'No, I'm no',' Morgan snapped. 'But she can be mad mental when the mood takes her. You know I'm right, Virg.'

'Aye, I dae,' he replied, placing the bottle on the table so they could help themselves. Even though his nonna had said it was safe, he still didn't want any. He was determined never to touch alcohol again.

While everyone else returned to the food and conversation, Virgil wandered back down the hall and into the lounge. The window overlooked the front street. Peering out, he saw Ember standing at the top of the road, staring at the house, the light of a street lamp cast over her. As he'd left the light off in the room, Virgil knew she wouldn't be able to see him. The way she stood so still was a little spooky. He'd always known she wasn't a full shilling, but he'd never been able to help himself around her, the chemistry between them was incredible. At first it had been her ungovernable temper that had been the problem, as well as the fact that she'd thrown things at him for no reason, but she'd gradually become more unstable throughout the course of their marriage. Their relationship hadn't done her mental health any favours but now they'd definitely split up her behaviour was becoming more erratic. If only she could have caught a grip of herself then perhaps their marriage would have stood a chance. But he couldn't put all the blame on her. Half the responsibility lay squarely on his own shoulders. He'd been far from the perfect husband. Now they were further from each other than ever.

Ember remained where she was for another two minutes before turning and slowly walking away.

Virgil grabbed the cardboard box the whisky had come in, which still sat on the hallway floor, and began folding it up ready to go in the recycling bin when a note fluttered out.

He picked it up and recognised Ember's handwriting.

Have a drink on me, babe, it read. *Laugh and have fun before your world goes up in flames.*

Virgil raced outside and down the street in the direction he'd seen Ember go but she was nowhere in sight.

He looked down at the note he still held. 'So much for an amicable divorce.' He sighed.

Virgil didn't tell the rest of his family about the note until the next morning as they'd all been in such a festive mood the previous night and he hadn't wanted to ruin it.

'What do you think?' he asked them all after showing them the note.

'Well, it's hardly surprising,' said Maria. 'Ember was never going to go quietly.'

'You don't think she means she's gonnae set the houses on fire, do you?' said Warren.

'She's no' called Ember for nothing,' replied James between mouthfuls of cereal.

'None of us are safe from her vengeance,' said Maria. 'In a way, I can understand. If Jimmy had ever dared divorce me, I would have made him suffer for it. There is nothing as vicious as a woman scorned. Virgil, you need to be careful.'

'We all need to be careful,' said Ludovica. 'She may blame us all for Virgil's decision to divorce her.'

'Can't you do something to her, Nonna?' said Wyatt. 'Put some sort of binding spell on her to make her behave?'

'No.' She scowled. 'I never interfere with anyone's free will.'

'I don't know what you're all worried about,' said Newton with another of his smug smiles. 'She's just one wee woman.'

'Aww, my naïve Newton.' Maria smiled, patting his shoulder. 'You continue believing all women are harmless if it makes you feel better.'

Newton narrowed his eyes at Morgan when he laughed.

The phone on the sideboard rang and Maria went to answer it. 'Virgil,' she called. 'It's Gordon from the corner shop. He wants you to escort him to the bank this afternoon. He asked for you personally,' she added, a twinkle in her eyes.

'Aye, all right,' he replied.

'Wonderful. He says to be at the shop at two o'clock.'

'I'll be there.'

Maria passed the message on to Gordon before hanging up. 'This is very good for our family. Soon everyone will be wanting our services.'

'It's no' surprising,' replied James. 'Callum Young is highly respected. He's supposed to be one of the best fighters in Glasgow. And Virgil took him down,' he added with a proud smile his brother's way.

Newton, in contrast, shot Virgil daggers. If it hadn't been for him, this could have been his moment of glory.

Virgil stared back at his older brother and thought that Ember wasn't the only one he should be wary of.

10

'I heard you absolutely hammered Callum Young,' said Gordon. 'Pow, pow, pow, you beat him to a pulp.'

'I wouldnae go that far,' replied Virgil as he escorted Gordon to the back door of his shop. He was trying to put Gordon's chatter to the back of his mind but it was difficult as the man never shut up. The shopkeeper was plump, round and cheerful with rosy cheeks, but he was also an enormous fantasist, so no one really listened to him, even when he wasn't making up a lot of lies.

'You're too modest, son. I mean, Callum's a baw hair away from being a professional and you took him down like he was a Girl Guide.'

'That's no' a fair statement,' said Virgil. 'Callum's a very talented fighter.'

'No' talented enough judging from what I've heard. You should be the one going professional, no' him.'

'No thanks. I prefer to stick to the amateur fights.'

'Perhaps it's for the best. You'd have to lose your wee pal here.' Gordon grinned, patting Virgil's stomach. Gordon's smile dropped at the storm that gathered in his eyes. 'Sorry, I never know when to shut my mouth and I cannae talk about anyone's belly,' he added, patting his own stomach.

'We'd better get to the bank.'

'Aye, all right.'

Gordon unlocked the back door. Virgil opened it and peered out.

'All clear,' said Virgil. 'Let's go.'

The two men stepped outside.

'Look after that while I lock this door, will you?' said Gordon, handing him the bag containing the week's takings. 'I've got Marcus watching the shop, but I always keep this door locked because he's a stupid streak of piss who wouldnae notice if someone snuck in and started nicking everything.'

'Why did you hire him then?'

'He's a good boy at heart and his family needs the money. He's honest too, so I know he'd never steal from me.'

Gordon continued to witter on, jiggling the door as it decided not to cooperate with his attempts to lock it.

Virgil looked up and down the alley. He was rather startled to see four men dressed in black appear at one end. He turned and another three appeared at the other end, penning them in. The fact that they all wore bike masks obscuring the lower halves of their faces indicated they weren't here with any good intent.

'Gordon,' said Virgil.

The man was so involved with whatever nonsense he was talking about that he didn't even hear him.

'Gordon, for God's sake, hurry up,' barked Virgil.

'There, finally.' Gordon smiled, satisfied that he'd finally managed to lock the door. 'I really should get that fixed.'

'Get in the fucking car,' said Virgil, grabbing his arm.

Gordon finally noticed the approaching menace, which had begun rushing towards them.

'Shite,' he exclaimed, leaping into the passenger seat of Virgil's car.

Virgil got into the driver's seat and started the engine.

'What are you gonnae dae, run them over?' exclaimed Gordon as he hit the accelerator.

'If they don't move then, aye,' he replied, revving the engine aggressively.

When the approaching gang didn't take the hint and move, he sent the car lurching forward, forcing the three men to leap aside as the car sped past them and exited the alley.

Gordon breathed a sigh of relief. 'Well, that was easier than I thought it would be.'

'You changed the time you were leaving for the bank because you booked an urgent doctor's appointment this afternoon and they didnae know. If we'd stuck to your original timetable then we would have been in the shop with the takings when they turned up.'

'Shite, you're right.'

'Who else knew you were leaving at two o'clock for the bank?'

'Well, just me, you and Marcus. Oh, and I called your maw and let her know but I'm pretty sure it's no' Maria or any of your lot. It wouldnae make your family look very good if you'd got your heid smashed in by a bunch of neds.'

'True,' said Virgil as he drove them out of Garthamlock. 'Are you sure you can trust Marcus?'

'Aye. He's worked for me for three years. He's like a second son to me; he'd never do anything like that. Naw, it must be someone else.'

'And you definitely didn't tell anyone else?'

'I told my Lucy but she wouldnae tell anyone either. She's always terrified when I do the bank run. She wants me to make the shop card only.'

'You really should.'

'Aye, but there's a few auld people around here who only like to use cash. I don't want to take that away from them.'

'Fine. Get your heid bashed in by a bunch of neds then.'

Gordon paused before saying, 'Maybe Lucy has a point?'

'Were they the same gang who've caused you trouble in the past?'

'Come to think of it, I don't think they were. The other lot were just a bunch of weans, but that gang looked much more organised and scary. The neds have never dressed like fucking ninjas before.'

'Then it's possible they've been watching you and learning your routine.'

Gordon paled. 'Creepy.'

'I'll look into it and see if I can find out who they were, because they might no' stop at your shop. They could decide to target other business owners too.'

'I wouldnae put it past them. Take it from me, I've served years in the hardest prisons in the UK, so I know these things.'

Virgil sighed. 'You served three months in Greenock Prison for shoplifting. You're no' Charles Bronson.'

'Still, I've seen their type before. They're nasty bastards and they've been denied their fun, which means they'll only hit their next target even harder.'

Gordon might be a bit of a prick, but Virgil knew he was right.

* * *

Thankfully Gordon made his deposit at the bank safely and Virgil drove him back to the shop where they found the gormless Marcus leaning against the counter, reading a magazine. When asked if there'd been any trouble, he told them no, it had been quiet.

Gordon had a pretty decent camera set up at the back of the shop, so he emailed the footage of the gang to Virgil, who returned home to discuss the matter with his family and show them the video.

* * *

'Thank God Gordon changed the time,' said Maria.

'There were only seven of them,' said Morgan. 'Virgil took out more than that on his own at Old Skool.'

'Gordon's certain it's no' the same gang who targeted him before,' said Virgil. 'They were just weans. This lot are something different. The question is, how did they get their information about his routine?'

'Gordon's a gobshite,' said Newton. 'He cannae help himself. I bet he blabbed to someone and didnae even realise.'

'It's possible but I think they've been watching him, learning his routine. This crew was tooled up and organised. We should find out who they are because they could attack another target in Garthamlock.'

'Like it,' said Morgan, slapping his palm off the table. 'We've got a quest.'

Warren blinked at him. 'What is this, *Lord of the Rings*? Actually, you do look a bit like a hobbit.'

'Shut it, ya dick.'

'Warren,' said Virgil. 'Could you speak to Rose, see if her

family knows who this lot could be? It's possible they come from outside Garthamlock.'

'Nae bother,' he replied.

'I don't think they're from around here,' said James. 'I cannae think of anyone who fits the bill.'

'I'm wondering if this is linked to Lucas Blair or Henry Allan,' said Virgil.

'Revenge?'

He nodded. 'Aye.'

'I think that is much more likely,' said Maria.

'There's one other possibility,' said Newton. 'Ember.'

'How could she know that I would be working for Gordon?' replied Virgil.

'That woman is smart and sly. It would be just like her to try and sabotage one of our main sources of income.'

'Would she though?' said James. 'Surely she'd want Virgil to get some cash behind him so she could take it all in the divorce?'

'Ember's well aware that I'm always paid in cash and no records are kept of our bodyguarding work,' said Virgil. 'As far as HMRC are concerned, the only money I have is what I earned at the distillery, which won't be anywhere near enough to keep Ember in luxury for the rest of her life.'

Warren's phone beeped and he checked the message he'd received. 'Rose will be here in half an hour,' he said. 'I can ask her then.'

'Good,' replied Virgil. 'I heard that Lucas Blair's been released from hospital.'

Everyone noted the twinkle in his eyes.

'Do you actually want to see him?' said James.

'How no'?'

'Because you might end up giving him another battering.'

'That won't happen. I only did that because I thought he'd kidnapped Ember.'

'And what if he winds you up?'

'He's no' that stupid.'

'Are you sure about that?' Morgan smiled.

'I don't think hassling Lucas again would be a good idea,' said Newton. 'Don't forget, he's working for Toni McVay. The fact that we all still possess our eyeballs indicates she's no' gonnae seek revenge for your attack on him but she might change her mind if you do it again.'

'That's a very good point,' said Maria. 'I don't think you should visit him, Virgil.'

'All right, Maw, if you think it's for the best,' he replied.

'I really do. Well, get to it, boys. Speak to everyone you know and find this gang. They could be a big threat to your body-guarding business, which I anticipate will become even busier in the wake of your latest underground fights. And before you go,' she said as they all began to get to their feet. 'I hope you havenae forgotten that in three days' time it will be the first anniversary of your father's death.'

The brothers all stopped and nodded solemnly.

'Of course we havenae forgotten, Maw,' said Newton gently.

'And you recall what we agreed we would do to honour that.'

'You don't mean...' began James, face falling.

'Yes, I do. You're going to dress up as the Earp brothers.'

'Christ,' he sighed.

'I've already ordered your outfits. I'm collecting them tomorrow.'

Wyatt became agitated, his twitching going into overdrive. 'I don't want to dress up as... him,' he muttered.

'I'm sorry, son, but this was a dear wish of your da's and we must honour it. Don't worry, you'll all look wonderful. You can get ready here then we'll make a pilgrimage to the pub where we'll all raise a glass to him.'

'You mean we've got to walk through the streets dressed up like nineteenth-century cowboys?' said James.

'It's what your father wanted and you will do it,' she said, the steely look in her eyes telling them all that she would not be dissuaded.

'Can't we at least drive there?' said Warren.

'No. You don't drive on a pilgrimage. Now this is what we're doing and you will give it your all. It's only what your father deserves,' she yelled.

Wyatt shifted from foot to foot. 'I don't want to dress up as *him*,' he pressed.

'You should be honoured to be named after such a great man,' said Maria, tilting back her head. 'And you're doing it for your father. Stop being so selfish. You're lucky the cemetery's too far away to walk to, otherwise we'd be going there too.'

Wyatt huffed but nodded.

Maria smiled triumphantly. 'Good boy. Now get to work, all of you. Stop this gang of robbers before they do our family any damage.'

The brothers left the house, their enthusiasm dampened a little by the news that they'd have to walk through the streets dressed as the Earp brothers.

'At least the outfits are pretty cool,' said Morgan. 'Black trousers, white shirt, black waistcoat, boots and one of those awesome long black coats.'

'Don't forget the cowboy hat,' said James. 'That's the bit I'm no' looking forward to.'

'We'll have people taking the piss out of us if we walk through the streets dressed like that,' said Warren.

'They wouldnae dare,' retorted Morgan. 'No' after what Virgil did to Callum Young.'

James patted Wyatt's shoulder. 'You'll be fine, pal. It's only for a few hours.'

Wyatt shook his hand off and rounded on him. 'Don't fucking touch me,' he snarled.

James held up his hands. 'Sorry.'

'I don't want to be *him*. I can never be like *him*. Da wanted me to be; he had the highest hopes for me because he gave me that name, but I always let him down. I was just a disappointment to him.'

'That's no' true,' said Virgil sympathetically knowing Wyatt had wrestled with this particular sense of inadequacy since boyhood.

'He always thought I'd do great things, but I never have and I never will.'

'You're only twenty-four; there's still plenty of time.'

'No, there isnae. No matter what I do, I'll never be a legend like Wyatt Earp.'

'You're no' the only one. I'll never be like Virgil Earp.'

'And I won't be like Morgan either,' said Morgan. 'At least, I hope I won't be. He ended up getting shot to death. At least Wyatt lived a long life and went to Hollywood.'

'Warren was shot to death too,' said Warren. 'So you're pretty lucky, Wyatt.'

'Why don't we forget about people who died decades ago and concentrate on the job in hand,' said Newton. 'We are not the bloody Earps, we're The Bloody MacGregors and that means a hell of a lot more to everyone around here.'

'Yeah, you're right,' said Morgan. 'We might share their first names but that's it. So you see, Wyatt, all that stuff doesnae matter. You've nothing to live up to.'

'That's easy for you to say,' he grunted.

'Roughing up a few people will make you feel better.'

'We're no' roughing anyone up,' said Virgil.

'For God's sake,' he sighed. 'I thought after last night we'd got the old Virg back.'

'I'm more willing to inflict violence when necessary but we're no' gonnae run around the scheme battering people just for the fun of it. We'll be smart about this because you know what it would do to Maw if another of us was put in prison. Speaking of which, I've got another visit booked with Nick this afternoon. I'll find out if our warning off Henry Allan worked.'

'I hope it hasnae made things worse for him,' said James.

'That's my worry too. Anyway, where do you suggest we start asking about this gang? I've been away for six months, so you'll all have a better idea than me.'

'Let's go to the pub,' said Newton. 'Big Billy Begbie knows about everything that goes on around here.'

The nearest pub to Garthamlock had been at the Glasgow Fort, the local shopping and leisure park, until Big Billy had decided he wanted to be a landlord, so he bought and renovated an old church in Garthamlock. He'd named it The Big Hoose, to the mystification of all the locals, as that was a slang term for Barlinnie, the most infamous prison in Scotland. Big Billy had intended the name to refer to his own nickname and not the prison's, so he'd stuck to his guns and refused to change it. The locals had flocked to try Big Billy's watering hole but he was a bad-tempered, violent individual who saw his customers as inconveniences rather than assets, so all the decent people had soon stopped patronising his establishment, leaving it to the local dregs and criminals.

'No' Big Billy,' sighed Virgil.

'What's wrong with Big Billy?' asked Warren.

'He's an arsehole.'

'He's no' that bad.'

'Aye, he is. He punched Jason Phillips in the throat for saying his lager was flat.'

'Jason's a prick. Everyone wants to punch him in the throat.'

'I see what this is really about,' Newton told Virgil. 'You don't drink any more and you don't want everyone finding out because they'll call you a jessie.'

'I don't care what they call me,' he replied.

'Aye ya do. Beating Callum Young restored your reputation and you don't want it damaging again.'

'We don't have to buy a drink,' said James. 'We can just go in and speak to Big Billy.'

'You know he won't give any information without us all buying a round first,' replied Newton. 'That's how he works.'

'Then I'll order an orange juice and tell everyone I'm no' drinking because I'm driving,' said Virgil. 'We'll take my car and Morgan's.'

This silenced Newton, to Virgil's satisfaction, and they all piled into the two cars and headed to the pub. The church was a lovely old building with a vaulted ceiling and arched stained-glass windows. The elegant exterior had been preserved but the interior was a different matter. The unsuspecting visitor may expect to walk in and see polished tables and glasses, a beautifully swept stone floor and friendly bar staff waiting to greet them. Instead, they would find themselves entering a cold, echoing creep fest. Big Billy had attempted to play on the gothic beauty of the building and failed miserably. Instead of a dark, luxurious interior, he'd filled it with tacky Halloween decorations, the beautiful stone floor covered in cheap lino stained with spilt alcohol. The bar was equally cheap and badly put together. People standing at the top end of the bar would find their glasses leaning to one side, the surface chipped, and in some places chunks of wood had been gouged out.

Fake cobwebs were strung from the windows hiding the beautiful stained glass. Plastic spiders adorned the walls and bats and crows hung from the ceiling on string. Skeletons, witches and ghosts were strewn about the room seemingly at random, taking up wall space or on sentry duty beside the tables. The pièce de resistance was an inflatable horse-drawn carriage six feet high and eight feet long with a zombie coachman and a skeleton peering out of the window. Big Billy had placed a barrier around it after multiple drunken customers had attempted to sit on the back of the horse and almost popped it.

A motion-activated witch with glowing red eyes popped out at every unsuspecting customer as they entered while cackling uncontrollably. The witch's face was even more twisted and deformed than its makers had intended thanks to the many punches it had received from startled punters over the two years it had been in situ.

'Jeezo, I hate that stupid thing,' gasped Warren as it cackled at him.

'The witch has been there since this place opened,' said Morgan. 'But it makes you jump every time.'

'Aye, don't go on about it,' he muttered.

The brothers strode up to the bar where Big Billy awaited them. He certainly lived up to his name. The man was enormous, standing at six foot four and weighing twenty-three stone. His head was huge and pumpkin-shaped, which most of his customers joked fitted in well with his pub's decor. His forehead was huge and sloping, the scalp covered in thinning, slicked-back, dark brown hair. His beefy arms were covered in fading tattoos. He always wore blue jeans and a white T-shirt, even in the depths of winter. Despite the fact that the vaulted, stone building could get rather chilly, Big Billy was cheap and only put the heating on when he really had to, but he never felt the cold, even when his customers began to moan about the temperature.

'Well, well, well,' said Big Billy when he spotted Virgil. 'If it's no' the champion.' Big Billy's voice was surprisingly high-pitched, but he'd made everyone who had pointed that out in the past instantly regret mentioning it.

'You heard about the fight then,' replied Virgil.

'Course I did. Everyone's talking about it. There were some fannies who were saying you'd lost your bottle and had turned into a pacifist, but you proved all those pricks wrong. Luckily, I don't believe anything I hear.' He peered at the bruising to Virgil's face. 'Looks like Callum gave you a good run for your money.'

'Aye, he did. He's an excellent fighter. Anyway, we're here to ask you a few questions.'

'Oh dear.' Big Billy grinned unpleasantly. 'Sounds like I'm in trouble.'

'Not at all. We just want some information.'

'Fine, but you know the rules.'

'Aye. What do you want, boys?' Virgil asked his brothers. 'It's on me.'

The brothers all ordered pints except Morgan and Virgil.

'What do you want poofy orange juice for?' demanded Big Billy, screwing up his face.

'Because we're driving,' retorted Morgan.

'Oh, aye, fair enough.' Big Billy began pouring their drinks. 'Ask away then.'

'Have you heard of a local gang dressed like ninjas going around robbing businesses of their takings?'

'This is about Gordon Maitland, isn't it? The gobshite's been blabbing about what happened all over the scheme. He said he took down five of them on his own while you dealt with the other two.'

'He didnae go anywhere near them.'

'Just as I thought. He's a coward. His arse collapses at the slightest sign of violence.'

'We're wondering if you've heard of who that gang could be.'

'Gordon made them out to be a bunch of international diamond thieves.' Big Billy chuckled. 'All organised and intimidating.'

'For once, he's no' far off the mark. They were.'

'Wow, that's a first. And you're asking if I've heard of anyone like that in the neighbourhood?'

'Aye.'

'Well, there is something. The last couple of days I've felt like someone's been watching me when I've been leaving here.'

'To drop off the takings at the bank?'

'Naw. Why, do you think it's connected to what happened to Gordon? Because he said they were there to rob him.'

'Aye, they were and they knew he was on his way to the bank.'

Big Billy produced a tyre iron from under the bar. 'If the fannies try to take my cash I'll shove this right up them.'

'There were seven of them.'

'I don't care if there were seventeen of them, I'll batter the living shite out of them.'

'This wasnae a gang of wee neds. They looked too professional.'

'What is this? Are you trying to sell your bodyguarding services?'

'No, we're just trying to find out who they are.'

Big Billy sighed and replaced the tyre iron under the bar. 'I've no' heard who they could be. Certainly no one who comes in here.'

'Which means it's someone outside Garthamlock.'

'I reckon so.'

'No one around here would be stupid enough to mess with you, Big Billy.' The landlord insisted his full nickname was always used. Anyone not following the rule would suffer a life-changing trauma.

'There's always someone with more baws than brains,' replied Big Billy.

'So you've no idea who it could be?' Newton asked him.

'Nope, but I'll make a few discreet enquiries and let you know.'

'Cheers. In the meantime, if you need our services...'

'I won't.'

Newton held up his hands. 'Fine.'

The MacGregor brothers quickly finished their drinks and left.

'Where to now?' said Morgan once they were outside.

'Can you drop me off at home?' replied Warren. 'Rose should be there by now.'

After dropping Warren off, the brothers drove around the houses of a few acquaintances, asking if they knew anything about this gang, but no one could give them any information, so they headed home.

They entered the kitchen to find Warren with Rose and her older sisters Jane and Carly Savage.

'Hey, beautiful.' Morgan beamed at Carly. 'I knew you wouldnae be able to stay away from me for long.'

Carly, as lovely as her younger sister, gave Morgan a disdainful look. 'I'm very happy with my boyfriend, thank you.'

'Shame,' he said crouching beside the chair she was sitting on. 'I'll be here, sweetheart, when it goes pear-shaped.'

'It won't go pear-shaped,' she coldly told him before turning in her seat, presenting him with her back.

'Still got it.' James grinned at Morgan as he straightened up, looking sheepish.

Wyatt stood beside Jane's chair, the oldest of the Savage Sisters, and stared down at her creepily. Jane, however, wasn't in the least intimidated.

'You still married to your wife?' he asked her.

'Aye,' she replied, eyebrow raised. 'How?'

'Well, if you and her ever want a man to...'

'No' another word, you,' Maria told him. 'I brought my boys up better than that,' she yelled, clipping first Morgan and then Wyatt around the back of the head.

'Ow.' Morgan frowned.

'Now sit down,' she told her sons. 'We have things to discuss. By the way, this is Virgil,' she told Carly and Jane.

'Congratulations on your fight last night,' Jane told Virgil. 'Toni's over the moon with your performance. Most of the money was on Callum, so she cleaned up.'

'She bet on me?' He frowned.

'Aye. She knew you'd win.'

'And that is why she's remained on top for so long,' said Maria. 'Now, to business. Did you find anything out?' she asked her sons.

'Big Billy at The Big Hoose said he's felt someone's been watching him this past week,' replied James. 'He's nae idea who it could be and he's no' heard anything from any of his customers.'

'We've got an idea of who could be behind it,' said Carly.

'Who?'

'It's a crew put together from various areas around Glasgow. It's no' just men but women too.'

'Put together by who?'

'Mick Jones from Easthall. He was released from Barlinnie three months ago after serving two years for robbery. He also has a history of mugging and breaking and entering. We think he made connections with other prisoners and organised them into a crew once he was released.'

'How did he make connections with the women?' said Morgan. 'Bar-L's an all-male prison.'

'Either he knew them already or they were connected to another member of his crew.'

'So you've been hunting them then?'

'No, because they're no' stupid enough to come onto schemes run by Toni McVay, but Garthamlock isn't part of her turf, so it's fair game. We've mentioned it to her, but she's said we're no' to get involved. However, she did say we could give you Mick's name. Do with the information what you will.'

'Cheers, doll, we really appreciate it,' said Morgan, running a hand up and down her back. 'It's a shame you cannae join us on the hunt. Then you'd get to see me in action.'

Virgil was astonished when Carly shot to her feet and drove her fist into Morgan's stomach. His brother doubled up before dropping to his knees, coughing.

'Good girl.' Maria smiled. 'He asked for that.'

Morgan straightened up, wheezing. 'She hits like a hammer,' he gasped. 'You've changed, doll,' he told Carly. 'What happened to you?'

She just stared back at him coldly.

Jane got to her feet. 'We have to go now – we've work to do – but you will continue to have the pleasure of Rose's company.'

'Thanks for coming, ladies,' Maria told the sisters. 'It was good to see you again.'

Virgil was surprised that his mother seemed to be so warm towards the sisters, especially after one of them had just walloped her son.

'You too,' replied Jane before the two women left.

Morgan flopped into a chair, arms wrapped around his stomach. 'There was no need for that,' he muttered. 'I'm telling you, that lassie's been through a bad experience. She wasnae like that before.'

'The first time we met them she punched you in the face,' said Newton.

'Aye, but did you see her eyes? There was something dark in them.'

They all looked questioningly at Rose.

'It's best you don't ask,' she replied. 'So, are you going to look for this Mick Jones?' she added, wanting to change the subject.

'Definitely,' replied Virgil. 'I don't know anyone in Easthall. Do any of you?'

'I've got an ex-girlfriend who lives there,' replied Warren.

Rose's eyes hardened. 'Oh aye?'

'Don't worry, babe, she's nothing compared to you.'

'She'd better not be,' she glowered back.

'It was over between us two years ago. It's no' like I see her any more. For all I know, she's moved.'

'Don't tell me you're jealous?' Newton asked her with another of his smirks.

'No, of course not,' said Rose, tossing back her head. 'I'm just curious.'

'Aye, course,' he said knowingly.

'Does anyone else know someone in Easthall?' said Virgil.

They all shook their heads.

'Then Warren's ex-girlfriend it is. Sorry, Rose.'

'There's no need to apologise,' she replied. 'I trust him. Besides, he knows I'd turn him into a eunuch if he cheated on me.'

'The sexy thing is that's no' an idle threat.' Warren smiled, taking his girlfriend's hand. 'She really could do that to me.'

'If you find the prospect of being castrated sexy then you need serious help,' said James.

'Let's head over there right now,' said Virgil. 'If Big Billy was right and someone is watching him, then they could attack again at any moment.'

* * *

The brothers decided not to go en masse to the home of Warren's ex for fear of frightening her, so Warren just went in with Virgil. Fortunately, Sharon was still in the flat she'd lived in when she'd dated Warren, who was sad to see what his ex-girlfriend had been reduced to. Once she'd been tall, willowy and beautiful with gorgeous long dark hair. Unfortunately, she'd got into drugs and now her hair was lank and greasy, her skin pale and spotty, a sore at the corner of her mouth and the weight had dropped off her to the point of emaciation.

'Warren.' She smiled, revealing brown teeth. 'This is a surprise. Long time no see.'

'Aye,' he murmured, stunned by the change in her. 'It is.'

'You're looking good,' she said, eyes running up and down him appreciatively.

'Aye,' he repeated. 'Err, you too,' he added, feeling it would be rude to say otherwise.

'Thanks.' She smiled. 'But if you're here to try and get back with me, you'll be disappointed because I have a boyfriend and he gets so jealous.'

'Actually, we're looking for someone and I thought you might be able to help,' he said, finally managing to shake himself out of his shock.

Sharon's smile faltered. 'Look, Warren, I'm happy to help and everything but life's difficult at the moment...'

'We'll pay you for the information.'

'Aye, that's great. Hey, Virgil.' She smiled. 'It's good to see you too. Come away in.'

They followed her into the flat and Warren was even more dismayed. What had once been a pleasant, clean and well-maintained place had degenerated into a stinking rat's nest. The brothers didn't comment in case she decided not to help them.

'Do you want a brew?' Sharon asked the two men. 'Or something stronger?'

'We're good thanks,' Warren hastily replied.

'Okay.' She gestured to one of the couches. 'Sit.'

As Warren pushed aside a heap of magazines, which spilled onto the floor, he spotted the dubious stains on the beige cloth, so he gingerly sat on the edge of the cushion, as did his brother. It disgusted him to think that he'd had sex with Sharon on this very couch, although back then it had been pristine.

'So, what can I help you with?' she said pleasantly.

'Have you heard of someone called Mick Jones?'

Sharon's smile dropped. 'Why are you asking about him?'

'We think he could be behind some trouble that's happening in Garthamlock, although we're no' sure about that yet.'

Sharon shot to her feet. 'I cannae tell you anything about him.'

'How no'?'

'Because... I just cannae, okay? You'd better leave now.'

'He's your dealer, isn't he?'

'I am not on drugs,' she retorted.

'Aye, ya are. I hate to break it to you but it's obvious. I'm just no' sure what drug yet. Meth? Heroin?'

At the mention of the last one, Sharon coloured and cast her eyes to the floor.

'Jesus, Shaz, what are you playing at? You used to be so together. You were studying to become an accountant; you had a nice part-time job in a restaurant, a smart wee car and this place used to be immaculate. The only place I'd seen smarter than this flat was my maw's hoose and now look at it,' he said, gesturing around him. 'And look at the state of you.'

Her head snapped up and she scowled. 'What about me?'

'You know exactly what I mean,' he said, voice filled with sadness. 'I never thought you'd start taking that shite. You used to be into healthy eating and working out at the gym. What happened?'

Sharon sighed and sank heavily onto the opposite couch, seemingly not noticing the newspapers strewn across it, which crinkled beneath her. Warren also noticed all the used scratchcards and spent lottery tickets amid the mess.

'I started seeing Wayne,' she said. 'He was into smoking a bit of weed and he took coke when he went clubbing and I began doing the same.'

'Jeezo,' he sighed.

'How dare you?' she snapped. 'You do exactly the same.'

'Correction, I don't touch coke any more and I smoke a bit of weed now and then but something tells me Wayne's into the harder stuff.'

'He started taking smack and somehow I started too. It was at a party one night. I was stressed because the restaurant I worked at was going under and I knew I was gonnae lose my job. He said

it would stop me worrying for a while and it did. Then things
started to get worse. I dropped out of uni, so I needed more and
more and I couldnae stop.'

'And Mick Jones keeps you supplied?' Virgil asked her.

'Aye. He got into dealing the moment he was let out of prison.
His parole officer has no idea; he thinks he's reformed. Mick's
always taking the piss out of him for being a stupid bastard. I
knew Mick before he went inside. He was bad to begin with, but
prison made him even worse.'

'You need to get off the heroin,' Warren told her. 'If you don't
it will kill you.'

'I don't want to get off it. It takes the edge off.'

'That's bollocks, doll. You can beat it, but you won't be able to
while you're going out with that fucking loser of a boyfriend.'
Warren was enraged on her behalf. This bright, beautiful
woman had been destroyed and it frightened him that she was
right when she said she lacked the strength to fight the drug.

'Don't worry about me; I'll be fine.'

Warren was about to continue trying to convince her to give
up the drugs, but Virgil spoke over him. 'We need to know everything you can tell us about Mick Jones,' he said, placing some
cash on the grimy coffee table.

Sharon's eyes settled greedily on the money before she
snatched it up and hastily counted it, totting up how much drugs
she could buy with it before stuffing the cash inside her bra.

'He lives on Ware Road. Number eleven.'

'Does he live alone?'

'Naw, he lives with his maw. He was renting a place before he
got sent down, so of course he lost that. It looked good for his
parole moving in with his mother.'

'Who does he hang around with?'

'He doesnae have many friends around here; he's pissed off

too many people over the years. He's pretty nasty and will have a go at someone for the smallest thing. He also has incredibly bad road rage. He drives around with a baseball bat in the back of his car and he's battered people's motors for the slightest thing. Everyone in Easthall is pretty scared of him.'

'Is his maw scared of him too?'

'Naw, but she has no control over him, if that's what you're wondering.'

'Have you noticed him hanging around with any faces outside of Easthall?'

'Aye. A few times when I've gone round to pick up my, well, you know,' she blushed. 'There have been some faces I don't recognise, women as well as men. It tends to be the same faces too, like they spend a lot of time together. I always get the feeling they're discussing something they don't want anyone to overhear and they cannae wait for me to leave.'

'Have there been any robberies or burglaries in Easthall since Mick was released, especially business owners getting attacked?'

'No' that I've heard of but if Mick is doing stuff like that he'd be bloody stupid to do it on his own doorstep.'

Virgil nodded. Sharon was an intelligent woman and it was a shame to see her brought so low. 'Is there anything else we should know about Mick?'

Sharon paused to think before replying. 'He has weapons stashed all over his house. When I was there once, a customer turned up for his next fix but he didnae bring the cash he'd promised. Mick took a machete out of this hidden panel cut into the wall in his maw's front room and threatened him with it. That's just one example. He has at least one weapon in each room and no' just machetes but bats, crowbars, knives, that sort of thing. He's mad if you ask me. One raid by the polis and he'll be back in prison, but that's Mick all over. He's pretty mental and he's afraid of no one. But he's far from stupid, which is what makes him so dangerous.'

'That's all very useful, Sharon, thank you,' said Virgil. 'And you won't tell Mick that we've been asking about him?'

'Course not. He'd kill me.'

'I hope we've no' put you in any danger?' Warren asked her.

'Naw, just as long as he doesnae find out.'

'He won't.'

'That's all right then.'

Virgil got to his feet. 'Thanks for the information.'

'Could you gi'e us a minute, Virg?' said Warren.

'Aye, course.'

Virgil left and Warren turned to Sharon. 'You've got to get off the smack, doll.'

'Did it ever occur to you that I don't want to?' she replied.

'Why the hell wouldn't you want to?'

Her face hardened. 'Look, we're no' going out any more, so my life is none of your business.'

'I still care about you and I hate to see you going down this path. You'll end up either in prison or deid.'

'I'm fine. I can handle myself.'

'Take a look around you, doll. This place used to be a show home. Now it's a...'

'A what?' She scowled.

'A tip. You had a good life and you're destroying it for the drugs.'

'I'm no' destroying it; I'm happy.'

'How can you be happy getting aff yer tits on heroin all the time?'

'It's none of your fucking business, Warren, so piss off,' she yelled back at him.

'Shaz, I want to help you.'

'I don't want or need your help. I'm a grown fucking woman who can do what she likes. Now get out of my flat. If you don't, I'll tell Mick you've been asking about him and he'll cut your fucking feet off with his machete,' she screeched.

Warren sighed. He knew he was wasting his time, but he couldn't stand seeing her like this. 'Fine, I'm going, but you know where I am if you need me.'

Sharon just glared back at him, eyes blazing.

Warren left and joined Virgil in his car.

'You okay?' Virgil asked him.

'No' really. I offered to help her but she told me to piss off. She's no' interested.'

'You're better staying out of it. Junkies only drag you down with them.'

'So you're saying I should just let her kill herself?'

'It's her life, Warren. You cannae help someone who doesn't want to be helped. Besides, if you get tangled up trying to help Sharon, one day you'll end up losing Rose and that lassie is far better for you than your druggie ex.'

'Aye, I know. It just makes me sad, that's all.'

'I get it but there's nothing you can do.'

Virgil's phone rang and he was pleased to see Cecil's name pop up on the screen.

'All right, pal, how are you?' He smiled as he answered the call. His smile dropped. 'What the fuck?' he yelled. 'On my way.'

Virgil hung up, stuffed the phone back into his pocket and started the engine.

'What's going on?' said Warren, hastily pulling on his seat belt as his brother slammed his foot down on the accelerator and the car lurched forwards.

'My caravan's on fire.'

11

Virgil sped up the road towards his caravan. He and Warren were forced to abandon the vehicle further down the road because of the fire engines and run the rest of the way.

'Oh Christ,' exclaimed Virgil when he saw the smouldering remains of his beloved van. Everything had gone except the metal skeleton, the fire having eaten through the rest. His plants and vegetable patch had either been saturated with water or trampled by the emergency responders. Everything he'd loved and worked so hard to nurture and grow gone in an instant. The sight was almost soul-destroying.

'Virg,' said Cecil, rushing to his side. 'I'm so sorry.'

'What happened?' demanded Virgil, eyes on the wreckage.

'We were all having a drink in the clubhouse when we saw the smoke. By the time we got here, the whole caravan was an inferno.'

'Was it an electrical fault?'

'I cannae say for sure but I heard one of the fire officers mention the word *accelerant*.'

Virgil's thoughts immediately leapt to Ember's note. 'Accelerant?' he repeated numbly.

'Aye. Like I said, that's just what I heard. I don't know what they meant by it.'

'Was anyone hurt?'

'Naw. Just your lovely caravan,' said Cecil sympathetically, patting Virgil's shoulder.

A firefighter approached them. 'Mr MacGregor?' he said, eyes flicking between the brothers.

'That's me,' replied Virgil.

The two men stared at each other in surprise. Virgil recognised the firefighter as a member of the crowd at his fight with Callum Young.

'Do you know what started the fire?' said Virgil, the first to snap out of his shock.

'There was a strong smell of petrol when we went in. The neighbours informed me gas bottles are used on the site but petrol isn't.'

'That's right. Thank God I disconnected the gas bottle before I left.'

'Aye, that's very lucky. I'm afraid I've had to call in the Fire Investigation Unit. Sorry, pal.'

'It's okay, I understand.'

'The officer dealing with the case is called John Simpson. He's a big fan,' he added in a whisper.

Virgil nodded in understanding, although the fact that the fire investigator would be on his side did nothing to lift his spirits. His wee haven was gone.

'It's no' so bad,' Warren told his brother. 'You can always buy another caravan.'

'But I loved that one. It was my home,' he said, staring at the tangle of wreckage with dismay.

'Here, Virgil,' said a woman called Mona, one of his near neighbours, bustling up to him holding a plant pot. 'I know it's no' much but I managed to save something.'

Virgil's spirits lifted slightly when he saw it was the geranium he'd thrown through the window. It seemed it was quite the survivor. 'Thank you,' he said, taking it from her. 'I hope you didnae put yourself at risk to get it?'

'Naw, it was far enough away from the van to be safe to grab it.'

Virgil cradled the plant pot to him, the last link to his old life. Now his caravan had gone it felt as though that had been permanently taken from him.

'How much stuff did you have in the caravan?' Warren asked him.

'Nothing I'm too bothered about losing,' he replied. 'All the important stuff is at Maw's.'

'That's lucky. Who could have done this?'

Virgil wasn't about to discuss that there and then. It was too complicated to even start to think about in that moment, especially if Ember turned out to be behind it. Instead, he watched a Land Rover Defender roll to a halt and a tall, powerful-looking man climb out. He was one of those individuals who looked completely square – body, shoulders, jaw and head. He had a buzz cut, which only enhanced the impression.

'I'm looking for Virgil MacGregor,' said the man even though his gaze had already settled on his target.

'He's here,' said Cecil, helpfully pointing at Virgil.

The man strode up to Virgil, hand extended. 'My name's John Simpson. I'm from the Fire Investigation Unit.'

'You got here fast.'

'Time is of the essence in cases like this, especially as it's forecast to rain later. I don't want to lose any evidence. Can I speak to you in private?'

'Aye, course.'

The two men moved away from the others.

'What can I do to help?' Virgil asked John.

'First, I'll need some contact details.'

'Nae bother,' said Virgil before rhyming off his phone number and his address in Garthamlock, which John scribbled down in a notebook.

'Nasty,' said John, looking at what was left of the caravan. 'It's fortunate you weren't inside.'

He then asked Virgil a few questions about the caravan, such as how long he'd lived on the site. Once he'd finished John said, 'Well, I'll get to work and let you know my findings when I'm done.'

'Thanks,' replied Virgil while staring wistfully at the van.

'I take it this is a big loss for you?'

'Aye, course it is. It's my home.'

'I hate to ask but was it insured?'

'No. Bloody stupid of me, I know, but it never crossed my mind that something like this could happen.'

'By the way,' said John, lowering his voice. 'Great fight last night. You made me a ton of money.'

'You bet on me over Callum?'

'Course. You're a MacGregor. I wondered, do you do private fights?' John glanced around again to make sure no one was paying them any attention but everyone was too busy watching the caravan and the firefighters.

'I mean would you put on a show for me and my pals fighting an opponent of our choice?'

'I don't know, I've never been asked that before.'

'We'll make it worth your while. You'll make more than

double what you earn at the other fights, which could come in useful,' he added, nodding in the direction of the caravan. 'You will probably even earn enough to buy a brand-new one. You don't need to give me an answer now. Think it over. You're free to go; I'll catch up with you later.'

With that, John wandered over to the firefighter who'd spoken to Virgil earlier and the two started chatting.

Warren approached his brother. 'So what's happening? Are you allowed to leave?'

'Aye,' replied Virgil while continuing to stare at John.

Warren looked from his brother to the fire investigation officer and back again. 'Something wrong?'

'No' here. I'll tell you in the car.'

Virgil was forced to delay his explanation to Warren when Cecil, Mona and the other residents of the site cajoled him to join them in the clubhouse for a drink. Warren said he'd drive so he could enjoy a pint but, to his dismay, not only did Virgil order an orange juice but the other residents ordered soft drinks too. After the residents had commiserated with Virgil for a good half hour, the brothers left.

'Hold that,' Virgil told Warren after they'd got in the car, handing him the pot containing the geranium.

'You're seriously taking this thing?' he replied, taking it from him.

'Aye, I am. I grew that from a seed and it's all I have left of my home, so be bloody careful with it.'

'I'll guard it with my life.'

Virgil didn't speak until they'd reached the main road, continually glancing back in his rear-view mirror, feeling as though he was saying goodbye to a part of his life that he really didn't want to let go of. 'The fire investigation officer asked me a weird question. He saw me fight Callum and he made a lot of money betting on me to win. He asked if I do private fights.'

'Private fights?' Warren frowned.

'Aye.'

'Sounds dodgy to me. Does he want you to fight naked or something weird like that?'

'I don't think so. He said it was for his friends and I'd face a fighter of their choice. He also said I'd make more money than I could at Toni's fights.'

'I don't like the sound of that. He could be some weirdo.'

'Or it could be the chance to earn some really big money. I might be able to replace my caravan.'

'He's taking advantage of you. He clocked that you'd just lost something big and thought he'd exploit you while you're vulnerable.'

'Maybe, maybe not.'

'Don't tell me you're seriously considering it?'

'I might have to.'

'You should run it past the rest of the family first. Personally, if I were you, I'd gi'e it a body swerve. You might find yourself chained up in someone's torture dungeon.'

'I didnae get any weird vibes off him.'

'Some people are good at hiding their crazy. Anyway, who do you think burned down your caravan?'

Without a word, Virgil plucked Ember's note from his jacket pocket and handed it to him. Warren held it with his free hand, the other wrapped around the plant pot on his knee, and read out loud, '*Have a drink on me, babe. Laugh and have fun before your world goes up in flames.* Well, I think that's case closed. And she did say she hoped the caravan burned down with you inside it. We all heard her.'

'Maybe.'

'Oh, come on, Virg. It's got to be her.'

'No' necessarily. It could have been Lucas Blair or this gang of robbers.'

'The gang of robbers has no reason to do this to you. All you did was get Gordon in your car and drive off. Lucas and Ember are much more likely culprits. My money's on Ember.'

'I cannae see her buying petrol, tipping it all over the van and setting it alight. She might singe her hair or break a nail,' he said determinedly. He had no idea what he would do if his own wife was responsible for taking so much from him just for her own selfish needs.

'Wow, you sound really sexist. A woman is just as capable of starting a fire as a man.'

Virgil raised an eyebrow. 'When did you become a feminist?'

'Rose has taught me a lot.' He smiled happily. 'Honestly, Virg, she's fucking amazing.'

'So I believe,' he said, relieved at the change in subject.

'Some women would have dumped me for losing to Morgan, but no' her. She thought I was brave for fighting my own brother.'

'Brave and stupid,' replied Virgil, earning himself a scowl.

The brothers returned home and called a family meeting in their mother's house. As they got out of the car, Virgil took the geranium from Warren and placed it in a sunny spot in the garden.

'You really love that thing, don't you?' Warren frowned when Virgil stood there, smiling down at the little plant.

'Don't call it a thing,' Virgil shot back. 'Plants can hear you, you know.'

Warren's jaw fell open as his brother headed inside their mother's house. It was hard to believe the man had beaten a boxing champion only the night before.

'Why can't I smell anything cooking?' said Warren as he followed Virgil inside.

'Because your gran's doing a tarot reading in the lounge,' replied Maria, who was sitting at the kitchen table, reading a magazine.

'But I'm starving.'

'Then make yourself something. You're a grown man.'

'The stuff I make never tastes any good.' He sighed, sinking into a chair.

'Then you obviously need more practice.' Maria looked up and frowned. 'Why do you both smell of smoke?'

'Virg's caravan burnt down.'

Maria looked to her older son in astonishment. 'What? I'm so sorry, Virgil.'

'Really?' he replied, scepticism in his tone.

'Of course. I may want you living back here but that doesnae mean I wanted that to happen. I know it meant a lot to you.'

'Thanks, Maw,' he said, taking the chair opposite her.

'Can it be saved?'

He shook his head. 'It's been gutted.'

'Such a shame. How did it start?'

'I'm no' sure yet. The firefighters smelled petrol, so they brought in a fire investigation officer. He's up there now, looking over the scene.'

'Arson?' she said, eyebrows shooting up.

Virgil nodded.

'My money's on Ember,' said Warren. 'Show Maw the note, Virg.'

Virgil did and Maria's face twisted with rage. 'The vindictive wee bitch,' she hissed, crushing the piece of paper in her hand.

'We don't know that it was Ember,' said Virgil. 'It could be Lucas Blair.'

'Lucas Blair, my arse. It's her. I can feel it in my water.'

'I don't want to accuse her without being certain.'

'I know you still love her, even though you're divorcing her, so don't let sentiment get in the way of justice.'

'Justice? What do you suggest I do? Beat her up? Because that's no' me.'

'No, of course not. I would never condone any of you raising a hand to a woman, no matter how insane. I'll sort her out,' she said, eyes narrowing.

'Let's just wait and see what the fire investigation officer comes back with first. It might no' even be arson,' said Virgil, still too overwhelmed by everything he'd just lost to consider the issue too deeply.

'All right, that does sound sensible. Did you find out anything from Sharon?' she asked Warren.

'Aye, she gave us some good information on Mick Jones.'

Before he could speak further, Maria held up her hand for him to be quiet. There came the sound of the lounge door opening followed by Ludovica talking. A tearful female voice answered her in return and then they heard the front door open and then close. A few seconds later, Ludovica entered the kitchen.

'What's burned down?' she asked.

'How did you know that?' replied Warren. 'Is it the smell of smoke?'

'No. A fire came up during the tarot reading. I knew the message was for me, but poor Philomena panicked and insisted on leaving to check on her house. She is a silly, skittish creature.'

Virgil related the saga of his caravan to his grandmother, who also sympathised with him, saying how sorry she was.

'I guess you've got what you wanted now,' said Virgil. 'Me back in Garthamlock permanently.'

Maria's expression turned frosty. 'I hope you're no' blaming us for this?'

'No, of course not but, you have to admit, it has worked out conveniently for you.'

'So you're no' going to replace the caravan then?'

'I don't know yet. There's no point if I'm gonnae be staying here, but the site still feels like my true home.'

'You don't even have the money to replace it,' said Maria with cold disdain.

'But I know a way I could get it.'

'No, Virg,' began Warren.

'Silence,' Maria told him before looking back at Virgil. 'What do you mean, you could get it?'

Virgil then went on to tell her about John Simpson's offer.

'Don't you think it's dodgy?' Warren asked his mother and grandmother after his brother had finished explaining.

Maria shrugged. 'It could be legitimate.'

'I'm gonnae hear John out,' said Virgil. 'I'm interested in what he has to say.'

'I don't get you,' said Warren. 'First you're saying you'll never fight again and now you're considering any dodgy old offer.'

'Because I need the money to replace my caravan.'

Maria's lips pinched. 'I thought this would encourage you to realise that your real home is here.'

'My home still feels to be back at Milngavie,' he countered.

'Maw, will you please talk some sense into him?' said Maria. 'Surely this fire is a sign from above that he belongs here, with his family.'

'Virgil is in control of his own destiny,' replied Ludovica. 'And you must respect that.'

When it appeared that Maria was going to argue further with

her mother, Ludovica gave her the full force of her dark, beady stare and Maria backed down.

'Fine,' she said, waving a hand at her son. 'Do as you wish but don't come crying to us if Warren is right and this John has an ulterior motive for offering you this fight. Besides, what if Toni finds out?'

'So what if she does?' he exclaimed. 'She doesnae own me.'

'She might no' like one of her fighters partaking in someone else's match.'

'I'm no' one of her fighters. I just happened to replace Newton, that's all.'

'Still, it might upset her. She doesnae see things the way the rest of us do.'

'You're saying I need to ask her permission if I do go ahead with it?'

His mother's response was an unhelpful shrug.

'See what the others say,' Warren told him. He looked to his gran. 'I'm really hungry, Nonna.'

She planted her big hands on the table and pushed herself to her feet. 'Then I will cook,' she announced.

'You should let him make something for himself, Madre,' said Maria. 'He relies on you far too much.'

'I like cooking for my boys and watching them enjoy my food.' She smiled, pinching Warren's cheek so hard he grimaced. 'It is my main pleasure in life.'

'You shouldnae take Nonna's pleasures from her, Maw,' Warren joked.

One by one the rest of the brothers returned to the house. By the time they were all settled around the table, Ludovica was dishing up a variety of delicious dishes along with some bread she'd made just that morning.

'This looks smashing, Nonna.' Warren smiled before eagerly tucking into some lasagne.

As they ate, Virgil told them all what Sharon had related about Mick Jones.

'Why didn't you go and see him straightaway?' said Newton.

'We were sidetracked by my caravan burning to the ground, so we had to head over to the site instead.' Virgil then told his brothers everything, including John Simpson's offer.

'You should take him up on that,' said Morgan.

'Warren thinks John could be luring me into a trap.'

'Maybe but if he's not then you could be passing up the chance to make a ton of cash.'

'We'll discuss that later,' said Maria. 'First, we need to talk about Mick Jones. If his crew are behind the attempted robbery on Gordon then he could come for our family.'

'Let's burst into his hoose and twat the lot of them,' said Wyatt eagerly.

'Amen to that,' replied Morgan.

'He has machetes and all sorts of other weapons stashed all around his home,' said Virgil.

'Then we tackle him somewhere else.'

'If he's no' behind it then we might force him to retaliate and that will bring us a whole fresh heap of shite to deal with. I think we're better working with Big Billy and setting a trap for whoever's watching him.'

'What if he's just paranoid and no one's watching him?'

'Big Billy's no' stupid.'

'Is he likely to go for it?' said James.

'Probably,' replied Virgil. 'Despite what he said, I don't think he wants to risk getting beaten up and robbed. We can see him this evening at the pub. I've got to visit Nick soon and ask him if Henry's backed off.'

'The Allans could have set fire to your caravan,' said Newton.

'I doubt it. They don't even know about it.'

'You assume.'

'It's possible, I suppose. I'll bear it in mind.'

Virgil hated conceding that Newton could be right about anything but he was forced to admit that he was speaking sense. He wasn't sure he could ever forgive him for sleeping with Nick's girlfriend when their brother was so fragile. If he could do that, what was to stop him from sticking the knife into the rest of their backs?

* * *

Virgil was relieved that Nick seemed much improved. His little brother had more colour in his cheeks and his eyes were brighter.

'Well, you look much better,' said Virgil as Nick took the chair opposite him.

'Henry and his crew have backed off. Whatever you did, it worked, so thanks.'

'Nae problem. I hope they stay away too.'

'I think they will. I heard Danny got a finger snapped.'

'Aye. That was Newton.' He frowned.

'Good on him.' Nick smiled. 'But that's no' the best news. Debbie came to see me this morning.'

'That's great,' replied Virgil, forcing a smile.

'She said she still does love me; it was just hurting her seeing me in this place, but she's promised to wait for me and she'll be there when I'm released.'

'Brilliant. So I hope that means you'll kick the drugs now you know you've still got Debbie?'

'Aye. I want to be the man she deserves.'

'You already are that man, but I'm glad to hear you're kicking the habit.'

'Everyone's talking in here about your fight with Callum Young. I've gone up a hell of a lot in all the men's estimations. Some of the top dogs in here have warned off Henry and his crew, saying they'll kill them if they touch me, so I've got double protection.'

'That's a relief, and the next thing you know, you'll be out of here. Just keep your heid down and don't do anything to piss off the governor.'

'I will, Virg, I promise.'

'Good.'

Nick glanced at someone entering the room and nodded their way. 'That's Henry Allan.'

Virgil immediately saw the likeness between Henry and his father Stan. Although Henry wasn't as obese, he was still very round around the middle and he was losing his hair. He looked more like Stan's brother than his older son, the man having aged prematurely, prison no doubt contributing to that. Henry glowered at the brothers before sitting down opposite a frail, grey-haired old lady.

'That's Henry's gran,' Nick told Virgil.

Henry said something to the old woman, who then glared their way, her look so furious it was almost satanic.

'Jeezo, I bet she could give Nonna a run for her money,' said Virgil.

'She's a nasty old bag,' said Nick. 'She's had to be warned several times by the prison officers for shouting and swearing. Once she even went for another inmate who'd had a row with Henry and set about him with her handbag. I'm amazed they let her back in.'

'She's still glaring at us.'

'Because she's crazy.'

With one final haughty look, Granny Allan turned her attention back to Henry.

'If Nonna was here she'd say she'd cast the evil eye on us,' said Nick.

'I wouldn't be surprised if she had.'

* * *

Virgil left the prison feeling happier. Nick was definitely doing much better and with a bit of luck he'd kick the drugs before he was released.

As he reached his car, he saw Granny Allan climbing into a taxi just outside the prison gates. The driver leapt out to open the back door for her, clearly familiar with the ways of this particular customer. Before getting in, she paused to look back at Virgil, treating him to another death stare so potent he felt a chill run down his spine. Then she climbed into the taxi, breaking the spell. As the car rolled down the street, the old woman continued to glare at Virgil through the window, eye contact only being broken when the vehicle turned the corner and disappeared.

'Creepy auld bat,' Virgil muttered to himself before getting into his own car.

* * *

On his return to Garthamlock, Virgil stopped by Debbie's house and told her that she'd better keep her promise to stand by Nick. She promised him that she would. Virgil could see the fear in her eyes, but he didn't attempt to reassure her. Fear would keep her with Nick and away from Newton.

The moment Virgil entered his mother's house, there was a cry from the direction of the kitchen.

'What's going on?' he demanded, racing deeper into the house, almost colliding with his grandmother as she rushed out of the kitchen door.

'Something is wrong,' she said, taking his face firmly between her hands, her grip so strong he could barely move his head.

'What are you doing, Nonna?' he demanded.

Maria and Newton also exited the kitchen. At the sight of his younger brother's face being squished between their grandmother's slab-like hands, Newton smiled, folded his arms across his chest and leant against the door frame to watch.

'What's going on, Madre?' Maria demanded of her mother.

'Malocchio,' she hissed. 'He's riddled with it. I don't understand, we have all visited that prison before and never returned like this. We need to deal with it immediately before it can cause any harm.'

Ludovica took Virgil by the ear and hauled him into the kitchen.

'There's no need for that, Nonna.' He grimaced. 'I'll come quietly.'

'If only all those people who saw you fight Callum Young could see you now.' Newton grinned.

'Shut it, you,' retorted Virgil.

To his relief, Ludovica released him and pointed to a chair at the table. 'Sit.'

Virgil obeyed, Maria and Newton watching as Ludovica produced the same white bowl she'd used before and repeated the test with the water and oil. The oil drops merged in the centre of the bowl rather violently.

'This is strong,' muttered Ludovica, shaking her head. 'I don't believe this malocchio was sent unintentionally. Whoever did it knew what they were doing.'

'It can't be Nick; he'd never do anything like that to his brother,' said Maria.

'It wasnae Nick,' replied Virgil. 'It was Henry Allan's gran. She was visiting him when I was there and she kept throwing me these really ugly looks. I saw her outside the prison too and she did the same thing. She's an evil old crone.'

'Did you feel anything when she was looking at you?' Ludovica asked him.

'Aye. She made me shiver.'

'Big bad Virgil MacGregor spooked by an auld biddy,' taunted Newton.

Ludovica clipped him hard around the back of the head.

'Ow,' he exclaimed, rubbing his head. 'There was no need for that.'

'There's every need,' retorted his grandmother. 'This is very powerful negative energy and should not be mocked.'

Ludovica then went through the routine with the scissors and the prayer to Archangel Michael, followed by the charm to remove malocchio. Virgil sighed with relief as the pressure behind his eyes that he hadn't even realised was there suddenly lifted.

'Feeling better?' said Ludovica knowingly.

'Aye, thanks, Nonna.'

She handed him a pair of scissors. 'Place these under your bed open, the points facing your feet. I have some desiccated seahorse for you to carry too. It will protect you against more malocchio because that woman is not finished with you; I can feel it. In fact, we can all carry some because I think she will target our entire family.'

'I am no' going around with a lump of dead seahorse in my pocket,' said Newton.

For once, Virgil found himself agreeing with his older brother.

'Fine, if you're going to be little girls about it then I have special keys you can carry instead. They will do the trick just as well.'

Ludovica produced a handful from a kitchen drawer and dumped them on the table. 'Take your pick while I place the broom at the front door to prevent the evil eye from entering our home.'

Determinedly, she grabbed the broom propped up in the corner of the room and stormed through the house with it towards the front door. Virgil selected his key and slipped it into his pocket while Newton regarded them with disdain.

'Pick a key, Newton,' Maria urged him.

'The whole thing's ridiculous.'

'No it's not and if you don't take a key then your nonna will punish you.'

'Fine, I'll take one,' he muttered, picking one at random while Maria selected her own.

Ludovica returned to the kitchen and regarded them all suspiciously. 'I hope you've all selected a key?'

The three of them nodded.

'Good. Keep it with you always. I want to know more about this Granny Allan,' she said, taking a seat at the table. 'What can you tell me?'

'No' much,' replied Virgil. 'I only saw her for the first time today. Nick did say that she's pretty aggressive. She started battering another prisoner who'd got into a row with Henry with her handbag and the prison officers had to escort her out. They let her back in though.'

'Probably because they were too afraid to keep her out. They know there is something strange and frightening about her. I will make my own enquiries. I think it would be wise to find out as much as possible about Granny Allan.'

* * *

That evening, Virgil headed over to The Big Hoose with James, Morgan and Warren, who was feeling stronger. Newton and Wyatt were on another bodyguarding job for a local drug dealer.

Big Billy was behind the bar, serving a couple of customers in his usual surly way.

'I've been graced with your presence twice in one day,' he said when he saw the MacGregor brothers approaching the bar. 'What have I done to deserve such an honour?'

'Can we have a word in private?' replied Virgil.

'Aye, I suppose, as long as you buy a round of drinks.'

James, Warren and Morgan ordered pints while Virgil opted for another orange juice.

'Come on through to the office,' the landlord told them. 'Oy, Dezzie,' he called to the young man at the other end of the bar who was staring at his phone. 'Dezzie, ya daft wee sod,' he added when the man failed to reply. 'Wake up before I scoosh you with the post mix again.'

The younger man's head snapped up. 'Aye. Billy?' he eagerly asked him.

'It's Big Billy, ya fanny. I'm gonnae be in conference and I don't want to be disturbed. Watch the bar.'

'Will do, Boss.'

Big Billy gave him a curt nod before leading the MacGregor brothers through a side door and into a chaotic room that was overflowing with piles of books stacked on the floor, cardboard boxes and heaps of clothes. Shoes were also scattered about the place.

Big Billy shoved a heap of clothes to the floor that was piled up on the chair behind the desk and took a seat.

'Sit down, boys, if you can find anywhere.' He chuckled.

'You living out of your office?' Morgan asked him.

'Naw, I'm just a messy bastard. My cleaning lady's always having a go at me; she says it makes her job a hell of a lot harder, the whinging coo that she is.'

Warren managed to find a stool to perch on, leaving his brothers to stand.

'So, boys,' said Big Billy. 'What do you want to discuss?'

'We want to set a trap,' replied Virgil. 'We believe whoever's watching you could be linked to the crew that tried to rob Gordon Maitland.'

'Why do you think that?'

'Call it a hunch.'

'What are you, a fucking polis?'

'Fine. We can leave you to get your takings stolen. It's no skin off our noses. Let's go,' he told his brothers.

'Just hold it right there,' said Big Billy when they all made for the door. 'Fine, you've called my bluff. I'm due to go to the bank tomorrow afternoon, as it happens. You can set your trap then.'

'Perfect,' said Virgil.

'How will you work it?'

'We'll hide outside the pub and see if anyone approaches you when you come out. Do you always go to the bank alone?'

'Aye, unless you count the cosh in my pocket.'

'Good. Then they won't be expecting anyone else to be there.'

'Any idea who it is yet?'

'We do have a suspect but we're hoping this will confirm it. What time will you leave for the bank?'

'One o'clock.'

'Then we'll get here at eleven. The gang will probably arrive early too and we want to beat them to it.'

'Fair enough. You'll be the ones hanging around like spare pricks, no' me. What do I need to do?'

'Nothing. Just go to the bank at one o'clock like you normally would and leave the rest to us. It would be a good idea if you leave the takings in the safe and fill whatever bag you normally transport them in with something else in case the plan goes bad.'

'Well, that's reassuring,' he muttered.

12

Brian, Lucas Blair's bodyguard, opened the front door of his home when someone knocked. One side of his face was covered in a large bruise from Virgil's fist.

'No' you,' he sighed when he saw Ember standing on the doorstep. 'Why don't you piss off? You've brought the boss nothing but misery.'

'Ask Lucas about the last time I saw him. He wasn't miserable then.' She smiled. 'Now, why don't you run along like the obedient wee poodle you are and tell him I'm here. I want to talk to the big man, no' his fucking monkey.'

'You mouthy bitch,' he spat. 'Do you know what happens to tarts like you?'

He took a hasty step back when she produced one of her small knives. 'And do you know what happens to people who don't do what I want?'

Brian glared at her but, before he could retort, Lucas's voice echoed from inside the house.

'Who's there, Brian?'

'Ember MacGregor,' he called.

'Why are you keeping her on the doorstep? Let her in.'

Brian grudgingly stepped aside to allow Ember to enter. She was pleased to note that he was limping after being thrown against the bar by Virgil.

'Good boy.' She smiled before striding inside, leaving him to slam the door shut in anger.

Lucas was stretched out on the couch drinking a cup of tea. The bruises to his face had turned an ugly yellow colour, but he appeared less swollen. His injured arm was still in a cast and rested on his chest.

'Hello, Ember,' he said. 'You're looking as beautiful as ever. Splitting up with that prick appears to agree with you.'

'I feel like a new woman,' she replied.

'I bet you do. Would you like a brew or something stronger?'

'No, thanks. What I would like is to talk to you.' She gave Brian a pointed look. 'In private.'

Brian looked to his boss, who nodded.

'Fine, I'm going,' muttered the bodyguard. 'I don't want to be around if your psycho husband turns up again.'

With that he left the room and headed into the front garden so he could keep an eye on his boss through the window.

'Don't mind him,' Lucas told Ember. 'He's still hurting after being thrown against my bar. His back's covered in bruises. I think it hurt his pride more than anything.' A nervous look came into Lucas's eyes. 'Virgil doesnae know you're here, does he?'

'Of course not. He'll be far too busy crying over his caravan. It mysteriously burnt down yesterday.'

'I wondered who would do something so terrible.'

The two of them smiled knowingly at each other.

'I must say I'm surprised,' said Ember. 'I had thought if you were going to give an order like that, you'd ensure Virgil was trapped inside it before starting the fire.'

Lucas's smile dropped. 'Hang on, you think I did it?'

'Yes. Why, didn't you?'

'No. I thought it was you. I have been planning some sort of revenge on Virgil but burning down a shitey caravan didnae seem enough.'

'So who did it then?'

'Nae idea but we should find them and thank them. Now, why don't you sit down, hen?' he said, patting the couch.

Ember perched on the edge and smiled at him.

'Did you come here about Virgil's caravan burning down, or something else?' said Lucas, resting his hand on her knee.

Ember picked up his hand and placed it on his own lap. 'I didnae come for that.'

'Oh, I see. You're waiting until I'm back at full strength.'

'I just came here to talk.'

'You've changed your tune. I thought we'd finally made some progress back at the hospital.'

'We've more urgent matters to deal with.'

'Such as?'

'Making sure I get everything in the divorce. Virgil wants to sell our house and split the profits, if there are any, but I don't want to leave my home. Why should I be forced out of my house just because he's decided he doesn't want to be married to me any more?'

'You're right, doll, it's no' fair. The man must be mad to leave a cracker like you.'

'I need your help to ensure I keep my home.'

'What can I do? This is private business between husband and wife. You're better talking to a good solicitor.'

'I already have one but unfortunately he insists on no' breaking the law. I need a man who can get things done, who's no' afraid of Virgil and his family, and I know that man's you,' she said, leaning into him, her breasts pressing against his chest.

Lucas coloured and cleared his throat. 'You know I'll do whatever I can to help you, doll, but I really don't want to get stuck in the middle of a divorce.'

'So you won't help me?' she said, pressing herself harder against him.

'I... I didnae say that,' he breathed.

'It sounded like you did,' she pouted, hand sliding down to his crotch.

'No, I didnae. You know I'll do anything to help you, sweetheart.'

They both looked to the window at the sound of a knock and saw Brian staring in at them with disapproval.

'Don't let her talk you into anything, Boss,' he called through the glass. 'Whatever she's planning will go bad for you.'

Ember got up, stomped across the room and yanked the curtains closed.

'There,' she said, returning to Lucas. 'All alone.'

She kissed him and he wrapped his good arm around her and pulled her tight against him. Ember thought it was fortunate he had an injured arm otherwise she would have found it very difficult to escape his grip, which she did, sitting up and smoothing down her hair.

'I don't get you,' exclaimed Lucas. 'You keep blowing hot and cold. What the fuck's going on?'

'I can't yet because I'm still married to Virgil.'

'So what? You're getting a divorce; you're a free agent.'

'Not in the eyes of the Lord.'

Lucas gaped at her. 'I never had you pinned as a Bible basher.'

'I am not a Bible basher,' she retorted. 'I just take my vows seriously. I could never give myself to another man while I'm still married to Virgil.'

Lucas sighed and dragged his good hand down his face, willing away his straining erection. 'But a divorce could take months, sometimes even years if it's dragged out.'

'Ours won't take years; it's not like we have a lot of property to dispose of. Just a few months at the most.'

'I cannae wait months for you.'

'Why not? You've already waited years.'

Lucas sighed resignedly. 'What can I do to make your divorce go through faster?'

'I want Virgil distracted, not thinking clearly. That will give me the advantage. You and your men need to keep him busy. Harass him, cause him some trouble but nothing too severe.'

'Why, so he can go into one of his rages and kick the living shite out of us all again? You're also forgetting that I've got my new deal to concentrate on and my business partner is no' someone I want to piss off.'

'You can say Toni's name; I do already know you made your deal with her and, by the way, if you think you're equal partners then you're wrong. She will always be the dominant one.'

'I don't care. She's making me a hell of a lot of money.'

Her eyebrows rose. 'Really?'

'I thought that would grab your interest. You always did want the high life, didn't you, doll? You used to dream about living in a big mansion with a fancy motor on the drive, all those five-star foreign holidays. Tell me, Ember, how many mansions, fancy cars and foreign holidays has Virgil given you?' He smiled when she frowned. 'Oh,' he continued. 'I forgot about the holiday to Blackpool he took you on.'

'What are you trying to say, Lucas?'

'That I can finally give you everything you want. You're so

close to fulfilling all those dreams of yours, Ember. The only thing standing in your way is your husband.'

'Not for much longer, but you need to help me, Lucas, if you want that life with me.'

'I do, more than anything,' he said, taking her hand and kissing it.

'Then you need to mess with Virgil.'

'Don't worry, I know exactly how to do that and the best thing is he won't see it coming. Stick with me, sweetheart, and you won't go wrong. Now, how about a little fun like we had back at the hospital? Your vows didnae stop you then.'

Ember repeated what she'd done for Lucas in his hospital room, the act easier for her this time as she was now sure she'd got him onside. All she had to do was string him along until she'd got her revenge on Virgil. However, she was also starting to look at Lucas in a different way. He was right: he could give her everything she'd ever wanted. He would never rock her world like Virgil but perhaps that shouldn't be her priority any more?

* * *

Virgil struggled sleeping that night. So much had happened in just a day and, if he was honest with himself, it had left him reeling. He tried not to think about his caravan; it was too painful. The thought that Ember had been responsible for burning it down kept haunting him, but he would not condemn her without any proof. He also had the fire investigation officer to contend with. What if he was blamed for the fire? The fact that the caravan wasn't insured went greatly in his favour because it meant he had no motive to burn it down.

The next thing Virgil knew it was daylight. Glancing at the

clock, he saw it was half eight in the morning. At least he'd got some sleep.

After showering and dressing, he headed into his mother's kitchen where all his brothers were already gathered, tucking into breakfast. They'd never been ones for lying in late. Their father had always been an early riser and he'd drummed that into his boys. Anyone who hadn't been out of bed by eight thirty had a bucket of cold water thrown over them. Virgil watched his brothers eating the food their grandmother and mother had prepared for them and it suddenly seemed ridiculous to him. None of them had even considered moving into their own place. They seemed to think that living in the houses either side of the family home meant they were independent, but they still came here for all their meals and to get their laundry done. Overgrown children pretending to be grown-ups. Before moving out, Virgil had never seen anything wrong with it. His perspective had changed once he'd married Ember and left home.

'You're up late.' Maria frowned disapprovingly.

'Sorry, I slept badly,' he replied, taking the spare chair between Wyatt and Warren. 'I had so much going through my mind.'

'That is no excuse. If your father was here, he would have drenched you in cold water.'

'Aye, I know,' he muttered, pissed off about being chastised like he was still a little kid.

'We need to work out how we're gonnae handle this job today,' said Newton. 'James has got me and Wyatt up to speed seeing how you were no' here to do it.'

'Good, then I don't need to go over it again.'

'Have you come up with a plan?' said Morgan.

'It's simple. We'll split into pairs and hide in various spots outside the pub. If this gang shows up, then we beat the shite out of them.'

Newton's look was withering. 'And if this gang is Mick Jones and his pals, who we know are tooled up, what then? Do we take weapons of our own?'

'I don't think that's a good idea. If we get caught with them by the polis, we could end up getting sent down.'

'So you want us to face a violent, armed gang with nothing but our fists. Is that what you're saying?'

Virgil's eyes blazed. 'If anyone's got a better idea then feel free to speak up,' he snapped back. 'I'm sick of all the responsibility being put on my shoulders. You're all just as capable as I am, so someone else come up with a fucking plan. Well?' he added when no one spoke. 'Have you all gone fucking mute? You're always complaining that you're the oldest, Newton, that you should be the one leading us all. Well, here's your chance. What?' he barked when someone tapped him on his right shoulder. He turned and saw his grandmother staring back at him with hard, cold eyes. In one hand she held a bowl of cereal. 'Oh, sorry, Nonna. I didnae mean to shout at you.'

With a glare, she dumped his bowl before him, slopping milk onto the table before stomping back over to the stove.

'You're right, Virg,' said James. 'I suppose we do put too much responsibility on your shoulders. It should be up to us all to come up with a plan, no' just you.'

Virgil rolled his eyes when his brothers all looked at each other blankly. He was starting to see why his mother had wanted him to come back.

'It is difficult,' said Maria, saving them all from having to speak. 'On the one hand, you don't want to face armed men without weapons and on the other, you don't want to be arrested.'

'We tackled Gary Wilson and his bawbags without weapons when they were armed and that went well for us,' said Morgan.

'Gary's a fud,' replied James. 'He'll never be as big a threat as this crew.'

'We need to assume this gang are very dangerous,' said Newton. 'It's the sensible thing to do. If they do turn out to be a bunch of disorganised fannies, then all the better for us.'

Virgil sat back as his brothers continued to talk, content to let them come up with a plan. He had enough on his mind.

After much discussion, they finally decided on a plan of attack. Morgan and Warren had a reputation for being good at fixing cars. People often came to them for help rather than pay a garage, consequently they often carried tools around in the boots of their cars. The two brothers would visit the spots they would hide in to wait for the gang and plant wrenches and screwdrivers there, that way the brothers couldn't be caught carrying them about the streets. Virgil was pleased; it was a sensible idea and he hadn't come up with any of it.

Just as breakfast ended, the fire investigation officer turned up. Virgil led him straight into the lounge so they could talk in private.

'Bad news, I'm afraid,' opened John. 'Petrol was used to start the fire. Someone broke in and poured it in every room, leaving a trail throughout the caravan. Whoever it was knew what they were doing; they used it for maximum effect, ensuring the caravan would be completely destroyed.'

'Shit,' breathed Virgil, grinding the palms of his hands together. 'I was hoping the firefighter I spoke to was wrong.'

'Unfortunately not. As it was arson, the case has been handed over to the polis.'

'Is that necessary? I just want to move on with my life and forget about it.'

'There's no choice. The site owners want this investigating too. We want to make sure this is an isolated incident and no' a case of a serial arsonist with a grudge. The time of day the fire was started is very telling. Whoever was responsible knew the other residents would be in the clubhouse, leaving them free to get to work. That indicates inside knowledge. The polis will be around soon to talk to you.'

'Marvellous,' muttered Virgil, thinking of the job they were going on that very day. What terrible timing.

'In a way, it's lucky you didnae have insurance, as it means you don't have a motive for burning down the caravan.'

'I suppose. It's worrying though. If this isn't the work of a serial arsonist and someone is targeting me, what's to stop them from coming here and setting fire to this place too?'

'It is something to consider. Speaking of considering, have you thought about my offer?'

'I'd like a bit more information first.'

'Fire away. Sorry, no pun intended.' John grinned.

Virgil didn't like that smile; there was something strange about it.

'Two fighters and five rounds, just like at the other underground fights,' said John. 'Don't worry, I won't ask you to fight one of your brothers. It will be fighters of my own choosing.'

'Who are these other fighters?'

'We have a few Eastern Europeans. There's a couple of savage Irish fighters who work for us regularly and an English lad too.'

'No other locals?'

'Toni McVay snapped up the best of the local talent.'

Virgil's eyes filled with suspicion. 'What is this, some sort of sting operation? Are you working for the polis?'

John laughed. 'You must be joking. Outside my professional life, I do my best to stay the hell away from them.'

Virgil wasn't sure he believed him. 'Why have you approached me if you don't use any local fighters?'

'Because my clients heard about your latest match against Callum Young. You can speak to Callum if you like; he's fought in our matches a few times. My clients want to see what you can do for themselves.'

The mention of Callum's name reassured Virgil a little. 'What's in it for me?'

'Thirty grand per fight. Double if you win. You can buy another wee caravan with all that.' John smiled at the surprise in Virgil's eyes. 'That's much more than Toni pays, isn't it?'

'Have you considered what she'd do if she found out about your matches?'

'Other people organise their own underground fights and she doesnae bother them.'

'I suspect those other people aren't raking in as much money as you are.'

'That's because I was sensible and rounded up the richest clients. Toni lets in any low-order bastard with a bit of cash. My fights are VIP events. Only a privileged few are allowed in and the betting gets wild. One of the Irish fighters walked away with just a few quid shy of a hundred grand a couple of weeks ago.'

Virgil tried to ignore the voice that whispered at the back of his mind that such a huge sum would get him back his peaceful life in the countryside. 'I take it these fights are no-holds barred?'

'Aye. Absolutely anything is allowed, even eye-gouging. I'll be up front with you, a fighter from Poland lost an eye a few months back. The only thing that's banned is an outright kill. We don't want to be clearing away any bodies. I have men on standby who split things up if it looks like a fight's going too far.'

'Has it ever gone too far?'

'Naw. I don't employ animals. I choose fighters no' just for their physical skills but their mental ones too. That's why I want to recruit you. I've heard how smart you are.'

'Toni will probably expect me to fight for her again.'

'Aye, and I don't have a problem with it. You won't work exclusively for me. Besides, if the Queen of Glasgow's happy then everyone else is happy too.'

'Do you want my brothers involved in this?'

'I havenae been asked for them. So far, it's just you. We can see how you get on and take it from there.'

Virgil was thinking of replacing his caravan and fighting for a divorce that Ember may contest. Solicitors weren't cheap and this was money he wouldn't have to declare to the taxman. 'I'll do it.'

'Great.' John smiled. 'The fight's arranged for ten o'clock tomorrow night at this place,' he added, holding out a card.

Virgil took it from him and saw there was just a number and a postcode printed on it.

'Knock three times and ask for me,' added John.

'My brothers will want to see this,' said Virgil.

'Fine, bring them along but don't fetch the whole clan, will you? These events are quiet and understated. Don't bring more than two of them with you. I should stress that my clients are rather cultured, so they don't appreciate...'

'You're saying bring the least neddy of my brothers?'

John smiled. 'Aye. Nae offence.'

'None taken – I understand.'

'I'm glad you've agreed to this; it's a great opportunity for you. In the meantime, I'll see what I can do to get the polis to go easy on you. I know the detective who's been put on the case: DS Twining. He's an ambitious wee sod and will do anything to advance his career but we're good pals and he won't go all in on you if I ask him not to.'

'Why, does he go to your fights?'

'Aye, he loves a good flutter and the adrenaline of a no-holds-barred match. He won't be there tomorrow night though because he's working.'

'I thought only rich people were invited to your fights?'

'A polis is a very useful thing. He gives us protection. Play your cards right and the arson case will go nowhere.'

'I understand.'

'Great. Well, I'll see you tomorrow night then,' said John, getting to his feet. 'And don't be late. My clients hate tardiness.'

Virgil escorted John to the front door. He closed it behind him and turned, almost jumping when he found the entire family congregated in the hallway behind him.

'Jesus,' he gasped.

'What did he say?' asked Maria.

'That it was definitely arson. Petrol was found inside the caravan.'

'Does he know who did it?'

'No. The case has been handed over to the polis.'

'Did he mention the match he wanted you to fight in?' said Morgan.

'He did and it's tomorrow night.'

'You agreed?' said Maria.

'I'd have been mad to turn it down. He was offering big money.'

'How big?'

'Thirty grand per fight. Sixty grand for a win. One fighter recently won a hundred grand.'

'So much for your principles,' said Newton.

'What choice do I have? I want to replace my caravan and I'm about to divorce a very vindictive woman, so I need to pay a good solicitor.'

'What's the big deal with the divorce? It's no' like you've weans or a load of cash to think about.'

'Ember could try for spousal maintenance,' said Warren. 'A pal of mine got hit pretty hard by that. It cost him a fortune while the divorce was going through. The good news is it ends when the divorce is finalised but the cow he was divorcing dragged everything out so she could get as much from him as possible. When it was over, he didnae have a pot to piss in.'

'And Ember's vicious enough to do that to you, Virg,' said Wyatt.

'Good luck to her,' replied Virgil. 'I barely have anything.'

'I'm just saying, divorces can lead to a lot of trouble,' said Warren. 'I think it's smart getting some cash behind you.'

'Yes, but what do we know about these fights?' said Maria, addressing this question to Virgil.

'Only what John told me,' he replied. 'They sound very similar to the ones Toni runs, except the people who watch his fights are rich. He only lets in a select clientele.'

'And he told you nothing else?'

Virgil shook his head.

Maria tilted her head down in warning. 'Don't lie to me, Virgil.'

'Fine. He said there are no limits in these fights. You can do what you like to each other as long as you don't kill your opponent. Anything else goes.'

'I don't like that at all. Even Toni has rules for her fights, certain things the fighters cannae do.'

'Aye, but sixty grand, Maw,' said Morgan.

'Sixty grand is not worth being maimed for life.'

'That won't happen.'

'You can't possibly know that.'

'The fight's tomorrow night and I promised John I'd be there,' said Virgil.

'Excellent.' Morgan smiled.

'What is this?' exclaimed Maria. 'One minute you're refusing to fight anyone and the next you're selling your soul to the first person to wave a lot of money before your face. What is happening to you, Virgil?'

'Nae idea,' he sighed. 'All I know is I could really use the cash. It wouldnae be so bad if my caravan hadn't burnt down. Anyway, we need to make tracks and get into position before that gang show up at The Big Hoose.'

'Virgil, we need to discuss this more,' said Maria as he made for the door, his brothers following.

'I don't have time.'

'Virgil...'

Without another word, he pulled open the door and stalked outside, his brothers following.

'I do hope you were nothing to do with his caravan burning down,' Ludovica told her daughter once the men had gone.

Maria regarded her with surprise. 'Why on earth do you think I might be? Can you honestly see me going to that sordid wee site with a petrol can?'

'No but I can see you paying someone else to do it.'

'I have never been so insulted.'

'Please don't act innocent with me. If you didn't arrange for it to happen then I know that you are pleased it has. You'll be disappointed though if you think losing his caravan will make Virgil stay in Garthamlock. He's different.'

'He's turning back into the old Virgil.'

'The old Virgil would not have walked out when you said you wanted him to stay and talk. The old Virgil would have obeyed and listened. Whoever burned down his caravan has created a brand-new man, one even stronger than the old one. You have no sway over him any more and neither does Ember. He's a law unto himself and I fear what this means, not just for him but for us all.'

'You're right, he is different, but I will get him back under my control.'

Ludovica chuckled and shook her big head. 'You'll be wasting your time. He won't listen. You would be wiser to accept this new Virgil and try and work with him because you will lose if you fight him. It is much better to accept the change.'

'I accept nothing,' Maria hissed back.

'True wisdom is choosing the battles you can win.'

'I never back down from a fight, no matter the odds.'

'You sound just like Jimmy. That is something foolish he would say. Very well, try and fight Virgil. It will only lead to misery,' said Ludovica before heading back into the kitchen, leaving Maria to plot how she would crush the rebellion out of her son.

* * *

Virgil had elected to team up with James for this particular job, so the two of them were watching the street below from the window of a first-floor flat close to The Big Hoose owned by a friend of Morgan's. This gave the two men a bird's eye view of the street. They could see Newton and Wyatt crouched behind a transit van. Morgan and Warren were out of view in some bushes on the wasteland opposite the pub.

'I'm hoping this is all in Big Billy's imagination and no one is watching him,' said James.

'You no' in the mood for a fight?' replied Virgil, eyes glued to the window.

'No' if we're facing off against people armed with machetes. I don't want to lose an arm.'

'Aye, we need to be careful. I hope the others don't get carried away.'

'While it's just the two of us here, aren't you worried about going to this exclusive fight tomorrow night?'

'A wee bit. I'm no' an idiot; I know I need to be careful. John said I could take two of my brothers with me. I want you and Newton to come.'

'Newton?' replied a surprised James.

'John said nae neds.'

'The others aren't neds. Well, maybe they are a wee bit,' added James when Virgil raised an eyebrow.

'Newton may be a dick but at least he can behave himself when he has to. Morgan and Warren will get carried away and Wyatt might get twitchy.'

'Fair enough.'

'Do you think I'm mad for going?'

'A wee bit but if this turns out to be everything John said it is then you could be onto a massive earner; but I thought money wasnae that important to you any more?'

'I'm an optimist, no' a daftie. Hey, Big Billy's coming out.'

The brothers watched as the landlord strode confidently out of the pub with a backpack slung over one shoulder. If he was worried a gang of robbers might attack him, he didn't show it.

Big Billy walked over to his car parked at the kerb. Producing the keys, he unlocked it, opened the door and got into the driver's seat.

'Looks like we won't see any action today,' said James.

The car started rocking violently from side to side. An arm had snaked around Big Billy's neck from the back seat and he was struggling furiously against it.

'Christ, they're in his car,' exclaimed Virgil.

The brothers tore out of the flat, downstairs and outside, racing towards the car but Morgan and Warren, who were closer, had almost reached it. Wyatt and Newton had also emerged from behind the transit van and were rushing to assist.

Morgan grabbed the handle of the rear driver's door and pulled but it refused to open. He drew back the wrench he held and smashed the window. Reaching inside, he grabbed the man who had his arm around Big Billy and attempted to drag him out of the car. The man released Big Billy to struggle furiously against Morgan.

Before any of the brothers could assist, more men rushed out of their own hiding places to tackle them.

'Holy shit, they've got machetes,' exclaimed Newton before raising the hammer he held to deflect a blow from one of the large blades.

When one man ran at Virgil, he grabbed him by the waist and threw him onto the bonnet of Big Billy's car. The man hit it with a loud bang, bounced off it and rolled to the ground, the machete falling from his hand. Virgil kicked the weapon down a drain.

'What did you do that for?' exclaimed Warren. 'We could have used that.'

'We don't use blades,' he retorted. 'Use your strength and speed against them.'

James followed his lead and threw one man against a lamp post. He then hastily snatched up the machete he'd dropped and sent it the same way as his friend's.

Big Billy hauled himself out of his car, tore open the backpack and pulled out a whip. Hooks were tied to the tail of the whip.

'What the fuck?' exclaimed James, leaping back as Big Billy

wielded the vicious weapon, cracking it through the air, the hooks scratching one man across the back, tearing through his clothes to the skin beneath and making him scream.

Big Billy cracked the whip again with all the dexterity of Indiana Jones and caught another man across the ribs, ripping his jumper, revealing deep scratches and torn skin.

Warren threw another man, who also bounced across the bonnet of Big Billy's car.

'Watch my fucking motor, ya dicks,' yelled the landlord.

When he cracked the whip once more, one of the masked men yelled at the others to run.

'Get 'em,' roared Virgil.

He and his brothers made chase, but the men leapt into two cars and sped off before they could reach them. Big Billy, however, doggedly continued the chase, waving his whip around in the air as he rushed after the cars.

'Try and rob me again, ya bastards, and I'll rip off your foreskins with this bad boy,' he yelled.

'Nasty.' Morgan grimaced.

The cars sped up and turned the corner with a screech of tyres, vanishing from view.

Big Billy, due to his enormous size and poor health, soon slowed to a sweating, panting halt.

'Take it easy, big man,' said Newton, patting his back when he doubled over to catch his breath.

'Well that was a waste of time,' said Wyatt. 'We've still nae idea who they are.'

'And how the fuck did they get into Big Billy's car?' said James.

'That's... what I... want to know,' gasped Big Billy. 'It's a... brand-new... motor.'

'Check it out, Morgan,' said Virgil. 'This is your area. You've broken into enough cars in the past.'

Morgan nodded and rushed to examine the car. 'There's no sign of force being used. Big Billy, does this car have keyless entry?'

'Aye,' he replied, finally catching his breath.

'I bet they used a relay transmitter and an amplifier to trick the car into thinking the key was near. But then again, they could have used car key code grabbing, compromised the on-board diagnostics or cloned the key.'

The others all blinked back at him blankly.

'I tell you, keyless car entry is shite,' continued Morgan. 'Have you taken the car to a garage recently?' he asked Big Billy.

'I had it valeted a couple of days ago,' he replied. 'I had nae choice, my wee nephew spewed his guts up in it.'

'Who did you use?'

'A mobile one. I didnae want to drive it stinking of puke.'

'Have you used them before?'

He nodded. 'A few times.'

'And did you leave the key with them?'

'Aye. Why, do you think it's him?'

'It's possible.'

'I'll kill him,' he seethed. 'I'll rip the fucking weasel's heid right off.'

'Take it easy, big man, we don't know that it is him yet. We can go and talk to him though.'

'Aye, I'll get you his business card.'

'I'm guessing the takings weren't in that bag?' said Virgil, nodding at the backpack Big Billy had discarded on the ground.

'Course not. I just stuck a couple of bricks in it to make it look like it contained some cash.'

The pub door swung open to reveal a rough-looking man in a tatty leather jacket and torn jeans.

'You coming back in, Big Billy?' he called. 'Only Dezzie's struggling to replace a barrel of lager.' He frowned, noting the spots of blood on the ground, the men's dishevelled appearances and the whip in the landlord's hand. 'What have you lot been up to?'

'Nothing,' said Big Billy. 'Get back inside and keep an eye on Dezzie. I'll be there in a minute.'

The man nodded and returned inside.

'You've earned yourselves a pint on the house,' Big Billy told the brothers. 'Come on in while I dig out that card for you.'

The MacGregors followed him inside, ranging around the bar while he headed into the office with his bloodied whip.

'Why did Big Billy just walk through here carrying a whip with hooks on?' Dezzie asked the brothers.

'He uses it on lazy barmen who don't know how to change a barrel,' replied Wyatt.

Dezzie paled. 'It's no' my fault. He's only shown me how to do it once and that was months ago.'

Wyatt chuckled when it looked like Dezzie was going to cry.

'Boss,' said Dezzie when Big Billy returned. 'I will get the hang of changing a barrel, honest. Please don't hurt me.'

Big Billy frowned. 'What the fuck are you on about, ya whinging wee fanny?'

'They said...' he began.

'Never mind what they said and pour the men their drinks, that's if the barrel's been changed.'

'Aye, I managed to do it. It took me a few goes but I got there in the end.'

'Good. Well don't just stand there,' he barked. 'Start pouring.'

Dezzie jumped and started hastily producing the glasses.

'Here you go,' said Big Billy, tossing a business card onto the bar.

'Thanks,' replied Virgil, picking it up and pocketing it. 'We'll get right on it.'

'Let me know as soon as you know, okay? If it is that wee bastard, then he'll be getting a visit from me.'

'Will do.'

'It's quite a common practice,' said Morgan. 'Garages and car valeters are given the keys without the customer thinking twice about it, so it's the perfect opportunity to clone the key.'

'Would you need to leave the key with a mobile valeter?' Virgil asked Big Billy.

'Aye,' he replied. 'He didnae wash it here, he did it outside my hoose because the missus needed it later that day, so I got a lift in here. He locked the car when he'd finished and posted the key through the letterbox.'

'Giving him plenty of time to clone it.'

'Aye. Bastard,' seethed Big Billy.

'Take it easy. Like we said, we're no' sure that's what's happened yet. The mobile valeter could be innocent.'

'No, he isnae.' Big Billy glowered. 'I can feel it in my water, but I'll leave it up to you lot to find out.'

13

After leaving The Big Hoose, the brothers drove off in Virgil and Morgan's cars and went to talk to Gordon.

The other brothers waited in the motors while Virgil, James and Newton went into the corner shop to ask Gordon if he'd had his car valeted recently. He said he'd had it cleaned by a mobile valeter three weeks ago. The business card he handed them matched the one Big Billy had given them.

After asking around their contacts, the brothers managed to track down the valeter's home address. This time, only Virgil and James went to the door. The woman who answered their knock said Reece was out on a job and she didn't know when he'd be back. They both thought the woman seemed rather wary of them and they weren't sure if that was because she was nervous about two strange men knocking on her door or because she knew her husband was involved in criminal activity.

'I reckon she knows exactly what he's up to,' said Virgil after he'd got back into his car with James.

'Then let's get it out of her,' replied Newton, who was sitting in the back seat.

'No. We don't do that to women,' retorted Virgil when Newton moved to open the door.

'You might have a problem with it but I don't.'

'You're no' laying a fucking finger on her,' snarled Virgil, turning in his seat to face him.

James shifted uneasily when Virgil and Newton exchanged glares, praying he wouldn't get caught in the middle of another of their fights.

'We cannae burst into the woman's house in broad daylight and rough her up,' said James in his calm, reasonable tone. 'We're better tracking down Reece.'

'How do you suggest doing that?' retorted Newton.

'We call the number on the card and book a valet,' said Virgil.

'Good idea.' James smiled, enjoying the annoyance on Newton's face. 'That sounds better than roughing up some wee woman.'

Virgil dialled the number, and the call was answered within a few rings. He gave his address and arranged for Reece to come to the house the next day to clean his car.

'Couldn't you have booked him sooner?' said Newton.

'No, he couldnae fit me in today. Luckily, he had a cancellation for tomorrow or we'd have to wait even longer. Now we need to go to Easthall to find out what this gang will do next,' said Virgil, starting the engine and setting off before Newton could object.

Virgil gripped the steering wheel hard as he drove, disheartened by how easily he was being dragged back into his old life. However, there was a part of himself that was enjoying it all, and he knew that dark seed would only continue to grow.

* * *

The brothers were never ones for sneaking around and subtlety, so they decided to make their presence felt in Easthall to see what happened. They freely wandered around the area, talking to the locals. They went into the convenience store before heading into the barber's a couple of doors down to get haircuts and chat to the staff. They even asked them about Mick Jones.

'You can talk to him yourself,' replied one of the barbers. 'Mick's due in here any minute for his shave.'

Sure enough, five minutes later a man entered the shop. He was very tall, standing at just under six foot three. His hair was wavy and jet black, slicked back at the front. His stubble was also black and his thick eyebrows were just a whisper away from becoming a monobrow. It was instantly clear he was a dangerous man; it showed in his brown eyes, which constantly flicked from side to side, assessing and seeking out weakness. His body, although lithe, was strong-looking, the tight black T-shirt he wore clinging to the muscles in his stomach and shoulders.

'Here he is now.' The barber smiled. 'This is Mick, boys.' He looked to Mick. 'These lads were asking about you.'

'Oh, aye,' he replied, studying one brother carefully before moving on to the next, taking his time.

'Nasty scratches on your arm,' commented Virgil, noting the fresh marks to Mick's forearm. 'It looks like you've been scratched by hooks.'

Mick's gaze locked with his, the corner of his mouth lifting. 'Aye, I went fishing,' he replied.

'Do you go *fishing* often?' said Virgil.

'As much as I can. I enjoy it.'

'You like the adrenaline?'

'Something like that. There's nothing like *fishing* to get the blood pumping.'

'I went fishing once,' said one of the barbers. 'It was really boring.'

'You're doing it wrong,' replied Mick with a diabolical smile. He looked back at Virgil. 'So, what are you lot doing in Easthall?'

'What does it look like?' replied Virgil, gesturing to his hair. He glanced in the mirror and frowned when he saw the barber had cut it a little shorter than he liked. 'No more off the top,' he said.

The barber nodded in understanding, put down the scissors, picked up the clippers instead and began tidying up the back.

'Bit of a strange place to come for a haircut, given how you live in Garthamlock,' said Mick.

'So you do know who we are?'

'You already know I do. You're The Bloody MacGregors.' Mick sank into the vacant chair beside Virgil. 'Just my usual shave, Ben.'

One of the barbers nodded, put down the scissors he was using to cut Warren's hair and turned his attention to him instead.

'Hey,' said Warren. 'You've no' finished with me yet.'

'I'll get back to you as soon as I've done Mick's shave,' he replied, wrapping a barber cape around Mick and fastening it at the back.

'That's no' right.'

'It is around here. Mick's in charge of this place, no' you.'

The door opened and seven more people piled inside: five men and two women. Some of them sported bruises and scratches to their faces, indicating they'd all been at the fight earlier. The last man to enter bolted the door and pulled the blind while one of the women pulled the large blind covering the window that looked out over the street. The barber shop was quite small, so it was a little cramped with so many bodies inside.

'We're no' all here,' said Mick. 'One of my men is in hospital having his back sewn up after what that mad bastard did to him with his whip.'

'I hope you're no' expecting us to feel sorry for him?' Morgan frowned.

'Nope,' said Mick casually, leaning back in his seat while the barber began lathering up his face. 'But I am pissed off that I'm a body down.'

'So fucking what?'

'I've got a big job coming up and I need a replacement. I want one of you to be that replacement. I've heard you lot are very capable and I've already seen that you're as hard as fuck. I don't care which one of you it is, just as long as one of you fills the vacancy you made. You'll get half my man's share, the other half will go to him.'

'We're no' doing it,' said Virgil.

He was watching the barber who'd been cutting his hair from the corner of his eye, who'd stood on his other side, thinking Virgil wasn't paying him any attention. Slowly the barber put down the clippers and picked up the scissors. As he moved to put them to Virgil's neck, Virgil drove his elbow into his stomach, snatched the scissors from his hand and shoved the barber over while leaping to his feet. Three of Mick's men ran at him, but James grabbed one by the throat and threw him to the floor, Wyatt elbowed another in the face and Newton knocked the third man out with a punch to the head. As the barber fell, his T-shirt rode up and Virgil saw the scratches across his belly, telling him the barbers were part of Mick's crew too.

Mick chuckled. 'The rumours about your family's speed and

strength are true, which makes you even more valuable to me. Rather than fight us, join us.'

'What, doing over shopkeepers and pub landlords?' Newton sneered. 'We have our sights set a bit fucking higher than that.'

'Naw. All that was just to limber up, keep us sharp. We've got a much bigger target in mind.'

'What?'

'I'll only tell you if you agree to work with us.'

'No,' said Virgil.

'Aren't you being a bit hasty?'

'We're no' working with you and we don't gi'e a shite what you get up to as long as you keep it out of Garthamlock. That's our territory and we don't tolerate anyone robbing the local businesses. Do you get it?'

Mick regarded his own foamy white face in the mirror thoughtfully before replying. This showed Virgil that he was a strategist, thinking out every move before acting. Virgil had only just realised that all his muscles had gone rigid with tension, so he took a deep breath and allowed them to unfurl. He felt he was negotiating for his family's very lives. This crew was dangerous and it was clear Mick was a man used to getting what he wanted. It was vital he didn't allow him to gain the upper hand and drag him and his brothers into a situation that could only hurt them.

'It's a bloody shame, that's all I can say,' said Mick. 'Together, our crews could have gone a long way. I know your family's always in need of cash. Are you gonnae stop your brothers making the biggest payday of their lives just because you havenae got the bottle?'

Virgil noted the gleam in Newton's eyes. His brother, who was a selfish, greedy bastard, had caught the intoxicating whiff of money. 'It's nothing to do with bottle,' said Virgil. 'And everything to do with no' teaming up with a crew who'd stab us in the back the second they got the chance. And you were sent down for robbery, which shows you're no' very good at it.'

This comment clearly angered Mick, but he reigned it in. 'I've learnt a lot since then,' he replied. 'We've pulled off robberies that the polis and the local underworld have no clue about. I can make you all rich.'

'You mean you'll get us all sent to prison,' said Virgil, noting the gleam in Newton's eyes was only increasing.

'Take some time to think it over,' replied Mick, ignoring his objections. 'I want an answer by midnight tonight. You know where to find me. If I don't hear from you then I know you're no' in.' He waved a hand at his crew. 'Let them pass.'

Virgil tossed the scissors to the floor. 'Let's go,' he told his brothers.

'Hey, he's no' finished cutting my hair,' said Warren, pointing to the barber attending to Mick.

'You can get it sorted somewhere else,' Virgil impatiently replied.

Warren huffed but didn't argue, following his brothers to the door, the eyes of the two groups locked on each other, wondering if the other was going to attack.

The MacGregors left, the bell over the door ringing as they exited.

'I look a proper fucking state,' said Warren, self-consciously touching his hair as they returned to the car. The top had been cut shorter but the sides hadn't been attended to and his hair appeared to stick out over his ears.

'You could have come out looking a lot worse,' said James.

'No way. We could easily have taken them.'

'Maybe, maybe not.'

'What do you all think of Mick's offer?' said Newton.

'You're no' seriously considering it?' exclaimed Morgan.

'He said he could make us rich.'

'That's shite. He only wants one of us there to use as a patsy so he and his crew can get off scot-free.'

'You're right,' said Virgil. 'That man's a snake; he cannae be trusted.'

'What if you're wrong and his offer's genuine?' countered Newton. 'We could be missing out on the biggest payday of our lives.'

'If it really is the biggest payday of Mick's life then why the hell would he want to share it with anyone else? Think about it, Newton, or are you that greedy you're willing to take the chance with your freedom?'

'I'm no' fucking greedy,' he snarled back. 'I just want this family to finally earn big.'

'So do I, but teaming up with that prick isnae the way.'

'I agree,' said James. 'Teaming up with Mick and his crew would be a big mistake. There's only one place they're going and that's prison. All we can do is hope they stay away from Garthamlock.'

'Unfortunately, I don't think they will,' said Virgil with a sense of foreboding. 'Mick's no' done with us yet.'

* * *

Reece the valeter knocked on the door of Maria's house at eleven thirty the following morning.

'Hi,' he said and smiled when James answered the door. 'I've come about a motor that needs valeting.' He was an unimpressive man: small, bald and scrawny.

'Oh, aye,' replied James before grabbing him by the front of his hoodie and dragging him inside.

'What are you doing?' cried Reece. 'Get off me.'

He went abruptly silent when four more men appeared in the hallway and he allowed himself to be led into the lounge. The brothers hadn't dared disturb the sanctity of their grandmother's kitchen for this interview.

Virgil was waiting for them, standing in the middle of the room as Reece was dragged in. The hardness in his eyes terrified Reece far more than the rest of the men.

'Did you clone Big Billy's car key?' demanded Virgil while James and Newton between them held Reece in a death grip.

'B... Big Billy?' he stammered. 'Who's he?'

'Morgan,' said Virgil.

Morgan punched Reece in the gut. He would have folded in two had James and Newton not been holding him. His legs went weak and he coughed and gasped, attempting to catch his breath.

'Don't mess us about,' said Virgil. 'You know full well we're talking about the landlord of The Big Hoose. Everyone around here knows Big Billy.'

'Oh, that Big Billy,' rasped Reece. 'Aye, I remember now. What's that about his car key?'

'We think you cloned his key while you had access to it for valeting and then you gave the cloned key to Mick Jones in Easthall so his crew could rob him.'

'What?' he said, attempting to look outraged and failing. 'I'm a respectable tradesman. I've been valeting for four years and I have lots of satisfied customers.'

Virgil sighed impatiently. 'Listen, it's perfectly simple. If you don't tell us what we want to know, then we'll kick the living shite out of you. We'll then torch your work van with you inside it. Now fucking talk,' he barked.

Reece could tell the man was serious, so he nodded. 'All right, I did.'

'Did you do the same with Gordon Maitland's?'

'No, because Gordon's car's so fucking old.' He also went on to name other business owners not just in Garthamlock but all around Glasgow whose car keys he'd cloned.

'How much does Mick pay you for each key?' said Virgil when he'd finished.

'Two hundred quid.'

'That's no' very much.'

'Aye, well, I've got debt and child support. Cleaning people's cars isnae enough to cover all my bills.'

'We don't gi'e a shite about your money troubles. What we do care about is you messing with the people of Garthamlock. Do you choose your targets or does Mick?'

'I'll let Mick know what cars I've got booked in that week and who owns them and he'll tell me which keys to clone. It's also useful if he needs a motor for a job. He'll use one of the cloned keys to nick a car.'

'You do know it's only a matter of time before the polis work it out, if they haven't already? If we found you then they could too.'

Reece swallowed hard and nodded. 'That thought has already occurred to me.'

'Is there anything else you do for Mick?'

'Naw, that's it.'

'Would you have cloned my car key if we hadnae known what you were up to?'

Reece blanched and shook his head.

'Tell us the truth,' said James. 'Unless you want another whack to the gut.'

'Fine, I might have done,' mumbled Reece, hanging his head, avoiding all their eyes.

'He cannae tell us anything else,' said Virgil. 'Give him a

kicking and then throw him out. Don't hurt him too badly though. We don't want to take him to the hospital.'

Virgil frowned. He hadn't thought twice about giving that order. Committing violence was just so easy. How much longer could he fight against his true nature?

He exited the room, leaving his brothers to deal with Reece. He could rely on James to stop them from getting carried away.

'Well?' said Maria, who was waiting for him in the kitchen, sitting at the table sipping coffee while Ludovica cooked at the stove.

'Reece confirmed he's been cloning his customer's car keys and selling them to Mick,' replied Virgil, taking a seat at the table. 'The boys are ensuring he doesnae come back to Gartham-lock again.'

'Good. You handled that very well, Virgil.'

'That's the easy part. We have to deal with Mick next.'

'Doesn't it feel good leading again?'

'No' really. It just feels like a weight.'

'But you're so good at it.'

'For months the only responsibility I've had is for myself and there's so much freedom in that. Now I've suddenly got to take care of my brothers who are all adults,' he muttered, the anger starting to rise inside him again.

'Your father never complained.'

'Because it was his job to look after us,' he exclaimed. 'But it's no' mine. I'm no' even the oldest son, but the responsibility has been dumped on me again.'

Maria glanced at her mother, who was throwing her a look telling her not to nag him, so she swallowed down her irritation. 'And how will you deal with Mick?'

Virgil exhaled heavily and his body relaxed, his anger

retreating. 'Nae idea. We need to think about it carefully. He's really dangerous. Intelligent too.'

There was a loud commotion as Reece was ejected out the front door. A few seconds later, Newton and James entered the room.

'You've no' left Wyatt, Morgan and Warren to see Reece off, have you?' said Virgil.

'All they're doing is escorting him back to his van,' replied Newton, taking the seat opposite him. 'They can handle that. Thanks, Nonna,' he said when she placed a plate before him that contained a maritozzi, a round brioche cream bun of a stunning golden-brown colour with honey, vanilla and orange zest. Virgil and James got one too. 'He'll never lose his flabby gut if you keep feeding him these treats,' added Newton while nodding at Virgil.

'As much as I hate to say it,' replied Virgil. 'You're right.'

'Eat,' Ludovica told him sternly. She took great offence at anyone who refused to eat her food.

'If you insist,' he replied, picking it up and biting into it. 'Wow, amazing, Nonna,' he mumbled through a mouthful of the bun.

A couple of minutes later, the rest of the brothers entered the kitchen too.

'I hope you went easy on Reece?' said Virgil. 'We need him to run to Mick telling tales.'

'Aye, we did,' replied Warren. 'He drove off no problem.'

'What will Mick do when Reece does tell him?' said Maria.

'Nae idea,' replied Virgil. 'So we'll have to be prepared. He might no' even do anything if he was being honest about wanting our help.'

'Well, changing the subject, I do hope you've no' all forgotten what's going to be happening this afternoon?'

'How could we forget, Maw? It's the first anniversary of Da's death.'

'Exactly, so I don't want any of you creeping off. You're gonnae wear the costumes I got for you and you'll like it.'

'Yes, Maw,' her sons all said in unison.

'Good. Now I'm going upstairs to start getting ready.'

'But we're no' leaving for two hours,' said Morgan.

'I'm well aware of that, but a lady needs time to prepare. I've put your costumes in your rooms. I expect you to be ready to go on time.' As she spoke, she looked pointedly at Wyatt, knowing that out of all her boys he was the most likely to object.

Wyatt stared back at her rather harshly and she glared at him, daring him to argue with her. When he looked away, she smiled with satisfaction and swanned out of the room.

* * *

'I feel like a prize cock,' commented Warren as he joined his brothers in the dining room. Fortunately for him Maria didn't hear as she was upstairs. He'd had his haircut completed by his usual barber, but it wouldn't have mattered because it was hidden by a black cowboy hat.

'I like it,' said Morgan, admiring himself in the mirror over the sideboard, straightening the lapels of his long black coat. 'The birds are gonnae go wild over these outfits.'

'I hope Rose doesnae think I look like a prick.'

'She won't. These outfits are dynamite. Trust me.'

Warren stood beside his brother and regarded his reflection doubtfully.

Ludovica entered the kitchen, leaning heavier than usual on her walking stick.

'You're no' ready, Nonna,' said James. 'We need to leave in a few minutes.'

'I'm not going,' she replied, slowly sinking into a chair at the table. 'My knees are playing me up. I'm not up to that long walk to the pub.'

'Since when have you had trouble with your knees?'

'They've tortured me for the last five years. Why do you think I carry this walking stick?'

'To hit people with.'

'It's to help my poor, aching knees.'

The smile that accompanied this statement told the brothers all they needed to know.

'I wish I'd thought of that.' Warren sighed.

They went silent when Wyatt entered the room wearing his costume.

'You all right, Wyatt?' said Virgil.

His brother was twitchier than usual, standing in the doorway, his left eye and limbs going ten to the dozen.

'No,' he said sullenly. 'I look like *him*.'

'That's the idea,' said Newton flatly.

'I don't want to look like *him*.'

'You don't look like him,' said Morgan. 'You don't have a moustache.'

'I hate this,' huffed Wyatt, anxiously tugging at his collar.

'It's just for a wee while and then you can take it off again,' said Virgil. 'We're doing this for Da.'

'Aye, which is the only reason why I'm wearing it.' His fingers began plucking at the buttons of the waistcoat. 'Da would have preferred to be the real Wyatt's father instead of mine.'

Before any of them could reassure him, there was a knock at the door.

'That'll be Rose,' said Warren. He moved to answer it and hesitated. 'And she really won't think I look like a walloper?'

'Of course she won't,' said James. 'That lassie's mad about you.'

Warren nodded and rushed out of the room, reappearing with his girlfriend and a big smile on his face. Rose was dressed as a cowgirl in a brown dress with fringes around the chest and hem, a darker brown belt around her waist and a cowboy hat and boots.

'Doesn't she look great?' He beamed.

'I didnae know you were joining us for this?' Newton sniffed.

'Maria invited me,' replied Rose. 'I hope you don't mind but she said she wanted me to come. This is the outfit she picked for me.'

'Course we don't mind,' said James. 'And you look lovely.'

'Thanks.' She smiled.

'I didnae know someone outside the family would be taking part,' said Newton haughtily.

Warren was about to tell his brother off, but Rose got there first.

'Fine, I'll go home if you insist but you can explain to Maria,' she said.

The way Rose addressed Newton made Virgil realise that she wasn't at all intimidated by him. Newton had scared off plenty of his brothers' girlfriends in the past. Only Ember had been immune, until now.

'She doesnae think I look like a walloper either,' Warren told his siblings.

'Course you don't,' said Rose. 'You look so handsome.' She turned to address the rest of the men. 'You all do. So, who else are we waiting for?'

'Just Maw. I bet she'll be some prim and proper schoolmistress.'

'That's where you're wrong,' said a voice.

Maria entered the room wearing a burgundy burlesque dress, the upper half a tight-fitting corset, the lower a long skirt with stockings underneath. She also wore black gloves that stopped at the elbows. Her thick greying hair was piled on top of her head, a black feather sticking out of it. In one hand she held a matching burgundy feather boa. Ankle-length high-heeled boots completed the ensemble. The dress only accentuated her slim, statuesque figure and her hair being pulled away from her face showed off her lovely dark eyes and fine bone structure.

'Well.' Maria smiled. 'What do you think?'

'You cannae go out like that,' spluttered Morgan.

'Why not?'

'You're dressed like a tart.'

'Your father loved this outfit. I often wore it for him.'

The brothers all grimaced.

'We don't want to know about your sex life,' said Newton.

'I don't see why not; it was beautiful and very passionate. I could tell you things you've never even heard of.'

Rose smiled when Morgan and Warren clamped their hands down over their ears. 'I think you look beautiful, Maria,' she said. 'The colour really suits you.'

'Thank you, sweetheart.' She smiled back. 'That's what my dear Jimmy always used to say.'

'You cannae walk through the streets like that,' replied Morgan. 'You'll catch a cold.'

'I have this to keep me warm,' she smiled, wrapping the feather boa around her shoulders. 'Wyatt,' she added more gently. 'How are you?'

'I look like *him*,' he grunted. 'And I don't like it.'

Maria's expression hardened. 'No, you don't look like *him*. You look like you're in a costume. It's only for a few hours and you will tolerate it because you're a MacGregor and we can tolerate anything. Do you understand?'

Wyatt took a deep breath and nodded. 'Yes, Maw.'

'Good. Then let's go. Big Billy will be waiting for us at the pub.'

'Here goes nothing,' James quietly told Virgil as the two of them led the procession to the front door.

Morgan trailed behind the rest of his family. Despite his enthusiasm about their costumes, he still wasn't sure how the locals would react to them and he had no wish to be mocked. Morgan looked to his grandmother, who smiled at him smugly while remaining seated at the kitchen table, drinking coffee.

Virgil stepped outside first, relieved to see the street was quiet. James followed and then Newton. Warren exited next, holding Rose's hand, much happier about the situation now he knew his girlfriend approved. Maria was right behind them, looking the most confident of them all, a smile playing on her lips as she urged Wyatt outside. Morgan was last, reluctantly closing the door behind him and shuffling after the rest of the family. He'd decided to hang back behind the others until he was sure no one would take the piss out of them.

'We are MacGregors,' announced Maria as she joined Virgil and James at the head of the pack, taking her place between them and linking her arms through theirs. 'Act like it.'

This stirred something inside them and they all walked taller and more proudly, although Morgan still attempted to use the others for cover. Wyatt shuffled along beside him, constantly tugging at his collar.

They turned onto the next street where one man was washing his car while chatting with a friend. Three children were also playing in the garden of one of the houses. They all stopped what they were doing to watch the MacGregors pass by. The brothers glared at the men, daring them to say something, but they both removed their baseball caps in respect, word having got around as to the reason for the costumes. Jimmy had been highly respected in Garthamlock.

'Nice coats,' called one of the little boys.

Virgil nodded back at him.

'That went better than I thought it would,' James quietly told Virgil.

The closer they got to the pub, the busier the streets seemed to get. Everyone stood back to watch them pass, removing their hats if they wore them, as though they were in a funeral procession. Morgan finally stepped up to the front when a group of young women, ignoring the solemnity of the occasion, began wolf whistling.

'Looking good, boys,' they called, making the men preen, except for Warren, who was too wrapped up in Rose.

It was almost like a parade by the time they arrived at the Big Hoose, word having got around, and people coming out of their homes to see what was happening. Even the customers in the pub had poured outside to watch their approach. Virgil thought he saw Ember among the watching crowd, making his heart beat harder with excitement, but the red hair belonged to another woman. His heart rate slowed and the fluttering in his stomach eased. Despite everything she'd done, even the mere prospect of her could still affect him powerfully.

Just as the MacGregors reached the door of the pub, a breeze picked up, making the men's coats swirl around them.

'I bet it was like this at the OK Corral,' they heard one man say.

Silence reigned as the MacGregors entered the pub. Big Billy had done up the place in a western theme, with plastic cowboy tat such as toy guns, wanted posters of random faces, inflatable cacti and a large banner proudly proclaiming, *Yeehaw*.

'Classy,' commented Newton with a curl of the lip.

A table had been set up on which was a surprisingly lavish buffet. Beside the table propped up on a stand was an enormous framed photograph of Jimmy at the OK Corral wearing his traditional blue denim shirt, jeans, cowboy boots and hat, a big smile on his face.

Big Billy stood on guard duty before the buffet, defending it from those who would try to pilfer some of the food.

'Stay back, you greedy bastards,' he roared at the customers who were hovering eagerly around it. He sighed with relief when the MacGregors entered. 'Thank Christ you're here. It's like fending off an invading army,' he said, gesturing to the other customers, who had backed off in the wake of the family's arrival.

'Tuck in, boys,' Maria told her sons. 'I'm no' very hungry.'

They noted she was staring wistfully at Jimmy's image, her eyes misting up.

'Is she okay?' Rose asked Warren.

'Aye,' he replied. 'Gi'e her some peace and she'll be fine.'

Rose nodded in understanding, pained by the ache in Maria's eyes. She admired Maria enormously. Rose had lost her own mother a few years ago, so it was nice having an older maternal figure to look up to again.

'That went better than I thought it would,' said James as he nibbled on a sausage roll. 'I felt sure that at least someone would take the piss but everyone seemed really respectful.'

'Aye, it was actually pretty nice,' replied Morgan. He looked to Wyatt, who was suspiciously sniffing a cocktail sausage on a stick. 'How are you holding up, big man?'

'I'm okay,' he grumbled. 'I still cannae wait to take off this fucking gear though,' he added, gesturing to his clothes. 'I feel like *he's* hanging around, haunting me.'

'Really?'

'Aye. He's haunted me my entire life but now he's closer than ever, watching and judging me.'

Morgan glanced at his brothers, who all shrugged.

'Do you think this smells off?' said Wyatt, shoving the cocktail sausage under Morgan's nose.

'Urgh, get it away from me. I cannae stand those things.'

The MacGregors were given a shot of expensive whisky each and they all toasted Jimmy's image, as did the rest of the customers, who had to content themselves with cheaper drinks.

'Christ, this is so tacky,' said Newton.

'Aye it is,' replied Virgil. 'But at least Maw seems to appreciate it all,' he added, nodding in her direction. She was chatting with her friends, all of whom were admiring her outfit. A couple of male customers had too but Maria had rebuffed them with icy put-downs.

The atmosphere improved when Big Billy put on some music. Johnny Cash's moody 'God's Gonna Cut You Down' burst into life, an artist all the MacGregor brothers enjoyed and who had been Jimmy's favourite singer.

'Hey, Warren,' yelled a voice.

Everyone stopped to watch a tall woman in her early twenties storm through the pub towards them. She was very pretty with masses of long dark hair, but there was also a hardness in her face that was rather intimidating.

'You bastard,' she told Warren, striding up to him. 'We've no' been broken up five minutes and already you're with some tart.'

Rather than be offended, Rose merely smiled.

'What did I tell you I'd do to the next bitch you started seeing?' pressed the woman.

'Piss off, Gemma,' replied Warren. 'We broke up ages ago. What I do now is none of your business.'

'I'm gonnae batter her face in,' snarled Gemma, nodding at Rose.

'You can try.' Warren smiled.

'Fine,' she said, removing her jacket and tossing it aside. 'Come on then, you slag,' she told Rose.

'Shouldn't we do something?' said Virgil. 'Gemma's pretty hard.'

'Relax,' Morgan told him.

Gemma attempted to strike Rose, but Rose got there first and punched her right in the face. Gemma shook off the blow and attempted to fight back, but Rose hit her again and again, knocking her back over a table.

'Do you want to leave while you've still got some dignity?' Rose asked Gemma as she picked herself up and dusted herself off.

'Warren's mine,' she retorted. 'He'll never be yours.'

Rose sighed and drove her palm up into Gemma's nose. As Gemma's knees sagged, blood trickling from one nostril, Rose grabbed a handful of her hair and began dragging her towards the door backwards. Gemma shrieked, attempting to pull Rose's hands from her hair but she failed.

When she reached the door, Rose knelt to whisper in her ear. 'If you bother me or Warren again, I will smash your fucking face to pieces. I will then tear every strand of hair out of your head and make you eat it. I hope I've made myself clear?'

'Yes.' Gemma grimaced as Rose's grip on her hair tightened. 'I've got it.'

'Good. Now piss off and I'd better no' set eyes on you ever again.'

Rose hauled Gemma to her feet and shoved her out through the door before striding back to Warren in triumph.

'Savage Sister indeed,' commented Virgil.

'Aye,' said Morgan. 'You don't fuck with that family.'

Warren beamed with pride and held out his arms to his girl-friend. 'Come here, you total goddess.'

Rose smiled and embraced him before the two passionately kissed. Rose looked to Maria. 'Sorry about that,' she said.

Maria walked over to Rose and took her by the shoulders, smiling fondly. 'No apology is necessary. You handled that beau-tifully. Gemma will never bother Warren again.'

The rest of the wake passed peacefully and the MacGregors made the walk back home feeling a lot less self-conscious.

'Are you still going to that fight tonight?' James asked Virgil as they strolled down the road together.

'Aye.'

'I wish you'd reconsider. I've got a bad feeling.'

'So do I but I feel better knowing I'll have you and Newton watching my back.'

'I'm no' so sure about Newton,' said James quietly, glancing back over his shoulder at their older brother, who was walking at the rear of the group with their mother on his arm. 'Did you see his face when Mick was talking about making us rich?'

'Aye, I did.'

'I hate to say this about my own brother but I'm no' sure we can trust him.'

'He wouldn't go as far as to betray our family, would he?' Virgil added uncertainly.

James shrugged.

Virgil glanced back over his shoulder at Newton and caught his brother watching him. He was already walking into an unknown and potentially dangerous situation. The gleam in Newton's eye made Virgil wonder if taking to the fight a brother he wasn't sure he could trust was a wise move. If Newton did decide to turn traitor, then the consequences for both himself and James could be severe indeed.

14

Ludovica got off the bus and stared at the house mistrustfully. Already she could feel the darkness that dwelt there. It had seeped through the walls into the garden and onto the street, which was a shame as the house was neat and well kept.

Ludovica raised the small gold cross around her neck to her lips to kiss it before walking up the path to the front door, which was opened before she reached it by a small, dainty, sparrow-like woman with perfectly coiffed silver hair. Her limbs were like knitting needles and she looked very fragile, but the malevolence in her eyes spoke of immense strength and challenged the world to take her on.

'Betty Allan?' said Ludovica, feeling like a giant compared to this tiny woman. However, she wasn't foolish enough to think that mere physical presence would be enough to subdue a woman like this.

Betty's thin lips curled with pleasure. 'Judging by the Italian accent I guess you're one of the MacGregor clan?'

'I am Virgil's grandmother,' she replied. 'I had to see the woman who cast such potent malocchio over him.'

'Mal what?'

'Malocchio. The evil eye.'

'Oh, I see. I won't deny it. He hurt my family.'

'I understand that and I can respect it. Your family hurt my family and in response, my family hurt yours. I call it even.'

Betty's bird-like head tilted to one side, the malice in her eyes growing, the darkness continuing to gather around her. 'I do not call that fair. Henry didn't actually do anything to Nick, he only threatened to while your grandsons beat and tortured my son and grandson. That is far from even. Retribution and balance is still to be redressed and I swear I will redress it.'

'Using all the dark means at your disposal?'

'I know you have the same gifts I do – I can feel it – so you understand what I'm capable of.'

'You're right, so you should already be aware that cursing people will only bounce back on yourself. You bring negative energy to others, you will receive it yourself.'

'Only if you don't know what you're doing.'

'The negative energy has already done its damage; you're shrouded with it and while you continue to curse others it will only claim you more and more. I don't care if it consumes you entirely; however, it becomes my business when you begin attacking my family. I came here to warn you to leave us alone. Let our grandsons sort it out between them and we'll keep our gifts out of it. They are grown men. They do not need their grandmothers fighting their battles for them.'

'I disagree. I know I don't need to fight for my family, but I do it because I want to. I enjoy hurting others. This may shock you but it's what I live for and I will hurt your boys.'

'Then you will fail. I have placed powerful protections around them and all the dirty energy you send their way will rebound on you. I warn you one last time – do not do it, for your own sake.'

'Dear Ludovica – oh yes, I know your name, even though I noticed you were careful to keep it from me – I love the challenge you have set me. Finally, I have met someone whose skills equal my own. It will be fun.'

'It will be fun – for me.'

Betty cackled wickedly. 'How wonderful. I could really like you, Ludovica, even though I usually hate people. Let our grandsons fight with their fists. We have much more interesting weapons.'

Ludovica banged her walking stick on the ground three times before spewing a rapid stream of Italian at Betty. She ended this by crooking the first two fingers of her right hand and hissing like a snake.

Betty laughed again and clapped her hands together. 'Wonderful theatrics. I bet that has the morons shiteing their drawers, but it won't work with me.' She stepped back inside her house. 'I look forward to seeing what you're made of,' she said before closing the door.

Ludovica grunted in irritation and banged the walking stick again before turning and stalking proudly back up the garden path. As she went, she hit a garden gnome in the face with her stick, a malicious smile curling her thick lips when it shattered.

* * *

Virgil did decide to leave Newton behind and take a different brother with him that night, but Morgan and Wyatt were on another bodyguarding job and Warren was accompanying Rose on some event her family was having, so he was left with no choice but to take Newton. At least James would be there, whom he could rely on to keep an eye on their older brother.

The address John had given Virgil led them to a very upmarket bar and restaurant in an elegant Georgian building on Kelvingrove Street in the West End of the city. It was clearly closed for the evening, even though it should have been open, which went to show that what the owner made from John's fights earned him more than having the place filled with customers eating and drinking.

The door was locked, so Virgil rapped on the door in the way John had described. There was the sound of bolts being drawn back and the lock being turned before it was opened by what could only be described as a gorilla in a suit. The man was enormous and very hairy. Two beady eyes peered at the MacGregor brothers from under thick, bushy brows.

'What?' grunted the gorilla.

'I'm Virgil MacGregor and these are my brothers.'

The gorilla's harsh expression softened. 'Oh, aye. Come on in, boys.'

He refused to open the door more than halfway, meaning they had to squeeze inside. They were confronted by a second gorilla who wasn't as hairy as his friend but was just as big. The pair seemed rather friendly towards them now they knew who they were.

'I'll take you through,' said the least hairy of the two while his friend remained on guard duty at the door.

Virgil couldn't help but admire the luxury surroundings – the polished reception area, the high-class bar and restaurant. It made a nice change to the dilapidated venues Toni chose to host her fights. However, the advantage of Toni's locations was that they were always in quiet places or areas where the locals knew not to interfere. This venue, however, was in a much busier spot.

They were led through the restaurant and into what appeared to be a spacious function room. There was another gleaming bar off to one side, tables ranged close by it. The rest of the room was taken up by a large boxing ring. Rather than walk in to the excited chatter of a large crowd, they entered to the muted murmurs of a few expensively dressed people quietly talking. There were seven men and three women plus John. There was also a single barman behind the bar.

'Virgil.' John smiled when he entered. 'So glad you could make it,' he added, striding over to him. 'I don't need to be told that these are your brothers. The resemblance is pretty strong.'

'This is James and Newton.'

'Interesting names you all have,' said John as he shook their hands. 'Come and meet your fans,' John told Virgil, clapping him on the shoulder and escorting him over to the wealthy spectators. His use of the word *fans* made Newton scowl. If his own brother hadn't attacked him, he would have been the man of the moment instead.

Virgil had expected to be properly introduced, but instead John just gave them his name and failed to give him theirs. One of the women got to her feet. She was blonde and attractive, in her mid to late twenties. She began circling Virgil, studying him closely.

'Here she goes,' said a man with a strong Glaswegian accent, smiling.

'I'm just inspecting the goods,' replied the woman, her high heels slowly clicking as she moved. 'I like to ensure that all the fighters are up to scratch.' The woman kneaded Virgil's shoulders and arms before moving around to his back. 'Good. Strong and hard.' She winked at him. She stood before him and frowned at his stomach. 'But here, not so good,' she added, poking him in the belly.

'It's padding,' replied Virgil. 'Helps absorb the impact of the blows.'

The woman smiled, revealing extremely white teeth. 'So, your flabby belly's a strategy then?'

'Aye. It never fails.'

'He beat Callum Young,' John told her.

'So I heard,' she replied. 'I wouldn't have believed it if you hadn't seen it with your own eyes.' She turned to James and Newton. 'More fresh meat,' she said wolfishly.

'These two aren't fighting,' replied John. 'They're just here for moral support.'

'Shame because they look even stronger.' She trailed her fingers across James's stomach before doing the same to Newton. She smiled up at him. 'Hard and firm.'

Newton winked back at her.

'You're in good hands with Virgil,' James told her. 'He's the best fighter out of us all.'

This statement caused Newton's smile to drop.

'Really?' said the woman. 'Well, I suppose we'll see,' she added before retaking her seat.

'Anyone else wantin' to cop a feel?' said John.

When one large, bald, overweight man got to his feet, Virgil gave him such a ferocious look he hastily sat back down.

'Everyone satisfied then?' continued John.

The spectators all nodded.

'Good. Then let's bring in Virgil's opponent. Come on in, Marius,' he called.

In strode a man of very similar size and height to Virgil. The only difference was his stomach was the very essence of washboard. He wore a pair of black jeans, his top half bare. His flattened nose indicated he was an experienced boxer.

Marius was forced to stand there while the blonde kneaded

his flesh and smacked him appreciatively on the backside. His stony expression didn't change, showing he neither enjoyed nor resented the attention.

'Marius is a seasoned veteran of these fights,' said John. 'He's one of our best fighters.'

'And has made us a lot of money.' The blonde smiled.

'Aye, he has. He's extremely talented and no' to be taken lightly, a worthy first opponent for you, Virgil.' A rather sinister expression shadowed John's face. 'Let's hope he doesnae make it your last.'

'I'll never forget the way his last opponent's eye popped right out of his heid.' The large man grinned rather macabrely. He looked to Virgil. 'Keep your fingers crossed the same thing doesnae happen to you.'

'Right, boys,' said John. 'Limber up and let's get this show on the road.' He turned to his clients. 'It's time to place your bets.'

The betting was placed with quiet murmurs and secretive gestures, lacking all the noise and arguing of Toni's fights. Virgil was enjoying the rather peaceful contrast, but he got the feeling the peace would soon end and this would be the toughest and bloodiest battle he'd ever fought. He forced away the sadness this thought created because he knew this fight would probably destroy the peace-loving Virgil once and for all. The old adage about a man being master of his own destiny was a lie and this realisation burned like bile inside him.

Virgil removed his shirt, noting the derisive look the blonde was giving his stomach. Why was everyone so obsessed with abs?

He and Marius began warming up and stretching. Just as they'd finished and before they got in the ring, Virgil extended his hand to Marius to shake.

'Good luck, pal,' he said.

Marius regarded his hand with even more disdain than the

blonde had given his stomach before lithely jumping over the ropes into the ring.

Virgil followed, deciding to climb over and not risk jumping and making an idiot of himself. Two men wearing tracksuits emerged from a side door. One was the referee, an older, grizzled veteran of the ring. The younger man was there to bandage the fighters' hands.

The two men then took their places, ready to begin the fight. Virgil again attempted to be a good sportsman and held his hands out for a fist bump, but Marius snubbed him once more.

'All right, you two,' the referee told them harshly. 'As you know, this fight is no-holds-barred but no lethal moves, okay? None of us want the hassle of clearing away your carcasses. Understood?'

Virgil and Marius nodded.

'Good. Now get to it and put on a good show. These people are paying a hell of a lot of money to watch you two beat seven bells out of each other.'

The referee stepped back, the bell rang and Virgil had to immediately dodge a punch swung by Marius. The man moved even faster than Callum. In fact, Virgil was pretty sure he was just as fast as himself. Marius struck him in the solar plexus. Virgil immediately gasped for air, winded, but he fought through the urge to stop to catch his breath, drawing back his right fist before landing a blow in the area of Marius's liver. The effect caused his opponent to go instantly still, the pain of a liver shot intense. This gave Virgil the precious seconds he needed to get some air back into his lungs. However, Marius recovered faster than Virgil had expected. Normally a liver shot could incapacitate someone for up to thirty seconds, but it seemed Marius was made of tougher stuff.

As the two fighters exchanged more blows, Newton casually told James. 'I thought Marius looked familiar.'

'You've seen him fight before?' he replied.

'Aye, it was about a month ago. He took on Tommy the Titan Timpson. Marius took him down in thirty seconds.'

'What?' spluttered James. 'But Tommy's undefeated.'

'He was. Marius is an ex-UFC champion. He got banned from the legitimate fights for holding submission locks too long and ignoring the referee's warnings. He's a fucking beast. He punches bags full of sand every day to toughen up his fists. He also carries a tennis ball around in his pocket and squeezes it over and over. I heard his grip could snap iron.'

'Did you know that before Virgil got into the ring with him?'

'No, course not. It's only just occurred to me.'

James narrowed his eyes at his brother. 'Are you sure it's only just occurred to you?'

'Aye it has. I'm telling the truth,' he added when James stared at him mistrustfully. 'It wouldnae be to my advantage to have Virgil lose this fight. If he does well, then we could all get to enjoy this gravy train.'

This statement did reassure James somewhat; although he still wouldn't put it past Newton to keep Marius's strengths to himself simply so he could watch Virgil lose, he knew how jealous Newton was of their brother.

'Oh, thank God,' breathed James when the bell rang. 'The first round's over.'

He hurried up to Virgil, who was panting for air against the ropes. The trainer handed him a bottle of water, some of which he guzzled, the rest he poured over himself.

'This guy's serious business,' said James.

'You're telling me,' retorted Virgil. 'I can barely keep up with him.'

'He's an ex-UFC champion who beat Tommy the Titan Timpson. He punches sandbags and squeezes tennis balls for fun.'

'Tennis balls?' Virgil frowned.

'I can see why John pitched you against him: you're equally matched in speed and size but this guy's a total beast and he's capable of beating you. You need to bring out the rage monster.'

'No. I need to be able to start winning fights without that. Besides, this guy hasnae done anything to piss me off. He's only doing his job.'

'So was Callum but that didnae stop you going mental on him. You need to get the bloodlust up again.'

Newton joined them. 'Something wrong?' he said.

'I'm telling Virgil that he has to unleash the beast,' replied James.

'He's right; you do,' Newton told Virgil. 'Or you're gonnae take a severe beating. I've seen Marius fight before. So far, he's gone easy on you.'

'Easy?' said Virgil, eyebrows shooting up.

'Yes, Marius is a beast but so are you. You just defeated one of the top fighters in the whole city, so you can beat this guy too.'

Virgil nodded. Perhaps he'd been wrong about Newton after all. Just because he'd betrayed Nick didn't mean he'd stab all his brothers in the back. 'Thanks.'

'You're welcome.' The bell rang. 'Now tear the bastard apart.'

Virgil shoved his gum shield back into his mouth and returned to the fight.

'Hey, that was great,' James told Newton. 'You really increased his confidence.'

'Aye, which is more than you were doing. Stop panicking and let the man do what he does best.'

They turned back to watch the fight. Virgil moved with a

lot more confidence and focus, evading the first blows Marius sent his way. Virgil even landed a couple of punches that were delivered with such speed his opponent was unable to avoid them.

'Look at the prick.' James grinned, gesturing to Marius. 'That shocked him.'

'Aye, it did,' replied Newton. 'I bet he's never fought anyone who's as fast as he is before.'

However, this was no cause for celebration. It just encouraged Marius to change tactics and he did it just as Virgil was finally falling into the love of the fight, his bloodlust rising. Marius had raised his arms high against the onslaught of punches Virgil was sending his way, his hands covering the top of his head.

'He's got him and it's only the second round,' said James excitedly.

'He's showing that bitch that his flabby gut doesnae slow him down,' said Newton, nodding in the direction of the blonde, who was beginning to look a little worried as she'd put all her money on Marius, as had some of the other patrons. Only John appeared confident, as though he was expecting something dramatic to happen.

Marius suddenly stepped forward, so his raised forearms were pressed against Virgil's chest, the punch Virgil threw with his right hand missing and sailing past him. Marius then wrapped both arms around Virgil's chest, placed his left foot behind Virgil's right leg, bent his knee and threw Virgil over his shoulder. A stunned Virgil landed hard on his back while Marius landed on top of him and began pummelling him in the face.

James rushed over to the referee, who was watching from the edge of the ring. 'Hey, did you see that?' he demanded.

'How could I miss it?' replied the referee casually. 'I'm standing right here.'

'He's no' allowed to do that.'

The referee's look was withering. 'Did you no' hear me say that anything goes in this ring?'

'Oh, shite,' he breathed. 'Virgil, get up,' he yelled. 'You've got to get up.'

James didn't hold out much hope. Virgil's eyes were wide and dazed from the shock of being thrown, as well as from the punches Marius was delivering.

'He's no' used to fighting like this,' said Newton.

'Virgil, get the fuck up,' roared James. 'Use your legs, anything. Just do something.'

'He's done for,' said Newton.

'Don't talk like that,' spat James.

They were both astonished when Virgil managed to spin on his lower back, so he was side-on to Marius, and wrap his legs around his neck. Marius had failed to pin him down, thinking he could end this fight with repeated blows to the face.

'I didnae know he could do that,' said James.

Marius started turning a startling shade of purple as Virgil tightened his muscles, choking him. Even the referee was about to intervene, until Marius punched Virgil in the side of the right thigh. Virgil grunted with pain and released him, the two men collapsing back for a moment, Marius to catch his breath while Virgil waited for the pain in his leg to die down. They both scrambled to their feet at the same moment, Virgil limping slightly on his right leg as they turned to face each other.

'Oh dear,' said a loud voice. 'Have we missed some of the fight?'

James and Newton turned to see Lucas Blair enter with Ember on his good arm. His other was still in plaster. Ember wore an expensive designer dress, diamond earrings and a matching diamond necklace. She positively glittered as she walked across the room towards the bar.

'A bottle of your most expensive champagne,' Lucas told the barman, purposefully shouting so everyone could hear him.

The barman nodded and began preparing his order.

Virgil just stared at the pair of them, dumbfounded, while Lucas and Ember smirked back at him.

'Virg, look out,' called James.

Virgil was so busy gaping at the newcomers that he hadn't noticed Marius drawing back his fist. He was struck in the side of the face with such violence he was thrown back onto the ropes.

'Ignore them,' James told him. 'Get your heid back in the game.'

James hadn't even finished talking before Marius unleashed a vicious onslaught, pummelling Virgil's face and body. Virgil, still knocked sideways by the shock of seeing Lucas and Ember together, could only raise his arms to try and block some of the blows. He managed to push Marius back a few steps, so he was no longer pinned against the ropes.

'Get yourself together, Virg, for God's sake,' yelled Newton, seeing his chance of being offered such a lucrative fight slipping away. He pointed at Ember and Lucas. 'Those arseholes chose that moment to enter; they're trying to make him lose.'

'Probably,' replied James. 'All we can do is hope Virgil shakes himself out of it.'

Both brothers were disheartened when one punch from Marius caused blood to erupt from Virgil's mouth. He staggered back a couple of steps, eyes rolling about in his head. Marius sensed victory was near and laid into him with renewed vigour.

'Jeezo, he's gonnae kill him,' cried James. 'Virg, get angry. That prick is with your ex-wife.'

'He's done,' muttered Newton, eyes flashing angrily when Virgil dropped to his knees, blood and saliva dripping from his mouth and down his chest.

As Marius drew back his fist to land the blow that would end the fight, Virgil flung himself at his legs, wrapping his arms around them while throwing himself forward, knocking Marius flat on his back.

'Yes,' cried James and Newton.

The bell rang, indicating the round was over.

Virgil slowly released Marius, who shot to his feet, fury written all over his face. If Virgil hadn't pulled that move, he could have won by now.

While Marius stalked back to his corner, looking strong and full of energy, Virgil crawled back to his on his hands and knees, blood still dripping from his mouth.

His brothers rushed over to him, jumping into the ring to help him to his feet.

'How are you holding up, pal?' James asked him.

'Shite,' he mumbled, looking over at Ember and Lucas.

'Forget them,' said Newton. 'Concentrate on the fight. You've got to win; think of all the money and your new caravan.'

Virgil staggered slightly and James had to steady him.

'There's no shame in throwing in the towel,' said James. 'It's no' worth brain damage.'

Virgil hadn't even heard him, his gaze locked on Ember. The shock drove everything else out of his mind – Marius, the ring, the fight, the audience. All Virgil knew was that his wife was with the man he hated most in the world, the man who'd bullied and tormented him throughout most of his childhood. On top of that, one or possibly both of them had destroyed his beloved caravan. Virgil expected to feel anger but there was only shock and pain.

The bell rang again for the third round.

'Wait,' James told the referee. 'He's no' ready... Jesus,' he exclaimed when Marius charged towards Virgil, already swinging his fists, determined to end this.

James and Newton jumped back out of the ring. Virgil was still watching his ex-wife, so he hadn't even realised and the blow to the kidneys knocked him forward over the ropes. Caught with his back turned, Marius was free to attack him mercilessly.

'I'm gonnae do this bastard myself,' exclaimed James, rolling up his sleeves.

'Don't be fucking stupid,' said Newton.

'He's gonnae kill Virgil.'

'They won't allow it to go that far.'

'Then why isn't that fanny doing anything?' he said, frantically gesturing to the referee.

Virgil kicked backwards, catching Marius in the right knee. His opponent cried out and hopped backwards on his left leg. Virgil swung his fist as he turned and struck Marius in the solar plexus. The blow lacked the usual power of one of Virgil's punches, but it was enough to knock Marius back a few steps. It was clear Virgil was done. His face was a swollen, bleeding mess, his body was riddled with bruises and he shuffled more than walked, but he seemed determined to stay on his feet. He tried to strike Marius twice more. One blow hit his shoulder but the other missed and Marius retaliated with a punch that took Virgil's feet out from under him and he hit the canvas hard.

'Start the count, ya dick,' James told the referee before Marius could launch a fresh attack. It looked like he was trying to, frantically hopping towards Virgil on his uninjured leg but the referee got there first and began the count, forcing Marius to stop.

'Thank God,' breathed James when it was over, glad Virgil had done the sensible thing and stayed down.

'Shite, he lost,' muttered Newton.

'Just be pleased he's still alive,' spat back James.

He hopped over the ropes, Newton following. Meanwhile the small audience began to clap as Marius was proclaimed the winner by the referee.

'Virg,' said James, kneeling by his side and patting his shoulder. 'Virg, can you hear me?'

Virgil's one good eye opened, the other completely swollen shut. 'I lost, didn't I?'

'Aye. I know it's a first for you, but you did bloody well.'

'I blame Ember and that wee wanker she's with,' said Newton. 'He could have won if they'd no' come in when they did. They sabotaged him,' he yelled, voice carrying over to the pair sipping champagne at the bar. In response, they raised their glasses in a toast.

'Can you get up?' James asked Virgil.

'Well, I cannae lie here all night,' he murmured.

'Newton, gi'e me a hand.'

The two men between them got Virgil to his feet.

'If he gets out of the ring on his own, he'll get a bonus,' the referee quietly told the brothers.

'Did you hear that, Virg?' said James. 'Get out of the ring without our help and you'll get a bonus.'

Virgil took a deep breath and nodded. His brothers released him and he stood on shaking legs before slowly walking towards the ropes like a toddler who'd just learnt to walk. The clients got to their feet and started to applaud him, all except Ember and Lucas, who appeared rather put out.

'Why are they clapping?' Newton asked the referee.

'Because he's the first to fight Marius and still leave the ring under his own steam.'

Virgil slowly clambered out of the ring, grimacing in pain. He fell rather than climbed down, landing on the floor in a crouch.

'You have to stand up straight or nae bonus,' called the referee.

With a determined grunt, Virgil slowly pushed himself upright, legs continuing to shake until he was stood straight.

'All right, you've earned your bonus,' said the referee.

'Thank God,' said James before he and Newton jumped out of the ring and rushed to catch their brother before he collapsed.

John approached Virgil, an enormous smile on his face.

'Virgil, what can I say? You gave us a wonderful show.'

'I lost,' he mumbled through his injuries. 'But you already knew I would, didn't you?'

'Aye, I had an inkling. Marius is undefeated.'

The man himself proudly jumped out of the ring and made his way over to his adoring fans. James was very pleased to note that he was also cut and bruised and limping on his right leg.

'We wanted someone who could at least stand up to him for a little while,' continued John. 'I anticipated you'd only go two rounds, so to get to the third is a feat indeed. You should be proud of yourself, Virgil. In honour of that, you'll get the full sixty grand instead of thirty plus another ten for getting out of the ring on your own, so seventy grand altogether. I'm sure that'll get you a nice caravan.'

'He might have won if it hadnae been for that pair,' said James, angrily gesturing to Lucas and Ember.

'Why, what did they do?' John frowned. 'I know their entrance was a little noisy but I'm sure Virgil's fought in worse conditions.'

'She's his wife and she came in with his nemesis.'

The other patrons overheard this and were immediately concerned.

'What is this?' said a man. 'If he was distracted then it's no' a fair fight.'

'He's right,' said the blonde. 'I want to know that the right man won.'

'The right man did win,' objected Marius in a thick Polish accent. He gestured to Virgil. 'Look at what I did to him.'

'Only because he was distracted,' retorted James. 'He was looking away when you punched him. That's no' fair.'

'Please, everyone, let me handle this,' exclaimed John when a squabble broke out. He turned to Lucas. 'Is it true that she's Virgil's wife?'

'Soon to be ex-wife,' he replied. 'They're getting a divorce, which he instigated, so he's no' right to complain about her seeing someone else.'

'That's no' the issue,' said Newton. 'The problem is you knew seeing you both together would shock Virgil, so you purposefully came in late without any warning, knowing he'd be distracted and lose the fight. You sabotaged him.'

'I did not,' he retorted. 'Our taxi was late picking us up. We did intend to be here before the fight even began.'

'You're a fucking liar,' yelled back James.

'Take it easy,' Newton told him.

Virgil in the meantime had sunk into a chair, too sore and tired to remain on his feet. He looked at Ember, who stared back at him, clearly enjoying herself.

'I agree, it does sound like tampering,' said the large man. 'We all noted Virgil's reaction when that pair walked in.'

'We need a rematch,' exclaimed the blonde excitedly.

'Fine,' said Marius, storming up to Virgil. 'We will sort this out right now.'

James and Newton placed themselves before their brother. 'Then you'll have to go through us,' snarled the latter, who was itching for a chance to prove himself.

'Fine,' yelled Marius.

The referee and trainer rushed to intervene.

'Save it for the ring, laddie,' the referee told him, planting his hand in his chest.

'Get the fuck off me,' snarled Marius, shoving over the referee, catapulting him across a table.

The trainer leapt on Marius's back, the patrons all hastening out of the way as Marius spun around wildly in an attempt to shake him off, but the trainer clung on valiantly. When he realised it wouldn't work, Marius dragged the trainer over his shoulder and threw him to the floor.

'Marius, stop this right now,' exclaimed John, noting his patrons were all frantically placing fresh bets as Marius stormed up to the MacGregor brothers.

'I'm going to finish you off,' he roared, pointing at Virgil.

Virgil just stared back at him indifferently, too tired to care. Before Marius could reach him, Newton's fist met the side of Marius's face. The impact knocked the fighter sideways but it didn't take him off his feet.

'Great, you've just pissed him off even more,' James told Newton when Marius threw back his head and roared in rage.

'Marius, stop,' cried John. 'The fight's over.'

'Don't be a spoilsport,' the blonde told him. 'This is great.'

When the rest of his patrons agreed with her, John was left with no choice but to allow things to continue.

Newton stood fearlessly before Marius, determined to take him down.

'Keep your guard up, Newton,' exclaimed James when Marius punched him in the ribs.

While this chaos was going on, Virgil dragged himself to his feet and hobbled over to Ember and Lucas. When she realised he was approaching, Ember tossed back her hair and slid her arm through Lucas's.

'What the fuck's this then?' demanded Virgil. His voice didn't come out as strong and commanding as he'd hoped.

'Sorry, pal, what was that?' said Lucas, bursting with smugness as he wrapped an arm around Ember's shoulders. 'I cannae hear you properly because of your horribly swollen and split lips. Ha,' he added. 'How does it feel getting a taste of your own medicine?'

Virgil turned to Ember. 'You're really seeing this walloper?'

'I am,' she said proudly.

'Why? You think he's a wanker.'

'No, Virg, *you* think he's a wanker.'

They were interrupted by a loud crash. Marius had been thrown back onto a table, writhing like a wild beast while both James and Newton laid into him.

Virgil looked back at his wife. 'You're only seeing him to get at me.'

'Wow, someone's up their own arse,' Lucas told him.

Virgil ignored the man. 'I suppose he is loaded though,' he said bitterly. 'That's what you've always wanted, after all.'

Ember just stared back at him, although her smile had disappeared.

'You've no right to complain, pal,' said Lucas, prodding him in the shoulder. 'For some mad reason you dumped this amazing woman. You brought this on yourself.'

'I did it for her, because I cannae give her what she wants,' he replied more gently, still keeping his gaze on Ember. 'Aye, it gave me a shock seeing you both together but if you're the man who can finally make her happy, then good luck to you both. I won't interfere,' he said before returning to his chair.

Ember's eyes glittered with anger as she stared at his retreating back. Virgil smiled to himself, able to feel her fury. He chuckled as he knew Lucas would later bear the brunt of that anger. In a way it was a relief knowing he would no longer be the focus of her considerable rage. Satisfied with how that had gone, he watched his brothers struggling with Marius. James had managed to pin him down to the floor while Newton hunched over him, punching him repeatedly in the face, the patrons talking excitedly, wads of notes clutched in their hands.

When Newton finally knocked Marius out, the two brothers triumphantly got to their feet, fists bloodied, smiling at the cheers from the patrons, all of whom began showering them with money. Virgil enjoyed his brothers' delighted smiles as they eagerly caught the money and began stuffing it into their pockets. He only hoped they managed to keep hold of it longer than they usually did.

'Here's a little extra for you,' the blonde told Virgil, pressing a wad of notes into his hand. 'I was wrong. You were magnificent.'

'Thanks,' he said, taking it from her. 'That's good of you, doll.'

'I look forward to seeing you fight again, flabby gut or no',' she added, patting his stomach before returning to her friends.

'Congratulations,' said Virgil as his brothers strutted over to him.

'This isnae how things are done here,' exclaimed an astonished John. 'The fighting should stay in the ring. Hey, you,' he told Virgil. 'I said to bring the brothers who knew how to act in decent company and you chose this pair,' he added, gesturing from Newton to James.

'Don't blame us,' retorted Newton. 'Marius started it. The fight was over. We have the right to defend ourselves.'

'One of you pinning a man down while the other batters him is no' defending yourselves. I saw the looks on your faces, you were enjoying it. No wonder you're known as The Bloody MacGregors. You're a bunch of psychos.'

'Why are you so bothered? He's an arsehole.'

'He's my best fighter.'

'He still might be when he wakes up.' Newton smirked.

'Don't you fucking grin at me like that,' seethed John, storming up to him, coming to an abrupt halt when Newton squared up to him.

'Take the pole out of your arse, John,' said the blonde. 'This is the best night we've ever had here and we got two fights instead of one.'

All the other patrons nodded and murmured their agreement.

'Oh, well, the important thing is you enjoyed the show,' he said, looking much happier.

'More than you can possibly know.' A large man smiled. 'Especially as I put my money on these two boys,' he added with a sweep of the hand towards James and Newton. 'You should have all three of them here as regulars.'

'Aye, I will,' he said when the other patrons expressed their admiration for this idea.

'Is it true there are more of you?' the brunette eagerly asked the brothers.

'There are four more of us but one's in Bar-L,' replied Newton.

'You should bring the other three. Six lightning fights in a row, each fight two rounds rather than five with a different brother facing off against one of John's regulars.'

John's eyes lit up when they all began discussing the amount of money they'd be willing to gamble and the rich friends they'd bring along. 'All right, if you insist,' he said magnanimously. 'I will arrange that for you.'

'Hang on,' said James. 'We've no' agreed yet.'

'Are you telling me you're gonnae turn down a massive payday?' demanded John.

'Perhaps. Me and my brothers need to have a wee chat. We'll let you know our decision. Virgil's got your number.'

'I know you won't let us down, boys.' The blonde winked.

James turned to Virgil. 'Let's get you home. Nonna will sort you out.'

Virgil slowly got to his feet and James helped him on with his jumper. He stopped as he passed Ember, who stared back at him sullenly before he continued on his way, refusing to look back.

15

'Oh, sweet Mother Mary,' gasped Maria when Virgil returned home with his brothers.

'Bloody hell,' exclaimed Morgan, who was sitting at the table reading a newspaper. 'Who did you fight, a combine harvester?'

'It was Marius Zielinski,' replied Newton as Virgil carefully eased himself into a chair.

'That monster? The guy's a psycho. Nae offence, Virg, but I'm no' surprised you look like that.'

'This isnae down to Marius,' replied James. 'It's Ember's fault.'

'Oh no, did she have another of her maddies and jump into the ring?'

'No. She turned up halfway through the fight with Lucas Blair.'

'You mean they were together, like on a date?'

'Aye, and they made their big entrance at that moment to distract Virgil from the fight, giving Marius the chance to lay right into him. Until then, he was holding up against him really well; it could have gone either way. Virg got a big bonus for leaving the ring under his own steam. It's the first time an opponent of Marius's has managed it.'

'Madre,' Maria called up the stairs while the men talked. 'Virgil needs you.'

Her call was answered by an irregular thumping on the stairs as Ludovica descended with her walking stick.

'John wants all of us in,' said Newton. 'Rapid bouts of only two rounds, each of us fighting a different opponent. His customers loved us and they cannae wait. They're bringing more of their rich pals and we're gonnae make a ton of money.'

'Are you sure about this?' said Maria. 'I mean, look at the state Virgil's in.'

'That's no' his fault,' said James. 'But we will face really tough opponents too. It won't be easy.'

Ludovica entered the room and took Virgil's face between her hands to assess his injuries.

'Easy, Nonna,' he said. 'I'm in quite a bit of pain.'

'You'll be fine,' she said, slapping him on the shoulder. 'You are strong.'

'I really don't want to be hit again today,' he groaned.

'I will fetch my salve,' said Ludovica, propping her walking stick up against the table before heading over to a cupboard. 'Morgan, get me a bowl of warm water and a cloth.'

'Yes, Nonna,' he obediently replied, getting to his feet.

'I'm no' sure it's wise for you all to fight for this John,' said Maria. 'I have a bad feeling.'

Virgil plucked a wad of notes from his jacket pocket and tossed it on the table.

'How much is there?' gasped Maria.

'I'm guessing ten grand.'

'That's no' very much for all those injuries you've been left with.'

'That's just a tip I got from one of the punters. You can keep it as my contribution towards the housekeeping. I also got a ten-grand bonus, plus sixty grand for the fight.'

'You mean you made eighty grand from just one fight?' said Maria, scooping up the money and slipping it into the pocket of her cardigan.

'Aye, and I lost. Imagine how much it would have been if I'd won.'

Maria's eyes gleamed. 'Maybe it's no' such a bad idea after all, but I am still worried.'

'Relax, Maw,' said Newton. 'It's fine. Trust us.'

She nodded. 'I do.'

'So there's room for me too on this gravy train?' said Morgan, placing a bowl of warm water and a cloth on the table beside Virgil.

'Aye, all of us. Even Nick when he's released if he wants in too.'

'Hmm, good,' said Maria thoughtfully. 'Anyway, let's put that on the back burner for the moment. I want to discuss Ember. Is she in a relationship with Lucas?'

'He seems to think so,' mumbled Virgil as his grandmother began cleaning the blood from his face with the cloth.

'And what about her?'

'I think she's using him to get to me, but then again he is loaded and that's what she's always wanted.'

'She's definitely using him,' said James. 'Lucas is the only one who cannae see it. And her plan failed. Virgil might have lost the fight, but he got offered more work and was paid a fortune.'

'Meaning she will be cooking up something else in that wicked brain of hers,' said Maria, eyes narrowing. 'The wee bitch. I cannae believe I used to like her.'

'To be fair, Maw,' said Virgil, 'I knew from the day me and

Ember got together that breaking up with her would bring me no end of trouble, but I married her anyway. And she's still hurting after I started divorce proceedings. We cannae put all the blame on her.'

'Well, I can,' said Maria, already planning on having a word with Ember herself; but she wouldn't tell her son that, he'd only try and stop her. They needed a wee chat woman to woman.

* * *

Maria slipped out of the house early the next morning before any of her sons were up and walked to the house Ember and Virgil had once shared but which only Ember lived in now. She was pleased to see that her errant daughter-in-law was still maintaining the property nicely.

She rang the bell and when there was no answer, she kept on ringing it until the door was pulled open by an irritated Ember, her red hair ruffled. It was rare to see the woman without her make-up; Ember was the type to put on her face for a trip to the corner shop, but she was still beautiful, her ivory skin flawless. However, there were shadows around her eyes that weren't usually there and Maria was unsure whether that was because she'd just woken up or if they denoted the turmoil within. Ember's green eyes were dull, until they settled on her visitor and flamed into life.

'Virgil sent you, didn't he?' were her first words.

'No, dear,' replied Maria. 'In fact, he's no idea I'm even here. He's still fast asleep recovering from his injuries.'

Ember nodded, already gathering that Maria was aware of the previous night's events. 'You'd better come in then.'

'Thank you.'

Maria followed her through to the kitchen. 'This place is

sparkling,' she said approvingly. 'You were never this good at cleaning before. You're the cat's lick type of cleaner.'

'Lucas is paying for a cleaner for me,' she replied as she switched on the kettle.

'You mean your new boyfriend?'

Ember turned and smiled at the danger shining out of Maria's eyes. 'If you want to call him that.'

'So you are in a relationship with him then?'

'We're just seeing how it goes.'

'Men don't pay someone to clean a woman's house unless he's expecting something in return.'

'You're being very unfair on Lucas. He likes doing good deeds.'

'No' from what I've heard of him. The rumour mill says he's one very nasty creature.'

'Not to people he likes.' Ember's smile was provoking. 'And he really likes me.'

'Are you sleeping with him?'

'That's absolutely none of your business.'

'It is when you're married to my son.'

'In name only.' Ember produced a brown A4 envelope from a drawer and tossed it onto the kitchen table. 'This arrived yesterday from Virgil's solicitor. Divorce papers for me to sign.'

'Have you signed them?'

'Not yet. I know I should but sentiment's holding me back.'

'Is that all?'

'I still love Virgil. But I hate him too.'

'I can understand that. If Jimmy had ever tried to divorce me, I would have hated him too.'

Pain filled Ember's eyes. 'But he didn't divorce you because he truly loved you,' she exclaimed. 'Virgil doesnae love me.'

'Yes, he does, but he knows it will never work between you.

You may as well sign those papers because your marriage is over, but I warn you – don't try to sabotage my son again. He could have been killed last night because of your antics.'

'That wouldn't have happened; John doesn't allow things to go that far in his fights.'

'From what I've heard, it's only thanks to James and Newton that Virgil's still alive.'

'Your boys do like to exaggerate,' said Ember with a derisive smile.

'Perhaps. I don't believe you wanted Virgil killed, but I do believe you wanted him to take a beating; it's in your nature. Well, he's been punished, so you can leave him alone now. Start up with Lucas Blair if you wish – your private life really is none of our family's business any more – but if you try to hurt my boy again, it won't be his brothers or his grandmother that you'll have to deal with, but me.' Maria thrust her face into Ember's. 'And you know that I can be more dangerous than the lot of them put together.'

Ember took a step back from her mother-in-law. 'What is this, Maria? You know I was loyal to him right up until he said he was divorcing me. Even during the six months he was away, I never even looked at another man.'

'Yes, that is true and you're to be commended for it, but your actions last night hurt my baby and I could happily rip you to pieces for that.'

'Baby?' snorted Ember. 'He's a grown man.'

'My children will always be my babies, no matter how old they are. If you ever become a mother, then you'll understand.'

Ember's eyes widened when Maria plucked the biggest knife from the block on the counter.

'I will leave you with one last warning,' said Maria, thoughtfully studying the blade. 'If you cause my son any more trouble and refuse to give him a nice, smooth divorce, then I will come back here and slash the shite out of that lovely face. We'll see if Lucas continues to pay for your cleaner then.' Maria slipped the knife into her handbag. 'I won't stay for a brew. I've got things to do.'

With that, she departed, leaving Ember to glare after her fiercely. Maria smiled when she reached the door and heard her daughter-in-law scream the word *bitch* followed by a smash, indicating her kitchen was bearing the brunt of her fury.

'Such a shame,' Maria said to herself as she stepped outside. 'It was so spotless too.'

* * *

Ember banged on Lucas's front door until it was opened by Brian.

'Oh,' he said flatly. 'It's you.'

'Let me in,' she said, barging her way past him. 'I need to see Lucas.'

'He's still in bed.'

'Tough.'

Brian just shrugged and returned to reading his newspaper in the living room. The mad cow was his boss's problem.

Ember stormed upstairs. It took her a couple of goes to locate Lucas's bedroom in his large house and she walked in to find him sprawled naked on his bed, jaw hanging open and snoring. She'd never seen him naked before, so she took a minute to study him. Lucas's body was better than she'd thought it would be. His arms and chest were pretty toned. Although his stomach couldn't be described as muscular, at least it wasn't flabby like Virgil's. Her eyes moved lower and she was even more impressed with what she saw.

'Lucas, wake up,' she said, shaking him by the shoulders.

'Eh, what? But I don't want to go to school today, Maw,' he groaned.

'What?'

He forced his eyes open. 'Oh,' he said, hastily sitting up. 'Sorry, I was dreaming. I...'

'Never mind all that. Maria MacGregor just came to my house and threatened me with a knife.'

'Oh my God, are you okay? Did she hurt you?'

'No. She just picked up my biggest knife and said she'd slash my face up. The mad bitch said you wouldn't want me then. She's trying to split us up, Lucas,' she wailed, a tear artfully sliding down one cheek.

'Come here, gorgeous,' he said, pulling her into his arms, loving the feel of her pressed against his bare skin. 'You're shaking. I know Maria's a hard-faced bitch but I didnae realise she could be scary.'

'That's because you don't know what I know.'

'And what's that?'

'Do you remember the stabbing of Adrian Lovell two years ago?'

'Aye. I remember Adrian. He was a bit of a roaster and he loved his drink. He was a money lender too. Plenty of people around here were well into him for a lot of cash.'

'That's him. He was found bleeding in the street and taken to hospital. He died two days later. He was only thirty-nine.'

Lucas nodded. 'The polis never did catch who did it.' He frowned when she regarded him meaningfully. 'Are you saying Maria killed him?'

'He was stabbed around nine o'clock at night. It was almost winter, so it went dark early. It was a miserable night. Me and Virg were at home when Maria knocked on our door. Virg told me to wait in the living room while he took his mother upstairs to the bathroom. He came back downstairs while I heard the shower going upstairs. I went into the kitchen and caught him putting some bloodied clothes into the washing machine. When I asked him what had happened, he said Maria had fallen in the street and cut herself. He asked if she could borrow some of my clothes to go home in, even though we are not the same size.' She sniffed.

'Maria came back downstairs after her shower wearing my jogging bottoms I use for the gym and one of my baggy jumpers. She said she was fine and she didn't look at all injured to me. She was really pale with these horrible shadows under her eyes. I could tell that something bad had happened, worse than a fall. Virgil had gone really pale and sickly-looking too. He drove her home and when he came back I asked him over and over for the truth, but he just kept saying that she'd fallen in the street. When I heard about the attack on Adrian the next day, I just had this horrible feeling, so I went straight to Maria's house after Virgil had left for the gym. I snuck in using my key. All the brothers were out, and I overheard Maria and Ludovica talking in the kitchen. Maria was saying she didn't want to do it but it had been a necessary evil, and Adrian wouldn't be able to threaten their family again. When I walked in and asked her outright if she'd been responsible for attacking Adrian, they looked like they could kill me.'

'Did they try?' said Lucas, who was listening with astonishment.

'No. Probably because Ludovica didn't want blood spilled in her precious kitchen. Maria told me that I knew full well she'd fallen and hurt herself and it was nothing to do with Adrian. I told her someone had seen her at the scene and she had to flee immediately before the polis came for her. You know how convincing I can be and she fell for it. She jumped up like she was ready to run out, until she caught herself and sat back down. It was enough to confirm I was right. Ludovica got angry, then told me it was better to forget about it. I said how could I forget something like that and the look she gave me chilled me to the bone. You know me, Lucas; I'm no' easily intimidated but there's something... unearthly about that auld biddy.'

'Aye, I know. She's a spooky witch. But why would Maria kill Adrian?'

'He was causing trouble for her precious sons at the time. He'd already stabbed Wyatt in the side. Adrian was threatening to cut Warren's throat and castrate Morgan.'

'Aye, he was a mad rocket. But surely her boys could have fended him off? The only reason Adrian didnae stab Wyatt very deep was because Wyatt threw him out the pub window. Her sons could have easily taken him down. Maria took a big risk with her own safety.'

'There was another reason and it wasn't to do with her sons. Maria had borrowed a lot of cash off Adrian and he was wanting it back. You know how shite that family is with money. When she couldn't pay it back, he started demanding payment in kind.'

'But she's an auld woman.'

'She is not. Give Maria her due, she's still very attractive and a lot of men have been sniffing round her since Jimmy died. Adrian was threatening to tell Jimmy about her debts if she didn't do what he wanted.'

'So what? Jimmy would have turned Adrian into paste.'

'Jimmy wasnae very well. Now we know it was on the run-up to his heart attack, but at the time no one realised it was that serious. All the same, she didn't want him worrying when he was poorly. Maria probably felt she was left with no choice.'

'Maria told you all this?'

'No, Virgil did. He knew I wouldn't give up until I knew, and he was scared I'd keep pressing his maw and grandmaw. He only told me to protect me,' she added with a fond smile. 'Maria realised I knew her secret and she hates me for it.'

'Wow, this is huge. I could do a lot with this information.'

'You mean blackmail?'

'Or something even better. I need to think about it but if I do use it, the MacGregors will know you told me and they'll do anything to protect Maria. I don't want to risk your safety.'

'I'm willing to be put in danger if it brings down that family. Maria made a big mistake threatening me.'

'I swear that I won't let Maria, her mad maw or her sons hurt you. I'll see what I can find out about the investigation into Adrian's murder. The polis might have DNA evidence that they're just waiting to compare to a suspect's. If Maria's no' already in the database then they wouldnae be able to match her to the murder and – let's face it – I bet they were looking at all the other local roasters for Adrian's stabbing. They wouldnae even have considered a well-respected middle-aged woman.'

'I don't want to go running to the polis and I didn't think you would either given the line of work you're in.'

'You're right. Toni would take my eyes out if I did that; she'd think she couldnae trust me. No, this information needs to be used smarter than that. Let me mull it over. I'll come up with something.'

'Okay, thank you,' she breathed with relief, although inwardly she felt smug with satisfaction. The MacGregors thought they could get away with threatening her and ejecting her from their family but she would make them pay, and Lucas was going to be her weapon.

'I cannae believe you're here in my bedroom,' he said, sliding an arm around her and pulling her closer.

They kissed but Ember pulled away when things got more passionate. 'I'm gagging for a brew. I'll go and put the kettle on,' she added, ignoring his erection.

Lucas watched her go longingly before sighing with frustration and falling back into the bed.

* * *

Virgil's brothers began to applaud when he shuffled into the kitchen the next morning. His right eye was entirely swollen shut and his left one was just a slit.

'Jeezo, you look worse than I did after I fought Morgan,' piped up Warren. 'I bet you can barely see.'

'I wouldnae be able to see at all if it wasn't for Nonna's remedies,' he replied, slowly sinking into a chair at the table.

'That Marius is a fucking animal,' said Warren. 'Bugger, I wish I'd seen that fight.'

'Here, eat this,' said Maria, placing a plate of baked eggs before Virgil. 'It will give you your strength back and it's nice and soft for your sore mouth.'

'Thanks,' he replied, unable to smile because it hurt so much.

'Newton told me John wants all of us to fight in his matches, which sounds great,' said Wyatt. His left eye was twitching but this time with eagerness rather than emotional turmoil.

'Aye, if you want to look like this,' replied Virgil.

'I don't mind if I'm earning what you got paid.' Wyatt's face creased. 'Does that mean you're gonnae buy another caravan and move back to Milngavie?'

'I don't know yet,' said Virgil, far too tired and sore to get into all that.

'So what has everyone got on today?' said Maria as she placed a jug of orange juice on the table.

'I'm going back to bed when I've finished my breakfast,' said Virgil.

'You must be mad,' replied Morgan. 'If I had all the cash you just made, I'd be going on a shopping spree,' he replied.

'I've learnt to control my spending,' Virgil replied. 'And now I actually have some savings. You should do the same.'

'Sod that, you only live once. You've got to enjoy it while you can.'

Virgil shook his head and began gingerly tucking into his baked eggs.

'When does John want us to fight?' said Warren.

'He'll be in touch soon,' replied James. 'Just be patient.'

'I cannae be patient. I want all the cash Virg just made. I want to buy a new car.'

'You only bought one six months ago,' replied Maria.

'Aye, but I'm bored of it. Besides, a car's an asset.'

'What a load of shite,' said James. 'I love cars as much as any man, but even I know they only bleed you dry. You'll never make any money on them.'

'Fine. I'll use the cash as a deposit on a house.'

'You're moving out?' Maria frowned.

'I want to ask Rose to move in with me.'

'Really?' She smiled, this statement appeasing her. 'You're really that serious about her?'

'Course, she's amazing.'

'That's wonderful, sweetheart.'

Morgan looked across the table at James. 'You ready to go?'

'Aye,' he replied, wolfing down the piece of toast he still held before getting to his feet.

'Another bodyguarding job?' said Virgil.

'Yeah,' replied James. 'We've been even busier since we got back into Toni's fights.'

'I see,' he said, noting the way his mother gave him a triumphant smile.

'Me and Newton have got a job too this morning,' said Wyatt.

'You really should think seriously about starting your own legitimate business,' countered Virgil.

'If we were legit, all the dealers would stop using us and they're our main customers,' replied Newton.

'Then you'd get new and better customers.'

'We're fine as we are. Besides, we'd have to pay taxes and lose a load of the money we make to the thieving government. No thanks.'

The four men departed together, so only Virgil was left with Warren and Maria.

'Where's Nonna?' said Warren. 'I don't think I've ever known her not be around at breakfast.'

'She said she had an appointment,' replied Maria.

'She's no' ill, is she?'

'Don't be ridiculous. Madre has never been ill once in her life. Now mind your own business and get on with your breakfast.'

'Fine,' he sighed.

'I'll get it,' said Maria when there was a knock at the door.

'Let's hope it's no' Ember with a lit firework,' said Warren as their mother left the room. 'I remember her throwing one through the window when you had an argument.'

'She's moved on from fireworks,' replied Virgil. 'These days, if she's gonnae throw anything it'll be a hand grenade.'

Warren chuckled.

The two men looked at each other when there was the sound of shouting at the front door.

'Where is he? I want a rematch,' bellowed a male voice with a heavy accent.

'And I said you cannae go in there,' replied Maria's voice. 'He's no' well.'

'Get out of my way,' snarled the man.

Virgil and Warren got to their feet just as Marius charged in. He was bruised and his upper lip was swollen, but he looked nowhere near as injured as Virgil.

'You,' he spat, pointing at Virgil. 'I want a rematch. We need to find out who is the better fighter.'

'You're the better fighter,' he replied. 'If we had a rematch, you'd only beat me again.'

'We don't know that for sure, so we're going to find out right now.'

'You expect me to fight in this state?'

Marius removed his jacket and tossed it to the floor, his T-shirt following.

'Hey, you,' Maria told him. 'No one strips off in my kitchen.'

'Relax, I'm not taking anything else off.' He grinned at her lasciviously. 'Unless you want me to?'

'No I do not. Now get out of my hoose.'

'Be quiet,' Marius told her before looking back at Virgil. 'Now fight me.'

'No,' he replied.

'Do it.'

Virgil folded his arms across his chest, which hurt more than he'd care to admit. 'I said no.'

Marius tilted his face to the ceiling and released a frustrated roar, hands clenching into fists. 'Fight me,' he bellowed.

Virgil shook his head.

'I'll fight you,' said Warren.

Marius frowned at him. 'Who are you?'

'Virgil's brother. I'll gi'e you a run for your money, sweetheart.'

'Do not call me sweetheart,' grunted Marius, lower jaw sticking out, tendons tightening in his neck.

'Come on then, big man. Right here, right now.'

'No. Virgil is the one I want to fight,' he said before turning back to him. 'You can say no all you like but this is happening. Hey,' exclaimed Marius when something connected with the back of his head. He turned to see Maria wielding a broom, the bristly end pointed right at him.

'Get out of my kitchen,' she yelled.

'Fuck off.'

'I'll call the polis.'

'I've heard all about your family, so I know you won't.'

When he tried to lunge at Virgil, Maria smacked him with the broom again.

'You're really pissing me off,' Marius barked at her.

'Leave right now before I stick this up your arse.'

Maria went silent when he snatched the broom from her hand and snapped it across his knee before casting the two pieces aside contemptuously.

When he turned to Virgil, who still stood there impassively, Marius drew back his fist but Warren rushed forward and punched him in the side of the face.

'Bastard,' yelled Marius before rounding on him.

The two began exchanging vicious blows, Warren giving as good as he got. It was his first fight since his match against Morgan and he was revelling in it, until Marius's fist met his injured ribs. He felt a crack and groaned, stumbling backwards.

'Oh Christ, no' again,' exclaimed Warren.

As Marius moved in for the kill, infuriated by his audacity, Virgil grabbed Marius around the neck from behind, pulling him away from his brother, but he was still very sore and weak and Marius quickly shook him off, throwing him back against the wall.

'Leave my boys alone,' yelled Maria before throwing a handful of salt into his face.

Marius gasped and hastily wiped the salt from his eyes. Virgil took the opportunity to hit him in the stomach but it barely had any effect. Marius struck back at him but missed because he was still blinded by the salt.

'Watch out, Virgil,' said Maria, pulling him out of the way by his arm when Marius continued to throw wild punches, determined to hit him even though his vision was impaired. 'Warren, don't,' she cried.

Warren ran at Marius just as he managed to get the salt out of his eyes. Marius grabbed him by the neck, holding him at arm's length as he wrapped his second hand around his throat and began to squeeze.

'I'll kill you,' grunted Marius, squeezing harder.

Virgil tried to prise his hands from his brother's neck but Marius kicked him hard in the leg and he went down.

'No, stop,' screamed Maria as she watched her son slowly being strangled.

She ran to the kitchen drawer and yanked it open, eyes dancing over the contents before grabbing a knife.

'What's going on?' said a voice.

Rose entered the room and was shocked at the scene. When she saw what was being done to her boyfriend, a banshee-like scream left her lips, the sound chilling everyone's blood.

Throwing down her handbag, she launched herself at Marius and grabbed his crotch. She squeezed his genitals, twisting them as hard as she could.

Marius's scream was even louder than Rose's war cry. He

released Warren, who dropped to the floor, coughing. Marius fell onto his back and frantically tried to shake Rose off, but she remained firmly latched on. When Rose released him, he curled up into the foetal position and began to whimper.

Now the danger was over, Maria slid the knife she held back into the drawer. She glanced at Virgil and realised he'd seen her holding it.

'Jeezo, babe, you're a wee dynamo,' Warren told Rose.

She grinned back and threw her arms around him, concerned when he grunted with pain. 'What's wrong?' she said.

'That arsehole cracked my injured ribs,' he grimaced.

'Oh no. I really think this time you should get checked out at the hospital.'

'Aye, maybe you're right,' he said, sweating. 'It hurts even more than before.'

'Is everyone else okay?' Rose looked to Virgil. 'Jesus, did he just do that to you?'

'No, he did it to me last night,' he replied, dragging himself to his feet.

'What?'

'I'll explain later,' said Warren. 'I think I really need a doctor.'

'I'll drive you,' Maria told him.

'We cannae leave Virg alone with that nutter,' said Warren, pointing to the shivering Marius.

'I'll tie him up and call your brothers. They can come back and deal with him.'

'They're on bodyguard duty,' said Virgil.

'Then they'll just have to work something out. I will not have that animal in my house one second longer than I have to,' she replied.

Maria produced some duct tape from under the sink and tied

Marius's wrists and ankles together. She then phoned James and told him to return ASAP.

'Warren, get in the car,' she said. 'You're a terrible colour.'

Rose and Maria between them got Warren to his feet and helped him outside.

'How are you doing, Marius?' said Virgil when they'd gone.

'P... pain,' he rasped, body shivering with agony. 'Much pain. I think there is blood too.'

'If you hadnae come here today then your wedding tackle would still be intact. How did you find out where I lived, by the way?'

'A note was left in my bag at the restaurant last night.'

'The restaurant where we fought?'

'Y... yes,' he said before lapsing into silence, the pain too intense for him to continue talking.

Virgil knew Ember had given Marius his address. Once again, she'd betrayed him, only this time she'd thrown something even worse than a hand grenade into his home. Anger and pain vied inside him for supremacy. Did Ember really hate him that much?

16

James returned with Morgan and the two of them took Marius away. A few minutes after they'd gone, just as Virgil was about to head next door and go back to bed, Ludovica returned.

'What happened to my kitchen?' she demanded, taking in the knocked-over furniture, snapped broom and scattered salt.

'The man I fought last night came in demanding I fight him,' replied Virgil. 'He wasnae too happy when I said no. Maw and Rose took Warren to hospital after Marius cracked his ribs.'

'And where is this man now?'

'James and Morgan took him away, so he's probably been thrown into the Clyde.'

'Ember was there last night. Is this something to do with her?'

'Undoubtedly.'

'That little bitch will never stop.'

'I know,' he said resignedly. He thought of how his mother had picked up that knife and wondered if he should mention it to his grandmother, but he decided against it. He had no wish to drag up the past. 'Where have you been anyway, Nonna? It's no' like you to miss breakfast.'

'I had something to do.'

'You're up to something.'

'Such as?' she said, pulling on her apron and tying it around her waist.

'It's no' anything to do with Henry Allan's gran, is it?'

'What makes you say that?'

'Instinct.'

'Fine. I did go to her house and I met her.'

'And?'

'She is a nasty, evil old bitch who means our family a lot of harm. I have put certain safeguards in place but I worry she may find a way around them.'

'Hold on a minute, you think someone's capable of getting around your defences?'

Ludovica nodded.

'I've never heard you say that before.'

'I have only met someone like Betty Allan once before and that was back home in Naples. Giulia Borrelli was the worst of all the vipers. She thrived on creating misery for everyone around her. She wanted to make me miserable too because she wanted your grandfather for herself. I went through a terrible time when I became very ill. I could not eat. Every time I tried, I would be sick. My vision began to go and chunks of my hair came out. It was only thanks to my grandmother and her sister that I was cured. They realised someone had put the evil eye on me and traced it back to Giulia. She had done the same to other girls who liked your grandfather. She was very powerful and Betty is even stronger. Fortunately, my grandmother and her sister were even more powerful and they dealt with her.'

'I've never heard you talk about anyone like this before. You almost sound worried.'

'I am worried.'

'Seriously?'

'Yes, but I will make sure she can't hurt us. I have just been out visiting some friends I thought might know about her. They did and what they had to say proved my fears aren't groundless.'

'Okay,' he slowly replied. 'Right, I'm off to bed.'

'Are you feeling unwell?'

'No, just really sore.'

'You carry the key I gave you?'

'Aye,' he replied, producing it from his pocket.

'Good. You must always keep it near, even in the shower.'

'I will, Nonna. Promise.' He didn't quite share his grandmother's beliefs but he'd seen enough strange things happen around her over the years to convince him that there was more to the world than everyone thought, so he was willing to go along with her advice.

As he left, Virgil looked back and saw her lighting a pair of candles, no doubt to begin one of her rituals. It was strange. His grandmother was absolutely fearless; no one ever worried her, but now she was fretting over a thin little sparrow of a woman.

* * *

When Virgil had gone, Ludovica fetched her knitting basket from the sideboard in the dining room. She then returned to the kitchen, sank into a chair and began knitting a small doll with grey hair that was meant to represent Betty Allan. She continually murmured a charm to herself as she worked, eyes filling with an unnatural light as she sewed the doll's lips together.

Ludovica held up the doll to study and nodded, satisfied with her work. 'Your mouth is bound; you cannot hurt us now, you evil little bird woman,' she hissed.

* * *

It was Newton and Wyatt who brought the news. Maria deemed it so important she told Wyatt to wake Virgil and he followed his brother into their mother's house for a conference in the kitchen. Everyone was there except Warren, who was still at the hospital with Rose. Ludovica had already taken a taxi over there to see if she could be of any assistance to her grandson.

'We think we know what that big job was Mick Jones had planned,' began Newton.

'Jeezo, I'd forgotten about him with everything going on,' replied Virgil.

'A local security depot was robbed. They went through the friggin' roof like something out of a film. They made off with seven hundred and fifty grand,' said Newton, his eyes taking on that greedy gleam at the mention of so much money.

'How do you know it was them?' replied Virgil.

'I don't for sure but I reckon it was. No other crew around here is organised enough to pull off a stunt like that, except the McVays, and we all know Toni would never sanction something so splashy and showy.'

'If it was them then they'll soon be lifted by the polis.'

Before they could discuss it further, there was a knock at the door.

'I hope that isnae that madman come back to challenge Virgil again,' said Maria.

Morgan, Wyatt, James and Newton went to answer it and returned alone.

'Well?' said their mother. 'Who was it?'

'DS Twining,' replied Newton. 'He wants to talk to Virgil about the caravan fire; he's waiting in the lounge.'

'Wonderful,' sighed Virgil, slowly pushing himself to his feet and hobbling out of the room.

In the lounge waited a skinny, gangly man with a pale face, fuzzy blonde hair and large light brown eyes. His suit was light grey. It looked as though all the colour had been sucked out of him. Even his expression was rather lacklustre. The officer held out his hand for him to shake, which he accepted.

'If you don't mind,' said Virgil. 'I need to sit down. Please,' he added, gesturing to the couch while he sank into an armchair.

'Thanks,' replied Twining, taking the proffered seat and producing a notepad and pen from his pocket. 'If you don't mind me saying, you look a mess but then again, that happens to everyone who faces Marius in the ring.'

'You heard about that then?'

'Aye. John told me. I wish I'd been there. By all accounts it was quite the show, but I had to work.'

'That's a shame. Anyway, I expected to see you earlier than this.'

'Let's cut to the chase. We both know you're now one of John's fighters, so I was just gonnae mark this as unsolved, case closed. That was until Marius Zielinski was found a couple of hours ago battered to shite with both knees broken and his nuts half torn off.'

'What?' He frowned. 'That's a shock.'

'Don't act the innocent with me. He's already told me you and your brothers did that to him.'

'You're seriously saying we half tore his nuts off?'

'Aye, well, he did mention something about a *strzyga* doing that to him. I had to look it up. It's a female demonic creature in

Slavic folklore. Either the man's gone aff his nut with the pain or a woman did that to him. I believe your maw lives here?'

'If you'd met my maw you'd know she wouldnae go anywhere near his nuts. She didnae do that to him and neither did my brothers.'

'Don't worry, I'm no' here to lift any of you for it. That would only lead to everyone finding out about the fights, but John is very pissed off. Marius is one of his best fighters and your family's put him out of action for months, perhaps even permanently. I'm here to tell you that you and your brothers now belong to him.'

'You fucking what?' said Virgil, narrowing his eyes.

'You lot will fight for him as and when he demands, even if you're supposed to be fighting for Toni McVay at the same time. Oh aye,' he added when Virgil appeared shocked. 'I know all about that. If you fail to hold up your end of the bargain, then you'll be done for setting fire to your own caravan.'

'That's shite. I didnae do that; it was my home. Why the hell would I burn it down?'

'I'd come up with reason enough to satisfy any jury.'

'You dirty bastard.'

Twining smiled and shrugged. 'I've been called much worse.'

'I'll fucking bet.'

The detective got to his feet and stared down grimly at Virgil. 'You and your family are now John's bitches. One wrong move and you'll join your wee brother in Bar-L.' He smiled when Virgil glared at him. 'I'll see myself out.'

Twining whistled cheerfully as he left, setting Virgil's teeth on edge.

Virgil remained where he was, thinking over the detective's words. Once again, he experienced the sense of being trapped, as though his life were no longer his own and he was getting pretty bloody sick of it. His family, unable to contain their curiosity any longer, all piled into the lounge.

'Well that's just marvellous,' sighed James once he'd finished explaining.

'Fuck this Twining,' said Morgan. 'He's nae evidence.'

'Polis like him fake it,' replied Virgil.

'What if John wants one of us to fight when we have to fight for Toni?' said Newton. 'She won't like that at all. She'll take our eyeballs and cut off our cocks.'

'Or perhaps we could get Toni to get rid of John and this wee Twining,' said Maria.

'You mean convince her he's competition?' said James.

'Aye.'

'She probably already knows about him.'

'Perhaps but I could make her believe that John's a big threat to her.'

'I don't know,' said Virgil. 'Bringing her into it might make things worse. She could get angry with us for fighting for John in the first place.'

'What do you mean, *us*?' said Newton. 'You're the only one who took part in the fight.'

'You and James joined in too,' he snapped back.

'Perhaps you're right,' said Maria. 'We should keep Toni out of it and deal with these people ourselves.'

'How?' said Morgan. 'We don't have Toni's power or influence.'

'But we are just as violent as she is,' growled Wyatt.

'Aye, you're right,' replied Newton with a dark look.

'We cannae attack a polis,' said Virgil. 'It would be madness.'

'He won't be able to blame us if he doesnae know who attacked him in the first place,' countered Newton.

'No,' said Maria firmly. 'We do not attack polis. End of story.'

Virgil's phone rang. He pulled it out of his pocket and handed it to James. 'Answer it would you, mate? I'm too sore.'

'Nae problem,' he replied, taking it from him and answering the call. 'Hi, Big Billy. No, it's James. Virgil's no' well.' His eyebrows shot up with alarm. 'You fucking what? Aye, we're on our way.' He hung up and handed Virgil back his phone. 'Mick and his crew have turned up at The Big Hoose and chased out all Big Billy's customers. They want us over there right now. You too, Virg.'

'Oh, hell,' he sighed. 'I'm no' up to that.'

'There's no choice. If we don't go over there, they'll come here and start smashing the place up.'

'Did Big Billy say what they want?'

'Naw, they won't tell him.'

'This is the last thing we need,' grumbled Virgil, slowly getting to his feet. Why couldn't people just leave them the fuck alone?

'You cannae just walk in there,' said Maria. 'They obviously want to do something terrible to you.'

'Maw's right,' said Morgan. 'This might be a good thing, actually. It could be the perfect opportunity to get rid of them once and for all. That would be one less headache to deal with.'

'Aye, all right,' replied Virgil. 'Anyone got any suggestions?' He sighed when none of his brothers spoke. His brain felt foggy and wouldn't come up with an idea either.

'I think I have something,' said Maria. 'It's pretty wild but you have to trust me.'

'We do, Maw,' replied James.

'Good. I believe that Mick and his crew carry machetes?'

They all nodded.

'That means you have to one-up them, so this is what you're gonnae do.'

Maria could see her sons weren't comfortable with her plan but they were willing to go along with it, as there was no other option. She smiled with satisfaction. Virgil was the only one capable of standing up to her, but he was too unwell, so she was in charge once more.

* * *

The MacGregor brothers entered The Big Hoose to find only Big Billy, Dezzie the barman and Mick Jones and his crew present. Mick and his people were enjoying drinks that were no doubt on the house, especially as they all carried machetes.

The witch at the door once again cackled into life as the brothers entered. The eyes of Mick, his crew, Big Billy and Dezzie all widened at their entrance.

'Have you just been to a fancy dress party?' said Mick.

The MacGregors all wore the costumes they'd sported for their father's memorial wake.

'No,' replied Newton.

Mick glanced at his friends, who were all laughing and smiling, albeit a little nervously. He turned back to the brothers. 'Then why are you dressed like that?'

'Because we like it.'

'Okay,' Mick slowly replied, unsure what to make of all this. He was starting to think that the MacGregor brothers might be a bit mad. He looked to Virgil. 'What the fuck happened to your face?'

'I got into a row with an ex-UFC champion,' he replied. 'Now, why have you dragged us out here?'

'You didnae gi'e us an answer about joining us.'

'We agreed that if we didnae contact you that meant we were out. We want nothing to do with you and your crew.'

'Bad decision, boys. My motto is *if they won't join you, beat them.*' Mick smiled, pleased with this play on words before smashing the machete he held into the nearest table, creating a massive gouge in the wood.

'Watch what you're doing, you bastard,' exclaimed Big Billy. He went silent when Mick pointed the machete at him.

'Shut it, ya fat dick,' bellowed Mick.

All Big Billy could do was glare back at him impotently.

Virgil rolled his eyes. 'Look, I'm tired and sore and I want this wrapping up as quickly as possible. Just piss off back to Easthall. We've already told you to stay out of Garthamlock.'

'We go where we fucking like,' yelled Mick.

'No' around here you don't.'

'I've had enough of this shite. If you're no' with us, you're against us,' snarled Mick, spittle flying from his lips. 'Take a limb aff each of them,' he told his crew before pointing at Virgil with his machete. 'But leave that twat to me.'

'Fine,' said Virgil. 'But don't say we didn't warn you.'

From under their long black coats the brothers all produced rifles and aimed them at the intruders.

Only Mick appeared unconcerned. 'What are those, props to go with your cute wee costumes?'

Mick and the rest of his crew all jumped when Virgil fired and a shot blasted into one of the tables.

'As you can see, these are very real,' said Virgil, loading another cartridge into the rifle. 'Our da was a huge fan of the Old West and he collected a lot of illegal items from that time. Take this gun for instance. It's a heavy-barrelled Winchester 1876 rifle from Arizona. It might even have been used to hunt buffalo, so it'll have no problem taking down a few neds with knives,' he added, causing Mick to scowl. 'These guns are all antiques, but they've been looked after.' Steel filled Virgil's eyes. 'And they all still work. Me and my brothers aren't psychos. We don't usually go around threatening people with guns, but we're more than happy to when someone threatens to hack off our limbs. So, what will it be, Mick? Do you and your pals want to have a go? Is your ego really worth getting shot?'

Mick hesitated and looked back at his crew, who suddenly didn't appear so confident.

Virgil aimed his gun at another man. 'What do you think, pal? Do you want to have a go?'

The man reluctantly shook his head.

'I didn't think so. Now, fuck off the lot of you. You stay in Easthall and we'll stay in Garthamlock. That's the deal. If you break it then we'll come after you with these bastards and finish you. Got it?'

Mick's jaw throbbed with rage. He was furious at being outmanoeuvred but intelligent enough to know that he was in the weaker position. 'Aye, all right,' he muttered.

'Good.' Virgil gestured to the door with the gun. 'Now get out.'

Mick nodded and his crew began to file out the door, the witch continuously cackling, eyes lighting up as each person passed it by. The last man to leave became enraged by the mocking laughter and punched the witch in the face. To the surprise of the MacGregors, the witch rocked backwards before pivoting forward, its long, pointy nose jabbing the man in the left eye, making him scream in pain. The witch then rocked a few more times, still cackling, before going still.

'Get out,' grunted Mick, who had remained behind as his crew filed out. He shoved his injured man in the shoulder, sending him sprawling outside. He hesitated before leaving. 'This isnae over. No one gets the better of me.'

Virgil nodded. 'We'll be ready.'

Mick glowered at them before following his people outside.

Only once they'd gone did Virgil gently place the heavy gun on the nearest table and slowly sink into a chair. Keeping up the strong front had been difficult when he was feeling so rotten.

Big Billy came out from behind the bar and patted the witch on the shoulder. 'Good girl.' He smiled. 'I was fed up with people hitting her, so I put her on the base of an old rocking chair. Now she hits back.'

'We should warn Warren,' replied Morgan, dumping his gun on the table beside Virgil's. 'He's always punching that thing.'

'I appreciate you coming so quickly, boys,' said Big Billy. 'But I want those guns out of here asap. Do you think they'll come back?'

'One day,' said Virgil. 'Mick's ego won't be able to take being bested. He will want revenge.'

* * *

The brothers returned the guns to their hiding place in a storage unit outside Garthamlock that their father had bought to store his illicit antiques. Once that was done, they headed home to find Maria anxiously pacing in the kitchen while Ludovica cooked at the stove. Maria had already brought her mother up to speed on recent events, so she wasn't surprised by the fact that her grandsons were all back in costume.

'Did it work?' Maria asked the men.

'Aye, we got rid of them,' replied Newton. 'Nae bother.'

'How's Warren?' James asked Ludovica.

'He'll be all right. Two of his ribs are broken and they're worried about him puncturing a lung, so they're keeping him in tonight. Rose hasn't left his side. That girl is very loyal. She's a fine mate for our boy.'

'I wish you wouldnae call our partners mates, Nonna.' Morgan grimaced. 'You scared off two of my ex-girlfriends that way.'

'We still have to work out what we're gonnae do about John and DS Twining,' said Newton, removing his long coat and hanging it over the back of one of the kitchen chairs.

'That situation's a lot more complicated than Mick and his crew,' said James. 'We cannae go around pointing rifles at them.'

'I'll talk to John man to man,' said Virgil.

'He won't be interested in what you have to say after we broke Marius's kneecaps,' replied Wyatt.

'You mean after you and James broke his kneecaps,' retorted Virgil. 'Why did you have to do that?'

'Because he burst into our hoose, broke Warren's ribs, attacked you and threatened Maw,' he snarled back. With a growl of rage, he shot to his feet. 'I hate this fucking costume,' he bellowed before tearing the hat from his head and hurling it across the room. The coat followed suit, as did the waistcoat then the shirt, until he was just standing in the black trousers, bare-chested and breathing like a bellows.

Maria decided it wasn't a good time to chide him, so she just quietly picked up the clothes and hung them from a hook on the back door. The hat went into the pantry, out of sight.

'Your intentions were good,' Virgil told him. 'But it was the wrong thing to do. What Rose did to Marius's baws was punishment enough. Now I don't see any other way but to try and parley with John. He's a reasonable man, but first and foremost he wants to make money. He knows his clients really want to see us fight, so he won't do anything to put that at risk. I'm confident I can work something out with him. I'll gi'e him a call,' he added, taking out his phone and dialling.

The rest of the family listened in silence as Virgil spoke.

'He's agreed to meet me in an hour,' he told them after he'd hung up. Virgil sighed wearily. All he wanted to do was go back to bed.

'Where are you meeting him?' asked Newton.

'At a pub in the city centre. Can someone drive me there? I'm no' up to that.'

'I will,' said James.

'The rest of us will come too,' said Morgan.

'I told him I'd go alone.'

'We can wait in the car, just in case.'

'Aye, all right then. Let's get changed, then we can go.'

The encounter with Mick and wielding the heavy rifle had taken a lot out of Virgil and he worried that he didn't have the stamina for this confrontation with John, but there was no choice. His family's future as well as their freedom and safety depended on him being able to work out a deal with him.

* * *

John was already waiting for Virgil in the busy pub he'd selected for their meeting. As Virgil entered, he looked around, wondering which of the customers were with John because he was quite sure the man wouldn't have come alone. It was hard to tell because the damage to Virgil's face caused a number of people to look his way. Two big, muscular men standing at the bar gave him particularly hard glares, telling him everything he needed to know.

'You look like shite,' were John's first words as Virgil sat opposite him at the table he'd selected in a quiet corner.

'That's funny, because I feel like shite too,' he mumbled. 'What I really want is to be tucked up in my bed, no' here trying to negotiate with you, so let's get this over with.'

'I don't want to negotiate. Twining told you everything I had to say.'

'That's no' true. If it was you wouldnae have bothered coming out here in the first place. Your rich clients want to see me and my brothers fight, so you've no choice but to work something out with me.'

'I won't deny it's true,' he said coldly. 'But my clients will be furious when they find out what you did to Marius. He was one of their favourites.'

'Marius brought what happened on himself.'

'Who was the lassie who nearly tore his baws off? She didnae have red hair, so it wasn't your ex-wife and it wasn't your maw either.'

'It doesn't matter.'

'Actually, it does. I'd like to meet her. I don't have any female fighters and I'm sure my clients would love to see her fight.'

'Well, tough because they're no' going to. Now, I need to discuss what Twining said. You know we cannae possibly drop everything to fight for you because if we don't turn up at one of Toni's matches on your say-so then she will come straight for you. She'll consider you to be a threat and one day you'll mysteriously disappear. Don't forget, she's got a lot more polis in her pocket than one weedy sergeant.'

'Fine,' he grunted. 'We'll work around Toni's fights but you lot are mine,' added John, jabbing a digit in Virgil's face. 'If you or your brothers piss me about then you'll be sent down for arson. Twining is very good at making up motives. There are plenty of people sitting in their wee jail cells thanks to him and his creativity.'

'Understood,' said Virgil, the sense of being trapped tightening around him. It was starting to feel like he was wrapped in chains.

'It would also be a shame if any more property belonging to your family was set alight.'

The gleam in John's eyes caused something to click into place. 'You set fire to my caravan, didn't you?'

John's response was a smile.

Virgil's eyes blazed. 'You fucking twat.'

'Now take it easy,' said John, holding up his hands, knowing that violence usually ensued when Virgil MacGregor's eyes burned like that.

'Take it easy? You burned down my home, ya cunt.'

'You're fucking lucky that's all I've done,' hissed John. 'I could have gone for a much bigger target. Besides, I did you a favour. That caravan was a death trap. If you'd been in it when it went up, you wouldnae have stood a chance.'

'Why the hell did you do it?' glowered Virgil.

'I saw you fight Callum and knew I wanted you to fight for me. Burning down your shitey caravan ensured the lure of money would make you agree.'

'You manipulative dick.'

'Just bear in mind that I'm far more dangerous than Marius. Meatheads like him come at you head-on. I come at you when you're asleep.'

'It also makes you a coward.'

John shrugged. 'I know I'm no' a fighter like you. I have more effective weapons than my fists. I'll give you and your brother

Warren time to get over your injuries and then we'll host that round of lightning bouts. Cheer up, Virgil. We're all about to make a ton of money. Everything will be fine as long as you and your brothers play along.'

'And in the meantime, I'm your fucking puppet until you're done with me.'

'If you want to look at it that way.'

Virgil got to his feet and stared down at him coldly. 'I swear that one day I will make you regret burning down my caravan.'

'Perhaps, but no' until I've made all the money I can out of you.'

John's smirk rivalled Newton's for smugness. Virgil turned on his heel and left before he smacked him in the face. As Virgil made his way towards the exit, he glanced at the two men who'd been watching him earlier and saw they were staring back at him. They looked like boxers themselves and he wondered if he'd face them in the ring one day.

Only once he was outside did Virgil take out his phone to check it. He smiled. It had recorded everything John had said, including about DS Twining's penchant for fitting people up. The man wasn't as smart as he thought.

'Looks like I've got you by the baws, ya bastard,' he murmured to himself as he pocketed the phone. Violence got things done but it had its limits. Sometimes what was needed was a bit of brain power.

* * *

Maria opened her front door to a frail, elderly lady who rather resembled a sparrow. The repellent energy that rolled off her told Maria exactly who this woman was.

'Is Ludovica in, please?' she said politely.

'You're Betty Allan, aren't you?' gasped Maria, taking a step back, wanting to keep some distance between them.

'Aye, I am, dear. I take it you're her daughter?'

'Maw,' called Maria. 'There's someone here to see you.'

'I know exactly who it is,' called back Ludovica as she made her way down the hall towards the front door. 'I felt her evil the moment she came onto the street.'

Betty chuckled. 'I could say the same about you. Ludovica,' she beamed when she reached the door, 'how lovely to see you again. I just wanted to gi'e you a message.'

'Oh, yes?'

'I know what you tried to do but you failed. You're gonnae have to come up with something a lot better.'

'Is that it?'

Betty nodded.

'You came all that way out here just to tell me that?'

'I wanted to see you again; I'm rather enjoying our duel. It's such fun to finally meet someone with a strength that almost rivals my own.' Betty's laugh was light and tinkling but her eyes flashed with spite. 'I'm only just warming up. You havenae seen half of what I can do yet. Well, that's me. I'm away to get my messages. Goodbye,' she said politely before turning and walking away.

'What did she mean, Maw?' said Maria, closing the front door.

Without a word, Ludovica stomped into the dining room, opened the cupboard in the sideboard and took out her sewing basket. On top of the basket lay the small doll she'd made. She was astonished to see that the stitching through its mouth had been broken.

'What does it mean?' said Maria while her mother swore in Italian.

'It means I underestimated the little bird woman,' replied Ludovica.

Hastily she went into the backyard and got the fire pit going before tossing the doll onto it. The two women watched it be consumed by the flames.

'Already the bird woman's evil is in our lives,' said Ludovica. 'And we may never be rid of it.'

* * *

Three days later, just as Virgil was starting to feel a little better, his solicitor called to tell him that Ember had signed the divorce papers. Even though he knew it was the best thing for both him and her, the news made Virgil feel a little down.

He went out for a walk to clear his head. It was the first time he'd left the house since he'd met John in the pub in the city. Virgil soon found himself wending his way towards the home he and Ember had shared. Her car was on the drive, so he knocked on the door, not knowing why. All he knew was that he had to see her just once before their divorce was finalised and they were no longer man and wife.

'Virg,' she said with surprise. 'I wasn't expecting to see you here.'

'I'm no' disturbing you, am I?'

'Not at all. Come in.'

'Thanks,' he said, feeling awkward as he stepped inside, a stranger in his own home.

'I've decided I want to keep the house,' she said as she closed the front door. 'Lucas said he'd pay you half so I can keep it.'

'That's very generous of him,' he frowned. 'Are you shagging him? Sorry,' he sighed when she pouted. 'It's none of my business.'

'Aye, it's not.' Ember had in fact finally given herself to Lucas just the day before, after which he'd sworn she wouldn't lose her beloved home. The experience hadn't been as bad as she'd thought it would be. In fact, it had been pretty good, but it lacked the dynamite that exploded every single time between her and Virgil. She'd been forced to trade that in for money and financial stability. 'Actually,' she said more gently. 'Perhaps it's better that you do know. Yes, we're seeing each other. Do you have a problem with that?'

'I'd be a hypocrite if I said yes. I was the one who instigated our divorce.'

When Virgil leant into Ember, her cheeks bloomed with colour.

'Tell Lucas that if he ever hurts you, I'll rip his head right off.'

The corner of her mouth lifted. 'I'll pass on the message.'

'Good.' He planted a kiss on her cheek and headed for the front door. He hesitated and turned back to face her. 'I know that you not only sabotaged my fight with Marius but that you also sent that lunatic to my maw's house.'

'Me?' she said sweetly.

'Aye, you. Me and my brothers will be fighting regularly for John, so don't do it again. If you do, I'll put your new boyfriend in the ground.'

'So much for you not wanting to hurt anyone again.'

'I'll make an exception for slimy wee bastards who are giving it to my ex-wife.'

'I understand,' said Ember.

Lucas still hadn't decided what he was going to do with the information he had about Maria murdering Adrian. Ember wondered what Virgil would do if he found out she'd told her new lover. It probably hadn't occurred to him that she would ever reveal that secret. 'Wait, Virg,' she said when he made for the door again.

'What?'

Ember pulled down the sleeves of the rockabilly dress she wore, pushing the entire thing to the floor so she stood there in just a pair of black panties. 'How about one last fling for old time's sake?'

The familiar desire arose inside him. 'I'm no' sure that's a good idea,' he rasped.

'Please, Virg. Just let me feel that chemistry one last time.'

Virgil wanted to ask her if Lucas didn't do it for her like he did, but he didn't want to mention that creep's name. This was between him and his wife before the bond between them was forever severed.

He pulled her to him and kissed her, tearing down her panties as he pushed her up against the wall.

'Virg,' she moaned as he entered her.

Ember didn't go any easier on him even though she knew he was still recovering from his injuries. She clawed and bit and pinched his sore, bruised flesh, but Virgil revelled in it knowing he'd probably never experience chemistry like this again either.

Once it was over, they clung on to each other, Virgil burying his face in her hair.

'I love you,' he breathed before kissing Ember's cheek. He released her and hastily fastened his jeans before leaving.

He wandered down the street without glancing back at the house. As his father had always said, MacGregors never looked back. Ember was his past, not his future. Now he could concentrate on the fights for both Toni and John while trying not to get sent to prison or killed.

Ember pulled on her dress and watched Virgil from the window as he drove away, her green eyes burning. He might think she was already part of his past, but she would do everything in her power to ensure she remained in his present. Lucas might be her new man but soon Virgil would realise that he would never be rid of her.

* * *

MORE FROM HEATHER ATKINSON

The next gritty gangland thriller from Heather Atkinson is available to order now here:

https://mybook.to/NewAtkinsonBackAd

ACKNOWLEDGEMENT

The very excellent book *Italian Folk Magic* by Mary-Grace Fahrun was used in my research for this novel.

ABOUT THE AUTHOR

Heather Atkinson is the author of over fifty books - predominantly in the crime fiction genre. Although Lancashire born and bred she now lives with her family, including twin teenage daughters, on the beautiful west coast of Scotland.

Download your exclusive bonus content from Heather Atkinson here:

Visit Heather's website: www.thebooksofheatheratkinson.godaddysites.com

Follow Heather on social media:

facebook.com/booksofheatheratkinson
instagram.com/heatheratkinsonauthor

ALSO BY HEATHER ATKINSON

Wicked Girls

The Savage Sisters Series

Savage Sisters

A Savage Feud

A Savage Betrayal

A Savage Inheritance

Savage Blood

The Gallowburn Series

Blood Brothers

Bad Blood

Blood Ties

Blood Pact

The Alardyce Series

The Missing Girls of Alardyce House

The Cursed Heir

His Fatal Legacy

Evil at Alardyce House

The Bloody MacGregors

Fury

PEAKY READERS

GANG LOYALTIES. DARK SECRETS.
BLOODY REVENGE.

A READER COMMUNITY FOR
GANGLAND CRIME THRILLER FANS!

DISCOVER PAGE-TURNING NOVELS
FROM YOUR FAVOURITE AUTHORS
AND MEET NEW FRIENDS.

Boldwood

Boldwood Books is an award-winning fiction publishing company seeking out the best stories from around the world.

Find out more at www.boldwoodbooks.com

Join our reader community for brilliant books, competitions and offers!

Follow us
@BoldwoodBooks
@TheBoldBookClub

Sign up to our weekly
deals newsletter

https://bit.ly/BoldwoodBNewsletter